MW01645013

PRAISE FOR *A SONG AT DEAD MAN'S COVE*

"A chilling, atmospheric blend of contemporary mystery and gothic folklore, wrapped in lyrical prose and deep emotional undercurrents"

—Alex Norton from Likely Story

"Haunting, engaging, and heartbreaking"

—Anthony Avina

A Song at Dead Man's Cove

Ana Yudin

ISBN: 9798316967988

Cover art by Katarina Naskovski.

Please note that the following book contains potentially sensitive content that may not be suitable for some readers, including mental illness and death. If you require support resources, the following are some options:

National US Suicide Prevention Lifeline: Call 998
Crisis Text Line: Text HOME to 741741
List of suicide crisis lines by country:
https://en.wikipedia.org/wiki/List_of_suicide_crisis_lines
List for emergency telephone numbers by country:
https://en.wikipedia.org/wiki/List_of_emergency_telephone_numbers

For Nikolai

Part I

Zarya, 2023

Chapter 1

Zarya watched them through the stained-glass windows, those men and women underneath the canopy who spoke of tragedy. She could not hear them, but she could tell it was a tragedy they deliberated from the feverish excitement in their gesticulations. No one looked so excited unless something terrible had happened.

The townspeople's silhouettes were distorted through the curves in the glass, their bodies aglow in shades of violet and emerald green. One man shook his head at the others before heading toward the hotel. Then the front door swung open with a screech, and Zarya was face-to-face with him.

The man stood there, unsure how to announce the news. He looked from left to right and, when none of the guests paid him any mind, waddled toward the concierge desk.

When he was close enough for Zarya to smell the spiced scent of his deodorant, the man finally addressed her. "There's been a death, d'you hear?"

So, he was a harbinger of death, then. A real tragedy had occurred, it seemed—not even the fabricated kind she often saw playing on TV.

Zarya shut the book she had been hiding underneath the computer keyboard. "What happened?"

He looked pleased with himself to be the first one to tell her. His brows were furrowed gravely, but beneath those furrowed brows, his eyes revealed the hint of a smile. "Jessica, I think was her name. Her fiancé said she was swimming in the water one moment, gone the next. Coast guards looked for her for hours, but her body just now washed up on shore."

Zarya had heard the tales of those who went too deep into the water and never returned. Even strong swimmers on days when the ocean looked placid. The ocean was mighty, but there was something else out there—something less natural than the ebb and flow of the water.

She swallowed. "How old was she?"

"Twenty-six."

Just a year older than herself. Zarya's eyes drifted across the walnut desk, which glowed faintly under a prohibition-style lampshade. The name Jessica didn't ring a bell, but it could have. No one was safe from this. When the ocean called, it required no permission.

As her mind finally drifted back, it occurred to Zarya that the man before her had continued babbling on about the matter, and his monologue grew faintly back into focus. "She was the sweetest girl… model citizen, that's what they say… and no one knows what happened…"

She nodded along just like she had been trained to do by the hospitality industry, clustering her nods near the ends of his sentences to make it seem like she agreed with what he said. It was enough to keep the man going, and he remained fueled by the validation until eventually pausing to catch his breath. Zarya thought it was over then, but the man let out one last burst of energy.

"I say we drag those monsters out of the water and kill 'em all, anyway. That's what I say."

He had finally run out of steam. The man removed his palm from the polished wood and started looking around for someone else to talk at. When his eyes found a middle-aged couple in golf attire by the hearth, he aimed in their direction without so much as a goodbye.

Zarya quietly observed the scene. The man told the same tale to the hotel guests sitting fireside. The woman, who had just draped a cashmere sweater around her shoulders, looked up from her glass of wine. Right away, her eyes widened at the story. Her husband had his back to the check-in desk, but Zarya could tell he was not quite as entertained. His head barely lifted for the herald of death.

As the local repeated the same sequence of events as before, this time with greater gusto, Zarya's mind drifted. She tried to picture what the latest victim might have looked like. Perhaps brown-haired with a pretty face. Perhaps with big, blue eyes. Her life was over now, and for what? What did the creatures at the bottom of the sea want with her? Maybe the man was right that they were pure evil.

When the guests finally excused themselves and the local left to find another willing pair of ears, the lobby went quiet. There was only the hum from the fireplace, the quivering of light against the walls. Once upon a time, the hotel had been a Victorian mansion, as evidenced by the wood paneling and ornate furniture. Zarya stepped out from behind the check-in desk and sank into one of the pieces, a velvet-upholstered armchair with intricately carved handgrips. She allowed herself to close her eyes, even if just for a moment, lulled by the crackling of logs and the dim lighting.

But it was a short-lived reverie, for she was soon awoken by the sound of someone throwing more logs into the fire. It startled her upright.

Bruno stood before her with a disapproving look. At five foot five, he was not doing a great job of looking too menacing.

"Did I fall asleep?"

"Yes, you did. You're lucky it was me that caught you and not Mrs. Irving."

Zarya combed her hands through her hair, willing herself to stay awake. A copper strand fell right back to her forehead. "Did you hear the news?"

"What, that you're going to get yourself fired?" Bruno raised a brow.

"No, about the girl that washed ashore." Zarya winced at herself. Was she becoming like the man who had relayed the message, rejoicing at the chance to tell someone a piece of shocking news? On some level, maybe she thought it would make her more interesting. Clearly, her life was so dull that she could hardly stay awake for it.

Bruno let out a soft gasp. He put a hand to his heart and echoed, "Washed ashore?"

"So I hear."

"We have to go there," he said, resolutely.

"To the place where they found her?" Zarya did not need to guess where. She already had a pretty good idea.

"Yes," insisted Bruno. His eyes had a crazed glint to them. "Don't you want to?"

Zarya shrugged. Of course she did—but something felt wrong about treating this misfortune like a circus act. "I don't know…"

"We're going." Bruno grabbed her by the hands. His palms were clammy to the touch. "There's no talking me out of this."

Zarya knew there was no resisting it. Once Bruno got an idea in his head, it was game over. One time, he had forced her to walk all the way out of town on their lunch break simply because he was craving a very specific type of gelato. Lavender lemon, if she recalled correctly. They had returned drenched in sweat for the rest of their shift, and Zarya had spent the whole afternoon averting eye contact with the hotel guests who flinched at her summer stench.

"Fine," she said, returning behind the front desk. Someone was walking up toward the stained glass of the front doors. Zarya typed the password into the clunky computer, nails clicking against the keys.

The guests drew open the front door, and as they did, a strange fluorescent light seeped into the hotel, the kind of light that precipitated a storm. The rain was not here yet, but it was so close she could almost taste it.

"Welcome," Zarya called to the guests. She had already checked in the young couple yesterday afternoon, and now they made their way up to the room. They turned down the hallway without so much as an acknowledgment. Then it was just her and Bruno again, and she could feel Bruno's eyes mocking her. "What is it?" she asked, her tone snippy.

"You're just a kiss-ass is all." Bruno threw another log into the fire haphazardly.

"You're supposed to crisscross the logs," she reminded him for the fortieth time.

"Yeah, yeah, to 'let the oxygen fan the flames,' I know." He rolled his eyes.

Bruno came from money, and it showed. His family was one of the richest in Brazil (or so he said), but he liked the gossip culture in the service industry, so this job was as good as any. At least this was the fanciest hotel in town, with its 19th-century architecture and highly acclaimed restaurant.

The Friday afternoon surge came and went. Soon it was five o'clock, and Zarya handed over the desk to the night shift. She grabbed her satchel from underneath the chair and tossed it over her shoulder. Bruno was already out the door.

Outside, the air was sticky. Even with spring in full force, something about today felt like autumn. The overcast sky thickened the air beneath it. It made Zarya remember late August storms, the echo of thunder. Leafy trees turning to gold. The front lawns, currently filled with lilac bushes and verdant garden beds, seemed like they should be adorned with pumpkins, grapes, and fake ghosts. The ivy that ran up the brick walls seemed less like a backdrop for the summer, and more like a web of deceit, meant to conceal the ghouls within.

It was such thoughts that preoccupied Zarya. She panted heavily in the humid air. She could almost taste it on her lips—the sweet, dark nectar of autumn. With its gray skies and chilling breeze, its small bats winging their way across the murky undergrowth, carrying the same feeling as today—of air that is about to turn, not quite summer but not quite something else yet. She got like this sometimes, with a dread so all-consuming it clouded everything else.

"Earth to Zarya," Bruno said, snapping his fingers in front of her eyes. "What are you thinking about?"

How could she explain to him that she smelled death in the air? "Nothing, really."

They strode down the main strip, a road flanked by pastel-colored shops. Past a kitschy souvenir shop displaying ceramic mermaids out front, another donning its graphic tees and semiprecious gems, an art gallery where a woman with thick-rimmed glasses scribbled across canvas, a clothing boutique with overpriced dresses, and the bar and grill where Zarya had spent too many nights.

Past the main strip, the edifices grew sparse, replaced by evergreens and oaks. They were headed to a place called Dead Man's Cove. A place of trouble, nested off a peninsula where Washington and the Pacific interlocked fingers. Hundreds of sailors' skeletons were said to line the ocean floor, and sometimes you could still see the phantom ships floating through the fog.

The cove had earned had its name in 1853 when the Vandalia was shipwrecked, its sailors lifelessly carried ashore. The lighthouse on that peninsula had been abandoned around the same time, as if even the lighthouse keeper had given up on saving the sailors.

Bruno must have sensed her tension. "You're not scared, are you?" There was a slight jeer in his tone.

Zarya didn't answer. She never got too close to the water—her mother had forbidden it. All sorts of legends wafted through the air here.

Zarya could tell they were getting near, because even the chattering birds had gone quiet. They were in the thick of the forest now. Pacific madrones jutted out of the earth, their bark peeling to reveal smooth trunks underneath, reminiscent of wounds. Up ahead, a mist unfurled, and Zarya could hear the increasingly close sound of ocean lapping against ocean.

The air was filled with the overpowering scent of brine, clams, and algae. Zarya's stomach churned. She would have far preferred to be at Dave's Bar and Grill now, smacking down half a dozen oysters and some clams. Instead, she had let herself get dragged into Bruno's field trip. Again.

The ocean was in sight now, pale and marrow-colored and ferocious. Fog made it practically impossible to see much past the shoreline. Drops of condensation caught on Zarya's hair, little pearls of glass against amber strands. On the beach, bone-colored driftwood stacked atop itself.

Almost there. The cove was on the opposite side of the peninsula. She and Bruno crossed up an incline, and from there they could see the cove. It was a crescent-shaped stretch of sand, with small waves that foamed slightly at the mouth. There, standing with their shoes in the sand, stood a news reporter and a cameraman, the microphone and camera pointed at a man of about thirty. His hair was half-concealed by the hood of a raincoat, but Zarya could see the sorrow in his eyes. It poured out of him in streams of saltwater.

Zarya drew slightly nearer, where she could hear his voice ever-so-faintly.

"She was my everything… I loved her so much."

Zarya lifted her own hood over her head so that Bruno wouldn't see her getting rheumy-eyed.

"Can you walk us through the details of what happened? Did you see it yourself?" asked the news reporter.

The man shook his head morosely. "I had climbed up to get a look at the lighthouse." He motioned to the bluff on the westernmost edge of the cove, where the old lighthouse towered over them with its crumbling blue and white paint. The camera followed his line of vision. "Jessica wanted to stay down here and get a photo of me by the lighthouse. But by the time I was up there, she was gone." His voice shattered into a fit of sobs.

The newscaster retracted her microphone and looked squarely into the camera. "You heard it here first, folks. The fiancé of the woman who drowned at Dead Man's Cove told us the tragic story of how it happened. Stay tuned for more details." Then, she lowered the microphone, and her expression went from austere to blasé. She asked the cameraman, "Did you get all that?"

Zarya could not bear to watch anymore. She backed away from the precipice to turn home.

Bruno, seeming satisfied with their venture, trailed after her without protest. "Well, what do you think?" he asked.

Zarya grimaced. "I think it's very sad."

"You think it was a siren that did this?"

The word *siren* made the hairs on Zarya's forearms bristle. There were so many names for those water-spirits—*selkies, nymphs, naiads, nixies, melusines*… Every culture had a name for them. Zarya's own mother called them *rusalki* in Russian. If so many different civilizations had a word for the same thing, maybe there was something to the legend. But no one here had ever seen one, so how could Zarya be sure?

"I don't know," Zarya admitted. "I still don't know if I believe they exist."

"Oh, they exist, alright. How else do you explain all the deaths?"

Zarya shrugged. "Maybe it's rip currents. Or sneaker waves. Or a serial killer."

Bruno let out a scoff, unconvinced. "It's a siren."

They headed back to town just as the storm finally broke, giant towers of bruised clouds dropping tears across the coast. Zarya picked up the pace, her hood now fastened tight around her face.

When Bruno's street came up, she said, "Listen, I'll see you on Monday."

"Alright, see you." Bruno waved.

Zarya jogged the rest of the way to the hotel. For her, this was home—or the closest thing to it. Mrs. Irving permitted Zarya to live in what had once been the servant's quarters. This way, she did not have to pay Zarya as much, and she could at least make use of a room that was otherwise unpresentable to guests. Plus, Zarya didn't need to live with her parents. Win-win.

Zarya's fingers found the lock on the hotel's side door, jamming the key into it. The door had expanded in its frame from the humidity, making it hard to push open, but eventually, it gave in. Once inside, a narrow corridor greeted her, both sides lined with wallpaper in a peacock pattern of iridescent purple and green. All day and night, those eyes on the peacock feathers watched her. Zarya flicked on an electric lamp ensconced into the wall, though it did not do much to keep the darkness at bay.

Her room was past the corridor and up two flights of stairs, in the attic. She went up the winding staircase, ignoring the framed portraits of Victorian figures in tight-necked dresses. They were familiar to her by now, but she did not know their stories. Even their names eluded her.

The servants' quarters were tight, the ceiling built into a gable so that Zarya had to duck around the sides of the room. Still cold from the rain, she ached for a warm shower. Zarya turned the ancient shower valve and left her clothes in a heap on the ceramic tiles. Steam was already starting to unwind the tension from her body.

After her shower, she scarfed down a leftover burger in bed while the fluorescent light from the TV flickered against the walls. There was nothing good on tonight. She aimlessly flipped through the channels, almost ready to give up.

But right before she did, she saw him on the local news channel—the recent victim's fiancé. Zarya laid down her burger. The same scene as before began playing.

"I loved her so much."

"Can you walk us through the details of what happened? Did you see it yourself?"

"I had gone up to see the lighthouse." The camera panned over the deteriorating lighthouse. "Jessica wanted to stay down here and get a photo of me by the lighthouse. But by the time I was up there, she was gone." He cried.

"You heard it here first, folks. The fiancé of the woman who drowned at Dead Man's Cove told us the tragic story of how it happened. Stay tuned for more details."

Somehow, it was even more brutal to watch the second time. Zarya stayed on the channel, listening to the news anchors give their expert opinions. It must have been a slow news night otherwise, because their commentary seemed to drag on forever. One of the reporters was a middle-aged man who liked to think himself the voice of reason; the other was a woman with silky tresses who prided herself on her ability to cut people off. Tonight, for a change, they were on the same page.

"I just don't see what else can be done about this situation, except to bait out whatever is in those waters and extinguish it," said the woman. She was clever not to use the word *siren* on live TV, even though everyone within a ten-mile radius knew exactly what she meant. She was also clever to use the word *extinguish* instead of what she really meant—kill.

"No, I completely agree, Sandra. How many more of our family and loved ones have to perish before we do something? This simply cannot go on! It's only been a few years since the last victim. It feels like the disappearances are becoming more frequent."

"But what can realistically be done?"

"We need to band together, all of us. Get all the boats and ships we can out on the waters, whatever weapons we can muster up, and kill those things before they kill us."

Zarya felt her heart fluttering in her chest. She thought back to the victim's fiancé, how destroyed he had looked both on camera and in person. She could imagine herself in his shoes, losing someone beloved, and it frightened her. The sirens could take one of her loved ones next.

And she could see how, in times like these, a little piece of hate might wedge itself into her chest. It could happen all too easily.

Josephine, 1850

Chapter 2

Josephine hated the lighthouse from the very moment she saw it. She hated the suffocating scent of fresh paint on the walls. The way the tower hovered over the landscape like a rifle. Those winding stairs. Its stripes in navy blue and white, reminiscent more of inmate attire than marine life.

She had expected the Wild West to be beautiful, and certainly it was. The forested mountains were a sight to behold, their peaks so tall they remained dusted with white even in the depths of spring. But the place was astoundingly underpopulated and undeveloped. The town itself could hardly be called a town. On their way in, she had seen a few shops, as well as a gated estate she was told belonged to her husband's employer. Not far beyond that estate, she had seen an Indian settlement—a wooden longhouse with a gabled roof, a cluster of women on the grass weaving baskets, their eyes haunting as they fixed on Josephine through the prairie schooner's window.

Of course, Josephine revealed none of her sentiments to Thomas. She did not know him well enough to be frank with him yet. Thomas had given her a choice: come live in the lighthouse with him or stay in Maine. What newlywed bride would be satisfied with the latter?

So, here she was. This uncharted land was far from Maine, but Josephine told herself it would be similar in some ways. The gray, rugged coastline would feel like home. And, in time, perhaps she could find friends in town.

It was late May. When she heard the muted thumping of footsteps outside, Josephine hastened to the window. An unknown man traipsed across what was now her backyard, with hands clasped behind his back and a frock coat trailing after him. Josephine met him at the doorstep.

"Good morning!" she called out to him, peeking her head out.

The man met her gaze. His eyes were blue and deeply set.

"May I help you?" she asked. "This is private property."

Underneath his Broadway-style hat, the man's complexion was pinkish, with the faint traces of freckles. "Yes, it's in fact my property, madam."

Josephine felt her cheeks redden. Somehow, she had managed to bungle the first encounter with her husband's employer right from the start.

"I imagine you're Mrs. Byrne," he went on. He paused for a moment, as if searching for a word. Once he found it, he returned his gaze to her and said, "It's Josephine, if I recall correctly?"

She nodded. "My apologies for—"

"No need to apologize," he said, with an ease in his voice that suggested she had not offended him. "You're just looking after the grounds. That is, after all, your most important task as lighthouse keeper's wife."

He was close enough for her to get a good look at him now. So, this was the man responsible for Josephine's life in Maine being uprooted, then. He was neither tall nor short in stature, neither slender nor hefty. Despite his unassuming appearance, he must have been quite powerful if he needed to construct a lighthouse for his business.

Josephine clasped her hands awkwardly against the bodice of her dress. "Can I offer you a cup of tea?"

"Actually, I was hoping to speak with your husband." Hurley looked the lighthouse tower up and down. "Is he up there at the moment?"

"He is," replied Josephine. Thomas liked to spend his time in the lantern room even during the day. For cleaning and maintenance, he claimed—though sometimes Josephine wondered if it was more to avoid her. "I can go fetch him for you, if you wish."

Hurley shook his head. "No, no, I wouldn't want to impose. When do you think he'll be down?"

"He usually comes down around three o'clock for a refill of tea." She had already been counting down the minutes to one of Thomas' rare sightings.

Hurley stole a glance at his golden pocket watch. "Very well, then. I suppose a cup of tea is in order." He flashed a smile.

Josephine waved at him to follow. As he entered, Hurley removed the hat from his head and placed it on the dining table. The gesture revealed a head of golden-brown hair, fashionably oiled against his scalp.

Josephine occupied herself with the tea. She poured water and Assam leaves into the copper kettle, then affixed it over the woodstove.

"How are you liking it here so far?" asked Hurley.

Josephine found herself at an impasse. Would it be more favorable to tell her husband's employer a white lie, or should she perhaps tell the truth? Hurley seemed like a friendly fellow so far. And, in truth, she enjoyed purging herself of her emotions. It was cathartic somehow.

"It's very gloomy, sir. And not one lady with whom I can fraternize!"

Hurley sank into the nearest chair and let out a laugh. "Your frankness is refreshing, madam." When his laugh subsided, he added, "Perhaps I can help with that."

"Oh?"

"My wife and some of her friends have afternoon tea together once a week. Sometimes they read together, too. It's good fun for them."

"Is that so?" Josephine drew out the silence between them, hoping an invitation was imminent.

"I'm certain she would welcome you into their—what did you call it?" Hurley smiled, batting his lashes. "Fraternization."

He had walked straight into the trap. "Thank you, Mr. Irving, I very much appreciate it."

"Please, call me Hurley."

A better-behaved lady would have earnestly declined. But Josephine did not particularly pride herself on being a well-behaved lady. "Very well, then."

Just as the kettle was starting to let out a ghastly shriek, she heard footsteps coming from the tower. Then the door opened, and out swung Thomas. He was taller and wider than Hurley, with a wiry, blonde beard. He smelled of whale oil, and by the looks of it, the grease was all over him.

"Thomas, dear, Hurley has paid us a visit. Sit. I'm just making some tea."

Thomas wiped his hands against the backs of his trousers, preparing to shake Hurley's hand. It was difficult for Josephine to assess if underneath his beard there was a smile, but there were no traces of one in his eyes.

"Mr. Irving," he said, shaking his employer's hand. "I hope you haven't been waiting for me terribly long."

"Oh, not at all." Hurley pulled out a second chair before sinking back into his own. "Please, let's sit and talk awhile. Your wife has most hospitably offered up tea."

Thomas paid no mind to the mention of his wife. He accepted Hurley's invitation, clasping his wind-callused hands on the table in front of him. "What can I do for you, sir?"

Hurley pulled out a tobacco pipe and began taking puffs at it. "I was hoping to go over the lighthouse responsibilities with you."

"Of course."

"Now, I know you've been working lighthouses for a good decade now, but I figured it's always a good idea to be on the same page with my business associates."

Josephine turned away to pour boiling water over the tea leaves. She was gathering that Hurley liked to speak to people as if they were his equals—even when it was plain as daylight that this was not the case.

Hurley continued, "You will have no doubt noticed that the lighthouse is in good condition. This will change, in time. With the wind and brine out here, there will be plenty of cleaning, repairing, and repainting to do. There are frequent gales in the area. And, of course, those are the most crucial times for passing ships to spot the lighthouse, so you must make sure to keep the light burning throughout the night.

"Each evening, the lamp must be filled with flammables, the wicks trimmed so that they don't smoke. The Fresnel lens must be polished every morning, as well as the lantern room windows. The brass must be shined, the floors swept. Please make sure the light's rotation mechanism is in order. If there is a mechanical issue you cannot repair, do let me know right away. Keep an inventory of equipment so that I may provide replacements when necessary. Maintain the boat in case of shipwrecks. And, most importantly, lend a hand to any ships in distress. If you ever see a boat coming dangerously close, detonate the fog signal."

"Understood, sir." Thomas gave a stoic nod.

Josephine brought out a salver of sugar and milk. She poured the tea into three teacups, sliding two of them across the table. Then, she took the third for herself and began sipping. Resting against the stove, she watched the men intently. Thomas had an austere manner about him, whereas Hurley seemed nonchalant. The businessman always seemed to keep his eyelids half-closed, as if he had not a care in the world.

"Do you currently have everything you need?" Hurley asked Thomas.

Thomas again nodded. "Yes, sir."

"Excellent." Hurley took his first sip of tea. "Excellent tea,

Josephine. Quite refreshing."

Josephine's lip tugged into a half-smile. "Happy to hear that."

Now that the orders were out of the way, Hurley leaned back in his chair. He looked from Josephine to Thomas, then back to Josephine. "So, the two of you are from Maine, then?"

"Yessir," answered Thomas. He was making a valiant attempt at charisma, but his foot was already tapping against the floor. As if he couldn't stand to be away from the lantern room for long.

"Long journey."

"Indeed, sir."

Josephine caught the slight stall in their conversation. She asked, "And yourself? What brought you out here?"

A spark caught in Hurley's gaze. "The Gold Rush, of course. While I am not involved myself in the mining of gold, I thought it a wondrous opportunity to profit indirectly." He gazed out towards the misty forest outside the window. "In a few years, this land will be flourishing. You'll see. The lands are fertile, and more people East will hear of the gold. Wise men will be flocking to the West coast for trade and transportation industries."

"It must be a helpful talent to see opportunities before they arise," Josephine remarked.

He shrugged. "We shall see. I have made wrong predictions before, and I'm certain it will happen again."

Josephine's gaze darted towards her husband, hoping that her compliment toward another man had not been perceived as insolent. Thomas did not seem to mind, his face already carrying the expression of a man whose thoughts had wandered elsewhere.

"Have the two of you been married long?" Hurley went on.

"Just two months," Josephine answered.

"Only two months?" Hurley grinned. "How delightful. A new marriage, a new home… Many new beginnings all at once."

"You mentioned you are married, as well." Earlier, he had referenced his wife, but Josephine had found it surprising. She usually had a good sense about which men were married, and something about Hurley struck her as unmarried.

But Hurley nodded. "Six years."

"Ah." Her bachelor detector must have been getting rusty. "Any little ones?"

The man shook his head. "Not yet, unfortunately." He said it smoothly, but Josephine knew no man could be pleased with such a fact. Every man wanted a child to carry his name forward. Even the ones that claimed not to care. They wanted the immortality of a legacy. "But we are hopeful that it will happen soon."

"I'm certain it will," said Josephine with another sip of her tea.

"Thank you. Once upon a time, we were in your position, you know. Newly married and having just moved across the world to start something new." The way he rolled his words had long betrayed just how far he'd moved—Scotland, apparently. It had been a grueling journey for Josephine and Thomas to cross the country, but surely it did not compare to what Hurley must have endured by sea and land.

"Life is full of big changes," said Thomas. "We will adjust, won't we, Josephine?" For the first time since the conversation had started, he looked toward his wife.

"Of course, my love." She finished the last of her tea.

"Well, I should be going," said Hurley, standing up. He pushed his chair back under the dining table and shook Thomas' hand. Then, he turned to Josephine and bowed his head. "Thank you once more for the tea, madam." Before spinning out the door, he added, "Oh! I will bring by a man in the next few days to take a daguerreotype of you two."

Josephine gave a blank stare. "I'm sorry, I'm not familiar…"

Hurley perked up as if suddenly remembering the station of the woman with whom he was speaking. "Ah, how silly of me. A daguerreotype is quite remarkable. It's a big, wooden box, and it can make an instant portrait."

Now that he mentioned it, she had seen such images before. They were reserved for important people—people who did not fall in Josephine's category. She had no idea what the man could possibly want with a portrait of her and Thomas.

As if he'd read her mind, Hurley started explaining his reasoning. "I'm very proud of this lighthouse, you see, and honored by its first keepers. I should like to commemorate this wonderful new beginning."

He looked so eager that Josephine could not help a smile. "As you wish."

She followed him out just past the threshold of the door.

"I will see you next Tuesday at the house!" he reminded her.

Josephine nodded. She watched him vanish into the fog. Out of the corner of her eye, she thought she caught the glint of something to her left—a pair of eyes in the water, perhaps? She turned to look in the direction of the ocean, but it was just the crest of a swell.

Josephine turned back inside. She shut the door behind her. Thomas stood before her, the cup of tea still in his stubbly hands. For a moment, she thought he might demand an explanation for Hurley's passing comment about next Tuesday. But, to her surprise, Thomas said nothing about the matter. In fact, he said nothing at all before heading back through the door to the tower.

Zarya, 2023

Chapter 3

Zarya slept deeply that night, under the patter of raindrops falling hard against the attic ceiling. It rained and rained until the moment her eyes opened in the morning—and even then, the rain did not stop.

For most people, Saturdays were a day to rejoice. Not for Zarya. She threw on her work attire, a white button-down, slacks, and brown leather oxfords, then pulled her waves into a tousled ponytail. After tossing one last look at herself in the mirror, she headed downstairs to the lobby.

It was not Bruno who would be joining her on today's shift, but Mrs. Irving. The woman was needle-thin with a back rounded like a waning moon. Her eyes betrayed that she was no friendly neighborhood grandmother. She brought a sharp wit and an even sharper temper, known to flare during rush hour. On one occasion, Mrs. Irving had scolded Zarya on her way of walking, asking her if perhaps she had some sort of motor dysfunction. Zarya had blanched. Ever since, she tried to avoid walking in front of the woman.

The hotel had been passed along through Mrs. Irving's family's lineage for hundreds of years, since the days when Hurley Irving had constructed it. In fact, so renowned was the name Irving in these parts, that Mrs. Irving's late husband had taken her last name upon marriage. Mrs. Irving had insisted on it.

"Good morning," said Zarya, announcing her presence as she stepped out of the shadowy corridor.

Mrs. Irving peered at her from above spectacles. "Good morning, indeed." Her voice had a sardonic air to it, and she motioned at the rain streaming down the windows. "This weather on a weekend, huh? All the guests will be indoors and ready to pester us."

She wasn't wrong. Already, guests were pouring into the restaurant for the breakfast buffet, and a herd of children ran noisily through the hall.

"It'll be okay," Zarya said, half trying to convince herself.

But it was a long day, and neither the company nor the gloomy weather helped. Several times, Zarya's phone started buzzing in her satchel, but one look from Mrs. Irving was enough to let her know she'd be letting the call go to voicemail.

By the time her shift was over, Zarya could not wait to get away from the jade lampshades and the wainscoted walls and the fire that always seemed to lack sufficient firewood. She clocked out in the hallway and slipped out the side door, hoping it would go unnoticed lest Mrs. Irving think of one last errand she needed to run.

Still, the rain poured down. How long could it possibly go on? Zarya wondered just how far this storm spanned, how much water the soil could stand to absorb. She was used to the everyday drizzles in these parts, but rarely did she witness a storm like this one.

Rain seeped through her blouse until the fabric stuck to her skin. When Zarya walked through the door at Dave's Bar and Grill and the bell jingled to announce her arrival, she felt dozens of eyes on her. She scanned for a familiar face in the crowd, but most of them were middle-aged men whose names she did not know. She bolted towards the nearest empty chair at the bar.

As she waited for the bartender to turn around, Zarya peered at her phone. Four missed calls from her mom. Her thumb hovered over the call button, but it wavered. She couldn't quite bring herself to hear another barrage of instructions after a long day alongside Mrs. Irving.

"You look like you're ready for a drink."

It was Emily working the bar tonight, a woman with blonde ringlets of hair and a pair of bootcut jeans approximately one decade out of style. She had a beer glass in each hand.

"You and me both, I imagine." Zarya tilted her chin in the direction of an opened bottle of Smirnoff behind the bar top.

Emily caught her drift. She finished spouting beer into the glasses from the tap until the golden liquid frothed at the top, then slid them toward two men further down the bar top. When she was done, she placed two shot glasses between her and Zarya, poured in the vodka, and took one glass for herself.

"Cheers." The two clinked glasses and downed the liquor. It looked deceptively like water and tasted like something that was supposed to be under the hood of a car. Zarya's salivary glands temporarily throbbed with disgust.

Her face must have betrayed her, because Emily let out a chuckle. "Hey, you asked for it."

Zarya let the alcohol take effect for a moment, the baritone laughter in the background and the day's stress already fading. She was brought back to life by Emily tapping her fingers against the bar top.

"Hey, you want to eat anything? After this, it'll be another half hour before I can place an order." She motioned to the back of the bar, which had filled up with a swarm of tourists.

"Yes," said Zarya. "Fish and chips, please."

Emily slapped her palm against the counter. "Coming right up." Then, she sloped her head in the direction of something—or someone—standing behind Zarya.

Zarya looked over her shoulder, pretending to be glancing at the clock on the back wall. Instead, she saw a pair of eyes peering back at her, dark and almond-shaped, with the hint of a smile. A man in a red shirt stood waiting to place his order. Zarya had never seen him before—she would have remembered that deep, velvety skin and the bright smile that overtook his whole face when she locked eyes with him.

"Oh, I'm sorry. Are you trying to get by to place an order?" Zarya scooched her chair in by an inch. "I can let the bartender know what you want."

The man did not seem inconvenienced in the slightest. His smile somehow widened even more. "Sure, why not? I'll have whatever you're having."

Zarya looked down at the empty shot glass in front of her. "I'm not really having anything at the moment," she admitted. She blinked. "But that could change." She leaned over the bar top to tap Emily on the shoulder, acutely aware of the feeling that she was being watched from behind. "Hey, Emily—two whiskey Cokes, please."

Emily threw her a wink, and Zarya slid back down into her seat. As she did, she noticed the mystery man had inched closer to her chair.

"So, you're a whiskey girl, huh?" His voice was viscous like caramel. That smile persisted on his lips. "I'm Sean, by the way." He offered his hand.

His hand was warm, the fingers long and slender. Smiling, Zarya said, "Hi, Sean. I'm Zarya."

Sean stuffed his hands inside the front pockets of his pants, seeming pleased with the way the conversation was going so far. "So, you from around here?"

"Born and raised." Zarya bit her lip to stop herself from adding: *for better or worse*. "I imagine you're not?"

Sean laughed. "What gave that away?"

"You look too excited to be here."

Again, Sean let out a laugh and, without realizing it, Zarya found herself smiling.

"But your name sounds unusual," he said.

"It's Russian," she explained. "My parents moved here from

the Soviet Union."

Sean took a shuffle forward to better hear her over the commotion. "That's interesting. Are there a lot of Russians around here?"

"No," she replied, leaving it at that. Her parents had made sure to pick a place where it would be hard to find a sense of community.

By the time their drinks arrived, Zarya was so enraptured in the conversation that she hardly noticed them. Sean had to reach over her to grab their glasses. He handed one to Zarya, after which they clinked glasses, shouted cheers, and started downing the contents.

"I don't usually drink like this," she assured him, hoping he wouldn't see her as some sort of wild local harlot. She knew the ways men liked to put women into neat little categories. A box titled Harlot. A box titled Girl Next Door.

"Oh, yeah? What makes tonight special, then?"

"Well, it was the weekend shift at the biggest hotel in town. I shared the shift with my boss, who's kind of a pain in the ass. And it was rainy, so everyone wanted to stay inside and bug me." Her eyes skimmed over Sean's face. She wanted to see his reaction to this next part. "Not to mention, I found out yesterday that another young woman drowned out at Dead Man's Cove."

Sean blinked rapidly. "Whoa, whoa, back up a bit. A young woman died *where*? And what do you mean *another*?"

The bar grew louder with every minute, so loud that Zarya had to practically shout over the noise. The alcohol was helping with that a bit. "You've heard of sirens, right?"

"Sirens? Like mermaids?"

Zarya shrugged. "I guess you could call them that, but it doesn't really do them justice. Mermaids are a watered-down version of sirens, a fairytale we tell children. But real sirens are something else. They don't wear shell bikinis and sing about forks. Real sirens are deadly water-spirits."

It was a popular tale around here—of creatures in the water with tails made of fish scales, teeth like daggers, corpse-blue skin. No one had ever seen one up close and lived to tell the tale, but they liked to let their imaginations run wild all the same. Sometimes, they were said to take the form of seals. Sometimes they had tails, other times not. Their song was mesmerizing if you heard it—a death call. Too many souls had succumbed to its allure.

Sean seemed in disbelief. "You say this so casually. You really believe it?"

"I don't. But everyone else does." Zarya waved her hand at the sea of people surrounding them. "You'd have a really hard time finding someone from this town who doesn't take sirens very seriously."

Before Sean could open his mouth to ask a follow-up question, the burly man beside him inclined over the counter to better hear their conversation. "Are you all talking about sirens?" he asked through yellowed teeth.

Zarya nodded. "I was just telling this gentleman over here about what happened yesterday."

The yellow-toothed man scratched his beard. "You're not from here, I imagine?" he asked, looking Sean up and down. Zarya blushed, hoping he was not about to say something insulting.

But Sean merely shook his head.

"Well, let me tell you, son. There's evil reeking in that water out there." The local extended his arm out, presumably in the direction of the Pacific. "Every time there's a joyful event in this town, the sirens ruin it. This last victim, Jessie or whatever she was called—she had just gotten engaged that very morning. Can you believe it?"

Sean shrugged. "It could be a coincidence?"

"A coincidence!" It came out practically a roar. "This was no coincidence, boy. A coincidence is a one-time thing. This is a pattern—a formula as clear as day."

"It's never a good day to die," Zarya commented.

The local peered at her for the first time all conversation. "You two are young—there's still so much you don't know." He wagged his finger at her. "You should come by the vigil tonight, see for yourself. Maybe you'd learn a thing or two."

"There's a vigil happening?" Zarya exchanged a confused look with Sean.

"Yeah, something like that. Obviously, the girl is already dead, so there's not much we can do about that, but we can try to pray together. We're stronger as a group, you know." That was the last of what the man wanted to say before he chugged the rest of his beer and dumped some cash on the counter. "Vigil starts at eight. I'm headed over there early."

No sooner had the man gotten up that Sean had already taken his seat at the bar.

"I'll come a bit closer to eight," Zarya called to the local. "Still waiting on my fish and chips."

"Suit yourself." The man tossed a cap over his head and swam through the swarm of people toward the exit.

Sean took a sip of his drink. "You really gonna go?"

"Yeah, why not?" Zarya shrugged. Then, emboldened by the liquor, she added, "You should come with me. See what the local culture is really about."

"Alright, I'll bite." Intrigue gleamed in his eyes. "Could be an experience."

The rest of their time at the bar was a blur. Zarya had her fish and chips and took another shot—this time tequila. She licked the salt from her hand, winced at the liquor, and suckled on a lime wedge until her nausea dissipated. Before she knew it, eight o'clock was nearing, and there was a mass exodus from the bar.

"I guess everyone's got the same idea," she said. She got down from the bar chair and followed the crowd, Sean not far behind.

When the door swung open, everything was slick with rainwater. Hard rain droplets thumped against the already-flooded pavement.

"Damn it," Zarya muttered under her breath. "Still?"

"You need a jacket?" Sean offered, showing her his brown,

leather coat.

"Oh, I couldn't." Zarya was hoping he would insist. "Then you'll get wet, instead."

"Better me than you," said Sean.

He had walked straight into the trap. "Okay, fair." She took his jacket. It slouched far over her shoulders but got the job done.

Then they were out in the rain, following in the footsteps of the locals. There was a certain wickedness in the air, as though they were missing some pitchforks. Zarya had never traversed down to the cove at nighttime, and she thought about how different the route looked in the dark. The dangers of the daytime felt augmented, as if something might swallow her up from behind the trees' shadows.

"Is this what you do for fun?" asked Sean, playfully bumping his elbow against hers.

"I don't do much for fun. I work, and I eat, and I sleep." Just talking about it was making her depressed. "What do *you* do for fun, wherever you're from?"

"Honestly, kind of the same." Sean let out an icy chuckle that let her know he was not just trying to make her feel better. "I'm from LA."

The word made Zarya think of palm trees and sunshine and rollerblading down a beach walk. "I've never been," she said, "But I bet it's better than here."

Sean shrugged. "Eh, not by much."

"What do you do for work there?"

"I study journalism. Right now, I'm an intern at West Coast Media." In the flash of a moment, he pulled out a business card.

"Oh." Right—some people had *careers*, not jobs. Zarya pocketed the slip of paper.

"What about you?"

"I work at the hotel," she reminded him.

"Oh yeah, you mentioned that. Sounds like this hotel is kind of a big deal around here?"

Zarya wrapped the jacket tighter around her neck as another

torrent of rain slapped her on the crown of her head. "You're not staying there?" she asked. When Sean shook his head, she explained, "It's this old Victorian mansion that got repurposed into a hotel. It's practically a castle."

"Maybe after this, you can show me," suggested Sean. His tone feigned innocence.

Zarya tried not to think about his arm brushing against hers through the leather, or the fact that excitement had begun bubbling in her belly. "Definitely," she said, borrowing some of his feigned innocence for herself.

They were almost there. The cold from the rain was now made worse by the cold of the wind whipping from the ocean. As the cove came into their line of sight, the townspeople gathered around the precipice with their phone flashlights turned on. None dared to descend all the way down to the beach, especially with the high tide thrashing loudly against the rocks. Zarya found a spot to stand near the outskirts of the group. Sean stood beside her.

"Ladies and gentlemen," called a woman from the front of the group. Zarya had heard Mrs. Irving barking orders at work too many times to not recognize her voice, and now she was close enough to spot the woman's craned shoulders. "All of us are here today because we care about our people. We are tired of seeing our neighbors, our children, our parents, our spouses victimized at the hands of the sirens. We are tired of pretending we can coexist peacefully with these creatures." Mrs. Irving pointed out at the water, which was black as spilled ink. "Those *things* out there refuse it. They don't want peace; they want more souls for the graveyard of the ocean." Her eyes looked crazed in the dark, glinting like quarters. "We will not let them do this to us."

Zarya exchanged a look with Sean, who had begun to look increasingly uncomfortable. She did not know exactly where Mrs. Irving's tirade was headed, but every syllable was freighted with hate.

Zarya began to crave space. She inched away from the group,

so slowly that even Sean did not notice her slipping out. Several feet back, she found refuge under a cluster of trees. From there, she could see the water on the other side of the peninsula, growing more powerful and angry with every drop of rain.

The group went quiet now for a moment of prayer, their flashlights swinging from left to right like a concert audience. Now there was just the sound of water—water against leather, water against soil, water against water. Zarya still tasted the liquor on her tongue.

As she gazed out at the ocean, she saw something there, a shape that looked different from the rest. It was not the white crest of a wave, nor a rock. It was not far from shore—just where the water deepened—and close enough to get a good look at, if only it weren't so dark.

And then, a flash of lightning streaked across the sky, ripping the heavens open. With that flash of lightning, for the briefest moment, the ocean was filled with light. The contours of every surface shone crisply. Zarya could see the entire expanse of water, the edge of the peninsula, the trees, and most importantly, she could see the creature that locked eyes with her from the ocean.

Only her head, shoulders, and half of her chest were visible. Her skin was pallid and sallow like the moon. A bit sickly-looking, like she had been swimming in the water for far too long. Her cheekbones protruded out at a sharp angle, casting shadows across the bottom half of her face. Hip-length hair drifted behind her in the water, ink-dark. And her eyes were pale, their irises silver. Upon seeing Zarya, the creature opened her mouth to bare a set of rotting teeth. It was a smile of sorts, though certainly not a beneficent smile.

Just as quickly as the lightning had shone, everything went dark again. Next came the thunder, a peal so sharp that Zarya knew the danger was near. Moments ago, it had seemed like the sky had cracked open, and now it sounded like it.

She could no longer see the figure in the water. Zarya was not sure whether to scream or tell the others what she had seen. She was keenly aware of the alcohol burning through her bloodstream, how it would make her seem less than credible—and besides, how could she even show them what she had seen? The creature seemed to have gone underwater, and there was no more lightning. Her flashlight could not reach far enough to illuminate the entire ocean. So instead, she returned to the collective, heart still thrumming in her chest.

Sean spotted her. "Where'd you go?" he asked.

"Not far behind." Zarya trembled, unsure if it was from shock or rain.

Sean softly placed a palm on her forearm. "Are you alright?"

"Can we get out of here?" Zarya didn't give him a chance to answer, already starting towards the footpath. Behind her, the voices of the vigil faded with every step. Soon, she could hear only the sound of Sean jogging to catch up with her.

When they were off the trail and back on asphalted road, he asked, "What happened back there?"

Rain continued to streak the halos around streetlamps, though it was finally starting to slow down. Zarya hoped it would drown whatever she had seen in that water.

"Nothing," she said, determined to not have her sanity questioned tonight.

Sean was undeterred. "Look, Zarya, I know we don't know each other very well, but I can tell something changed after you came back from there. I promise I won't judge. Would you please tell me what happened?"

Zarya left a pregnant pause, but there was no point. She had already decided to tell him. She let out a sharp exhale and said, "I saw one of the creatures I was telling you about out there."

Sean had promised not to judge, but his look of incredulity revealed it was a battle to keep his word. He simply asked, "A—siren?"

Zarya nodded, grim. "I did say you wouldn't believe me. Go on, blame it on the liquor."

Sean sighed. "Look, it's not the craziest thing I've heard."

"No?"

"Don't get me wrong, it *is* crazy," he said, letting out a chuckle. "But I know people who claim to have seen ghosts and demons and all sorts of stuff."

"Well, good, I guess." It was good enough for her. "Do you still want to see the hotel?"

"I do."

When they approached the place, Sean recognized it before Zarya could point it out. From the outside, it was a broad building with violet panels and windowpanes painted pine-green. There were too many chimneys and towers to count, jutting out of its sharp gables. Zarya showed him through the side door, mortified at the possibility of her boss or a patron seeing her bring home a stranger. But Mrs. Irving was at the cove, so hopefully no one would notice.

"Damn, this is nice," mumbled Sean, looking up at the electric chandelier above their heads with its lightbulbs shaped like candle flames.

Zarya showed him into the lobby, and on their way in he marveled at the somber paintings encased in thick, gilded frames. She showed him all the rooms that weren't guest rooms—the green room, once a place of dining, and the foyer painted the color of boysenberry sorbet, and the cigar room in pastel orange. She showed him the grand piano made of maplewood and the circular room at the top of the tower with windows on all sides like a lighthouse. Beneath their feet, tiles were arranged in a mandala pattern, circles encased in squares and more circles.

"What exactly was this place?" Sean asked, clearly grasping that this was no ordinary hotel.

"It belonged to Hurley Irving, a Scottish businessman who brought his family out to the Pacific Northwest. He was one of the first to populate the area."

One of Sean's brows arched. "I wonder whose land he claimed as his own."

Zarya peered at the opulence all around. Hurley Irving had surely built a fortune, but she was not sure from what exactly.

She showed Sean to the attic next, her headquarters. She apologized for the heaps of clothes sprawled all about, uttering a quick word about how she had not expected company. It was the truth, but a measly excuse. Her place always looked like this.

Now that they were alone, Zarya had the sudden feeling of not enough air. She cracked open the window, trying to get the oxygen deeper into her chest. When Sean joined her by the windowsill and wove his fingers between hers, she froze. She thought she had wanted this, but now she was not so sure.

"Are you alright?" His fingers tarried.

"Yeah, I'm fine…" She could feel his warm breath on the back of her head, and it made her pulse quicken. "Listen, Sean—I think I've misled you tonight."

He took a step back to give her some space. "How so?"

"Nothing can happen between us."

A flash of disappointment flickered across his face, but it was soon replaced with a smile. "Let me guess—you have a boyfriend?"

Zarya shook her head.

"You're religious?"

Again, she shook her head.

"You don't like me in that way?"

Reluctantly, more head-shaking.

Sean looked caught off-guard. "I'm out of ideas. What is it, then?"

How could she explain to him the truth? Intimacy felt to her like a cast-iron cage. She had wanted to bring him back to her room when she thought he was just a pretty face, but his kindness had surprised her. It would complicate things if she slept with him.

She ignored his question for a question of her own. "Where are you staying?"

"It's a bed-and-breakfast a couple blocks from Main Street."

Zarya nodded slowly, hoping he would take the hint and that

she would not need to be too blunt. When Sean said nothing to fill up the awkwardness, she said, "Oh, I should give you back your jacket before you go."

She walked barefoot across the room to the armchair where she had tossed his jacket on the way in. Sean approached, and she handed it to him.

"So, I guess this is goodnight, then?" he asked, clamping the jacket under his arm.

"I guess so," she echoed, giving him a perfunctory smile. "Get home safe, okay? Hopefully, the rain has stopped by now." She could hear through the window that it had not.

"I will." Sean lifted his arms out like wings for a hug, and Zarya approached. She felt small inside his broad wingspan. Then Sean was headed for the door.

Before he turned away, she said, "I'm sorry."

"What are you sorry for?"

With a shrug, Zarya said, "I feel like I led you on."

"You have nothing to apologize for." As he stepped over the threshold, he said, "You're a strange girl, Zarya. You live in a Victorian hotel, you see sirens in the ocean, you kick me out even though you like me, and you apologize when you've done nothing wrong."

Zarya shrugged again. "I guess so."

And then he was out in the hall, giving her a nod goodbye. She shut the door behind him, but it was with that same feeling of something about to turn in the air.

Josephine, 1850

Chapter 4

Josephine carefully threaded a strand of hair beneath her bonnet. She rouged her cheeks and trimmed her overgrown nails. She tightened her corset an extra inch.

Today was Tuesday.

Thomas escorted her to the Irving estate, which hosted perhaps the biggest house Josephine had ever seen. It had a many-gabled roof with turrets, decorated trims, and dormer windows. As soon as they had walked up to the stained-glass details of the door, a butler swung it open for them. Josephine stepped inside, a vermilion carpet underfoot. The mansion was illuminated by a gold-plated chandelier and oil lamps.

"I should say hello to Mr. Irving," said Thomas, waiting idly by the doorstep as Josephine ventured in deeper.

The butler clasped his hands behind his back and stood tall. He peered at Thomas from above a hawkish nose. "Mr. Irving is occupied with business at the moment."

Josephine shrugged at her husband. "It's alright, Thomas. Go back to the lighthouse."

"What time should I return for you?" he asked.

Again, the butler interjected. "Mr. Irving informed me that he will send your wife a carriage home."

Thomas cocked his head to the side. "Very well, then." He

blinked at the man. "Good day."

Josephine bid him goodbye before waltzing into the motley of rich jewel tones. Already, she felt lighter without Thomas' heavy presence weighing her down. She had never before found herself surrounded by such wealth, such beauty.

Not recently, anyway.

It was perhaps the most unfortunate aspect of being poor that she should rarely ever find herself amidst beauty. All the ornate craftsmanship, fine-tuned music, decadent food, fresh aromas, and tactile comfort were reserved for the wealthy. Once, she had known a life like this, but it grew more distant by the day, its edges fading.

She heard the clearing of a throat behind her and turned around. Standing in the doorway to another room was a woman in a flounced skirt and matching bodice, both stitched from cloth the color of sage. Her hair was rolled up into a neat braid at the base of her head.

"You must be Mrs. Byrne." A smile flicked across the woman's face as she approached. "I'm Amelia Irving."

Hurley Irving's wife. Josephine examined the lady of the house. She had an oval face with plump, dewy cheeks, and her brows were beautifully arched.

"Pleased to meet you." Josephine knew it was the duty of the woman with the higher status to initiate shaking hands, but she reached for a handshake regardless. "Please call me Josephine."

If Amelia was offended, she hid it remarkably well. "Very well. And you should please call me Amelia."

Amelia waved Josephine into the parlor, where a three-faceted bay window unfolded to the garden. Roses crept their way up to the diamond windowpanes, their heads bobbing gently in the wind.

"You have a beautiful home," remarked Josephine, folding her skirts beneath her onto a settee.

"Thank you!" Amelia poured steaming water into a teacup. Then, she handed the ceramic cup to Josephine. "I look forward to introducing you to the other ladies. They should be here soon."

As soon as she had said it, there was a clamoring from the corridor. A handful of ladies poured into the parlor, some young and some older. Josephine had never seen so many beautiful dresses at once, with their lace trimming and ruffles and trumpet sleeves. The women plopped down like hens, cooing at each other and welcoming Josephine into the group.

Josephine latticed her hands together across her lap. Though the other women were all being lovely, she had the distinct feeling of being a fish out of water. She became acutely aware of the simplicity of her own dress and her limited vocabulary. These were reading women—they spoke of the latest literature and the burgeoning Industrial Revolution and all sorts of other things about which Josephine knew little.

At one point, Amelia's gaze wandered over to her. Perhaps sensing something, Amelia announced, "Ladies, why don't we tell Josephine a little bit about ourselves?"

As such, the introductions began. One of the women was Hurley Irving's sister, arrived from Scotland a few years ago. The others were the wives of Hurley's business associates, including Hurley's sister-in-law. It seemed the whole town revolved around Hurley. When the women's introductions were done, it was Josephine's turn.

"Very nice to meet you all," she said. "I'm Josephine Byrne. I live up in the lighthouse with my husband Thomas. We moved from Maine not long ago."

They erupted into a cacophony of compliments and local recommendations, after which the conversation drifted back to other tropics—gossip and art and housework. Why they pretended to be the housekeepers of their homes, Josephine was not sure. She had seen at least half a dozen servants since stepping in. Josephine faded into the background, once more feeling as though she were still locked up in the lighthouse. How could it be that she felt alone even in a group full of people?

She decided right then and there that there are two kinds of loneliness: the kind borne of solitude, and the kind that swelters in a crowd full of people. In both cases, loneliness was the same—it emptied the soul until there was nothing left. No distractions could ever be enough to feel full again.

She drank her tea and nodded along and smiled kindly at the other women, but inside she was listless. The minutes seemed elongated as they passed by. Even so, the hour passed, and eventually, the clucking hens prepared to head home.

"Josephine, I believe my husband has arranged a carriage for you," said Amelia. With the snap of her fingers, the butler was back in the doorway.

"Thank you," said Josephine, casting a glance at Amelia. "I appreciate you including me today."

"Of course, dear. Come back every week, if you so desire." Amelia gave Josephine's hands a faint squeeze.

The butler showed Josephine to the study, a room chock-full of black cherrywood and books. Behind the desk sat Hurley, his brows furrowed as he pored over a piece of vellum. When he saw the flash of skirts at the door, his eyes darted up to Josephine.

It was curious, thought Josephine again, how much Hurley behaved like an unmarried man. It was something about the way his gaze fell upon her, the way his eyes lingered on her a moment longer than they needed to. Either the man was remarkably charming, or his desire was unbound.

"Mrs. Byrne is ready for her carriage home," announced the butler.

"Thank you very much. I'll take care of it, Charles." Hurley rose from his leather-upholstered chair, signaling for the butler to leave. His unspoken request was swiftly obeyed.

Hurley circumnavigated his desk until he was standing at the front of it. Once there, he leaned against the wood and stuck his hands into the pockets of his suit.

"I hope my wife and her friends were hospitable."

"Oh, most hospitable."

"I'm so glad. And how is Thomas?"

For a moment, Josephine had forgotten herself. They had just been a man and woman speaking freely. The mention of her husband's name brought her somberly back to reality. "Oh, his usual self. He works most of the time."

"The two of you have everything you need?"

"We do."

"You must certainly let me know if there's anything you're missing."

Did he mean to be hospitable, or was there a hidden meaning in his words? Josephine had the sensation that, beneath every word Hurley uttered, there was the weight of all that he left unspoken.

Then, as if struck by inspiration, Hurley uncrossed his arms and went into the drawer beneath his desk. "Ah! I have something to show you."

Out of the drawer, he pulled a silver-varnished copper plate—the daguerreotype of Josephine and Thomas at the lighthouse that he had sanctioned last week. Josephine inched her face closer to the image. She had seen herself in the looking glass before, but never like this. Here, it was as if she were watching herself through Hurley's eyes.

She knew the effect her appearance tended to have on men. They liked to stare at her, as if peering through a faceted piece of glass that glinted differently based on the angle. And now, Hurley was staring at her, but at her image rather than her face in flesh and blood.

"It's a most fascinating invention," she concluded.

"Isn't it?" Hurley tilted the plate in the lamplight, admiring it. Josephine watched the movement of his eyes, how they hovered over her figure in the image.

"What will you do with it?" she inquired.

"I'll have it sent out to the newspaper to announce the erection of the lighthouse." Hurley finally whisked the daguerreotype away, gingerly placing it back in the drawer. "Well, I should walk you to the carriage, then."

They walked out of the study and through the corridor again, past tapered candles in brass sconces and darkly patterned wallpaper. Outside, a buggy awaited. Hurley opened the door for Josephine, and in she stepped.

Once she was inside, he leaned through the buggy's window opening. "I do hope to see you again, Josephine."

As he said it, he took her hand in his palm and kissed the back of it. A perfectly respectful goodbye between man and woman. And yet, his lips hovered over her hand a moment longer than they needed to. Josephine felt a flurry deep inside her belly.

She was sure of it now: this was not the behavior of a married man.

Zarya, 2023

Chapter 5

After Sean left, Zarya did not sink straight into slumber as she had hoped. Instead, she found herself drawn to the window, perching herself on the cushion by the windowsill. The downpour had settled into a faint dripping outside, and all she could think about was the siren she had seen out by Dead Man's Cove. It was true what they said, then—there was something out there luring innocent people to sea.

The more she thought about it, the more she could hear a song calling to her from outside. It was ever-so-faint, low enough in volume that it would not even catch on her phone's microphone, but the melody drew her in sweetly. Angelic—a woman's voice as crystalline and light as diamonds. It undulated up and down the octave in exotic, unexpected ways. Yet there was something recognizable about the song—Zarya could not pinpoint exactly what, but she knew the melody deep in her core.

Surely, this was not a voice of evil. It was a voice of love, drenched in butter and honey. Once Zarya found the person singing these tunes, she would certainly be somewhere warm and safe. That was what the voice promised her.

But even as the whiskey withdrew from her body and fatigue tugged on her limbs, Zarya knew she was being tricked. Although she did not know much about sirens, a few things were certain.

Firstly, sirens had a seductive song, which they used to entice their victims seaward. Secondly, even those who knew of the siren call could fall prey to it. And lastly, for those who were unable to resist the melody, death was imminent.

So, Zarya did the only thing she could think to do, which was to quickly shut the window and put headphones over her ears.

Somehow, this did not deter the music. It seemed to be coming not from outside, but rather from within. The siren had imprinted onto something *inside* of Zarya.

And Zarya had no idea how to unbind herself.

Only when the music started playing through her headphones did she finally fall asleep. Her last thought before slipping into dreams was that, in the morning, the music would surely be gone.

To her dismay, when Zarya awoke just before noon, she could still hear the music trickling faintly in and out. It did not help that her body was working overtime to pump the alcohol out of her system. Her heart beat fast and heavy in her chest, the muscles in her temples tense. Zarya shielded her eyes from the light blazing through the windows, hoping for one last hour of sleep.

But her fantasies of rest were interrupted by a loud pounding on the door. Her heart sought to leap out of her chest, and it quickened even more as Zarya reached for a pair of pajama pants and a sweatshirt.

When she opened the door, she let out a glad sigh. It was only Bruno. He had a Gatorade in hand, which he thrust at her.

Bruno waltzed in, making himself comfortable on the armchair. "Little birdie told me you had quite the eventful night."

"Word travels that fast, huh?" Zarya unscrewed the cap on the Gatorade and started sipping. She sank back into bed.

"So, who was the mystery man?" Bruno cupped his face with both hands. "I heard he was handsome."

"Yes, he was handsome. Look, honestly, it doesn't even matter. Some guy from California. I'll never see him again, and I don't care to."

"Was it that bad?"

Zarya was finding it difficult to talk and to relax her heart at the same time. With Bruno here, she would have to choose one or the other. At last, she said, "We didn't do anything."

Bruno let out a small gasp. "Why not?"

"I don't have time for bullshit in my life. And people always bring bullshit." Her guard was down, saying things she shouldn't say out loud. But hiding how she really felt took energy, and she didn't have energy right now. At least the chaos of this conversation was turning down the volume of the song stuck in her head.

"Damn, Zarya," said Bruno, his mouth twisting uncomfortably. "You sound a bit paranoid."

"I am a bit paranoid," she conceded. "How could I not be? You see the way people treat us in our line of work. The way they treat each other, too. Don't you?"

Bruno gave a slow, reluctant shrug. "I guess…? But I don't know, I feel like there's both good and bad. Sometimes people are nice, too."

He had a point, and Zarya hated how bitter she was sounding right now. Bruno was probably thinking it, too. Eager to change the subject, she noted, "I didn't see you at the vigil last night."

"No, I was on a date," he replied, his face aglow at the thought of it. "But since you refuse to talk boys, I'm not spilling any tea either."

"Fine." In truth, Zarya didn't care all that much about his latest fling. There was a new one every week, and every time it was the love of Bruno's life.

"But you went to the vigil, right?"

Zarya swallowed, recalling the events of the prior night. "Yeah."

Bruno must have seen something flit across her face, for he cocked his head to the side inquisitively. "What is it?"

Zarya took a deep breath and leaned in. "I saw something in

the water last night."

"Saw what?"

She said it in a whisper. "A siren."

The flecks of gold in Bruno's eyes lit up like flames. He leaned in closer. "You're not joking around?"

"I'm serious," she said, shaking her head. "I saw a creature out there in the water. It was unnatural. Looked half-dead."

Bruno leaned in. "We should let Mrs. Irving know."

"Bruno, you cannot tell anyone about this."

"Why not?"

"Please, just promise me you won't. *Especially* not Mrs. Irving." Zarya reached over to squeeze his hands. "Promise me."

"Okay, fine." Bruno pulled his fists out of her grip. "Are you—okay, though? Don't they say, if you see a siren, it's put its mark on you—"

"I'm fine," Zarya assured him, her tone clipped.

Bruno didn't look convinced, but he started towards the door regardless. "Okay, if you say so." He looked her up and down. "You should really get yourself cleaned up."

He was right. Zarya caught a glimpse of her reflection in the corner of her floor-to-length mirror, and it wasn't pretty. After Bruno was gone, she tugged the knots out of her hair and made her breath minty-fresh. Then, she changed into something more respectable and headed out into the corridor.

Now that the sun was out and people had gone out for the weekend, the hotel was less cluttered with people. Zarya relished the quiet.

She had grown to hate it every time a patron approached the concierge desk. Every interaction felt laden with tension. On one occasion, she had greeted a patron hello and asked how she could help them today. The patron, an older woman with a frozen face, had glared at her and remarked that, obviously, she was here to check in. After that incident, Zarya had stopped asking people how she could help them, instead just greeting them hello and waiting for their lead with a smile. But even then, a patron had found this form of greeting disrespectful, simply standing there and tapping her foot as she waited for Zarya to offer her assistance.

But the worst interaction had taken place last December, during rush hour. A young woman with husky-blue eyes had come up to the concierge desk. Zarya recognized her right away—it was one of her high school classmates, with whom she had shared many classes. Zarya began checking the young lady in, waiting to see if she was recognized before mentioning anything. After all, Zarya looked a bit different now. She had lost the baby fat in her cheeks and stopped straightening her hair, so she wouldn't have blamed the patron for not recognizing her.

As it happened, Zarya's classmate never had a chance to recognize her, because she never looked even up at Zarya. She was checked in, then sent on her way, not once making eye contact with Zarya. After she was gone, Zarya had stood there, stunned. She had never noticed it back in high school, but now she understood it well—certain people were the help, and they were too insignificant to even look at.

Now that the place was empty, Zarya headed into the library, where free coffee awaited. It burned scalding-hot through her cup. As she waited for it to cool, Zarya gazed at the leather books along the bookshelves embedded in the walls. Most had no obvious title, only gilded embossing along the spines. She had seen this bookshelf countless times before waiting for her coffee to cool, but this time felt different. This time, Zarya could feel that this old mansion held secrets—just like the ocean did.

One book was different from the others. It was slightly less hoary than the rest, its hardcover less faded. When she pulled it out of the shelf, trapped dust floated through the air. The motes sparkled golden in the sun's beams.

Zarya traced the title with her index finger: *THE GRAVEYARD OF THE PACIFIC.* She flipped to the table of contents, where shipwrecks were listed in chronological order from 1852 to 1962.

Quietly, she read the words aloud to herself:

"Before Europeans settled into the area, the coast of Washington was populated by Chinook and Clatsop tribes. These peoples survived on a diet of seafood, berries, game, and roots. As traders of fur and explorers began inching further west, smallpox outbreaks began decimating the indigenous communities. By the time Meriwether Lewis and William Clark made their way to the coast, few tribe members remained alive. For those that did, relations were tense with the white settlers. The Native Americans and the white settlers oscillated between co-survival and war. The natives taught the settlers about hunting, fishing, whaling, and gathering. They traded furs and pottery. But every now and then, violence broke out. Land treaties were signed, then broken. By 1855, even the faraway West was not spared from the Indian Wars.

"After the indigenous were pushed further and further from their land, it was the white settlers whose deaths rose to notoriety along the ocean. The Graveyard of the Pacific earned its name during the Victorian Era. This graveyard spans the coastal waters between Vancouver Island and Tillamook Bay, where two waterways clash, creating furious currents. The unpredictability of these waters, combined with secret sandbars and impossibly thick fog, make for a deadly combination.

"The lighthouse up on the peninsula Rock was erected in 1850 to guide sailors from these stormy seas. Yet, in the aftermath of its construction, the number of documented shipwrecks skyrocketed. The following manuscript chronicles the thousands of ships that have capsized since that time.

"In 1853, the boat Vandalia sank at the mouth of the Columbia River, and the corpses of sailors washed ashore at what was dubbed Dead Man's Cove.

"In 1869, the ship Anna Anderson was bringing oysters up north from San Francisco when a severe storm erupted. Seven men and the captain all vanished at sea.

"In 1875, the vessel Sunshine floated ashore belly-up. That

same year, the SS Pacific was going from Victoria to San Francisco when it crashed into Orpheus in the waters near Cape Flattery.

"In 1881, the Lupatia sailed into fog and struck the lighthouse Rock, sinking to the bottom of the ocean. Of the sixteen souls that perished, four bodies were never recovered.

"In 1882, a beachgoer at Dead Man's Cove on multiple occasions swore he saw ghost ships floating through the fog. He returned many times and kept a record of these instances. During his nighttime expeditions, he could hear the wailing of tormented souls coming from the water. One day, it frightened him so deeply that he refused to ever return to the beach.

"In 1883, the schooner JC Cousins crashed aimlessly into the shore. Local onlookers approached as soon as the tides turned low, but to their great surprise, there was no one on the ship. The sailors had simply vanished in the ocean."

Zarya shut the book with a sudden thud. The melodic ringing in her ears was growing louder. She closed her eyes and pressed two fingers into her forehead. Perhaps it was still the alcohol from last night weighing her down. She took a sip of coffee hoping it would help.

When she reopened her eyes, an idea struck her. It seemed that the majority of documented shipwrecks began roughly around the time that the lighthouse was built. Perhaps they had simply never been documented before, or perhaps the lighthouse was somehow related to the wrecks. If that were the case, how could a tower of safety and light bring on so much death?

She dug through the bookshelf some more, pulling covers just enough to read their titles before sticking them back in their nooks. There were books on the coal business, others on the railroad business, and encyclopedias of local plant life. At last, she found one that might be of use—a history of the Irving family's influence on the area.

Zarya sank into the armchair, book in hand. This time, she read silently. She read about how Hurley Irving and his wife emigrated from Scotland to Washington state in 1845. Hurley took up business in the mining industry. He brought his brother, as well, to manage sales and shipping for the coal company. Hurley's business enterprises then expanded to include a sawmill, a quarry, real estate, dyking, ship manufacturing, and railroad engineering. He quickly became the richest man on the West coast, accumulating dozens of acres of property. It was thus that he decided to build a mansion in 1949—now known as the Irving Hotel.

As Hurley expanded into the ship and rail businesses, he was incentivized to construct a lighthouse up at the Rock. The lighthouse was completed in 1850 and, that summer, Hurley hired the first lighthouse keeper, a man by the name of Thomas Byrne. His wife, Josephine Byrne, joined him at the lighthouse. In 1851, the keeper's wife vanished from the premises. Rumors spread around town that she had gone mad and returned home to Maine. Or worse, that her husband had killed her. The lighthouse keeper did not last long at the lighthouse after that.

Despite the failure of the lighthouse in its early years, Hurley's legacy continued to ascend. Later that year, his wife had their first child. She was initially believed to be infertile, but the Irvings went on to have six children.

Whereas the first half of the tome was filled with such historical facts, the second half contained illustrations and photographs. Black-and-white, washed-out snapshots of Hurley Irving and his family tracing back to the 1850s. The further back the photos went, the poorer their quality. Formidably blurry images of Hurley showed a young man with wavy hair combed into a side parting, revealing a dapper face. The later photos showed him more clearly, as a middle-aged man with hollowed eyes.

The photos went as far back as 1850, to the construction of the lighthouse. Zarya saw the snapshot of builders working on the tower. The next photo she saw was labeled: *Lighthouse keeper, Thomas Byrne, and his wife, Josephine Byrne.*

When she saw the photograph, Zarya's hands froze. On the

flimsy piece of paper, she saw a man with thick sideburns. And beside him, a woman with dark hair, sharp cheekbones, and pale eyes. She wore a dark skirt and bodice, the latter clenched tightly around her throat with a lace collar. The image made Zarya want to swallow. But when she tried, she could not.

She recognized those eyes.

Last night, they had been more silver than gray—or perhaps it had just been an illusion from the lightning reflecting off the ocean.

The siren had a name. Apparently, it was Josephine.

Josephine, 1850

Chapter 6

When the invitation to attend a party at the Irving estate arrived, Josephine's first thought was one of turmoil. What could she possibly wear that would be respectable enough for such a wealthy family? She owned only one dress that might have been elegant enough—but Josephine had long ago decided that the only place she would ever wear it was to her own funeral. The dress was too delicate to risk wearing otherwise, and it brought back memories that she would have preferred to be buried with her.

Her second-best option was a plum-colored skirt and bodice set. It had a simple cut, with none of the frills and lacework of the other dresses she had seen in town, but Josephine knew it suited her coloring.

Josephine begged Thomas to trim his beard until the very last moment. It had grown scraggly and uneven, but he did not seem to care. Each time she uttered her dissatisfaction, his only reaction was a grunt. If anything, Thomas' rugged appearance would be more damning of their social status than her dress.

Hurley had arranged for a boy to look after the lighthouse tonight in Thomas' place so that the couple could attend the party. Josephine was not sure what to expect of the night. She knew about the Irving festivities only what she had heard from the other women at teatime—that they were lavish and decadent. Hurley had a fortune to spend, and he intended to do just that.

But when she stepped through the front gates, the opulence still swept away Josephine's breath. The front doors were wide ajar, and inside she could see servants holding silver trays of seafood and drink. Amber lamplight flickered against the dishes—oysters plucked from the ocean not far away, caviar on crackers, preserved peaches, brandy in balloon glasses, and sparkling wine in crystal flutes. Josephine was so overwhelmed by the array that she almost forgot to thank the servant who shoved a glass in her hand.

"Thomas, isn't this a marvel?" she whispered in her husband's ear.

Thomas snatched a cracker from the tray and swallowed it in one efficient bite. "Yes."

She entered deeper into the lamplight. All around swayed women in sequined dresses, grasping the stems of their glasses delicately through gloved hands. A troupe of violists and cellists played their instruments, making the guests' chatter rise louder above it. From the looks of it, a few of the invitees were already feeling the influence of the wine. Their movements were fluid, their lips loose.

Josephine squinted her eyes through the crowd for a sign of Amelia. She found the lady of the house near the window, beaming at one of the guests in an embroidered dress. Josephine headed towards her.

When Amelia spotted her, she squealed in joy, reaching to embrace Josephine. "Welcome! I am so glad you could make it."

"Of course. When we heard Hurley arranged for it to be possible, we could not decline." Josephine looked around again, wondering where Hurley was, after all.

"Wonderful. So, Thomas is here, as well?" asked Amelia.

Thomas had been right behind Josephine when she had started across the room, but somewhere along the way, he had gotten lost amid the bustle. Josephine could see only the edge of his face in the distance as he reached for a second serving of caviar.

"Yes, he's here. I believe he's busying himself with the food."

Amelia let out a chiming laugh, but Thomas' rudeness was not lost on Josephine. With an apologetic smile, she said, "I'll go fetch him to say hello."

"It's quite alright if he's busy—"

"Nonsense." Josephine wove through the crowd to tap her husband on the shoulder. Thomas was downing the remnants of his wine and reaching for a second serving.

"You should come say hello to Amelia," Josephine said. Parties such as this one were the faint relic of a memory in her mind, but she did recall it was customary for guests to at least greet the hosts.

"I'll say hello later."

Josephine clamped down her jaw. She would need to be tactful if she were going to convince him. After all, flat-out commanding a husband to do something was a guaranteed way to ensure his refusal. With a pleading smile, she said, "She specifically requested to see you, Thomas. I think she wants to thank the man who's been keeping her husband's ships safe."

Thomas might have been a wild species, but even wild men were men. "Alright," he conceded.

Josephine looped her hand through his arm, showing him the way through the crowd to Amelia. The lady of the house was politely directing a servant when they found her. The servant left with a nod, and Amelia directed her attention towards Thomas. "Welcome!"

"Good evening." He gave Amelia a perfunctory kiss on the glove.

"I'm so glad you could make it," she repeated, as if she only had a few pleasantries in her repertoire. There was warmth in her demeanor, but Josephine could tell the woman was running out of topics to discuss with them. After all, what did she have in common with a lighthouse keeper and his wife?

Josephine scanned the room, searching for a subject of conversation. Her eyes befell a man who had clearly imbibed more than the others. He was bowing theatrically at a woman who did not seem quite impressed with his display.

"Who's that?" she asked.

Amelia followed her gaze. When she saw who Josephine was staring at, her face soured. "Oh, good lord. Let's not even speak of him. That man is foul."

"He seems quite friendly with the ladies," Josephine pointed out as the man began attempting to dance with a different woman. The second woman also rebuffed his advances with a stern gaze.

"That he is," sighed Amelia. "In the words of the very wise John Wesley, we must not associate with those 'who live an easy, indolent way,' but alas. Hurley insists that we open our home even to the basest of people. He does not believe in the moral values that keep our society in order."

"Is that so?" Josephine wondered what other laws of morality Hurley ignored.

"Yes, Hurley thinks himself avant-garde." Amelia lowered her voice to a mere whisper. "That man is a miner, you see. Hurley drinks with him sometimes at the saloon, to get a sense of the miners' grievances."

"That's most honorable."

Amelia shrugged her shoulders. "I love that my husband cares about his workers, but it does not mean we need to open our home to those who defile good Christian values."

But before Josephine had a chance to answer, she spotted the man of the house across the room. There, among the sea of men and women, his pale, freckled skin glowed in sharp contrast to his dark suit. For a moment, there was a pause in time, and Hurley's gaze found hers. They locked eyes.

He was not a particularly handsome man, but something about his appearance was starting to grow on her. And when Hurley smiled at Josephine, and there was something wolfish in those icy eyes. It was more than a cordial smile. If looks could speak, his would have communicated, *I am very pleased to see you here.*

She could not help the devious look she returned to him. She kept it there a moment longer than she should have, after which Josephine guilelessly averted her gaze. It was plausible deniability. If anyone had seen the exchange, she could simply claim they had misinterpreted a friendly smile. But, as far as she could tell, neither of their spouses had followed her line of sight.

She could still feel his eyes on her, and suddenly Josephine was overwhelmed by a desire to speak with him. If her instincts were right—and they usually were—Hurley would follow her if she wandered from the room.

"I feel a bit stuffy," Josephine announced to Amelia and Thomas. "Please excuse me just a moment."

Amelia's arched brows furrowed. "Oh, dear. Are you alright? Do you need assistance?"

"Perfectly fine." Josephine laid a hand on her corset, as if to signal she just needed some air in her lungs. "Thomas, please take good care of Amelia while I'm gone."

Thomas said nothing. He simply stared at the golden liquid in his glass, and Josephine took his silence as an opportunity to walk towards the dimly lit corridor. She took her time with each step, giving Hurley ample time to catch up with her. As she stepped out of the parlor, she could see her shadow's silhouette in the wainscoted walls. And, with each footstep, another silhouette approached hers, one in the shape of a man.

At the end of the hall, she turned slightly so that her profile was facing him. She fanned herself as if needing a moment to catch her breath. She knew she had a pretty profile, with sharp cheekbones and a sloping jawline, and she wanted him to see it. And, when Hurley was finally close enough, she pretended to catch him walking towards her. As their eyes met again, she smiled in delight.

"Needed some fresh air?" he asked, bowing to kiss the back of her hand.

"I did," she said. When his lips came into contact with her hand, something spidery crawled up her spine. "This is like no party I have ever seen, so I needed a moment to collect myself."

"To good effect, I hope."

"Certainly."

"If you would like even more air, I can show you to the garden." Hurley's eyes glinted in the candlelight like glass before a fire.

"Sure, I'd like to see the garden."

He motioned in the opposite direction to which they had come. "Ladies first."

She took his invitation, certain with each footstep that he was drinking her in. She kept walking forward until Hurley instructed her to take the first exit on the left. There, he held the door open for her. She stepped foot into a covered veranda where the air had already cooled.

Outside, the moon was sheathed behind a sheet of clouds. It was dark, only the lights from inside the house casting diamond-shaped patterns through the windowpanes and onto the grass. Josephine felt the cold air prick at her bare chest.

"You look stunning, you know," said Hurley, in a tone his wife surely would not have appreciated if she were present.

"Thank you."

They stood there, beside a lilac bush, in silence for a few moments. Then, Hurley asked, "Do you feel less faint now?"

She had never stated she felt faint, but his assumption was as good of an excuse as any. "Yes, I feel much better, thank you."

"Good." He stuck a hand into the pocket of his trousers. As he did, his jacket flapped in the breeze. "How is life in the lighthouse?"

Josephine shrugged. "It can be lonesome at times."

"Even with ladies' teatime?" He motioned at the house behind him. "Even with parties like this?"

"Even so."

"Why is that?"

No one had ever asked her that before. "Loneliness isn't about the quantity of acquaintances or the frequency of seeing them," she said. And even if it were, a party here and there was not enough to keep the loneliness at bay.

"No? What is it about, then?"

Josephine considered the question for a while. Then, she said, "It's about knowing you won't be alone in your time of need. That there will be somewhere to turn."

"Well, you have that. You have Thomas. And Amelia and the other ladies. And me."

At this last word, Josephine sensed a shift in his tone. Before, it had been amicable. Now, it once again seemed to harbor secrets.

"Do I?" she asked.

"Yes, of course. Anything you need, simply let me know."

His boldness was emboldening her, too. "And what is it *you* need?"

"Me?" Hurley let out a chuckle. "I have everything a man could want."

Everything except a child.

"Sometimes, I think I have too much."

"What do you mean by that?"

He sighed, though still with a smile on his lips. "I have many businesses, Josephine, and they are big responsibilities. Take the mining business, for instance. I need to look after my men, or else their families will turn to me if something happens."

He spoke like someone who truly cared about his workers. And yet, Josephine wondered, would a man who truly cared about his workers be speaking so intimately with one of his workers' wives?

"That is very honorable of you," she said.

"I try to do the right thing. I don't always get it right, but I try."

The trajectory of the conversation seemed to have gone too deep for him, because Hurley at once whisked her by the hand and back into the house.

"I love this song," he said, just as the faint echoes of violin made their way to them.

Puzzled, she followed his lead.

He had pulled her back into the parlor in the flash of a moment. Suddenly, Josephine was back in a sea of people and laughter and music and glamor. There, in the middle of the room, couples had started dancing to a peppy waltz rhythm. Hurley released Josephine and found his wife in the crowd, pulling her onto the dancefloor. Josephine watched them dance, gliding so elegantly across the hardwood. She peered around for a sign of her own husband, but Thomas was nowhere to be found. She longed more than anything to be there among the dancing. This moment was so fleeting. Soon, it would vanish.

When the song came to an end and another began, Hurley and Amelia stepped off the dancefloor.

"Where is Thomas?" asked Hurley, perhaps sensing Josephine's ache for dancing.

"I'm not quite sure." She felt so pathetic saying it, but Josephine was growing accustomed to Thomas' unexplained absences.

"He went to go speak with one of your associates," Amelia explained to her husband. "Though he's been gone a while, so I don't know exactly…"

"Then I will dance with you," announced Hurley to Josephine. Then, turning to his wife: "You don't mind, do you, darling?"

Amelia shook her head. "Of course not. Go right ahead."

Josephine did not have time to assess whether the lady of the house was indeed unbothered. In an instant, she felt Hurley's hand pulling her own. It was warm and cushioned, unlike her husband's calloused skin. Before long, Hurley had drawn her into the middle of the room, where he put his other hand just beneath her shoulder blade. He had so much zest in that moment, and the music was so lively, that Josephine could not even think of propriety. She could not consider the fact that she was dancing with someone other than her husband. She could only think of how much she enjoyed it.

The music seemed to have sped up, because now her head was spinning from all the motion. Aside from Hurley's beaming face, everyone else was a blur. Josephine let out a laugh. She did not know what was happening to her, only that her heart pulsed heavily every time Hurley was around.

At last, the song came to an end, and Hurley gently dropped her hand. He bowed in thanks. "You are a radiant dancer, madam."

Josephine blushed, though luckily her cheeks were already rosy from the dancing. When she returned to the sidelines, she found her husband there. Thomas had been watching them dance—though she could not tell if there were traces of anger in his gaze. He looked the same as always, uninterested in her.

"Where were you?" she asked. "I wanted to dance. I was looking for you, and you were not there."

"You found a dance partner," he responded, matter-of-factly.

Before Josephine could think of something to say, she saw Hurley and Amelia approaching. Hurley must have found his wife among the guests. Josephine grabbed the nearest wine glass, not quite sure whether it was hers, and took a hefty gulp.

"You found him," Amelia noted.

Josephine cast a look in her husband's direction. "I did."

"Thomas, your wife is a marvelous dancer," interjected Hurley. Apparently, it was not enough for Hurley to dance with someone else's wife—he needed to openly acknowledge it, too.

Josephine eyed him curiously. Was Hurley *trying* to flaunt the flirtation in front of their spouses? Something about it felt like a bid for power. Like he wanted to see how far he could go without getting caught. Like he wanted them all to know that he could do whatever he pleased.

But Amelia did not seem bothered at all. "She truly is!" she agreed.

Josephine placed her glass on the table next to her. "This wine is decadent, but I don't know if I can finish it." She put the back of her hand to her temple, feeling the warmth there.

"Then don't," said Thomas.

"But I wouldn't want to let it go to waste."

Across from her, Hurley listened to the exchange carefully. "I'll take it," he offered in a nonchalant tone.

The space between the four of them seemed to have

compressed. Josephine tried to swallow, but her throat was constricted. It was one thing to dance with a lady, and quite another to drink from her glass. Hurley was communicating something to her, though she was not quite sure what—that he did not mind sharing her saliva, that he was not disgusted by the exchange of bodily fluids, that he wanted to make her comfortable in his home? Josephine shot a glance at Amelia, but even she had gone white as a piece of papyrus.

Josephine cleared her throat. "Are you—certain?"

"Of course." Hurley extended his fingers toward the stem of her glass. "I'm not squeamish."

"Well, alright." Josephine handed him her glass with reluctance. She watched him bring the rim to his lips, then drink from her glass. He seemed utterly unbothered about the matter.

Across the room, Josephine caught sight of the miner Amelia had mentioned earlier, who was now attempting to dance with a third victim. His hands were too low down her back, by the cinched part of her corset where it was improper to touch. The woman, in turn, was keeping as much distance as possible between their torsos.

It occurred to Josephine at that moment that there were two kinds of men—the kind who openly expressed their desire to bed as many women as possible, and the kind like Hurley.

Men who pretended to be concerned with decency.

Wolves in sheep's clothing.

Zarya, 2023

Chapter 7

Zarya paced back and forth across the room. Her shoes thudded quietly against the rug, a threadbare relic of the past with the same peacock feather motif. She noticed once again the feeling of being watched, though she was not quite sure what to do about it.

She was almost certain now that the woman in the photograph was the same creature she had seen in the ocean. Josephine Byrne, apparently.

Even now, Zarya could hear the siren call echoing through her head, lulling her out to sea. She could not trust herself to be alone today—not with yesterday's tequila still trimming her impulse control and the sun searing through her eyes.

She was startled by a loud vibrating noise in her pocket. Zarya lifted the phone to her face.

Her mother. Again. Third call today.

It would not have been her first choice, but Zarya needed to go home. Out of this ghost of a building and near familiar faces. She had ignored too many of her mother's calls, and she knew what came next. The pop-up visits. The yelling. The threats.

Zarya tossed the empty coffee cup into the trash bin and headed to the parking lot, where her Honda awaited beneath the baking sun. Already, the Sunday morning exodus had started a trail of light traffic on the one-lane street. Children along the sidewalks pranced around, eager for a last scoop of ice cream before heading home to wherever they had come from.

Once she was out of the town center, it was mainly black cottonwoods and Pacific yews that spanned the sides of the road. The spring storm having passed, the greenery was lurid. Verdant blades of grass jutted out of the earth, and buds dangled heavily through the balmy air. When spring came to Washington, it came with unparalleled freshness.

Zarya's childhood neighborhood was not far off. She found herself slowing down to peer through windows to the insides of homes. In one home, a family gathered around the dining table. A young boy reached for the carton of orange juice while his grandpa helped himself to lunch. At the house next door, two women baked in beach chairs, holding champagne flutes filled with mimosas. A bottle of Chardonnay glinted in the grass between them.

The sights made Zarya's heart drop into her belly. She was always watching love from the outside looking in, never from within it.

Her parents' house came into focus next. Zarya pulled up to the driveway and stepped out of the car, even if her body resisted it with each second.

The house was a cream-paneled Dutch colonial. Window shutters flanked the windows. Through the window, Zarya saw none of the cheerful hustle and bustle from the other houses on the street. There was only an apron-clad woman standing before the stove, her back turned to the glass.

Zarya unlocked the front door and heard right away the scurrying of slippers against hardwood. Her mother turned the corner with her blonde hair and mint-blue eyes.

"Zarya!" The woman ambled to her head-first, eventually latching onto Zarya with a tight grip. Zarya gave a gentle squeeze before disentangling herself.

"Hi, Mama."

"You didn't tell me you were coming. I would have made something nicer for you." She threw a lingering look toward the pot on the stove. "All I have today is *borscht*."

Despite her thin frame, Zarya's mother was far stronger than she looked. She grasped her daughter's hand firmly.

"That's fine, Mama," said Zarya, inching towards the dining table.

Her mother leaned over the parapet toward the staircase. "Oleg, come here! Zarya is home!"

There was no response from his office.

Rivulets of tension were starting to pulse in Zarya's forehead. Already, her mother began hovering around her, toying with her hair and dissecting her every item of clothing. Though Zarya was further from the ocean here, the hymn between her ears grew more forceful by the moment. It washed over her, the pressure building in her head. Like a train growing nearer, the rhythmic chugging growing to a deafening horn.

She momentarily excused herself to the bathroom for a slice of solitude. When she returned, her father had materialized in the kitchen, too.

"Hello," he said with a curt nod.

"Hi, Papa."

It was like nothing had changed. With just a five-minute drive, Zarya had arrived right back where she had started—surrounded by the constant stream of chatter from her mother and the silence from her father. They were like a ball of gas and a black hole, one producing nuclear heat and the other swallowing it whole. Together, they had produced Zarya, whose main purpose in life was to avoid being completely engulfed.

When there was a momentary gap in her mother's stream of consciousness, Zarya interjected. "Have you heard about the woman who drowned?"

"Oh yes, how terrible," her mother said. "I so worry about you being at that hotel without us, Zarya. You're too far for us to look after you! When I hear news like that, it makes my stomach turn."

"I'm five minutes away, Mama."

"Yes, but why not live at home? That way, you could save up your money and—"

"Mama, please." Zarya felt her thighs starting to clench up against the chair. "We've had this talk before."

"Yes, but I still don't understand your reasons..."

For the first time, Zarya's father decided to use his voice. "Enough." One word, as if it was enough to change anything. Where he came from, one word of reprimand from a husband *should* have been enough.

Eager to change the subject, Zarya asked, "What do you think happened to that girl? The one who drowned, I mean."

Suddenly, a hush fell over the kitchen. There were a few long moments before her mother spoke again. When she did, it was to say, "Well, all I know is what my mother warned me about, and her mother before her."

Zarya's father rolled his eyes but said nothing. His wife went on.

"They're called *rusalki* where we come from. Women of the water. They are very dangerous, Zarya, so please be careful anytime you go out to the water."

Zarya recalled those ghastly eyes that had latched onto her. "But what are they?"

"Usually, they're young women who have died a violent death near a body of water—some of their own volition, others at the hands of others. Their spirits linger in the water, and they seduce the living for revenge. Their voices draw out the prey, and then their hair ensnares the victims. They are said to wear combs in their hair made of fishbones."

"This is nonsense," said Zarya's father, shaking his head. "Old wives' tales, Zarya. Don't listen to her."

Across the kitchen, Zarya's mother was overtaken by a burst of fury. "It is not nonsense!" she screeched, her voice shaking. Her eyes looked like blue marbles about to pop out of her eyes.

"But it is," he went on, using the tone he reserved for his eight-grade students. "*Rusalki* were originally a legend from Slavic Paganism. They were not considered evil. Rather, they helped with fertility and watering the fields of crops. The legend took on a more sinister connotation over time, as Paganism itself started to develop a bad reputation. And besides, the legend pertains to freshwater spirits in Russia, not ocean creatures."

"Don't listen to him, Zarya. There are evil spirits out there, and you see the proof for yourself. Those who died violent deaths never stay underwater forever. Their spirits are angry. They want retribution."

Little did she know just how much proof Zarya had seen. If she had, Zarya would never be able to leave this house again.

"So, what's the solution, then?" asked Zarya. "How can a person protect themselves from *rusalki*?"

Her mother answered, "Well, definitely avoid bodies of water. Especially during Rusalka Week."

"When's that?"

"In early June, when they come out from the water to swing from the willows at night."

"Okay. What else?"

Her mother gathered her thoughts for a moment. Then, she added, "There's only one thing that can stop a vengeful spirit, Zarya, and that is justice. Justice for the original violence that occurred. The death that lurks in murky waters will only be stopped when it's pulled out to the surface. What is hidden beneath the surface must be brought out."

That was the last that they spoke of *rusalki*. Zarya drank the sour beet soup her mother had made, then headed to her childhood bedroom. As suffocating as the air felt inside this house, it would be better to stay home tonight. Her mother was right that staying away from the water was wise, especially if Zarya was the next target.

Her bedroom was empty but for the eggshell-colored

furniture—a white desk, white leather on the bed's headboard, a white bookcase on which hardly anything sat. Zarya had never taken the time to decorate her room, because it had never felt like a permanent home. What point was there in making something feel like hers when she knew it was just a temporary stop?

Of course, that hadn't stopped her mother from decorating the place according to her sterile, minimalistic style. According to Zarya's mom, the two of them were indistinguishable. Two peas in a pod. Just like sisters. Best friends. Sometimes, Zarya got the distinct feeling that her mother wanted to crawl under her skin and live there. Zarya's body was not her own—it was a mere replica, an extension of her mother. Zarya had spent every day since adolescence trying to outrun her mother's asphyxiating attention. Sometimes, she wondered if the only way to truly escape it would be through death. Maybe then, her mother would finally understand: *My body is mine, not yours.*

It must not have been easy for her parents to move all the way from St. Petersburg to a small town in Washington, of course. Life in the Soviet Union must have been hard, even for a well-educated, newly married couple of teachers. They had left behind everything and everyone for a life of unknowns. Traded one gloomy land for another. But sometimes, Zarya wondered—why did the burden of filling her mother's emptiness fall onto her? And how was she expected to fill it? Her mother was like a leaky bottle that, no matter how much Zarya tried to pour into, would always end up empty again.

Sleep was shaky that night. Zarya heard the footsteps outside her door, pacing deep into the night. She even heard her door creak open around two in the morning, saw the silhouette of her mother's head in the doorway. It was as if the woman needed to check whether her daughter was still there—still breathing, still in existence. She was like a cat who could not understand where a toy went when it was placed under a carpet. To her, Zarya did not exist unless she had proof of it right before her eyes.

The figure in the doorway stepped back out momentarily, but the gesture had unnerved Zarya. She had trouble sleeping after that. How could she sleep, knowing that someone was monitoring her?

In the morning, Zarya tiptoed out of the room as quietly as she could. She grabbed herself a cup of coffee and prepared to head back to work. When she turned around from the espresso machine, her father sat in one of the dining chairs shaking his head, phone in hand.

"What is it?" she asked.

"This is only going to fuel your mother's superstitions," he replied, flashing his phone screen toward Zarya.

Zarya drew nearer. There, in black letters against a bright backdrop, were the words: *Days after local's tragic passing, thousands of dead fish wash up on shore near Dead Man's Cove.*

Zarya placed her lips on the rim of the coffee mug, inhaling the tendrils of aromatic steam. "Papa, what do you think caused it?"

Her father shrugged. "High tides retreating very quickly, perhaps. I'm not a scientist, but I'm sure there's a scientific explanation."

"Well, what if there isn't?"

"If there isn't a scientific explanation, it's because we haven't found it yet. But it's there." For a moment, he looked at Zarya, as if noticing her skepticism. "What is it *you* think about all this?"

Zarya retreated towards the kitchen island. If she told the truth now, her father would surely be calling the nearest inpatient facility. So, she said the closest thing to the truth that she could muster.

"I think there are a lot of things we don't understand. I don't know what to make of them, but I'd like to find out."

It was then that her mother's footsteps resounded down the staircase, the soles of her plastic slippers slapping against the floor with each step.

"Good morning!"

"Morning." Zarya tossed the last sip of coffee into the sink. "Alright, I gotta go."

"What, so soon?" Her mother took Zarya's words like a slap. "What time do you start work? Don't you have time for breakfast?"

"I have to run an errand before work."

Zarya's mother looked at the clock pinned flat against the wall. "It's only seven, and the hotel is just five minutes away..."

"I have to go," Zarya reiterated. She grabbed her car keys from the bowl on the counter.

"Well, when will we see you next? I want to see you more often, Zarya..." Zarya's mother gave her another excessively tight embrace. Zarya tried to wiggle out of it as discreetly as possible without wounding her mother's feelings.

"I'll let you know." She headed out the door.

The sun was once more sheathed today behind a layer of bruise-blue clouds. Zarya drove past the town, to the peninsula that hosted Dead Man's Cove, the headland called the Rock, and the lighthouse atop it. She parked along the shoulder and stepped out. Her ears were ringing now, a note so crystalline that she would do anything to get closer to it. With each footstep toward the ocean, her wish came true.

To reach the ocean, she needed to pass the forest. It was so dark underneath the canopy that only slivers of light shone between tree trunks. Along the trail, tall stalks of purple foxglove bobbed in the breeze, their flowers dangling like bells. Roots ran through the path in much the same way that veins ran through a person's wrist, bulging in some parts before disappearing under the skin. Zarya stepped over them.

She crested the bluff, and then the water came into view. There was no sea-creature out at sea today, no leviathan slithering across the surface. But she could smell the putrid stench of death before she saw it. Zarya buried her nose into the sleeve of her jacket. In the strip of sand known as Dead Man's Cove, thousands upon thousands of dead fish had washed ashore. Not the pretty, silver-glittering kind, but fish as black as gangrene. There were pools of them, each larger than the next.

Zarya felt her stomach tighten with the sudden urge for reflux. She gagged up acrid saliva, managing to keep down the morning's coffee somehow. She didn't care what her father had to say about the matter—this was no act of nature. It was preternatural, something unclean. Whether it was a ploy meant to drag out more victims or a foreboding threat, she did not know. But as she caught a glimpse of the derelict lighthouse on her way back to the car, Zarya knew one thing for sure.

Whatever monster swam in these waters, it had been created in that lighthouse.

Josephine, 1850

Chapter 8

When Josephine had envisioned marriage during her maidenhood, she had pictured nights spent cocooned in the strong arms of a husband, and so much laughter that it made her cheeks sore, and fresh flowers at her bedside every week. She had not imagined a husband who spent his nights locked away in a tower, the sheets on his side of the bed cold and unruffled, the ache in her belly for a love that did not exist.

She had expected the love between her and Thomas to grow over time. After all, that was what people said would happen. Marriage was a partnership, but affection could be kindled over the course of years. And yet, how could love possibly sprout when they hardly saw each other? When, in the times that their paths did intersect, Thomas uttered hardly a word to her? When he visited their marriage bed so seldomly?

He is not interested in socializing, Josephine told herself.

Then why, she wondered, was he so eager to take Hurley up on his offer for a drink at the saloon a few weeks after the Irving party?

Hurley once again arranged for a boy to take up the lighthouse in Thomas' place. The boy was no older than fifteen. He was Chinese, speaking not a drop of English. He arrived at the lighthouse wearing linen trousers and suspenders, but the professional attire did not conceal his poverty well. The undersides of his nails were dark with grime, his skin already sun-beaten despite his age. The boy gave Josephine a cordial nod before heading up the staircase to the lantern room.

Hurley had arranged for a carriage to transport Thomas to the saloon. She watched her husband get behind its slick, black door. Watched as the coachman gave his horse a slight flick and the carriage disappeared between the trees.

When Josephine had arrived at the lighthouse, the foliage had been bright and algae-green, but now the leaves hung heavy and dark in the forest. Their canopy shaded the area. She watched them rustle for a moment before heading back inside the house.

Thomas had left right after dinnertime. He would be gone no longer than an hour or two, she told herself. After all, he did not enjoy speaking with people.

Two hours passed, and Josephine peered at the clock curiously. She could not imagine what Thomas and Hurley had in common to discuss for so long. *They must be heading back soon*, she thought.

At three hours past Thomas' departure, the last of the light drained from the sky. The house was so quiet and still that Josephine began wondering whether she really existed. In an attempt to verify, she took a cup of tea up to the boy. He thanked her with a few words uttered in a language she did not understand, and with a look of gratitude that was enough to confirm she was in fact real. Then she headed back down and wondered whether to head to sleep.

Josephine rustled beneath the bedsheets as midnight came and went. By the time the hour hand of the clock crept into the small hours of the night, a rage was boiling inside her.

Thomas was so quick to cut their interactions short, so uninterested in getting to know her, and yet he had now spent six hours out with Hurley. The obvious conclusion was that Thomas was not uninterested in *people* so much as he was uninterested in Josephine. She wondered what she had done wrong to be so uninteresting. What had she done wrong that she was once again so unimportant?

By the time two in the morning struck, the tears had dampened Josephine's pillowcase. It was sometime between two and three that she heard the clomping of hooves out in the forest, followed by the clamor of voices.

She did not care that she was in her nightgown. She did not care that her hip-length hair flowed down her breasts. She did not care that it was indecent for any man other than her husband to see her in this manner. Josephine hurried to the kitchen regardless. There, through the window, she saw the carriage door open and a man in a woolen frock coat jump out. Illuminated only by moonlight, she could not see who it was, only that it was not Thomas. Then, a second figure dropped out of the carriage, holding on to the first one as if he were a life raft. His movements were lethargic and wobbly.

The door to the kitchen opened, and she saw now in the candlelight that the two shapes belonged to Hurley and Thomas. Hurley wore a sottish smile, but it was nothing compared to Thomas, who dangled from his shoulder like a man risen from the grave.

"Good evening, madam," said Hurley. Most men would have had the decency to keep their eyes averted, but Hurley made no attempt to conceal the way his eyes were drawn to Josephine's bosom.

"Evening?" Josephine crossed her arms over her chest. "It's been nearly eight hours since you took my husband to the saloon. I would not call this time of the morning evening still."

"My deepest apologies. It turns out your husband is quite a good sport. Maine folk sure can drink, can't they?"

Josephine pursed her lips harder. "How is he to tend to the lighthouse now, in this state?"

"You are right, he is in no state for it. We'll need to put him to bed, and the boy will need to work through the night."

"The boy is far too young to be staying up all night."

Hurley responded, "The boy is keen to make some coin. I'm sure he is not bothered by the prospect."

She had no retort to that. "Fine. Bring Thomas in this way."

She showed Hurley to the bedroom, where he dropped Thomas into bed with one hefty movement. Josephine untied her husband's shoelaces and tossed his shoes onto the floor. As she did, the strong scent of Scotch permeated the air. Thomas let out a weak groan but was in no state to say much of anything.

"Turn him on his side," instructed Hurley. "We wouldn't want him to choke on his vomit." Something about the way he said it sounded sinister.

Josephine turned a scathing eye over to Hurley before doing as told. Once Thomas was a fetal position, she motioned for the kitchen and showed Hurley out of the bedroom. When they were both standing in the dim light, she shut the door behind them.

"Again, I'm deeply apologetic," Hurley said, but he wore an impish smile on his lips that indicated otherwise.

"You are a terrible influence." Josephine did not care if the words offended him. Her temper had long ago tipped over into rage.

But her words did not seem to affect him. "You are probably right."

Hurley had seemed sober in comparison to Thomas, but she noticed the drawl to his words, the woodsy scent of his breath. He was looking her up and down, and not very discreetly, either.

Though she would have liked nothing more than to strike him with her fists, Josephine could not deny that there was still some magnetism between them. Some sort of connection there. Hurley was a man who did a great job of wanting her, and Josephine was a woman who did a great job of being wanted. Their needs fit together quite nicely.

"You look even more lovely at nighttime," said Hurley, putting into words the palpable tension that spun around them.

Still angry, she refused to thank him. Instead, she replied, "Well, it won't be of much use now that my husband is unconscious, will it?"

"That's a shame." Hurley's smile expanded. "A veritable waste."

She knew the impulses she was having were sinful. After all, she was a married woman. Her husband was just past that door. But at that moment, Josephine hated Thomas with all her heart. She wanted to teach him a lesson. She could not force him to be more considerate of her wishes—or really influence him in any way whatsoever. The only tool at her disposal was revenge. Since she could not get what she wanted, she could only get even.

So, when Hurley brushed the backside of his hand against her cheek, she did not smack his hand away and shriek in astonishment. She merely held his gaze until he dropped his hand and walked towards the door.

"Don't be too harsh on him," said Hurley as he put on his hat. "He is but a man, and we men are weak to temptation."

It almost seemed like Hurley *expected* Josephine to give her husband an earful tomorrow.

And then the thought occurred to Josephine that perhaps that had been his intention all along. Had Hurley taken Thomas out for a rowdy night at the saloon specifically because he knew it would create tension in their marriage?

As Hurley stepped out into the night, his figure was again shrouded in darkness, but Josephine could see him clearer than ever.

He knew how to sacrifice a pawn to get the queen.

Summer at the lighthouse was tolerable. Occasionally, Josephine could see whales peeking over the horizon, especially if she looked through the set of spyglasses that Thomas kept on the table. Water spouted from their backs, and sometimes they flipped over the water, sending heavy ripples in all directions.

At dusk, a bat frequently winged its way over the treetops, until the very last traces of periwinkle were lost from the sky. And, most excitedly, she saw a seal in the cove. Its fur was speckled, pale with darker streaks, and the slippery blubber beneath it glistened in the sun. Josephine had stepped outside to greet it, and the creature looked back at her through black, marbly eyes. Maybe she was seeing things, but she swore there was love behind those eyes.

"So, *you're* who I saw in the water that day," Josephine whispered, recalling the day she'd first met Hurley, when a pair of eyes had glinted at her from the ocean.

Once upon a time, Josephine's mother had told her a story about *selkies*. It was a tale that had been told across the islands of the frozen north for many moons, though it deviated slightly based on location. In some places, the legend started with a woman being drowned. In others, it started with her willingly walking into the sea. Even yet, some places said she was never a woman. But now, she was a *selkie*, a seal-woman.

Josephine's mother had learned the story in her hometown, a little fishing village on the east coast of Ireland. She had always started the story by saying that the sea was graphite-colored beneath a stormy sky. White summits zipped through its surface, rising and falling beneath the wind's incantation. There, a woman dove into the sea to die. When she opened her eyes at the bottom of the sea, between plumes of seaweed and glittering sand, she was reborn as a *selkie*. She roamed the vast waters with unparalleled freedom.

Until, one day, she was captured by a fisherman. His net dug into her sealskin, and she wriggled to get free. But the fisherman could see something in her eyes—some sort of human essence—and he insisted on taking her home, where he propped her by his hearth. Overnight, the *selkie*'s tail melted by firelight, and she was left only with her human flesh. The fisherman fell in love with her, and for seven years she stayed with him. She bore his children.

The years passed. She was content on land, but she could not forget the taste of freedom. And anytime she smelled the scent of brine, it called to her. She missed the feeling of arctic-cold water against her blubber, the plumpness of the oysters she cracked open with her teeth, the depths she used to explore of her own accord.

She could not stay here.

So, one day, as the midnight sun dropped behind the horizon, she jumped once more into the water. At contact with the sea, her sealskin returned to her. She cried a tear for the family she had left behind on land.

It was a most sad legend, thought Josephine. Why should a woman have to choose between freedom and companionship?

There were other tales of water-women, too. Josephine's father, though not as loquacious as her mother, would sometimes tell Josephine tales from his own home country, France. According to him, there were *melusines* in the freshwater, creatures that were half-woman, half-fish. In the original legend, such a creature named Melusine married a human man. She made him vow to never look upon her on a Saturday. But one day, Melusine's husband broke his promise. He peeked into her chamber, where he glimpsed her bathing in half-fish form.

In all the tales of water-women, there was a common thread—the betraying husband. Josephine was not sure why, but she had understood, even as a little girl, that certain legends spoke to something so true that they permeated across country borders and cultural dialects. Certain tales ran so deep that they were recognized in every part of the world.

So, yes, Josephine hoped to one day see a water-spirit. But despite the summertime visits, autumn would soon whisk away even her whale and bat and seal friends. Ghostberries would bloom on every bush that bordered the lighthouse—the first sign of the oncoming season of death. Fog would spill from the ocean, some days so thick that Josephine could see nothing around but white. She would wonder if this was how death felt. Then the foghorn would blow without warning, and she would startle so hard that her heart tried to leap from her chest.

Thomas was out today, on one of his infrequent ventures into town to pick up supplies. Josephine sat idly at the dining table, gazing out at the whiteness. Then, out of the mist, the figure of a man materialized. Was Thomas back so soon?

She recognized that it was not Thomas by the fine cut of the man's coat. Then she saw those ice-blue eyes set deeply in his skull.

She was out by the door straight away. "Hurley," she said on an exhale.

Hurley removed his hat and stepped right in. "Hello." His features went from overexposed in the fog to shadowy in the dimly lit room. "Is Thomas around?"

"He just stepped out," said Josephine. Aside from her husband, Hurley was the first person she had seen in days. She had teatime with the ladies later in the week, but this was a welcome surprise.

"What unfortunate timing." Hurley's eyes spanned the contours of Josephine's face.

"Some tea, perhaps?" she offered, brushing past him toward the stove.

"Certainly."

As she started the tea kettle, Hurley dropped into a chair. "I hope you and Thomas have reconciled your differences since our night at the saloon."

"Of course." She would never give him the satisfaction of thinking otherwise.

In truth, the day after the saloon had been a dark one. Josephine had pleaded with Thomas to never stay out so late again, and he had responded by telling her to know her place and storming up to the lighthouse. By the time the teenage boy had come down from the tower, Josephine was sobbing. The boy gave her a sympathetic look but crept quickly out the door.

"Excellent." Hurley wore an expression that suggested he did not believe her for an instant. "And what of us?"

Josephine sent a scattered look in his direction. "Us?"

"You and me." Hurley had risen from his seat and was walking towards her. He did not stop until they were improperly close, until she could feel the warmth of his exhales on her forehead.

"I'm certain I don't know what you mean." Josephine kept her words innocent, but she lifted her eyes to him coquettishly.

"I'm not here for tea," he whispered, finally shattering the space between them as he pulled her to him.

They had been skirting around their desire for weeks now. Every time they got close to it, Josephine felt a flutter of excitement. But now that the distance was broken, desire flooded her.

Josephine's breath quickened in pace as she felt his eau de cologne washing over her. He smelled of citrus and lavender and the hint of something else—a woman's scent, perhaps? She forced herself to bring Amelia Irving's image to mind. His wife had been nothing but kind to her. Amelia did not deserve this. And, despite his faults, neither did Thomas.

But what chance did honor stand compared to the desire of a man in flesh and blood? Josephine hungered for his tender touch like a seal-woman longed for her sealskin. For too long, she had been trapped between these four walls, and now she had the chance to finally *feel* something. Something other than the maddening apathy she had come to know all too well.

Hurley whisked her closer. He planted a kiss on her lips, and she melted into him. His tongue tasted like spiced, nutty cigars.

They were up against the wall now. She kissed him with the hunger of a woman starved, and he held her head steadfast as he returned the kiss. Her arms turned to gooseflesh beneath his touch. Then, before she had a chance to fully grasp what they were doing, he was pulling up her skirts.

It all felt very different from lovemaking with Thomas. For one, Hurley was a bit shorter in stature, his mouth easier to reach for a kiss. Instead of Thomas' strong, square hands, Hurley touched her with long, supple fingers. His chin was clean-shaven, not like her husband's coarse beard.

But the greatest difference was Hurley's ravenousness. It was this ravenousness that made him tear at her clothes and kiss down her neck, all the way to the half-moon between her clavicles. Josephine could not remember the last time she had felt so wanted.

Thomas hardly ever looked at her when she passed by—even when she wore a particularly pretty dress or bent over to pick something up from his feet. She was rendered invisible. And if the one person there could not see her, she was starting to believe she truly did not exist.

Would a tree make a thud if it fell in the forest where no one saw it falling? Josephine was not sure it would.

There was nothing more inebriating than the feeling of being desired. And Hurley not only desired her, but he desired her in a way that he could not contain. He desired her more than he desired his own honor.

Josephine had changed her mind. Thomas did deserve this.

She had been with other men before Thomas, but none as high in rank as Hurley. She knew the seduction to which all men were prone to succumbing, but there was something different about a man of Hurley's status. It was as though he was well accustomed to getting what he wanted. Poor men desired and they took what they could get, but rich men desired with the full confidence that they could have whatever they wanted.

Hurley climaxed with a grunt. At that moment, he was at his most vulnerable, at her complete mercy. But it was only for that brief moment, for he soon regained his strength and smiled, spooling a strand of hair behind Josephine's ear. He looked so unbothered, so unweighted by guilt, that Josephine was starting to wonder whether he had done this before. Her own conscience began to crawl back to her.

She threw a glance at the grandfather clock on the opposite wall. Thomas had only been gone for ten minutes, and in those ten minutes, she had managed to desecrate their marriage.

"Thomas will be home soon," she said, though she knew it would likely be another half-hour before this was true.

"I see." Hurley pulled up the pants that had fallen to his ankles and brushed her scent off his collar. Then, he gingerly took her chin in one of his hands, peering into her eyes with rapture. "You are exquisite, Josephine."

She hated herself for how much she needed to hear him say it. Josephine combed her skirts back to their original position, hoping it made her seem unaffected.

"I will try to catch Thomas another time," said Hurley, putting his hat back on. "Wednesday, perhaps."

"Hurley, I—" Josephine tried to find the right words, but there was no elegant way to ask it. "What should I do about teatime with the other ladies?"

Hurley looked perplexed by the question, his eyes vacant as if he was not sure why it needed to be asked. "I'm not quite sure I understand."

"Your wife—Amelia, I—"

The sentience returned to him with a smile. "Ah! You mean to ask whether you should still attend teatime?" Hurley grabbed both of her hands in his, beaming ear to ear. "Of course, my darling Josephine, this has no bearing on your social life. This is simply what people do sometimes. There's no reason why it should affect your camaraderie with Amelia or any of the other ladies."

Josephine wondered if he was not at all worried about what would happen if she told the truth about them. But then, of course, she would have far more to lose than him. She would be out on the streets without even her low-status husband to keep her safe. The whole town would shun her. Amelia would have no choice but to forgive Hurley, so there was not much her husband had to fear. A week or two of chiding, perhaps, but no more than that. Some forbidding glances tossed in his direction. Surely, Hurley was aware that the newfound secret was more a burden on his lover than on himself.

"Very well," said Josephine. "Will I see you there on Tuesday?"

"I will be there, and I will manufacture some excuse to see you." Fire churned in his eyes. "Discreetly, of course."

With that, he pressed one last kiss on her lips and stepped out.

While she waited for Thomas' return, Josephine was not sure

what to do with herself. She heated a kettle for tea after all, her hands going through the motions thoughtlessly. But surprisingly, with each sip of her tea, the guilt burned away from her insides. A new feeling replaced it—the feeling of knowing something that her husband did not. Of having a secret. What was that feeling called, exactly?

It dawned on her. That feeling was called power. She had been chasing it for as long as she could remember, delighted with even a sliver of it.

Thomas returned within the hour, his hands full of mechanical equipment, which he dunked haphazardly onto the floor. Josephine waited to see if he could sense her betrayal immediately, but he did not even look at her long enough to catch the new spark in her eyes.

"Hurley Irving came by looking for you," she said.

"Aye, he did?" Thomas started digging through his boxes. "What a scatterbrained man."

Her heart fluttered. Was Thomas insulting him because he knew? Quietly, she echoed, "Scatterbrained?"

"I distinctly told him I would be out at this time."

Josephine peered out into the nothingness outside her window.

She understood now.

From the moment he had laid eyes on her, Hurley had calculated step-by-step how he intended to take what he wanted. She was starting to see why he was such a profitable businessman.

Zarya, 2023

Chapter 9

Bruno knelt beneath the mantle, stoking the fire when Zarya approached him.

"There are thousands of dead fish at Dead Man's Cove," she told him.

He looked up from the fire. "I heard."

"No, I mean—" Zarya let out a short sigh. "I *saw* them."

"You did what?" Bruno set the iron poker back onto its hook. He rose from his crouched position. "Zarya, you shouldn't be going near the ocean, not with everything going on. You need to be more careful."

But before she had a chance to respond, the lobby door swung open, and out came Mrs. Irving. She looked particularly stony today, with coils of white hair curled around her ears like ram horns.

"Zarya. Bruno. I need to speak with you both in the back."

Zarya exchanged a look with Bruno, and something lurked behind his expression. He quickly averted his gaze before following Mrs. Irving.

Mrs. Irving led them to what had once been the cigar room. She motioned for them to sit in a velvet loveseat, while she sank into a chair made of carved wood, with red cushions fit for a throne. On the coffee table next to her, old apothecary jars and whiskey decanters lined up, gathering dust. A fern also spilled down the table.

"Zarya, I know you saw a siren." Mrs. Irving was nothing if not straight to the point.

Zarya shot a look at Bruno, who was already starting to inch away. "You promised!"

"I'm sorry, I—"

Mrs. Irving cut him short. "I have no time for pinky promises. This isn't a playground. Did you see the creature or not?"

Zarya thumbed the hem of her sleeve, still aflame from Bruno's betrayal. At last, she answered Mrs. Irving with a terse nod.

"You are the only person I know who has ever laid eyes on them, Zarya." Mrs. Irving added, "The only one still alive, at least."

"I don't know what I'm supposed to do about what I saw," Zarya admitted.

"I'll tell you what you're supposed to do. Help the people of this town. Now, what did you see, exactly?"

Zarya tucked her hands beneath her crossed legs. Quietly, she said, "It's just like in the legends. A woman in the water who looks half-dead, half-alive. Menacing, with sharp teeth and clouded eyes."

She would not tell them that the siren in the water matched a photograph of the old lighthouse keeper's wife. No, she had learned her lesson about telling secrets. Besides, how was she to know Mrs. Irving's intentions with this information? The woman seemed oddly invested in her hatred for the sirens—if there even was more than one siren.

"Was there a tail, like a seal's or a serpent's?"

Zarya shook her head. "I don't know. I only saw her up to her chest."

Mrs. Irving pressed the nail of her thumb between her teeth as if about to bite her nails. She stopped herself right before her jaw clenched down and asked, "What color was her skin?"

"Grayish-white. Maybe a bit blue. Like I said, she looked half dead."

"Alright, alright. Let me think." Mrs. Irving glared into the distance, past the lace drapes and the stained-glass windows depicting poppy flowers in braided circles. Finally, she brought herself back. "A few of us have started a neighbors' watch of sorts. We're calling ourselves the Defenders. We meet weekly, sometimes more, and discuss our plans for how to protect our people and get rid of the sirens."

Zarya could picture them already, pitchforks out as they pored over a chalkboard with their crusade mapped out. What was their plan, exactly? To toss her into the ocean as bait and shoot at any fish that dared come near? It seemed like a terrible idea—and illegal, most likely.

"Will you join us?" pressed Mrs. Irving. "Our next meeting is tomorrow evening."

Zarya shook her head. "This all sounds crazy."

"You should be more motivated than anyone to end these monsters," said Mrs. Irving, her pupils dark as scorched coal. "It's your life on the line."

The woman had a point. Zarya *should* have been more worried. Just this very morning, she had found herself back by the ocean. That couldn't possibly be rational. The siren must have been messing with her head, the song making it impossible to concentrate. But there was something about the allure that felt tempting to surrender to, that promised Zarya all her problems would go away if only she stepped into the cool water. Perhaps a part of her wanted to get pulled under.

That was a scary thought. Zarya looked to Bruno, who still would not meet her line of sight. Then she looked back at Mrs. Irving, let out a sigh, and gave one faint nod.

After a long day of ignoring Bruno at the concierge desk, Zarya could no longer contain her headache. The siren's song, although beautiful and metallic as windchimes, had inflamed her brain. Zarya wanted nothing more than to go for a drive to the ocean on a day like this. But she remembered Bruno's warning, and she stepped into the shower instead, turning down the water as cold as it would go.

It was a jolt to her nervous system. A much-needed jolt.

When she was out of the shower, Zarya saw her phone light up on the bathroom counter. Her mother, again. This time, a text.

When are you coming home again? I miss you.

She chucked the phone out of the bathroom and onto her mattress. It was hard enough to withstand one creature luring her out to a deathtrap, let alone two.

That night, after she had heated up a pack of mac-and-cheese in her ancient microwave, Zarya tossed and turned in front of the TV. She was unable to find a comfortable position, as if her legs couldn't lay still. She kept twisting and cracking her ankles, repositioning her feet as if that might help. But every time, she continued to feel a deep ache from within her bones, a desire to start walking and not stop until she reached water.

To quiet her mind, she dug through her nightstand, looking for a weed gummy. When she finally found one lodged beneath an old notebook, she removed the wrapper and popped it in her mouth. It took a bit, but Zarya finally fell asleep. Eventually, even her legs grew too heavy to keep rubbing against each other like a cricket.

In the morning when she awoke, the deep ache in her bones was stronger than ever. But the sun was out, filtering through the cracks of Zarya's curtains with reassuring warmth. Surely, it was safe for a stroll by the ocean today. She would make a point to avoid Dead Man's Cove, to go someplace where people would be around. The siren wouldn't risk luring her to the water in front of an audience, would she?

Zarya stretched her legs as hard as she could. The gesture helped for a bit, but then the feeling of restlessness came right back. The siren's song was getting louder between her ears, as if serenading her good morning. Zarya didn't even glance in the mirror before grabbing her keys and starting for the door.

Half an hour later, Zarya was back at the ocean, perched on a piece of driftwood. Across the water, sunlight gleamed like fish scales. In the shallow part, she could see through to the bottom. A persimmon-orange jellyfish floated near the surface all kite-like, its limbs dangling lithely underneath.

In her ears, a series of angelic notes continued to play, looping so that the end of each verse flowed into the beginning of another. Zarya was beginning to believe, more and more, that going into the water was a good idea. It looked so refreshing from here, promising to stop her racing thoughts with its icy embrace. She could easily slough off her clothes, go for a dip, and return ashore with newfound vigor. The waves were mere ripples out here, with hardly any whitecaps. Surely, she would be fine. She could just go in knee height. Maybe up to her hips. No higher than her waist, of course.

Where else was she meant to go? Back to the hotel, with its stuffy rooms and vigilante owner? Or perhaps back home, where she might as well sign away her right to freedom? The ocean was her only refuge.

Zarya thought about what her father had once told her about the ocean—that all life originated from it. The first single-cell organism, their most primeval ancestor, first formed out of that vast body of water.

And when a child is in the womb, he had explained, tilting his glasses to the tip of his nose, *it is like being in those primordial waters, in a sense. As an unborn child, you are cushioned in an oceanlike amniotic fluid. You go through the same process of evolution as the human race did—first resembling something like an amoeba, then a fish, then an amphibian, then a reptile, and finally a primate.*

It had been the most Zarya had heard him talk. But of course, he did not mind lecturing her about biology when it came time for a science exam. It was everything else he struggled to talk about.

As she stared out at the massive ocean, Zarya also thought about how much she hated people. She hated the way they spoke to each other, with needless cruelty and disproportionate defensiveness. She hated the way they tried to rope her into their twisted games, like Mrs. Irving with her vendetta, or Mama with her possessiveness. For just once, Zarya would have liked to be her own person, left alone to mind her own business. It felt like she had been running from people her whole life.

The Pacific was her only true friend. Its power was unparalleled, and sometimes she liked to fantasize about how it could cleanse this town of its impurities. Even now, a jolt beneath the earth's crust could send a wall of water lurching toward Zarya at inconceivable speed. Within seconds, the ocean could wipe her clean. After all, the Very Big One could strike at any given moment. The ground would shake, and minutes later the entire coastline would be submerged. Zarya's mother had long ago warned her to never turn her back on the ocean–but even with her face turned towards it, Zarya was at its mercy.

She would have loved to remove her sandals and dip her toes into the shallow water up ahead. Others had done so, summer tourists and children splashing around with their plastic shovels. If they could, why couldn't she?

Then her phone began buzzing again. Zarya prepared to temporarily mute her mother's calls, but it was only a text from Bruno, reminding her that the Defenders meeting was about to start soon.

Where are you? he asked.

She had the faintest feeling that he already knew. Zarya mustered all the strength she could find to tear herself away from the beach.

Soon she was back in the confines of the Irving Hotel, corralled into the cigar room with a dozen other people. The ringleader was, of course, none other than Mrs. Irving. She stood behind her desk with brutish eyes. It was the same look Zarya had seen in the bald eagles that passed through town—the eyes of a hunter, of an apex predator. And she had seen that same calculated aggression in the siren's eyes.

In the corner of the room, Bruno helped himself to a bottle of water. Zarya pretended not to have seen him and enfolded her arms at her chest.

"Come in, come in," said Mrs. Irving, waving down the last of the Defenders. After the door shut, she cleared her throat. "Thank you all for being here, especially on such short notice."

On short notice? Zarya's jaw clenched. Mrs. Irving had made it sound like the meeting was regularly scheduled at this time. Had she only scheduled it after speaking with Zarya?

Mrs. Irving went on, "Whatever is out there in the water, it has terrorized us for long enough. Those creatures have targeted our brothers and sisters, our sons and daughters. How many souls have washed ashore at Dead Man's Cove? How many families have our local police had to call up with news of tragedy?" She was pacing now, and occasionally she would thwack her hands against the desk for emphasis.

The old woman was starting to sound like a fire and brimstone preacher. Or a militia leader. Her passion and her ability to rouse passion in others came naturally, and Zarya wondered where the woman had picked up the habit. The rush of self-righteousness seemed to be fueling her.

Without warning, Mrs. Irving turned her attention to Zarya. "This young woman right here will be our ticket to freedom."

Zarya felt the white-hot pressure of eyes on her.

"She has seen a siren, and this thing has imprinted onto her. Tell them, Zarya."

Zarya looked out at the crowd of spectators. "I saw one."

A series of sharp inhales ensued.

"She is likely to be the next target," continued Mrs. Irving. "Because of this, she can take us straight to the sirens, and we can end them once and for all."

"This sounds dangerous," pointed out a middle-aged woman from the crowd. Zarya turned to get a good look at the woman and realized she recognized that face. She had seen it on TV—it was the face of the latest victim's mother. Deep trenches had formed under her eyes.

"What's more dangerous is letting her go about her life,

knowing damn well she won't be able to resist the urge for a swim one of these days." Mrs. Irving's lips had pursed into a forbidding glower. "You, of all people, should know how heavy a risk that is."

Across the room, Bruno raised his hand. Zarya looked at him sidelong.

"Yes, Bruno." Mrs. Irving gave him a wave of her hand.

"I don't know what the plan is, but I think someone should keep Zarya company as much as possible. I want her to be safe."

Zarya let out a huff of disbelief. "You want someone to tail me?" She met his eyes head-on for the first time since learning of his broken promise. "Why don't I just give you my Social Security Number, too? Would that make you feel more comfortable?"

Bruno opened his mouth to protest the insinuation, but Mrs. Irving had already wedged herself between them. "Come on, you two." She turned to Bruno first. "It's her choice, of course." Next, she turned to Zarya and said, "Zarya, you know Bruno cares about you deeply. Your safety is our top priority. Now, how would you feel about someone keeping you company when you're off work?"

"Absolutely not." Zarya spat out. It was starting to feel more and more like the walls were closing in on her. Like she was a bird in a golden cage. Already, Zarya was marking her escape through the nearest door.

"Okay, okay." Mrs. Irving took a moment to gather her thoughts. When she had recollected herself, she said, "Can you at least call me or Bruno if you ever feel the urge to head to the water?"

Zarya nodded. It was a promise she had no intention of keeping.

After the meeting had concluded and the Defenders started pouring out of the cigar room, Zarya moseyed over to the mother of the most recent victim. The woman was busy piling all her personal objects into a handbag when she spotted Zarya approaching.

"Excuse me." Zarya lowered her voice to a hushed volume. "My condolences, Mrs.—"

The woman frowned as if suddenly reliving her loss. Zarya

imagined it must have been the hundredth time today.

"Please, call me Mallory."

Zarya nodded. "Mallory, then. I was really sad to hear what happened with your daughter. Her name was Jess, right?"

"Yes, Jessica. Her friends sometimes called her Jess."

"I see." Zarya tried to find the right words to say. In her head, it had all been much easier. But now, face-to-face with the woman's grief, everything she had envisioned saying seemed insensitive somehow. "If it's not too much, I'd like to ask—"

"I'm an open book," Mallory assured her. "Especially when it comes to this."

"That's good to hear. Because I guess I was wondering—did Jessica mention seeing anything in the days or weeks leading up to her disappearance? Anything strange at all in the water?"

Mallory pursed her lips. "This might not be what you want to hear."

"I should hear it anyway."

"I agree." The woman's eyes darted around the room to make sure no one was listening in on their conversation. When she was satisfied with how the room had emptied, she whispered, "Jessica didn't mention seeing anything in the water, but she was spending a lot of time by the ocean in the days leading up to her disappearance. It was out of the ordinary for her. She wasn't a very outdoorsy type, but all of a sudden, she wanted to read by the ocean, have a picnic by the ocean, bathe in the ocean."

"Did she mention seeing anything strange while she was there?"

Mallory shook her head. "No, but it was like something kept pulling her there. She said she had a song stuck in her head, like, all the time. Day and night. During the day, if she had other things to keep her busy, she could resist the ocean's call, but the nights were harder. She even developed restless leg syndrome."

Zarya felt a knot in her throat. She tried to swallow it, but the knot stayed put. "What do you mean?"

"That's what the doctor called it. She couldn't stop rubbing her legs together. Jessica went to the family doctor to get it checked out, and the doctor said she might be anemic. Ran a bunch of blood tests on her." Mallory let out a scoff. "The results just came in, actually. A bit late."

"And was she anemic?"

The woman shook her head, slowly. "Everything was within range. There was no medical cause for it, but Jessica said the restlessness would only go away when she was in the ocean."

"I'm so sorry." Zarya wasn't sure what else to say.

"You should be scared, not sorry," Mallory replied. "I don't want what happened to my Jessica, to also happen to you."

"Did anything help? With drowning out the song or the restless legs, I mean?"

"Nothing at all. Towards the end, she started sleepwalking, too. And she started having horrible nightmares that wouldn't let her sleep. She even tried leaving town for a day, but it made things worse."

"How come?"

"She said the song just kept getting louder and louder the further from the ocean she got. It almost drove her crazy. She said her ears wouldn't stop ringing."

"So, getting away from the ocean makes the song louder, and getting closer makes it softer." That explained why Zarya felt a bit better every time the water was in sight.

"Exactly." Mallory pinned her gaze to Zarya's. "Which is why the only way out is to find this creature and kill it for good."

She didn't need to say the second half of what she was thinking. Zarya could see it in her eyes.

Before it kills you first.

Josephine, 1850

Chapter 10

Teatime was different now. Josephine kept her eyes averted when Amelia spoke to her, guilt knotted in her stomach and mangled with something else that she could not quite pinpoint.

The servants had removed the summer flowers from the vases of the house, swapping them with tall pampas grass and dried wheats. The bowl in the parlor was now filled with apples and grapes, the fruits of the season. As the ladies chatted about the newest literature, Amelia passed around trays of blueberry pie and blackberry scones. The pastries, though buttery enough to crumble in her mouth, tasted insipid to Josephine.

"Josephine, are you quite alright? You look pale today."

Josephine took a sip of scalding-hot tea, flinching as it seared her tongue. "Fine, thank you. I've just been feeling a bit ill is all."

"Oh, dear. Nothing serious, I hope?"

She was starting to hate the sound of Amelia's voice. The way it always managed to be cordial. Hurley must have intentionally married a woman with a surplus of compassion. It probably made things easier for him.

"No, nothing serious. I should probably find a physician one of these days," answered Josephine, hoping that would be the end of it.

"Oh, well, do you know that Myra's husband is a medic?" Amelia rang a bell, and in came one of the servants. When the servant arrived, she asked, "Could you be a dear and fetch my husband?"

Josephine's heart thrummed. Fear and excitement surged through her. She was unsure where one started and the other ended. Before she knew it, Hurley was standing in the doorway, bowing deferentially at the ladies.

Had he gotten more handsome since the last time she saw him? Josephine was not sure. Now that they had joined their bodies in carnal pleasure, there was a familiarity to his features that made her yearn to be in his arms. Want churned through her stomach.

"Darling, could you fetch Dr. Ainsworth while Josephine is here? She says she's not feeling quite well, and she hasn't seen a medic since her move."

Hurley gave a cordial glance in Josephine's direction. He was careful not to reveal his appetite for her in front of others. Now, as she sat before him, Josephine could finally pinpoint that other feeling that intermixed with her guilt.

Put plainly, it was envy. She wanted to spill her tea all over the hardwood floor every time Hurley and his wife exchanged a pet name or a look of affection. She could uproot his entire life right now, if she so desired. How was he so sure that she would not?

"Certainly, my dear," said Hurley. "I will send a telegraph at once." He nodded at the other wives. "Ladies." Then he stepped out.

Josephine's mind was elsewhere as the discussion reverberated back towards women's matters. She was not even sure how many minutes had passed by the time the servant girl returned in the doorway, hands clasped at her apron.

"Mrs. Byrne, the medic is in the other room for you."

"Already?" asked Amelia. "Good God, the man is speedy when someone is in need. Please, Josephine, feel free to see him. We will be right here when you've finished."

Josephine got up from the sitting area and followed the servant into a separate room. Not to the study where she had seen Hurley, but rather a bedchamber. A bed with wooden frames was pressed up against the wall, the coverlets wrapped tautly around the mattress. There was a hearth on the other wall, its mantle and surround gleaming with chestnut-colored tiles. Burgundy curtains had been pulled over the windows for privacy.

Josephine sat at the edge of the bed, waiting for the physician. At last, the door opened, and in entered a man with a silver beard and head of hair. She measured him up and down, assessing whether he could be trusted. When he flashed a warm enough smile, Josephine allowed herself to ease the tension in her body.

"Good day, Mrs. Byrne," he said.

She offered her hand, which he kissed delicately.

"I'm Dr. Ainsworth. I understand you've been dealing with an ailment?"

"Well..." Josephine thought about a lie he might find credible. Then it occurred to her that, while she had him here, it might be the best use of her time to speak frankly. She said, "The adjustment out West has been a bit—challenging."

Dr. Ainsworth sat in a cushioned chair in front of her. He crossed his legs and folded his hands onto one knee. "Please, do tell."

She was not sure what to say, exactly. "Sometimes, it feels like the color has been drained from the world. Is that normal?"

The medic tilted up her chin slightly, peering into her pupils. "Do you mean that you no longer see the full spectrum of colors?"

"No," she said, after he had pulled his hand away. "I *see* them, but I almost don't—feel them?"

Panic dappled across her chest. She shouldn't have said that, shouldn't have spoken about feelings. He would think she was a loon if the disease was in her mind rather than her body. And yet, she wondered, was her mind not a part of her body?

"Yes, I see." Dr. Ainsworth frowned. "Well, the truth is that the weather is quite dreary here, dear. You live out at the lighthouse, is that so?"

She nodded.

"Even more so, then. It is a tough life out there for lighthouse keepers, let alone their wives. Now, tell me, is there a chance you could be with child?"

Josephine twisted her fingers together in her lap. "I don't believe I am."

"I ask because a woman with child may experience a whole host of physical symptoms. Some emotional, too—the female condition is erratic, you see."

"I am not with child," she said, this time more firmly.

"Very well. In which case, perhaps *that* is the cause? Many women, when they first marry, expect to be with child at once, and they feel a sort of emptiness when that wish is not gratified. An empty womb can sometimes feel like an empty heart."

Josephine had not given much thought to having a baby. Doing so would require regular relations with her husband, and Thomas seldom visited her side of the bed. He worked through the night, only occasionally stopping by for a quick grunt in the dark. Even then, it seemed more out of duty than anything else. Like he didn't want to give her the satisfaction of being able to say he was a neglectful husband.

Now that she had felt Hurley's seed inside her, the prospect of pregnancy seemed riskier. Still, Josephine wondered how it might feel to have Hurley's child growing inside her belly. With its beating heart and little kicks, she would never be alone. And she would always have a little part of Hurley with her. She quite liked that idea.

"Perhaps you're right," she told the medic. "I think my life would brighten if I had a child."

Dr. Ainsworth looked pleased with himself. He examined Josephine's heart and lungs, then lifted her wan wrists to the light, inspecting her hands. When all seemed well enough to him, he started towards the door.

"I will pay you a visit at the lighthouse in two months' time, to see if you are better. God willing, your womb will be brimming with life by then." He smiled grandly, then started revolving the doorknob.

The door had not opened as much as an inch before someone on the other side pushed it open. Hurley helped himself inside.

"All is well, doctor?" he asked, closing the door behind him.

"No signs of physical illness," Dr. Ainsworth assured him. If he found it unusual that a man other than Josephine's husband was expressing an interest in the state of Josephine's health, he did not show it. But then again, Hurley seemed above the law in this town. "Just the usual signs of a delicate disposition. It's all too common in women, I'm afraid. We menfolk must look after the ladies in our midst."

"Certainly." Hurley looked to Josephine. His brows were slanted with hunger, though there was an air of plausible deniability about it. "Well, thank you, doctor," he said, shaking the physician's hand.

"Good day," said Dr. Ainsworth, this time making a successful exit from the room.

Now that she was alone with Hurley, the temperature seemed to have risen by a few degrees. Josephine sat idly on the bed, wondering how long they had before the servants caught on to their whereabouts. Hurley traversed the room slowly, his footsteps soft enough to not arouse suspicion from the hallway. Josephine felt the tingle of desire between her legs.

When he had reached the edge of the bed where she sat, Hurley hovered over, smiling mischievously. He angled up her face similarly to how the medic had done. But this time was different—Josephine felt less like an experimental subject as she had with Dr. Ainsworth, and more like an animal ensnared in a trap. Was it unnatural for an animal to desire being entrapped?

He reached down and kissed her, his lips pressed voraciously against hers. Josephine's hands found the edge of his suit, and she pulled him down on top of her on the bed. She could hardly breathe, intoxicated by the way he stole her breath.

His hunger for her teetered dangerously close to a point of no return. Before it happened, Hurley pulled himself out of the trance. He got off the bed and inhaled deeply. A lock of hair had fallen over his eye, and he pushed it back with his gaze still transfixed on Josephine.

"How have you been?" he asked, buttoning one of the suit buttons that had come undone at his breastbone. He gazed out the window as if trying to distract himself from his lust.

"Eager to see you," Josephine confessed, still catching her breath.

Hurley responded in a measured tone, with the same cordiality he had provided the doctor. "That's very kind of you to say."

She had hoped he would reciprocate her sentiments, but now she searched for something else to say. "And yourself?"

"Business has been quite dreadful," he said.

"Oh! Why is that?"

Hurley wiped a hand drearily across his forehead, as if the very thought of it was upsetting him. "I needed to reduce the miners' wages, and now they're striking—well, the European ones are striking. The Chinese miners will work for half the wage. I've warned the Europeans that I can replace them with more Chinese men if they unionize once again, but they're stubborn men."

Josephine was not sure why he was telling her this. Perhaps Amelia was uninterested in talk of business, and he needed a woman's listening ear. But no, that did not seem quite right—Amelia seemed to have a knack for providing blind support.

Deep in her heart, Josephine wondered if she had already managed to gain his trust. Perhaps he saw her as more than just a pretty face, but rather more of a companion. Perhaps one day, he would be so smitten that he might leave Amelia for her. Things had already progressed so quickly between them. Was it really outside the realm of possibility?

As if sensing her perplexity, Hurley threw Josephine a look. "I should not bore you with such talk. My apologies."

"No, no," said Josephine. She approached him by the window

and clasped her hand into his. "I want to know these things. Please, tell me."

Now that they were just a breath apart, the passion stirred in his gaze again. His chest expanded as he took a deep breath. He looked as though he were trying to expel his unclean thoughts.

"You should return to the other ladies," he said, though desire lingered in his eyes.

Josephine gave a coy smile. "I hope to see you soon."

She headed towards the door, the air between them still thick with yearning. She was not ready to leave him. In his presence, she felt truly alive. In fact, it was the only time she felt like she existed.

But leave him she did, making her way back to the parlor. The other women were nearly done with their tea, the pastries gone but for a few crumbs fit for a mouse.

"Josephine!" called out Amelia when she spotted Josephine in the doorway. "How was your visit with Dr. Ainsworth?"

Truthfully, Josephine had already forgotten about the doctor's visit. Amelia's undue hospitality was beginning to grate her. But Josephine relished in the notion that she at least knew something Amelia did not. Something terrible about her husband.

"Nothing to be concerned about," she answered, and the other hens clucked in joy at the news.

"I'm very happy to hear that, Josephine," said Amelia, reaching over to give her hand a squeeze. Little did she know that her husband had been touching the same hand just moments before.

The gathering ended shortly thereafter, and Josephine was back in the buggy headed to the lighthouse. With each clop of the horse's hooves, her delight faded. Soon, the moment in the bedroom with Hurley and their stolen glances in the parlor would exist only in her memory. She would be back in the abyss, floating aimlessly through space. He was in that big, showy house with his lovely wife, while she was all alone in the lighthouse. Josephine was lucky for a scrap of him while Amelia had most of him.

Josephine wondered, did he forget about her as soon as she was out the door? Was it easy for him to toss aside her memory when she was out of sight? Was he able to kiss his wife with convincing zest? Worse yet—did he truly *want* his wife just the same?

By the time the buggy reached the Rock and the lighthouse came into view, Josephine decided that she would never go back to teatime. She would have very much liked to never see Amelia again. Yes, that was a lovely thought.

Zarya, 2023

Chapter 11

The Defenders started their vendetta against the spirits of the ocean. If there was any sign of a siren, they had their ringtones set to full volume, ready to head out to the ocean with their hunting rifles.

Zarya had never known just how many of the townspeople had deadly weapons in their possession. Even the little, old couple that came by the Irving Hotel on Saturday nights for dinner, calling each other sweet pea across the table. Even the mother of two. Even the gentle-mannered man who always carried around a bag of chocolate coins to hand out. Zarya wasn't sure whether to sleep more or less soundly at night because of it.

For a while, it seemed like the Defenders would let her get away with her limited involvement. But after some time, she started to notice that nearly all her shifts were scheduled with Bruno and, despite her efforts to keep him at arm's length, he persevered in his attempts at socializing after work.

"Do we have any vacancies today?" he asked, tucking his satchel under the concierge desk for the day.

"No." Zarya flipped to the next page of her book.

"Come on, Zarya, how long are you going to give me the silent treatment?"

She shot him a dark look. "This isn't the silent treatment."

"Look, you can't expect me to keep a secret like that when it concerns all of us. It wasn't fair of you to ask me that in the first place."

"You're right." Zarya shut her hardcover, since apparently Bruno was determined to not let her read. "Next time, I won't say anything at all."

Bruno positioned himself in her sightline and planted his hands on his waist. "Look, missy, you're being really harsh. I've seen you do it with others, and now you're doing it to me, too. People make mistakes sometimes, okay? I made a mistake." He mustered up as much sweetness as he could for these next words. "Please forgive me."

Zarya let out a tired exhale. At least he was trying. "Maybe you're right."

"Of course I'm right. I'm always right, remember?" It was his favorite expression, *I'm always right.* A more realistic motto might have been, *I'm rarely right.*

Bruno twined his arms around Zarya, and she gave a reluctant squeeze back.

He was jaunty for the rest of the shift, shuffling between the concierge desk and the fireplace, making small talk with the guests. Zarya kept her eyes transfixed on the time, ready to clock out on the dot.

But just moments before their time was up, Bruno drummed his fingers across the concierge desk with a look of mischief.

"Let's go to Dave's."

"I don't know…" Already, Zarya could hear the counterargument.

"What, you got something better to do?"

It was the same argument her mother used when guilting her into coming home. No—that was the honest answer. She had nothing better to do. And she wanted so badly to go out to sea and feel the sacred caress of the water, even just for a moment.

"Fine. But I'm not getting drunk tonight."

"Of course, of course." Bruno reached for his knapsack. "Can we stop by my house first? I want to change."

She nodded as if she had any say in the matter.

Bruno's home may have looked unassuming, just a stone house fringed with bushes, but his wealth made itself known through small details. The bushes were trimmed just so, the front gate made of wrought iron rather than its cheaper impersonator. When the Very Big One finally came, every house in the Pacific Northwest made of unreinforced masonry would be toast—but those accustomed to luck seldom assumed tragedy would strike *their* family.

"My parents are in New York today," said Bruno, typing his passcode into the digital door lock. Next came the rhythmic beeping of the alarm, alerting them that they had approximately sixty seconds to tap the next passcode before sirens went off. Bruno pressed that one, too, and then it was silent throughout the house.

Zarya slipped out of her shoes and placed them at the door.

"I don't know how many times I have to tell you. You don't have to do that," Bruno reminded her.

But as he stepped onto the polished parquetry in his muddied soles, Zarya winced. She followed him into the living room, where the aroma of vanilla oil must have been diffusing somewhere. Bruno explained that he would be done in his bedroom shortly and said to make herself at home.

Zarya cast a long look across his living room. It was not the first time she had seen it, but she marveled at it every time. On the console table was a pitcher of water, slices of lemon pressed against the ice. Beads of condensation bubbled against the glass. She helped herself to a cup, savoring the fresh taste of citrus.

Along the console table were silver-framed photographs. Someone must have polished and cleaned up the silver, because it dazzled, capturing what little light came through the windows. The picture frames encased images of Bruno as a young boy, surrounded by family. His mother and father had been stunning in their youth, with hair the color of rich coffee beans and light brown skin, big smiles across their faces. Bruno, on the other hand, had always been somewhat of an ugly duckling. He peered at the camera from behind out-of-style glasses with a lopsided smile.

Zarya wondered what it was like to have a sense of belonging like this. Her parents thought she belonged with them, of course, but it always came with strings attached. If she gave them a week of her company, it would quickly turn into more. She could already hear it:

Why must you close your door?

Are you going to spend all your time in your room, or will you come spend time with us?

You're going out again? Didn't you go out yesterday?

You can't seriously wear that to dinner. What will people think? Go put on that bolero I got you.

It was easier to simply extricate herself from all that.

Bruno was finally done ruffling through his room, and he stepped out holding a velveteen makeup bag.

"I want you to have this," he said, handing the bag to Zarya.

Zarya unzipped the top to peer inside. There was a richly pigmented lipstick, a trial-sized mascara, and several bottles of skincare. She was not sure, but she thought she recognized the brand names as expensive.

"Are you sure you want me to have this?"

"Yes, silly. My mom got this for free." He looked her up and down, disapproving of Zarya's faux-satin blouse and tattered jeans. "Besides, you need these more than her."

Zarya was never sure if Bruno meant to offend her or not. Sometimes, his banter felt more like a slap on the face than a caress of endearment.

"Okay, then. Thanks." She tried on the lipstick, which stained her cupid's bow so intensely that she could barely figure out how to clean up the contour. She had never tried such stubborn makeup before.

At Dave's Bar and Grill, the early bird diners were already

sitting in the booths, but the clamor of dinnertime rose by the minute. Bruno was slightly less snarky than usual, perhaps sensing that he was still on thin ice with Zarya. He ordered a round of shots despite Zarya's protests, assuring her that he would foot the bill tonight.

Zarya tossed back the shot despite her better judgment, tasting the acerbic aftertaste of tequila long after it was gone. Around her, the chatter grew muffled and slower, as if the whole place had been dunked in thick honey. Her head was swimming in it.

When a man at the bar shot her a dimpled smile, Zarya knew it was time to leave. She would not be pulled into the suffocating grip of one more person tonight. She thanked Bruno for the meal and returned to the hotel.

Around these parts, light and darkness were always in sharp contrast. Zarya had forgotten how sunlight tasted all winter, but now the sun lingered in the sky long past dinnertime. Summertime had barely started, but already the daylight dawdled. Overhead, a bat shot through the canopy. Its little body cast a black shadow against the fiery pink of the sky.

The hotel was quiet tonight, which made the melodic note in Zarya's head all the more pronounced. She was starting to think that the alcohol didn't help. If anything, instead of muffling the siren's song, it only made it harder to resist the urge to run asea.

Maybe it was the alcohol, but before she turned off her bedside lamp, Zarya took a scarf and tied her ankles to the bedframes. Not tight enough to cut off circulation, but tight enough that she'd be startled awake if she found herself sleepwalking towards the ocean. The pressure helped with the restlessness in her legs just a little bit. Then, she was fast asleep.

But even sleep was not safe tonight. Nightmares gripped her—or were they flashbacks? They clammed up her skin, Zarya's shirt sticking to her armpits, her feet drenched in a cold sweat. Half-asleep and half-awake, in this world of reverie, she tossed and turned. She was back in her childhood home, the sound of shouting pulsing through her ears. It was the sound of her mother's screams, and her own, too.

The scene replayed just as it had happened.

Zarya ran to her room for an escape, turning the latch on the doorknob to lock it. Her mother sank her weight into the doorknob on the other side of the door. When she discovered that the door would not budge, there was a frantic knocking at the wood. Her shouts had been unkind before, but now they took on a menacing pitch. Zarya stepped away from the door, inching closer and closer to her bedroom window.

Her mother's shouts dwindled at the realization that they would not convince Zarya to unlock the door. Next, they took on a more saccharine tone. She promised that she just wanted to talk. Sweetie, just let me in, *she begged.*

But Zarya knew by now that her mother did not just want to talk. She would not stop until she had stripped every semblance of selfhood from her daughter. And if Zarya let her in through that door, she might as well have been signing away her autonomy.

So, Zarya did the thing she did best—she hid. If she could hide for long enough, then people would forget about her.

That was exactly what she assumed had happened when the knocking on the door went quiet. She's given up, *Zarya thought.*

It was only when she heard something down below her window that it occurred to Zarya—her mother was not one for giving up. Zarya crept behind the drapes to get a look at the commotion.

There, against the side of the house, her mother was climbing up a ladder. She was halfway up already, each step bringing her closer to the edge of Zarya's window.

Zarya sprang back, trying to find a hiding place behind the legs of her desk. But it was too late. Before long, her mother had reached the window and was knock-knock-knocking on the glass, hard.

Zarya, you are not allowed to lock the door! *she yelled.* Unlock it right now!

Zarya did just that. She bolted to unlock the door, then bolted down the stairs, then bolted out of the house, letting her legs carry her as far as they could. In the dream, her legs were stiff and slow-moving, unlike how they had been on that fated day. Despite the gelatinous resistance of the air, she managed to flee to an underbrush beside a creek. An old man was walking his dog when he spotted her, wide-eyed.

Zarya pressed her index finger to her lips. The old man nodded and walked along.

Now, in the attic of the old hotel, Zarya was awoken by her own gasp. Her heart throbbed loudly, and tears blotted the corners of her eyes. Sometimes, she wondered if the events of that day had really happened. Her only witness had been the old man walking his dog. He must not have known what he had seen, but he had seen it, nonetheless.

Zarya had been sixteen years old back then. A few years later, the old neighbor had stopped walking his small dog through the neighborhood, and she heard whispers in the neighborhood that he had passed away. Her only witness was gone.

After that incident, Zarya got very good at running away.

And now, the ocean beckoned her, *Come to me. I'll whisk you away, and you'll be able to stop running forever.*

Josephine, 1850

Chapter 12

Josephine's moods were beginning to mimic the weather conditions. September had been difficult, but at least it had brought apples tumbling down from high branches. October had been harder yet, the sky a slab of gray the color of gunmetal. Now, November sapped the last of the color from the trees. The wind grew stronger, the ocean more violent.

Occasionally, there would be a sunny day, and Josephine felt her mood brighten. She sat on a chaise longue by the side of the lighthouse, face sloped up to the sun in hopes of soaking up its rays. In those moments, she felt bursts of energy and raked all the leaves off the edge of the bluff, eyes lingering on the sea stacks that protruded from the water. But the sunshine was so fleeting, and soon clouds swept over the sky once more.

Thomas worked hard as always. Josephine had always assumed he was a hardy man, that he put up a brave front because he did not like to complain. Yet she was starting to suspect that he genuinely enjoyed the busywork and the long nights. She wondered if he had always been this way, or whether he just wanted an excuse to spend time away from her.

Sometimes, she sat before the looking glass and examined herself. Her hair, once rich as cacao, now looked lifeless, like grave soil. It had grown considerably, tumbling down past her hips in unruly waves. The diagonal creases underneath her eyes had deepened, the skin above them a shade of mottled purple like bruises.

Some days, Josephine found her appetite very difficult to locate. As more and more of these days piled on top of each other, her cheeks lost their bounciness. The skin was wrapped taut against her sharp cheekbones, against her narrow wrists.

It was no wonder, she thought, as she looked in the mirror. No wonder Thomas avoided her like the plague. She had been staring at herself for so long that her own reflection was starting to morph into someone unrecognizable. She wondered if she was beginning to lose her mind.

It had been two months since Dr. Ainsworth's visit to the Irving estate. Just as he had promised, the medic arrived at the lighthouse's doorstep, leather trunk in hand. At first glance of Josephine, his mouth twisted into a frown.

She invited him inside, taking a seat by the table. She would have offered him something, but the energy was depleted from her body today. It felt like someone had thrown a very heavy quilt over her.

"How have you been, Mrs. Byrne?" Dr. Ainsworth peered at her from above the edge of his spectacles.

"Oh, I've been alright," she said, toying with the hem of the lace tablecloth.

"You may speak frankly, you know."

Josephine let out a small sigh. "Well, alright. I suppose I haven't been much better since our last meeting."

The doctor placed two fingers at her wrist, counting her pulse in silence. Then he lifted her arms to examine them for discoloration. When he seemed satisfied enough, he asked Josephine to open her mouth and peered inside at her tonsils. He guided her jaw closed, lifted her eyelids with his thumb.

"How has your sleep been?"

"Oh, very good. Some days, I sleep even twelve hours."

"Hmm." Dr. Ainsworth glided his hand across the back of her ribcage, then the front of it. His fingers found the hollow where her womb supposedly resided. "And still no child?"

She shook her head. It was not for a lack of trying—after all, Hurley paid her a visit every week when her husband was out. She would have liked a baby's fluttering kicks inside her belly more than anything, but perhaps her womb was barren. It certainly felt like it.

"Is there anything you can give me to help speed the process, doctor?"

Dr. Ainsworth rummaged through his trunk, eventually taking out an amber tincture. "This may help some."

"What is it?" Josephine rattled the liquid inside the glass bottle.

"Saw palmetto extract. It has numerous benefits, some of which include fertility."

"I see." Josephine cradled the pipette in her hands.

"Say, is your husband present?"

Josephine nodded. "I'll go fetch him."

She headed through the door connecting the house to the lighthouse tower. Past it were five stories of spiraling steps, each more dizzying than the next.

She found Thomas at the top, gazing over the horizon with squinted eyes. When he heard Josephine's footsteps, he threw a quick glimpse in her direction, then returned to his watch.

"Yes, Josephine?"

"Dr. Ainsworth has come to pay me a visit," she said. "He asked for you."

"Is something the matter?"

"I'm not sure."

"Alright." Thomas pulled himself away from the lantern room, following Josephine down the tower steps. The way down was silent but for the sounds of their footfalls.

Dr. Ainsworth sat idly in the same chair where Josephine had left him. He rose to shake Thomas' hand, then made an inviting gesture for both spouses to sit beside him.

"I hope you're well," Thomas told the physician.

"Very well, thank you." Dr. Ainsworth made the first semblance of a smile that Josephine had seen all day. She wondered if he reserved all his charisma for men.

"So, what news do you bring, doctor?"

"I've examined your wife, and she displays the typical signs of melancholia. Fatigue, lack of zest, low mood, hypersomnia..." Dr. Ainsworth's eyes trailed toward Josephine. "I imagine you are a devotee of God, Josephine, so please excuse my need to ask such an offensive question—but do you ever fantasize of death?"

"Death?" The word tasted queer on her lips. Was that not her current state of existence?

"Yes, death." He locked eyes with hers.

Josephine shook her head, afraid he would sense her reticence.

But Dr. Ainsworth was more preoccupied with getting the right answer than with getting to the bottom of the truth. "Very good. If you ever have such sinful thoughts, you must tell me at once."

Josephine's head was foggy. The man kept throwing around words like *melancholia*, words that meant little to her. "What is it that I have?" she asked.

Dr. Ainsworth leaned back in his seat as if preparing to give a lecture to a room full of medical students. "The term *melancholia* originates from the Greek word for 'black bile.' A few disgraced medics are beginning to question this notion, but we know that all ailments are caused by an imbalance in the four basic humours of the body. Black bile is but one of them. Patients who struggle with melancholia have a disposition like the one I described, weighed down by black bile."

Well, she certainly felt weighed down. Perhaps the man was onto something.

Thomas' forehead furrowed as if he was hearing new information about his wife. He asked, "Dr. Ainsworth, what can be done about this?"

"The treatment is quite simple," replied the medic. "Frequent, fresh air will help. I would like to arrange for her to walk through the woods at least once per day. Aside from this, she must have ample rest. Either warm or cold baths can help. After a cold bath, she must rub her body with coarse flannel. And, perhaps most importantly," said Dr. Ainsworth, looking at the patient again, "a child should help."

Josephine felt a wash of color spread across her otherwise pale cheeks. Thomas' eyes skittered to her. Was that a peal of embarrassment she saw in his eyes? Surely, he must have felt his virility called into question just as she felt betrayed by her lack of fecundity. Or did he simply blame it all on her?

"I see," was all Thomas said.

Dr. Ainsworth bid them goodbye, and once he was gone, the room felt tighter. Josephine squeezed the dropper he had given her, letting a few droplets of the tincture fall beneath her tongue. The saw palmetto tasted acrid and soapy.

She had expected Thomas to head up the tower right away, but he lingered. After a few minutes of silence, Thomas got up from the table and walked toward the bedchamber. He opened the door an inch and looked at Josephine.

"Well, we should follow the doctor's orders."

It took her a moment to catch on. It was only when she saw the bedsheets through the slightly ajar door that it occurred to her what he meant. She rose and followed him, standing clumsily beside the bed.

It was hardly lovemaking, mechanical in the same way she imagined Thomas handled the lighthouse. A perfunctory touch here and there. No direct eye contact or tender kisses. He seemed to be executing items from a list rather than lost in the throes of passion. Even at the moment when his pleasure supposedly reached its peak, his eyes were narrowed in focus, as though trying to get it done with. He let out an understated groan.

She wondered if she was really as undesirable as Thomas made her feel. When she was with Hurley, he certainly made her feel beautiful, but he had yet to prove his devotion. One of these days, Hurley would surely declare his love for her. It was only a matter of time.

Thomas tore himself from the sheets as soon as it was over. Buttoning his pants, he said, "You should do as the doctor said."

"Yes." Josephine's eyes were drawn to the window, where a sliver of light filtered through the clouds. She would have to get out of bed eventually, but she could not find the strength just yet. She lay there for quite some time.

Zarya, 2023

Chapter 13

The nightmares made it harder for Zarya to sleep at night, which meant the siren's call grew harder to resist after nightfall. And with fatigue clouding her head, the strength to fight her impulses was fainter during the daytime, too.

So it was no surprise when she found herself by the water once more, watching a seagull and a stork fight over mussel shells in the sand. The stork was most definitely winning.

A couple of boats were anchored by the shore, white dots nodding against the blue ocean. Zarya told herself she was safe this way. If something were to draw her out to sea, the seafarers would see it.

But she knew, deep down, that she was at the mercy of the ocean. She did not dare turn her back on it.

Zarya felt her phone buzzing in the back pocket of her jeans. Bruno's name glowed on the screen. He had greatly increased the frequency at which he called her lately.

"Yes?"

"Mrs. Irving wants you to come by the hotel for an impromptu meeting," said Bruno on the other line, his voice clipped.

Zarya let out a disaffected sigh. "I'm busy."

"It's important. Please."

"Fine." Zarya forced herself off the sand.

She made her way through the evergreen forest, finding her car by the side of the road where she had left it. Overhead, birds warbled. They had been making noise for weeks on end, filling the dawn skies with their mating chirps.

When she saw the hotel parking lot filled to the brim, Zarya realized that it was not a work meeting Mrs. Irving had called. Some of the cars she recognized as belonging to the Defenders. One of them was a police car, and Zarya suddenly wondered if Mrs. Irving had asked the police officer in their group to surveil her location. No, that was insanity. Even for times like these.

Zarya found the door to the cigar room closed, and behind it, she heard muffled voices. Gently, she pulled it ajar, and there stood all the self-proclaimed wardens. Their eyes followed her as she walked across the room, until eventually Zarya found herself a seat by the windowsill.

"Where were you?" Mrs. Irving's tone was getting dangerously close to maternal.

Zarya shot daggers at her. "I don't see how that's relevant. Why are we here right now?"

Mrs. Irving put aside whatever unspoken confrontation she had hoped for. She announced, "We're taking a more proactive approach. Standing by idly and waiting for something to happen to you is not a solution." She turned to the oldest man in the group, a fisherman. "Joe, tell her."

Joe looked at Zarya. "I have a boat, as you know."

She did not like where this was headed.

"The strongest of us are going to take to the sea, with you in the boat with us."

Zarya couldn't help but laugh. When she was done, she said, "You want to use me as bait." It was just as she had predicted.

The man was about to protest, but Mrs. Irving cut him off with a quick gesture of her hand. "Yes," she said. "There's no way around it."

It wasn't the wildest idea Zarya had heard. After all, the

creature lived in the water. And, truthfully, she wanted to feel the edge of the ocean beneath the hull, to maybe even dip her hand into the saltwater without fearing what might happen.

"Fine," she said, trying her best to mask her excitement with an unaffected look. She crossed her arms against her chest.

The others seemed nonplussed for a moment—most of all Joe, who had brought up the idea in the first place. The room was quiet until Mrs. Irving broke the silence.

"Very well. We go tonight. Joe, how many does your boat hold?"

"It fits a dozen or so if we're going on a quick ride, but only six can fit comfortably if we stay overnight."

"We may very well need to stay overnight," said Mrs. Irving. "We're staying there all night if we need to. Whatever it takes."

Zarya was not sure what she had just agreed to do. She looked at Mrs. Irving's paper-thin skin, the ease with which it creased into expressions of hate. Her lips pinched together into a small line, and a pair of wrinkles deepened between her eyebrows as if she were looking at the grisliest sight.

It was understandable that the people of this town hated the sirens. Their loved ones were being picked off, one by one, and taken to the ocean, from where they were never returned. But still, Zarya could not bring herself to hate that creature. She had seen through the razor-sharp teeth to the semblance of humanity. Once upon a time, before vengeance had settled its way into her heart, Josephine had been a human in flesh and blood just like any of them. What had happened to her? Was she really as bad as they all thought? Somehow, Zarya was convinced her embrace would be warm.

The meeting concluded with list-making. Mrs. Irving determined who was coming on the boat—herself, Joe the fisherman, Zarya, the police officer, one other brawny-looking man and, at his own insistence, Bruno. She also designated each individual to bring certain supplies. The police officer was to bring as many weapons as he owned. The fisherman was to bring his fishing supplies—a fishnet, gaffs, and the biggest gaff hooks he could find. Bruno was told to bring sleeping bags. The other man was assigned filming equipment. As for Zarya, she was to bring snacks. Mrs. Irving had given her an easy task, no doubt aware she was already asking for so much from Zarya.

"What about my shift?" Zarya asked.

Mrs. Irving eyed her slyly. Finally, she said, "You can start your shift late to buy snacks."

When the meeting was over and everyone poured out of the stuffy cigar room, Mrs. Irving motioned for Zarya to stop by her desk. Zarya approached.

"This is a big night for you," the old woman said. "I hope we're not asking you for too much."

Zarya shrugged. "It's not like I have much of a choice."

"Oh, of course, you have a choice." Mrs. Irving's eyes gleamed unnaturally, as if they were made of glass. "You know what I think?"

"What?"

She inclined over the desk, her voice hushed. "I think we can get rid of all the sirens if we kill the one who turned them."

Zarya thought back to those glacier-blue eyes. "But how can we possibly know which one turned the others?"

"I was hoping you'd ask that." Mrs. Irving started ruffling through a manilla folder on her desk. Zarya saw the flash of old papers with curlicues of handwriting, photographs in sepia and black-and-white. Mrs. Irving kept shuffling through them until she came across a stack of newspaper articles, cinched together by a paperclip. She handed Zarya the stack. "These are all the articles I've kept in my lifetime, detailing all the lives that have been lost."

Zarya rifled through the pieces of paper. They smelled of ink and wood pulp.

"Some of these articles contain images of the victims," Mrs. Irving pressed on. "Do you recognize any of them as the siren you saw?"

Already, Zarya could tell that these articles were nowhere near old enough. Dead Man's Cove had been taking lives for far longer than Mrs. Irving's lifetime. Despite her attempts at playing detective, Mrs. Irving was foolish to think she could find the original siren in this way.

"I don't think so," said Zarya, almost to the bottom of the stack now. "And besides, how can I know if the one I saw is the original siren?"

Zarya shook her head. Her eyes were fixed on the hotel keeper's hands as they moved the folder into a drawer underneath her desk. Mrs. Irving took a key from her giant, jangling keychain and locked the drawer. Zarya made a point to recite in her head that the key was small and silver, with two sharp ridges like a mountain's edge. When Mrs. Irving caught her line of sight, Zarya forced herself to look away.

"No," Zarya answered.

Mrs. Irving pressed her lips into a frown, seeming unconvinced. "You would tell me if they were, wouldn't you?"

Zarya manufactured a smile that surely did not reach her eyes. "Of course."

"Very well." Mrs. Irving fell back into her swiveling armchair. "Well, go ahead, then. You should get those snacks before the check-in rush." She proffered a handful of cash.

Zarya took the money and nodded. She went out the hotel's side door, breathing a sigh of relief once she was out beneath the open sky. It seemed like the leaves had grown threefold overnight, for she had to duck beneath the bough of a red alder out front.

The grocery store was just around the corner. Inside, she walked right past the rows of strawberries, peaches, and plums, as well as rhubarb, asparagus, and spring peas. Doubting the folks she was meeting on the boat had much of a predilection for fresh produce, she headed instead straight into the middle rows.

Her cart was overfilled with chips, crackers, and cookies. On her way out, Zarya lingered in the liquor section, adding in a couple of bottles of rum. If she was supposed to play pirates and sailors, she might as well get in the spirit. She tossed in a massive bottle of Coca-Cola for good measure.

The total amounted to slightly less than Mrs. Irving had given her, and Zarya pocketed the leftovers. She returned to the Irving Hotel with handfuls of plastic bags, which she nudged under the desk in the cigar room. With Mrs. Irving gone, Zarya couldn't help but give the desk drawer a little nudge, but the maple wood would not budge. She headed back out to the lobby.

Her shift ended quickly. The exhilaration of tonight's plans made the day seem a bit brighter, even if the boat trip was a terrible idea. Maybe she needed to do crazy things more often.

She supped with Bruno on the patio, watching darkness blanket the town as people walked their dogs and whizzed by in cars. Everything took on a gaudy, blue hue in the twilight, so pigmented that Zarya felt the need to keep blinking her eyes. Beside her, Bruno seemed unbothered. He dug into his burger.

"Are you scared?" she asked.

"Of what?" Bruno didn't bother to stop chewing while he talked. "Tonight?"

Zarya nodded.

"No, why would I be? Are *you* scared?"

Zarya wasn't quite sure how to answer that. "I don't think so," she said, but it sounded more like a question.

"You shouldn't be," Bruno told her, reaching for another bite. "It'll be fine."

They loitered until dusk pushed out the blue glow. Bruno was loud and jovial as always. Then, they heard a screeching from the screen door behind them, and there stood Mrs. Irving in the doorway. Her hands were stuffed into the pockets of a windbreaker.

"Ready?"

Josephine, 1851

Chapter 14

As the year 1850 came to an end, the world seemed to be in black-and-white, like in the daguerreotypes. Josephine could not remember the last time she had seen the blue of the sky.

In town, gone were the harvested pumpkins, corn husks, grapes, and blueberries of the autumn. Before, Josephine had admired the cherry plum out front, with its burgundy leaves in a shade so dark they almost looked black. It had been one of the last trees to hang fruits from its boughs, ripe and dark and succulent-looking. But now, the fruits and the leaves had both fallen from their branches, and Josephine had to bend down to find a cluster of desiccated cherry plums at her feet. Her fingers tightened around it.

There was a rustle in the forest behind her, then a familiar voice. "Josephine, what are you doing?"

She had begun to associate the sight of Hurley with happiness—her only source of happiness, in fact. Her heart fluttered. Hurley wore a flummoxed expression, and she threw herself in his arms at his approach. Thomas might have been coming home through the forest, for all she cared.

"I was just looking at the pretty berries," she said, nestling in the warmth of his chest.

"Well, try to refrain." Hurley checked her fingers for residues of the berries. "The cherry plum's pit is poisonous. It contains cyanide."

Josephine made a mental note of it. She started kissing the side of his face, hopeful that he would take her right then and there, against the tree.

"Josephine, good God." Hurley threw a cautious look behind him, untangling her limbs from around his neck. "Someone could see us."

She let out a sinister giggle. "Who, the deer? There's not a soul out here for miles."

Hurley's grip on her tightened. "I'm serious, Josephine. What if someone is coming to pay you a visit and they see us?"

"Let them," she said, her voice hoarse.

When he saw that she could not be reasoned with, Hurley drew her inside the lighthouse. Josephine was beginning to associate those rooms with the darkness inside her mind, but somehow the place felt lighter with Hurley in it. How ironic that a place designated to brighten the ocean was her pit of darkness.

Once inside, Josephine took his coat and placed it on a hook by the door. Hurley sank into a dining chair, apparently in the mood for conversation before their lovemaking. He had gotten bolder about the length of his visits. Perhaps he had assigned Thomas to a task he knew would be time-consuming.

"You seem preoccupied," Josephine observed.

"It's been a dreadful week," he said.

"What's happened?"

Hurley crossed his legs and clasped his hands over a knee. "The miners have continued to strike. I had no choice but to evict them from their homes, which were on Irving property. I tried to reason with them, Josephine. Truly, I did. But they would not negotiate, and so I did exactly what I said I would do. I replaced them with Chinese men."

"You evicted them?" Josephine's voice was faint.

"What choice did I have? What would you have proposed?" He seemed to be genuinely asking, not silencing her for speaking out of turn.

She scoured her mind for the right answer. When she couldn't find it, Josephine replied, "I don't know. But I know what it's like to lose a home, and I wouldn't wish that on anyone."

For a moment, Hurley looked at her with puzzlement, as if he was about to inquire what she meant by that. But whatever curiosity he harbored about Josephine's past, he batted it away with one swift motion. "I treat these men better than most would. Have you not heard what is happening in the South?" He shook his head with what seemed to be genuine aversion. "There is a reason we have no slaves here. It is a barbaric practice."

"Then why not pay the workers a living wage?"

But Hurley was not listening. "And the strikes are not even the worst of it. After I sent the Europeans on their merry way, there were a series of accidents."

"What sort of accidents?"

Hurley took a sharp inhale of air. "First, one of the Chinese workers was run over by a coal car. The very next day, there was an explosion in the mine. Sixty men killed—including a fourteen-year-old boy. I went in there myself amidst the smoke, digging out whatever men I could."

Josephine remembered the teenage boy he had sent to substitute for Thomas in the lantern room. He'd had a gentle look in his eyes, a sweet lilt in his voice. She wanted to ask if it was the same boy, but she feared the answer.

Hurley's eyes were glossed over as if reliving the moment. "The stench of burning flesh, the sounds of their screams… It still haunts me in my sleep. Despite what they say, I do care for these men, Josephine."

Josephine could not bear the sound of it. She sauntered to the windowsill, hoping for something with which to distract herself. Then, she asked, "Why was a young boy working in the mines to begin with?"

He averted his eyes. "The boy's father had died in the mine a few months ago. Was I meant to deny him a means of sustenance?"

"No, of course not. It's just so awful."

"Yes, it is. I keep explaining the safety precautions to these men, but they barely speak a drop of English—and even those that do, have accents so thick I can hardly comprehend them. You can lead a horse to water, but..." He shook his head. The second half of his sentence got lost along the way.

"Why don't you hire back the European workers, and pay them a bigger wage?"

"I'm running a business, Josephine, not a charity. I must find a way to make a profit."

Josephine recalled his opulent mansion, a stark contrast to the very lighthouse in which they sat. It seemed to her that Hurley had no issue making a profit—he just wanted *more* of it. And, although it was sick of her, his greed was what she loved most about him. It was his greed for her that made her head dizzy.

"I think I'll step away from mining altogether," Hurley said. "Let my brother step in instead. I've found other ventures that look more promising."

"Like what?"

"Politics. Building a grand railway. Due to the location of Indian settlements, there's currently no railroad headed north." He shrugged. "We shall see."

His demeanor shifted now. He looked like he had gotten what he wanted out of the discussion, and the fire returned to his eyes. Hurley drew himself close to Josephine, cupping her cheek in his palm. He kissed her with a fervor that bordered on anger, as if he were punishing her for not being more validatory during their earlier discussion. And yet, it was the first thing to make Josephine feel alive in weeks.

"You're the most beautiful thing I've ever seen," he whispered, running a finger across her cheek.

Josephine wondered, was it enough to make him leave his wife?

They moved to the bed, his cloying cologne all over her. This was the part that left her intoxicated. Somehow, Josephine always forgot the part that came next—the part where he got what he wanted and felt free to leave.

It felt like their acts of lovemaking were getting shorter. He needed less and less of her, while she needed more and more. It took but a few dozen thrusts of his hips before the rapt look in his eyes trickled away and the hunger in his touch subsided. Josephine was left yearning for more, but it did not matter. These acts weren't about what she wanted.

Hurley sat on the edge of the bed with painstaking politeness.

Josephine was still reeling from the lovemaking. Her moment of vitality would be gone soon, and she needed to do something to prolong it. Surely, there was something she could say that could keep him here a while longer. Some other way she could prove herself to him. She could find a solution to his mining woes, and maybe then he would see her value—

"I love you."

No, those were not the clever words she had been seeking. In fact, it was a very daft thing to say. Telling the truth was usually daft.

The words loitered in the air between them. For a moment, Hurley looked as though he had just received an unfavorable business proposition that he would politely need to turn down. And what was that she saw in his eyes—a trace of pity?

She was not sorry she said it. It was the truth, and it felt good to let out. Hurley needed to know how she felt. He needed to know the depths of her devotion. If he knew how deep it ran, perhaps it would make him love her, too.

Was it so unlikely that he might love her? He certainly loved being inside her. She had an intoxicating allure to him that he seemed unable to resist. But somehow, her spell seemed to end the moment he had what he wanted. Still, she was at least expecting him to lie and say he loved her back. He lied to everyone—so then, what was the difference?

But it seemed that, for once in his life, Hurley was determined to be sincere. With downturned lips, he said, "You deserve to be happy, Josephine."

The words were a hammer to her heart. "If you want me to be happy, then be with me. Order Thomas away and put Amelia in a separate house. You practically run this town—you can do whatever you want."

"You cannot be serious, Josephine." He recoiled from her, almost imperceptibly, but she noticed. "You knew when we embarked on this affair that we were both married. You knew the rules."

"Yes, but I cannot live like this!" She could not say what she truly felt, which was that she had expected him to fall in love with her, that his visits were the single frayed thread keeping her from insanity, and that she had grand fantasies of him risking everything for her. The frustration squeezed tears out of her eyes. She covered her face so he would not see.

"What do you need, then? A visit from family? An allowance for yourself? A friend in town—"

"What I need is you!" She tore her hands away, and now the tears were flowing like a deluge. "If you won't leave your wife, then at the very least visit me more often. Give me a child. Treat me as your true wife in secret, if not publicly."

Hurley's thin lips were agape. For a moment, it looked like he could think of nothing to say in response. Then, in an unruffled cadence, he said, "You know I cannot give you what you want, Josephine."

It was so little that she asked for, not even an ounce of respect, but it was more than he could give. Was she not worth even this little?

She cried and cried until she was not sure from where the tears came. Hurley sat uncomfortably beside her, occasionally extending a comforting hand to her. But long before the tears ended, he pulled out his pocket watch. It dangled in his palm.

"I need to go now, darling. I'm sorry."

Her wail was swallowed by a sob.

"Are you able to collect yourself before Thomas comes back? What did Dr. Ainsworth tell you to do when you get like this?"

Josephine shook her head. He must have thought her mad. And clearly, Dr. Ainsworth disclosed the contents of her consultations to Hurley. But Josephine could not stop herself. She felt as though she were regurgitating the nothingness inside her. No matter how much she cried, there was more nothingness to purge.

Eventually, Hurley had no choice but to leave. Josephine was crouched on the floor, and he gave her a gentle tap on the spine before ambling towards the door. She kept her eyes glued to the nape of his neck as he left. She hated how even the back of his head made her wobbly with infatuation. She had begun to associate every inch of him with excitement, but now that he was leaving, there would be nothing keeping her from falling into the recesses of her mind.

She allowed herself to cry a few more minutes. By now, Thomas could be back at any moment, and she did not trust herself to lie when questioned about her state of mind. She combed through her memories, trying to remember what treatment Dr. Ainsworth had recommended. Her mind was blank. The only thing she could think about was the feeling that the whole world had gone black.

Suddenly, she recalled the cherry plums out front, their plump bodies like polished garnet jewels. She stepped into the outdoors, still barefoot, planting the soles of her feet against moist grass and jagged tree roots, but she was numb to the sensations of both.

Once she was out by the tree, her hands trembled towards the fruits. She envisioned herself tasting from them, letting the pits trickle down her throat like marbles down a jar. She wondered if it would be a quick death. She wondered if Hurley would cry for her. She hoped so. She thought so.

The cherries dangled like a pair of earrings in her palm, but then her eyes were drawn towards something behind the branches of the tree—the ocean. It was gray and big and menacing. Josephine was reminded of Dr. Ainsworth's mention of cold baths. It was certainly cold out today, the wind rustling goosebumps underneath the hem of her dress. She moved away from the tree, forgetting all about her dreams of death, assessing a way to get down to the water.

The lighthouse was perched on the highest point of the headland, but the land sloped down toward the forest. She followed its slant to a horseshoe-shaped enclave of sand. Here, short wind waves crashed upon the shore, strewing pieces of driftwood across the cove.

Josephine stepped into the water, at first just up to her ankles. The cold was piercing against her feet, but it numbed the agonizing sensation in her chest just slightly. Upon this discovery, she wasted no time. She tore off her dress, first the bodice and then the skirt. Next came the corset and the bustle. She tossed them all in a pile on the sand, feeling the wintry air prickle her flesh.

Then, she crouched down in the water, covered in ocean water up to her neck. The shock of the cold made her breath halt, but it also anesthetized the feeling of emptiness in her core. Here, she could not think, could not feel anything but pain. There was something remarkable about replacing her internal suffering with external pain.

In time, her breathing evened out. All skin and bones, the cold took hold of Josephine quickly. She felt a dull ache across her ribcage, as if the ribs were starting to ice over. Her stomach constricted. For the first time in as long as she could remember, Josephine could not feel the emptiness inside her. Flinching across the underwater sand, her feet went yellow and stony. Josephine lost sensation in her toes, just a slight tingle that dissipated with each moment that passed.

The longer she stayed there, the easier it felt. She could stay in the ocean for an eternity, Josephine thought.

But the lovely numbness was cut short by Thomas' voice booming down from the Rock. She saw the outline of his head above the bluff, watched him climb down to the cove.

"What in God's good name are you doing?" He gaped at her clothes on the ground before stepping into the ocean to grasp her. The water where she sat crouched only came up to his knees.

"Following the medic's orders," she said, meekly. She felt his rough hands on her forearms, grabbing her as though she were made of twigs. He pulled her out of the water in the way a child might seize a doll. It was the second time today, then, that a man had made her feel like a mere plaything.

"Have you truly lost your mind? What if someone sees you, all indecent out here?"

"There's no one around," she pointed out. A giggle made its way out of her throat, echoing across the cove. Josephine became keenly aware of how insane she must be sounding.

He did not negotiate with her further. Josephine shivered all the way up the headland, even once she was inside the lighthouse, even after he had dried her off and put her into bed. Despite the violent quivers that overtook her body, Josephine felt a sense of clarity and lightness inside. Her racing thoughts had quieted, replaced by a rush that could only be described as euphoric. She lay in bed, staring at the white ceiling, with a smile on her lips. Even as Thomas prepared to send a telegraph to Dr. Ainsworth, the smile lingered.

Zarya, 2023

Chapter 17

It was so dark by the water that Zarya could see all the stars freckled across the sky. A crescent moon cast its silvery sheen across the wind waves that foamed and crashed into the shore. Further out projected black shadows—the sea stacks. Zarya wondered how many millions of years ago they had arisen from volcanic eruptions, what sort of creatures had resided in the oceanic waters back then.

They found the fishing boat docked in the harbor. It was a blue-and-white trawler, perfect for camouflaging with the ocean. Already, voices chattered from inside the cabin. Zarya could see the faint outline of the police officer in the moonlight, hear Joe the fisherman yapping about his tools. She followed Mrs. Irving's lead over the edge of the boat, Bruno not far behind. Once inside, the surface beneath Zarya's feet rocked left and right. Her heart thumped with trepidation.

Joe turned on the motor, and the smell of gasoline drifted across the water. The motor hummed angrily.

Zarya sat by the washboard. She looked out at the ocean, hoping to see that pair of eyes glinting at her over the surface. But there was nothing as far as she could see, nothing but the sea stumps that protruded from the water like arrowheads chiseled for war.

A burly man sank into the seat beside Zarya. He looked to be in his early sixties, with a handlebar mustache the color of moonbeams. The man Mrs. Irving had brought along due to his strength.

"I'm Dave," he said, offering a handshake.

Zarya took up his offer. Dave's clasp was firm. "Dave like from Dave's Bar and Grill," she noted, making little of the word association.

"Exactly," responded Dave.

She had been gazing toward the water, but now Zarya whipped her head to look at him. "Wait, really? You're Dave from Dave's Bar and Grill?"

"Yes, ma'am."

Zarya gave an impressed nod. "Huh. Very cool place you got there. I'm over there most weeks."

"More than me, then."

The motorboat had broken free of the dock now, and they started gliding slowly away from shore. Zarya let out a sharp sigh. "I really don't want to be doing this," she said.

"No, me neither."

"Really?" Zarya brightened. "They dragged you into this against your will, too?"

"Don't get me wrong—I want to protect the town. I just don't love being out on the water."

Zarya threw him a sidelong look. "Why not?"

"I can't swim."

At first, she thought she must have misheard him. But the more the words lingered in the nighttime air between them, the more they made sense. Of course, Mrs. Irving did not care whose life she was endangering out here. What she wanted most of all was vengeance. For what exactly, Zarya was not sure. As far as she could tell, no member of the Irving family had been personally harmed by a siren. But she had seen all those secret files Mrs. Irving kept locked away in her desk, and Zarya couldn't help but wonder whether she was covering something up. Something related to the hotel and her lineage.

Before she had a chance to respond, Zarya heard her name called from the cockpit. She traversed the deck to the front of the boat as the vessel exited the harbor. Beyond, the vast seas greeted them with open arms.

"Yes?" Zarya reached the place where everyone stood huddled. Joe was peering out into the darkness, his hands maneuvering the helm ever so slightly.

"We need to discuss the plan," said Mrs. Irving, stepping over to the bench seats by the bow. She lifted one of the leather cushions to reveal a cavernous compartment beneath it.

There, Zarya saw a handful of firearms piled on top of each other. They looked cold and black and weighty. Heaviness pressed against her chest.

"Do you know how to shoot?" asked Mrs. Irving.

Zarya shook her head.

"Okay. Best to let the rest of us handle these, then. Joe, show her the other equipment."

Joe stepped away from the helm and grasped a thick, black fishnet from the deck. "If you ever see movement in the water, holler at me. I'll cast this net into the water."

Zarya's eyes trailed over the deck, landing on a giant, silver hook. Its tip was brandished so sharply that it made her pity whatever would be on the other end of it. She flinched slightly. "What's that?"

"Gaff and hook. That's what we use to grab fish out of the water when they're circling the bait. But in this case, we'll use it as a weapon if you see something that's not ensnared in the fishnet."

"Do you need me to do anything?" asked Zarya, knowing damn well that she intended to do very little.

"If you're not a shooter and you're not a fisher, it's probably best that you just keep watch."

Mrs. Irving stepped in between Zarya and the fisherman. Though the top of her head only came up to Zarya's shoulders, the old woman seemed to loom large. "Remember, Zarya, your role tonight is arguably the most important, and that is to be the bait. So, keep your eyes open, but let the rest of us handle the tough bits."

Zarya threw a look across the ink-black water. What chance did they stand against the entire abyss?

"Why don't you go into the cabin and speak with Bruno," Mrs. Irving instructed her. "He'll show you where the sleeping bags are, in case we have to stay out here all night."

Zarya did as told, descending the steps into the covered cabin beneath the cockpit. The room was nothing like the luxurious yachts she'd seen in pictures, with their lacquered wooden walls and pale leather and marble bar tops. Down here, there was just a stale mattress crammed beneath two counters. Bruno had set out a few more sleeping bags on the floor, which she had to zigzag around to get to the bed. On the counter next to her, she saw a row of half-drunk liquor bottles. It seemed Joe was not the tidiest of boat owners.

"These are yours," Bruno said, motioning to the plastic bags sprawled out beside the sleeping bags.

"The snacks. Give me one of them, please." Zarya reached to grab the chips from his grasp.

Bruno sat on one of the polyester blankets, watching her crack open the bag. Cautiously, he asked, "So, how are you feeling?"

"Fine."

"Really? You look nervous."

"I'm the bait," she said, parroting Mrs. Irving. "Wouldn't you be nervous, too?"

Bruno considered the question for a moment. Then, he answered, "No. I'd be happy to kill the siren once and for all."

Zarya pretended not to hear him, occupying herself with the potato chips.

Bruno went on, "Do you ever wonder why she picked you to be next?" His voice was tinged with disbelief, almost like he could not see what was so interesting about Zarya.

Zarya shrugged. "I don't think there was a reason. She picked me because I was there. She would have picked whoever locked eyes with her first."

"So, just the wrong place, wrong time." Bruno frowned. "That's too bad."

Zarya peeked through one of the portholes. The water was almost up to the window, a billowing mass of darkness. The boat had sailed far enough from the shore that the town was just a smattering of light on the horizon, and now it traveled parallel to the coast, bobbing up and down on the water like a rocking chair.

Zarya played cards with Bruno for a while, after which she headed back up to the deck. She found Joe at the cockpit, his eyes transfixed on nothing in particular. Joe gave Zarya a polite nod as she joined him.

It was growing cold. The wind scraped across Zarya's skin, bringing with it the scent of kelp and fish. She huddled underneath her denim jacket.

"Do me a favor," said Joe. "Reach over to that cubbyhole and see what's in there." He motioned to what looked like a drawer on the side of the cockpit.

Zarya pulled the knob towards her and peered inside. There, a flask rolled along with the motions of the boat. She reached over, clutched the cold metal between her fingers. "What is it?" she asked, presenting it to Joe.

"Bourbon." He shook his head at her offer. "Ladies first."

She had been hoping he would say something along those lines. Zarya unscrewed the metal stopper and took a swig. The bourbon burned her throat, then her stomach. Once the burning subsided, a little warmth flickered through her insides. She handed it to Joe.

"So, you've never seen anything strange out on the water?" Zarya asked as he took a big gulp. "All these years of fishing, and nothing?"

Joe shrugged. "Once or twice, I thought I might've seen something. Turned out to be nothing. I know they're there, though."

"How?"

"I can feel 'em watching me." His eyes squinted. "They're

watching, waiting."

The moon had risen higher in the sky, and now a wisp of cloud swept across it like gossamer.

"Waiting for what, exactly?" asked Zarya.

"I dunno. Not gonna wait to find out."

The boat slowed down to a cruising pace, the swell tipping it to the side every few moments. It was quiet. Zarya scanned the waters for something—anything at all. If she did see something, she wasn't sure what to be more scared of: the Defenders catching the sirens, or the siren catching her.

She helped Joe finish the vestiges of bourbon from his flask, and soon her blood coursed slower, more viscous, like honey. Her tongue languished as she spoke. Her mind was starting to feel slackened, no longer as tense about whatever swam in the depths below them. That was, until Mrs. Irving rounded the corner and joined her on the cockpit bench.

The woman folded her hands in her lap. She turned to Zarya with those sensing eyes of hers.

"You shouldn't drink tonight," she said, turning away as if the scent of alcohol offended her. "We need you sharp."

Zarya exchanged a quick look with Joe. If Mrs. Irving knew that the captain was also drinking, they would all be in for an earful.

"What if nothing happens tonight?" asked Zarya, keen to change the subject.

Mrs. Irving let out one wry, singular chuckle. "If not tonight, then we get her another night."

Mrs. Irving's calculated composure did not fool Zarya. There was a blistering rage inside the old woman—it was plain in the flare of her pupils.

"Why do you hate sirens so much?" Zarya asked.

Mrs. Irving looked at her as though she had asked the most absurd question. "They have taken from us, so very much."

"But this seems personal for you." Normally, she would not have spoken like this to the woman, but bourbon unraveled the tight cords that normally kept Zarya's impulses in place.

Mrs. Irving threw Zarya a curious look. For a moment, it looked like she was not going to answer her. Then, in a low tone, she said, "My family has hated the sirens for as long as I can remember. They instilled in me a healthy fear of the ocean—my parents, my grandparents, and their grandparents before them. They seemed to know something I did not. I think you will find, Zarya, that there is wisdom in trusting your elders."

Zarya's mind flitted back to the image of the lighthouse keeper's wife she had found in the Irving Hotel library—the same face from the water. The history of this town ran deep, and something about the lighthouse was connected to the hotel.

The boat swayed atop the increasingly cragged ocean, and Zarya felt the taste of alcohol making a comeback at the top of her throat. She steadied herself on the banister of the boat, hoping to offset the nausea. Beside her, Mrs. Irving receded with a look of disdain.

Zarya flashed open her phone to look at the time. It was well past midnight now.

"I think I'll go downstairs to nap for a bit," she said.

"That's probably wise." Mrs. Irving avoided her gaze.

Zarya lumbered towards the cabin, where Bruno already lay sleeping with his face toward the wall. She lay down on the gauche, filigreed bedsheets of the cabin bed and closed her eyes. Though the waves still gnawed at her stomach, soon the rocking motion lulled her to sleep.

She was awoken at first by the sound of shouting, the soundwaves sharp against her eardrums. It was a woman's voice—Mrs. Irving's—and it ripped her out of her sleep like a gaff hook. Zarya sat up, startled. Bruno was gone from the sleeping bag on the floor.

Following the shouts, there was a thud from above, like heavy machinery falling to the deck. Zarya vaulted from the bed and up the stairs, where everyone stood scattered across the boat, weapons and fishing equipment in hand. Joe had the cast net ready to hurdle at the water, Dave held a rifle against his shoulder, and the police officer had a gun pointed at the water. Bruno rotated a filming camera from left to right while Mrs. Irving faced the ocean with a pair of binoculars.

"What's going on?" The adrenaline seemed to have melted the alcohol from Zarya's veins.

She looked out to the water, where waves splashed all around the boat. She thought she spotted the two-pronged tail of a flipper near a trail of foam, but it disappeared too quickly to know for sure.

"Joe saw something," said Mrs. Irving, her tone tart. She would not disentangle her gaze from the ocean.

The boat was anchored in place, and the lack of motion made fear unfurl inside Zarya. She felt the sudden and familiar urge to run—but there was nowhere to run here.

"What should I do?" she asked, gripping the handrail tautly.

"Go a little closer to the water. Lure it toward you." Mrs. Irving gave commands much like a lieutenant.

Zarya did as told, leaning slightly over the stanchion. The flashlight from Bruno's camera shone a circle of light on the water, a sharp contrast to the darkness all around. Zarya saw the undulating shape of a body underneath the surface. A gasp rose to her lips.

It couldn't be this easy. That creature she had seen in the water was no jelly-brained fish. Her eyes had been knowing, keen. She would never attack an armed boat like this. Besides, Zarya could no longer hear the siren's hums echoing through her ears. The siren was nowhere near here. Something felt wrong.

There was a gunshot behind her, the noise so loud it felt like a punch. Zarya curled up on the deck, instinctively covering her head. She saw that Dave's rifle had ricocheted into his shoulder, sending him backward into the stern. A chorus of screams took hold of the others in the confusion.

Zarya forced herself up, fingers curled against the rail. One look in the water told her that Dave's shot had been in vain. Despite his broad shoulders, the man could hardly operate a gun.

Then, there was a sharp bellow from the police officer. "I see it!" His finger pressed down on the trigger of his gun, and this time the gunshot sent a screech through Zarya's ears.

The bullet went exactly where he wanted it to go. His weapon did not kickback like Dave's had. Blood curled through the ocean, at first bright red, then paler as it blended with the seawater. Without wasting a moment, Joe tossed the fishnet down where the blood plumed, and the net tightened around something heavy. It pulled Joe toward the edge of the boat, only the traction from his boots and Dave's strong arms keeping him from being thrown into the ocean. Something very heavy had caught in the fishnet.

The police officer put the safety on his gun and tucked it underneath his belt. He grabbed ahold of the rope from the fishnet and, together, all three men heaved. They strained, grunting from the weight of whatever lay trapped in that net.

When the net came over the edge of the boat, horror tore through Zarya. She covered her eyes with her hands, unable to bear the scene. The others fell quiet, too, and the only sound for miles was the contents of the fishnet thumping against the deck. It sounded slick and rubbery. After an eternity of silence, Zarya willed herself to reopen her eyes.

The seal wriggled inside the net in pain, blood gushing out of its blubber so quickly that it spread across the deck like red varnish. Zarya peered into its big, black eyes. Its whiskered muzzle seemed to call to her, begging for mercy. Zarya let out a pained wail.

"This is just a seal," said Mrs. Irving, her voice cold.

"You sure about that?" Joe reached for his gaff and hook, ready to wrench it into the animal. "Let's make sure it's not just posing as a seal."

"Stop!" Zarya sprang in between him and the seal, grasping the gaff with two hands. "Are you out of your fucking mind?"

Across the deck, Bruno's camera still rolled, even as he retreated further away in disgust.

"Joe, this is not the creature we're looking for," said Mrs. Irving. She shook her head, though she did not seem particularly riddled with guilt. "We have to put it back into the water. Seals are protected by the Marine Mammal Protection Act. If anyone finds out about this, we can get in big trouble."

"It's dying," Zarya said, loading as much hate as possible into each consonant. "We need to get it to help."

"There's no helping it, Zarya. Look at it!" Mrs. Irving motioned toward the pool of blood at their feet. "And besides, do you know any marine life veterinarians up at this hour?"

Zarya's eyes brimmed with tears. The seal's eyelids were closing, the wound still gashing red. It would be dead before they ever reached shore.

She reached over to touch the creature's slippery skin. The blubber felt cold beneath her fingers. Then she pulled away, choking on a sob.

The men opened the fishnet and tossed the seal back over the edge of the boat. There was a huge splash in the water, which sent ripples of water shaking the boat. Zarya watched the gray body sink, until the blood dissolved in the massive ocean.

When it was gone, she turned to Joe. "Take this boat to shore. Now."

She brushed past Bruno to get into the cabin, eager to be alone. Tears soaked her cheeks and streamed down to her lips tasting like saltwater.

Bruno followed her in. He had gone pale despite his sun-kissed complexion as if the blood had dropped from his face.

"Are you alright?" he asked, sitting beside her on the bed.

"No." She wiped her tears to glare at him better.

"It'll all be okay," he said, trying to pet the side of her arm.

She jerked his hand away from her. "No, Bruno, it's not going to be okay. We just killed an innocent creature, and for what? To kill someone who's already dead?"

She did not expect Bruno's reaction. Without warning, his eyes grew darker. The compassion he had shown Zarya just moments before was wiped from his face all too quickly. He said, "They are *not human*, Zarya. Don't you understand? They might look human in some ways, but they are not. You can't see them as human, because then you'll lose sight of our mission."

At that moment, she looked at him and truly hated him. Her hate simmered and seethed. It churned at her insides. She wanted nothing more than to wipe that look off Bruno's face, and she knew that their friendship was forever gone.

"Get out of my face."

Part II

Zarya, 2023

Chapter 16

Entrapment was a feeling Zarya did not tolerate well. Yet she had a decision to make—should she stay entrapped in the Irving Hotel with people who had killed an innocent creature of the water, or should she return to a more familiar form of entrapment?

After the boat expedition, Zarya had returned to the attic with bile still on the edge of her tongue. She had dithered back and forth, shards of moonlight shifting through the curtains. She could not get those big, black eyes out of her head, their pleading gaze for mercy. A retch was incoming, and she swallowed it down by some miracle. Maybe it would have been better to let it out.

No, she decided. She could not stay in this mansion with Mrs. Irving and Bruno a minute longer than was needed. She would meet her parents for dinner right after her work shift and move back in with them.

There was, of course, a third option—one that whispered in her ear with melodic intonations. It promised an eternity of freedom underwater. But, of course, Zarya understood that nothing in life was free. There was a reason that creature wanted her seaside, and it was unlikely to be out of the goodness of her heart.

Already, dawn had begun to cast lilac shafts on the horizon. Zarya tried to close her eyes and sleep a bit, but every time, she saw that seal's body sinking to the bottom of the ocean. Her heart raced.

Her legs twitched, shocking her awake. She went out to the balcony, leaning over the wrought-iron banisters to gaze at the sunrise. Somewhere, a Pacific wren serenaded its mate, filling the sky with high-pitched chirps. Zarya was exhausted, but the day was just beginning.

By the time the garden was fully engulfed in sunlight, she pulled away from the expanse. She grabbed a cup of coffee from the foyer, hoping it would help with the churning sensation in her stomach. Unfortunately, it only made the sensation worse.

Then came time for her shift.

Zarya stood blankly behind the concierge desk. She did not have a book underneath the keyboard like most days. If she had, the words on the page would have certainly been meaningless to her.

Mrs. Irving did not make an appearance until two hours into their shift. But when she did, it was in a neatly pressed blouse and tailored pants. She seemed to have scrubbed the saline odor from her skin and replaced it with a thick scent of cherry blossoms. She did not look Zarya in the eyes before joining her at the desk.

But then, after a few moments, the woman said, "I trust that you won't do anything brash about last night."

Zarya pressed her fingertips into the side of her forehead. The muscle there responded with a throb of pain.

"I'd like to change my work schedule," she said, carefully tiptoeing around Mrs. Irving's insinuation.

"To what?"

"I don't want any more shifts with Bruno."

Mrs. Irving looked at her for the first time all day. For a second, she looked like she might chastise Zarya, but if that was her intention, she swallowed it. "Okay," she responded, her voice even. "Anything else?"

So, it was a negotiation, then.

"Yeah. I'm not coming to the Defenders meetings anymore. You'll need to find a way to stop the siren without me," Zarya said, resolutely.

Mrs. Irving gave one nod. "Fine."

"And I need a sick day."

"Today?" Mrs. Irving glanced worriedly at the weekend crowd already pouring in.

"Today."

Zarya did not wait for permission. She grabbed her satchel from the floor and started toward the stained-glass door. Mrs. Irving did not attempt to stop her. And if she had, Zarya would have already been gone.

She found her parents in their usual orbits, her mother in the kitchen and her father in his office. Zarya's mother squealed in delight when she saw her daughter ambling through the doors. The radiators were still on despite the May sun that lingered in the sky. Zarya took off her jacket, the skin beneath already sticky. It felt like there was not enough oxygen in the room.

"Have you come for the weekend?" asked Zarya's mom, hopeful.

Zarya dug through the refrigerator, half searching for a can of soda and half trying to cool herself down. She spotted a can of Coca-Cola and cracked it open, bubbles fizzing to the top. The cool, syrupy liquid frothed down her throat.

"I need a break from the hotel."

"Of course, sweetheart. You know you're always welcome here."

"I'm going to take a shower." Zarya hated that she had to announce it, but she knew her mother would summon her otherwise, wondering where Zarya had gone.

Zarya hated showering at home. She recalled all too vividly the times growing up when her mother had walked into the bathroom with no regard for the running water, shouting about how Zarya was taking too long, about how she wanted to spend some quality time before the day was over. Zarya had learned to shower in record-low time, but nothing could scrub the feeling of panic every time she showered. Any moment now, her mother might come swinging through the door.

She had hardly even rinsed the conditioner from her hair before turning off the shower valve. Zarya looked at herself through the steamed mirror, squeezing the water from amber strands of hair. She looked like she belonged in a tomb, fatigue tugging at the skin under her eyes. She threw a towel over her hair and stepped out.

Her mother had laid out a platter of food on the dining table—deviled eggs, slices of ham and salami, chunks of cheese, tomatoes, cucumbers, and olives. Zarya picked from the selection, careful to keep her facial expression flat. Any semblance of emotion and she knew the eruption that would follow. *Is everything alright, Zarya? What's been going on? You don't seem well. Talk to me, come on.* And then, after the initial resistance: *Why are you being so secretive? You can't talk to your own mother? I don't understand why you're being like this. Tell me what's on your mind right now.* Even her thoughts had no right to be private.

Before her mother had a chance to start with her questions, Zarya thought she might beat her to the chase. "Tell me about Rusalka Week, Mama."

Her mother looked out the window to the yard out front, where begonias and rhododendrons shot towards the sky. She seemed surprised by the question.

"I don't know so much about it. All I know is from my mother in the village where she grew up."

"Well, what did she say about it?" asked Zarya.

"She sometimes called it Green Week. She had a sister in Romania who called it Rusalii. It's a festival in early June, in the seventh week leading up to the Pentecost. But, to tell you the truth, the tradition always felt older than Christianity. My mother said it had to do with the cult of the dead."

Zarya swallowed, hard. "Why's that?"

"Well, some people thought the *rusalki* were their deceased family members. Some thought they were the unclean dead—you know, the dead that aren't dead as they should be, who cause harm to the living."

"What did people do during the festival?"

"Hmm." Zarya's mother started toying with Zarya's hair as she explained, "Your grandmother told me they used to honor a birch tree during Green Week. They'd name it after a *rusalka*. Some people would even cut branches from it and bring them home. Then, at the end of the week, they'd drown the tree."

"Why a birch?"

"Birches were historically symbols of death. On the Thursday before the Pentecost, girls would sing songs and pick flowers, using the flowers to make wreaths. They'd find a forest clearing, where one of the girls was chosen to be the *rusalka*, wearing a dress with flowers woven into her dress and hair.

"They'd bring offerings to the birch tree—fried eggs, beer, butter, and garlands. They would say incantations for luck with the crops. You see, they believed the *rusalki* were in charge of water and fertility, so they could either make floods or bring a healthy amount of moisture to the crops. Then, at the end of the week, they'd cut down the tree, dress it like a woman, tie colorful ribbons around it, and drown it."

"Drown the tree?" Zarya was not sure she heard correctly.

Her mother nodded, still digging through Zarya's strands. "To protect the community from the *rusalki*."

Zarya was not sure what to do with this information. "I see."

"Zarya, why do you keep asking about this?" Mama fixed her eyes on Zarya. It was too late to feign ignorance now—the questions had already started.

"No reason."

"Zarya…"

By some miracle, the smell of food seemed to have lured Zarya's father from his cave at just the right time. Zarya let out a small sigh of relief as he turned the corner and sat across from her at the dining table. He uttered a perfunctory hello.

"I'd like to go for a walk with you today," Mama suddenly

announced to Zarya. It didn't sound like a question. Now that the initial excitement of her daughter's visit had worn off, her mood was starting to sour. She needed more of Zarya, and she needed her alone. Time together didn't count unless they were alone.

"I'm so tired," replied Zarya. "I was thinking of taking a nap."

"All day?" Her tone, which had been syrupy-sweet before, now sounded curt and morose.

Zarya nodded. "Yeah, I didn't get any sleep at all last night." She tried to sound nonchalant about the matter.

But already, her mother's brows were drawn in worry. "None at all? What on earth were you doing all night? Not drinking, I hope?"

"No, of course not. I just haven't been sleeping well."

Her mother's expression went from worried to cloying in the span of a moment. She threw her arms around Zarya, squeezing with all her might. "You'll sleep here tonight, sweetheart. It's so much quieter and more peaceful than in that hotel. I just changed your sheets, too."

Zarya waited a few moments before pulling away from the embrace. If she waited even a second less, her mother's sense of rejection would alchemize into anger like the flip of a switch.

She got up from the table now. "I think I'll go for that nap."

"Alright. But don't sleep too long, okay? If you do, you'll have trouble falling asleep tonight. And I want to have some quality time with you, like when you were little. You remember, don't you? You're still my little girl."

Zarya threw a glance in her father's direction to see if he would at all intervene, but he was busy chewing on a piece of smoked ham. She pitied him, in some ways. He needed to live here no matter what. But then Zarya remembered all those years he had stood by and said nothing to protect her, and her pity melted away.

Yes, Zarya did remember being her mother's little girl. In the very beginning of childhood, her mother's attentiveness and warmth had been a refuge. Zarya recalled how sweet her mother could be—

how sweet she still was on occasion.

But as Zarya had grown up, she'd learned the word no. She'd started to have desires of her own. She'd felt the urge to become her own person. And, with each day, Sweet Mommy had receded, replaced instead by an angry, neurotic version of her. Mean Mommy. By the time Zarya reached adolescence, it seemed she could never do anything right. If she wanted Sweet Mommy, she needed to still be Mommy's Little Girl. It was a steep price to pay.

Zarya retreated to her bedroom, where she drew the blackout curtains and buried herself under the duvet. The sheets indeed smelled fresh, the cotton soft to the touch, and she allowed sleep to take hold of her. So deep was her tiredness that even the nightmares could not awaken her.

She awoke hours later, with her legs aching and the siren's song undulating in her head. The house was quiet, and the light coming in through the edges of the curtains seemed to have dimmed. Zarya peeked through the crack to see that a big, heavy cloud had swept in from the ocean. She checked the clock—three in the afternoon.

She sat in bed, trying not to make the mattress squeak against the bedframes. If she made a loud enough sound, her mother would know she was awake and come bursting through the door, demanding to spend time together. Zarya pressed her eyes closed, trying to think. She needed to get out of the walk with her mother, for she could sense the tension already rising. There was no chance the walk wouldn't end with one of them screaming at the other.

The waiting around and biding her time felt all too familiar. Zarya recalled her weekend mornings growing up, how she would postpone getting out of bed as long as possible because she wasn't sure what mood her mother would be in that day. On Friday afternoons, she would linger in the classroom, hoping for an excuse to not go home. And on weeknights, after her father picked her up from school, she would flinch at the sound of the garage door opening, the sound of her mother's shoes growing closer. Whether she would get Sweet Mommy or Mean Mommy was as unpredictable as the toss of a coin.

Now, having caught up on sleep enough to think straight, Zarya realized she had made a grave miscalculation. Yes, the Irving Hotel was a shadowy place, filled with terrible people and perhaps a ghost too many, but there she could at least lock her own door. She did not have to fear the sound of footsteps in the corridor. If someone wanted to violate her privacy, they did so surreptitiously, not in the light of day as if they had every right to do so.

She threw on the jacket she had flung across the floor and started opening the bedroom door, inch by inch. Once the sliver was large enough for her body to fit through, she slipped through and tiptoed towards the front door. Outside, it smelled of spring and rain and grass.

Zarya threw a glance at the windows to see if anyone had watched her slip out. There was no one there, so she skulked towards the car.

Josephine, 1851

Chapter 17

Hurley's visits began thinning after Josephine's declaration of love. He still came to her intermittently, as if unable to stop himself, but it was only when most convenient to him. He came with a ravenous appetite, with no pretenses of polite conversation before he dug into her body. Now that he knew she adored him, it was like he understood just how much leeway he would be afforded. He no longer tended after Josephine's pleasure, looking only after his own. When Josephine tried to pleasure herself during their lovemaking, he looked at her as though she was mad.

She had become nothing more than a vessel for his pleasure. Perhaps he figured that her heart was already broken, so what did it matter if he broke it any further?

Sometimes, he arrived at her doorstep with such a rapacious expression on his face that she was sure someone else had stirred his desire. He ordered her to quench his lust, getting bolder and bolder in the way he spoke to her. He knew just how little Josephine respected herself, and there was no reason for him to pretend he respected her any more than that, either. Even at noon on a Sunday, she was expected to be ready for him. The lighthouse was starting to feel like a brothel.

In truth, she was always ready for him. These minutes of rapture were the only time she was pulled out of her emptiness.

Josephine was addicted to Hurley, but moreover, she was addicted to being coveted. When she saw the crazed look in his eyes, it was the only time she held any power. He could not help himself from being drawn to her—even when it was obvious that he had tried to stay away—and that temporarily made her a very powerful woman.

Perhaps that was her destiny, to be the siren call he could not resist. One bat of her eyelashes, one downward tilt of her face, and he was done for. Neither his wedding vows nor his self-restraint could keep him from her.

But as soon as he found ecstasy in her body, the spell was broken. He removed himself from her touch effortlessly, already fastening his garments on the far edge of her bed. He made some small talk, inquiring about her plans for the rest of the day, then left with the blankest look in his eyes. Not even a kiss goodbye.

And, once he was gone, the emptiness settled back in like quicksand. Like any addict, Josephine needed more and more of him to feel alive, while he provided less and less. The high no longer produced enough of a rush to counteract the crash that followed.

Every moment of existence stung. Josephine knew only one thing that somewhat helped, and that was the ocean. Even now, in late January, she undressed before the Pacific and swam into the cove, knowing very well that Thomas might be home soon but willing to risk it over the pain. She no longer hyperventilated at first contact with the cold. Her body had grown accustomed to the ocean, even relied on it.

On this day, something formidable happened.

She saw the ripples of water coming from the edge of the cove, in two diagonal angles converging where a sphere popped out of the water. Occasionally, the sphere disappeared underwater, and the ripples evened out. Josephine scanned the water, hoping to see where the seal head had gone, but it popped back out in an unexpected place every time.

Now, the seal drew near her, so close she could see its husky whiskers and hoary hair, its dappled body and lustrous skin.

It was so close that Josephine could reach over to touch its muzzle. She felt its warm breath on her wrist. The water was steel-gray beneath the winter sky, and Josephine saw the contour of the creature's massive body right underneath the surface. It could have been a menacing sight, were the animal not so gentle.

The seal floated before Josephine. It rested its neck against Josephine's arm, and Josephine nearly crumbled at the kindness of the gesture. She could not remember the last time she had felt such affection. There was saltwater all over—saltwater in the ocean, saltwater pouring from her eyes…

She recalled the tale of the *selkie*. Once a tale of freedom, now a story of pain. In the legend, the *selkie* had not one but two husbands who loved her. Josephine, meanwhile, could not even find love in one man. This gesture of warmth from the creature of the ocean was all she had to live for.

Josephine decided that there must be something sacred about the water and the animals that inhabited it. Why else did all creatures need water to survive? Why else were humans at the mercy of water when growing crops? Why else did priests dunk newborns into a bowl of water? The baptism was but a cleansing initiation, a passageway into the kingdom of Heaven, a return to the cosmic womb. Josephine herself had felt the way the ocean washed away her suffering, even just for a few hours. She longed to curl up in it for all eternity. As the sinful thought appeared in her mind, her tears intensified.

She was seawater-sodden from head to toe. The seal lifted its head from Josephine's arm for the first time in a while, and its eyes were drawn to the Rock behind them. Josephine understood. Thomas was coming home, and she needed to return to the lighthouse. The seal, as if knowing Josephine would not pull herself away of her own accord, dove underwater and did not rise back up until it exited the cove. There, where the cove turned to ocean, it lingered a moment with bead-black eyes before plunging back into the water.

Josephine swam back to shore, running inside before her husband's return. Upon hearing of her ailments, Hurley had arranged for a washing basin to be delivered to the lighthouse. A gesture of kindness, Josephine had thought. Proof that perhaps he could still love her. Or just that he wanted to silence her tears.

Josephine had pre-filled the bath with water, and now she stooped inside it to hide the evidence of her swim. Even the tepid water, which had long lost its steam, felt hot by comparison. She felt the sensation return to her core, then eventually to her toes and hands as well. Patches of waxen flesh turned shell-pink.

She heard the door of the lighthouse swing open, and then Thomas was standing at the threshold with a look of dubiousness. "You're bathing?"

"Just as the doctor ordered," she said, avoiding his direct gaze.

Thomas approached, peering into the bath that reeked of brine. At the edge of Josephine's foot floated a tousle of kelp. He raised an inquiring brow.

"Oh, I decided to use saltwater for my bath," said Josephine.

"I see that." Thomas drifted towards the door. "I ran into Dr. Ainsworth in town. He said he'd stop by for a visit shortly. You may want to dry off."

"Certainly, dear."

Josephine toweled herself off, slipping into a fresh bodice and skirt, both of which were gray as clams. She ran a comb through her hair and pinned the hip-length mass into a braided bun. By the time she was done, she could already hear Dr. Ainsworth in the dining room.

The doctor palpated her body, grouching to Thomas about her lack of improvement. Her body temperature seemed abnormally cool, he noted, his fingers in warm contrast against her flesh. The medic checked Josephine's reflexes, then tapped against her back as if expecting a knock in return.

When the examination was done, Dr. Ainsworth grimaced. "Allow me to speak to your husband alone for a moment, Mrs.

Byrne."

Josephine excused herself, but she did not wander far, lingering by the wall with her ear pressed against it. Through the wall, she heard Dr. Ainsworth's tone of ennui. He was no doubt dissatisfied with her progress, and the failure of her treatment was due to her faults rather than his.

She heard only snippets. "Her melancholia … resistant to treatment."

Josephine wondered, did she have any hope at all of ever experiencing joy if her own physician was out of ideas?

"Still no update … conceiving a child?"

There was Thomas' low rumble. His voice was too muffled to make out the words, but Josephine could gather a pretty good estimation of what he might say. *No, doctor, her womb seems to be barren. It has nothing to do with my utter disinterest in our marriage bed.*

Dr. Ainsworth responded. "What family … in Maine?"

This time, Josephine heard her husband utter the word *sister.*

"I will write … letter."

Josephine had heard enough. She splayed onto the bed and stared at the ceiling as was becoming her habit. Already, the effects of her ocean swim were wearing off. The melancholia trickled back in, black as a seal's eyes and empty as Josephine's womb.

Zarya, 2023

Chapter 18

Since the moment she had snuck out of her parents' house, Zarya's phone would not stop buzzing. At the seventeenth unanswered message from her mother, Zarya decided to power off the phone altogether.

She arrived at the Irving Hotel just before the dinnertime rush. She lurked through the wainscoted corridor, peeping around the lobby corner to check if Mrs. Irving was still behind the concierge desk. When she found the woman occupied, with no one else to help her on the shift, Zarya pushed open the door to the cigar room where the Defenders held their meetings.

The drapes were drawn. Only a sliver of light poured into the room, dust motes dancing like gold flakes. Zarya pulled the drapes shut all the way. No one could catch her snooping. She turned on the lamp, which cast a ruddy aura across the room's already garish wallpaper.

Zarya started with the bookshelves. She pulled out entire rows of books, seeing if there was anything hidden behind them, then pressed her palms against the bookcase itself in the unlikely event that there was a secret latch. When nothing furtive revealed itself, she headed towards the desk where Mrs. Irving had sat during the meetings.

A couple of candlesticks flanked the desk. There was an

ancient-smelling chess set, which Zarya checked inside to find only pieces of polished ebony and ivory. Then, she moved to the drawers.

The top drawer was the one that Mrs. Irving had locked at the end of their last meeting in the cigar room. Zarya pulled on it once more, but the wood was fastened in place. She tried the other drawers instead. Stiffly, they opened, and Zarya peered inside.

There, she saw the camera that Bruno had been flashing on the boat last night. She seized it in one quick motion and pressed the on button. Surely enough, in graphic frames, Bruno had caught the killing of the seal. Zarya could not bear to watch until the end. She turned the camera in her hands, wondering why Mrs. Irving had not kept it in the locked drawer. After assessing the situation from every angle, Zarya determined that the camera was too bulky for the secret drawer. Mrs. Irving had had no choice but to leave it in an unlocked drawer.

Zarya slipped the camera into her jacket pocket. Before fleeing the scene, she checked the other drawers, as well, but there was nothing of interest. She found only a bottle of antiquated port, some matches to light kindling in the fireplace, and bookkeeping papers for the hotel. Zarya bit her lip, unable to contain her curiosity about what lay in Mrs. Irving's clandestine file. Family secrets, no doubt. Things that she would not want to become public knowledge.

Zarya turned off the lamp and prepared to exit the room. Then, with no warning, the door connecting the cigar room to the lobby started to jangle. She heard the metallic sound of keys on the other side, followed by a key jamming into the lock.

There was not enough time to get to the other door, the one that connected to the corridor. Unable to think, Zarya dove behind the velvet loveseat. Its back was to the window, so she had to crouch down in the narrow space just as the doorknob turned and Mrs. Irving came through the door.

Peering underneath the loveseat, Zarya saw the woman's narrow ankles make their way across the room. Mrs. Irving sank into the cushioned chair behind her desk. She gave an affirmative sound as if talking on the phone, and Zarya became aware that someone was speaking to her on the other line.

Zarya ordered her hands to stop trembling. She listened as the hotel heiress finally responded to the person on the phone.

"She vows she won't come to the meetings anymore," said the old woman, her voice throaty with contempt.

It took Zarya a few moments to realize that she was the "she" in question.

Mrs. Irving went on, "We'll have to find another way to do it." There was a pause while she listened on the phone. Then, she asked, "Are you still tracking her phone's location?"

Anger flowed over Zarya in waves. She was awash with it. She started to hear her own blood in her ears.

"Good," Mrs. Irving continued. "Then we'll just follow her anytime she shows up near the water, and we'll do it that way."

Mrs. Irving was using the tone of finality she reserved for wrapping up conversations. When she finally bid the person on the other line goodbye, she rose from her chair and lingered a moment. Zarya held her breath, hoping the old woman could not see her crouched behind the loveseat. But in a moment, the lobby bell rang, and Mrs. Irving left through the same door.

As soon as those frail ankles were out of sight, Zarya bolted through the other door. She lunged up the stairs to the attic, where she tossed the cell phone onto her bed. Even if the phone was off, she needed a guarantee that no one could trace her next step.

Her next stop was to the public library. Zarya hastened out of the hotel, bumping past patrons in the corridor but too preoccupied to apologize for once. She kept going until she reached the library.

It was an unassuming, one-story brick structure from the outside, and not much more impressive on the inside. Zarya sifted through the rows of children's books and fiction to the technology section at the back of the room. There, she ejected the camera's SD card and stuck it into the chubby computer. The camera's contents popped up in a brand-new folder on the desktop. Zarya peered over her shoulder to make sure no one could see.

In a different window, she opened her email. Under her breath, she inaudibly hoped that her email was not being monitored, too. She attached the file from the SD card to the body of the email, then pulled out the business card Sean had given her.

West Coast Media.
Intern line: (818)852-8000
Intern email: interns@westcoastmedia.com

She hoped—desperately—that it would be Sean who found her email and not another intern. If this file got into the wrong hands, her lifeline could turn into a disaster.

Zarya typed on the keyboard for five minutes straight, the keys loud, then took a look at the end result.

Subject line: *Follow-up for Sean*

Hi Sean,

You may remember me from your visit to Washington a couple of weeks ago. I have a big story for you on the topic we were discussing. I have attached a file but cannot say more over email or telephone. I need your help. Please let me know if you want to break this story.

Sincerely,
Zarya Petrov

Zarya highlighted the sentence that said *I need your help.* She pressed the delete key. She had never been one to ask for help from anyone, even in the direst of times.

She held her breath as she clicked the send button. With a loud whoosh, it was gone, and Zarya deleted the email from her sent folder, then her recently deleted folder. She changed the password on her email for good measure. Once she was done, Zarya logged out of the computer and headed back out.

She eyed the other library guests carefully, hoping to catch any lingering gazes, but they all looked engrossed in their books and laptops. Zarya let out a tremulous sigh.

The sky was still robin's egg blue despite the afternoon turning into evening. Zarya wished the sun would not set at all tonight, for with the sunset came the horrors that flashed through her eyes and the melody that enticed her out to the water.

That afternoon, she locked herself in the attic of the Irving Hotel, which had gotten stuffy as the May days deepened. Beads of sweat grew sticky against Zarya's skin, and she had no choice but to prop open the window. As she did, outside chatter floated through, as did the ever-heavenly song from the ocean.

Zarya kept the SD card from the camera in her wallet, on her person, and placed the camera itself in the safe. She knew very well that Mrs. Irving could open the safe if she so desired, but Zarya would be damned if she let the woman find the SD card.

Hours drawled on before the light leached from the sky, leaving behind puffs of pink clouds like cotton candy. Zarya watched a small bat careen above the canopy, heard tourists growing louder under the influence of liquor. She fell asleep once a cool nighttime draught blew in through the window, caressing her bare arms like a wraith's kiss.

Josephine, 1851

Chapter 19

It seemed like the winter would not end. Aside from the evergreens that barricaded the lighthouse, the other tree branches swayed bare across the sky. Thomas had not left the lighthouse in a while—likely because Hurley had not given him express instructions to do so—and Josephine yearned for a dip in the ocean, to see her friend from the water or just feel the cold slow down her heart.

If she could not go for a swim, then she would find solace some other way. Josephine layered multiple petticoats underneath a skirt with tiered flounces. Over her bodice, she drew an imitation cashmere shawl. She parted her hair down the middle into an updo and wrapped a Fanchon bonnet over her head. As she peered in the looking glass, Josephine was surprised by her prettiness. She had not put much effort into her appearance of late.

"Where are you headed?" asked Thomas, who was refilling his mug of coffee to take up the tower. He had asked it not with curiosity, nor even jealousy. He had asked it with the tone of a person inquiring about the whereabouts of a tool they had lent someone.

"Just following the doctor's orders." It was becoming Josephine's favorite expression, her favorite excuse to get outside. "I'm going for a walk."

"Unattended?" Thomas' forehead creased.

"There are no brigands in the woods, dear," Josephine assured him. And if there were, perhaps they could put her out of her misery.

Thomas cleared his throat. "Very well, then. Don't venture too far out."

She meandered down the trailway of the forest, searching for any semblance of life. Spider silk stretched between the fingers of an evergreen bough, but she could find no spider. There were opalescent pearls of dew on the brushes. Moss dangled from speckled tree trunks like algae. But there was no one with whom the share the beauty.

Besides the occasional squirrel that shot past the path and the corvids that watched her with coal-black eyes, Josephine was utterly alone. She took big gulps of air on the incline, feeling the crisp oxygen sting her throat. A thick fog obscured the trees, painting the forest white. Soon, she could see only a few footsteps ahead. The nothingness pressed up against her, making itself at home in her soul.

After a while, a brook made itself known, cymbal-like. Josephine followed its music until she found it. There, surrounded by ancient ferns, freshwater passed over the pebbles at the base of the brook, quickly and smoothly. She inhaled its cool scent.

She carried on through the forest for longer than she had anticipated, only realizing this fact when she was at the edge of the forest near the road into town. It was silly to stop here, she thought. Since she was so prettily dressed and already out of the house, why not see what was in town? It had been months since her last teatime visit.

A horse-drawn Brougham rolled past her, its wheels crunching against the cobblestone. Josephine waved hello at the coachman, who tipped his hat cordially but looked off put by the sight of a lady walking lonesome on the side of the road. Josephine wondered who he carried inside the carriage. No doubt, someone with more important matters to tend to than her.

It was a ten-minute walk into town. Turreted houses and brick buildings came into view—the local apothecary with its vials of herbal tinctures, the alehouse where men wearing English-style hats laughed raucously, and the train station that Hurley Irving himself had constructed to make a fortune. A vendor bustled past Josephine carrying a basket full of bread. An Indian woman loitered in the town square, beside a rack of bearskin rugs. She had a wide, soft jawline and eyes the color of deerskin. Josephine willed herself to smile at the woman despite the emptiness she felt inside. The woman smiled back.

All the men on the street wore shades of gray or black, and even the women's capes were dark over their skirts. Josephine was starved to find a single pop of color amidst the sights. It seemed like all the color had drained from the world. She gathered herself under an Italianate-style streetlamp. Despite the early hour, it would be dark soon, and the kerosene had already started burning.

It had been a mistake to come out here. This was where people came who had things to accomplish—friends to see, items to purchase, business to conduct. Josephine had none of these things. She had thought that being among the bustle of people would raise her spirits, but instead, it merely dawned on her how alone she was. She prepared to turn home.

"Josephine?" a woman's voice called from behind.

Josephine turned around. When she saw Amelia Irving beaming at her, her spirits dropped even lower.

Amelia was radiant, her cheeks plumper than usual, eyes twinkling with warmth as always. Beside her was another woman wearing a ruffled skirt. She did not look quite as jovial, instead eyeing Josephine up and down.

For a moment, Josephine fantasized about how lovely it would be to tell Amelia about her torrid love affair with Hurley. That should wipe the smile right off her face.

But it was a foolish idea. Although confessing the affair would hurt Amelia, it would hurt Josephine even more. It would surely end things with Hurley. The mistress may have seemed from the outside to have the advantage—after all, she was the one deceiving the wife—but in truth, it was the wife who had it better. The wife had at least earned the respect of her husband, the right to publicly be claimed by him. When affairs lost their steam, the wife remained. Neither woman could win in the situation, but the mistress always lost more.

Josephine managed a convivial greeting. "Amelia! How are you?"

"Oh, I've been quite well. And what about yourself? We've missed you at teatime."

"Yes, my apologies for missing teatime. I've grown a bit ill since our last encounter, unfortunately."

Amelia's face contorted with pity. "Oh, dear. I hope nothing too serious?"

"No, just a regular bout of melancholia." As soon as she said it, Josephine wished she had not. Amelia still held the traces of empathy, but her companion's face had flushed uncomfortably. Perhaps Josephine was not supposed to speak about her illness out loud to people. There seemed to be something shameful in the matter. Melancholia was not like illnesses of the body, which the sufferer was understood to have no blame for causing. For some reason, diseases of the mind were a reflection of the sufferer's character. And yet, Josephine wondered, was the mind not a part of the body too?

"Dear, if you need to see Dr. Ainsworth, you're happy to do so at our house. After all, he visits our house often these days." At this, Amelia's hand reached down to her belly. Josephine followed the trace of Amelia's hand with her gaze, and when she did, she noticed for the first time a swollen shape beneath Amelia's cape.

Josephine was in a stupor.

How could she have missed it? Amelia was with child—and just a few months away from giving birth, by the looks of it. Hurley's visits had diminished not only due to Josephine's profession of love but also to his oncoming child. He did not need a plaything anymore now that there was someone new coming into his life.

"Congratulations," Josephine blurted out, but her world was going white. She leaned against the streetlamp for support.

"Goodness, are you alright?" Amelia asked.

"Yes, yes," Josephine assured her, blinking fast to bring her vision back. "I should be getting back, though. Where are you headed now?"

Amelia's brows remained furrowed, but she was not one to rudely ignore a question. "Visiting my sister-in-law—"

So, she would be away from the Irving estate for a while, then. That was all Josephine needed to know.

"Marvelous, I hope you have a marvelous time." Josephine started in the opposite direction of the lighthouse, hoping Amelia would not notice. "Good day!"

She charged towards the Irving mansion, not looking behind to see if Amelia was watching. When the estate appeared before her, she squinted her eyes at the mullioned windows. Through the glass, she saw Hurley smoking a cigar at his desk, plumes of smoke curling around him.

Josephine clouted at the knocker, and shortly thereafter the door opened to reveal one of the servants. It was an older, female servant who answered, her lips drawn in a skeptical frown. The Irvings must have sent away the butler.

"May I help you?"

"Hello. I'm Josephine Byrne." Josephine caught her breath, which was still fractured after the fast walk through town. She wished she could loosen her bodice for more air. "My husband is the lighthouse keeper, and I have some—I would like to speak with Mr. Irving about business matters."

The servant stared blankly, unimpressed. "Mr. Irving is quite busy at the moment."

"I understand that. My apologies, it really is an urgent matter."

The woman threw a look behind her, then sighed. "Very well. Come on in."

Josephine stepped into the dimly lit mansion. She followed the servant down the hall and into the cigar room where she had seen Hurley sitting.

He was seated in a wide armchair, clutching a glass of wine with one hand and a cigar with the other. A fire churned in the fireplace, casting shafts of warm light across the chestnut-colored tiles of the surround.

"Mrs. Byrne, what a surprise!" Hurley jumped from his seat, a flash of panic darting through his eyes. He headed to the door where the servant lingered, thanking her profusely before shutting the door on her.

The servant's shadow was still visible in the crack underneath the door, but Josephine could not wait another moment. "Your wife is pregnant." She could not bring herself to say Amelia's name. To do so would make it all real. This way, Amelia was but a ghost, not even important enough to be mentioned by name.

Hurley placed a hand over her mouth, hushing her. "Settle down. Someone could be listening."

Josephine tore his hand away from her face. "I don't care." She felt like a serpent, extracting all the venom she could muster before sputtering it out at him. "Why didn't you tell me?"

"Tell you what? That my wife is bearing my child? Surely, this shouldn't come as a surprise. It's what husbands and wives do."

Josephine had spent many long, lonesome nights trying to convince herself that Hurley no longer visited Amelia's bed, but she had always known it was an unlikely scenario. Still, she had been so sure of Amelia's barrenness, her only comfort in the ordeal.

How ironic that Josephine herself could not create a child. It made perfect sense; she could see no reason why any living creature, including a baby, would ever want to live inside the empty walls of her body.

"Have you forsaken me, then?" she asked, the pressure starting to build in her eyes. "You'll go ahead and discard me like you must do with all your whores?"

He let out an amused laugh. "What whores? Josephine, you're dwelling on this too much." Hurley approached her now, the firelight dancing upon his face. He held her with both arms and peered into her face with instantly manufactured wonder.

Good God, he's talented at this, thought Josephine.

He went on, "We have a good thing. An escape from the shackles of life. It can be nothing more, but isn't it wonderful as it is?"

Josephine glowered at him. "No. You have used my body and discarded me as if I don't matter. I never want to see you again."

It was a lie, and it pained her to say it, but she had no choice in the matter. After her outburst today, she'd be lucky if Hurley came by the lighthouse even to talk business with Thomas. This way, at least Hurley would think it was her choice to never see him again. He would desire her more knowing that he couldn't have her, and this would bring him back to her doorstep eventually.

But he merely stared at her, with thinly veiled mirth. "As you wish, Mrs. Byrne."

She winced at his formality. After all the moments of passion they had shared, all the kisses he had spread across her body and the frissons she had given him, how could he relegate her to a mere acquaintance? Was she so insignificant to him that it had all meant nothing?

She was crying now, and she hated how weak she must have seemed. Lately, she cried every time they were together. No wonder he wanted nothing to do with her—she was not a good time anymore.

Josephine hastened out of the room. She saw the servant at the end of the corridor but did not wait to be escorted out. The front door slammed behind her, and she knew it would attract attention, but she did not care. Tears were still streaming down her face. She must have been a hysterical sight to behold, rushing through town without an escort. She cried as she hurried down the road, then cried as she hurried through the forest, and finally, she cried as she reached the miserable sight of the lighthouse.

He would be back soon to reconcile, she had told herself. Any moment now, he would emerge from the forest, take off his hat, and apologize for their quarrel.

But as the days leafed by like the pages of a book, it became increasingly apparent that her hope was a mere illusion. He did not care. It did not bother him that the affair was over. He did not love her and never would.

She spent her days pacing in the kitchen until the walls felt foreign to her, like how words sometimes looked after staring at the letters for too long. She had no appetite, for food tasted like nothing to her. She spun around the contents of her plate with her fork until she gave up eating altogether. She gazed in the looking glass and imagined a pair of hands wrapping around her throat, like Hurley had sometimes done during their moments of passion. She had enjoyed it when he'd done it, because it had confirmed what she already suspected. That he was a bad man. That she was a bad woman. That he saw her for what she was. That he was punishing her for it.

But those hands around her neck were also proof that he felt passion. That he felt so strongly about her, he could not contain himself. That he wanted to possess her entirely. Even if it meant killing her.

For a moment, Josephine wondered if he might want her dead. If he did, it could certainly be arranged. At least if he hated her, it meant he felt *something* for her. Instead of the indifference he had shown on their last encounter.

When it became clear that no one was coming for her, Josephine searched for something to alleviate her excruciating anguish. There was only one option left, one last person's emotions to rouse.

Thomas. She had betrayed him. Perhaps he was not such an abhorrent man, after all. Perhaps it had been Hurley she should have hated.

Yes, she liked this novel idea. Hurley was the bad man, and Thomas was the good man. She would rectify things with Thomas. She would find a way to repair their marriage, and that would show Hurley. She did not think long about the matter before deciding it was the right approach.

So, she picked up her skirts and started up the stairs of the tower, each step bringing her one step closer to calamity. When she reached the top of the lighthouse, she found her husband poring over the ocean.

"I need to speak with you," she said, heart practically bouncing in her chest.

"Not now."

"Please." Her torment was apparent.

Thomas turned to face her. "Very well. I am listening."

Now that she had his attention, she was not sure what to do with it. She was starting to forget why she had decided to do this. To give him an opportunity to prove that he cared, perhaps? Regardless, it was too late to turn back now.

"I've been having an affair with Hurley."

Silence spanned the space between them. Thomas stood there before the backdrop of ocean and fog, fingering the buttons on his waistcoat. His lips pressed together, but he said nothing. Josephine tried to read his face for a semblance of emotion—anger, grief, jealousy, anything—but there was nothing behind those eyes. She had seen him show more emotion while dragging firewood inside the house.

She severed the silence. "I'm sorry." Maybe this would pull a reaction out of him.

But still, Thomas said nothing. He stared at her resolutely, or rather stared *through* her. Josephine started to feel like an invisible specter. The longer the silence extended, the more she felt herself disappearing. She had pulled the most theatrical of her gestures out of her repertoire, but it seemed even those would not be enough.

"Please, say something."

Thomas broke his stare only to gaze out the window at the Pacific. A schooner rode the swell in the distance, its silhouette gauzy through the fog. Thomas watched it ride into the horizon before returning his attention to Josephine.

At long last, he said, "I did not want this marriage any more than you did."

He might as well have slapped her. At least then, he would have shown that he cared. Instead, Josephine was left with that gaping wound in her core that emptied her out no matter how much she tried to pour into it. No one could see her bleeding from the inside, but she longed for the wound to manifest externally. For all of them to see how much it hurt.

For a moment, she thought about going to the kitchen and dragging the blade of a knife across her forearms. But the only thing sillier than hurting herself was the possibility that no one would mind if she did.

"Then why did you marry me?" she asked.

Thomas shrugged, his shoulder pads falling limply back to their place. "It is easier for a lighthouse keeper to have a wife. Someone to cook and clean the house while I tend to the tower. You needed a husband, and I needed a wife."

So that was what she had been, then—a means to an end. A cook and a maid, but nothing more. He had never chosen her to be his wife because of who she was, but only because she was a woman. The same way that Hurley had never chosen her to be his mistress because of who she was, but only because she was a woman. Had it not been her, it would have been someone else.

"What will happen now?" she asked, her voice gravelly with shame.

"The same as before. We will go about our lives separately. Except this time, you will know your place. You will not bring any more disrespect to my name. You will stay out of my way. And that is the way your life will proceed."

It might as well have been a death sentence.

Zarya, 2023

Chapter 20

Zarya was facing away from the concierge desk, wiping the dust off the gilt frames of nautical paintings bolted into the wall. Her eyes lingered on the dark strokes of the shipwreck depicted, the paint dashed on as if in a fury. She was pulled away from the oil canvas by the sound of the concierge bell just behind her. Why would someone ring the bell when they could simply bid her good afternoon? She prepared to plaster a false smile on her lips, but when she turned around, relief poured into her.

"Sean."

"I got your email," he said. His voice was more honeyed than she remembered it, his frame taller.

Zarya looked around warily. "Not now," she whispered. Then, in regular volume: "Can I help you check in?"

He played along, "I don't have a reservation. I was hoping to book one today." Sean threw her a wink. "Last minute trip, you see."

"Sure, sure." Zarya clicked through the computer screen, growing more anxious with each click. No, this could not be. "I—unfortunately, it looks like we're out of rooms."

Sean responded with a placid smile. "I'm sorry, I'm not sure where to stay, then."

Zarya again peered over her shoulder to make sure Mrs. Irving was not haunting the corridors. When she saw no one there, she pulled out her leather keychain and handed Sean one of the silver keys. In a whisper again, she said, "Go up to the attic. Room 323. I'll meet you there as soon as my shift ends."

Sean peered down at his wrist, which donned a worn, leather watch. "Alright. What time is that?"

"Five o'clock."

He gave her a nod and headed down the hallway. Zarya watched him for as long as she could, taking in his cologne and well-fitted jeans. When he was gone, she planted her face into her palms. Was she making a mistake? Was it right to trust this near stranger?

She vacillated between yes and no before settling on yes, she needed to trust him. Despite barely knowing him, he was her only hope out of this. Nowhere in this town was safe from prying ears—the hotel, the bar and grill, her parents' home, and even the police station. Her best shot was an outsider.

As soon as her shift ended, she headed upstairs. She found Sean sitting in a chair beside her window, overlooking the trees and the main street. He had a pensive look about him.

Sean had gingerly transplanted her pile of clothes from the chair to the bed. Zarya blushed at the realization that he must have found her room in disrepair upon entering—again.

"Thank you for coming here," she blurted. "I didn't know what else to do or where to turn."

Sean rose from the chair to greet her. She was again distracted by the smell of his cologne.

"It's alright," he said. "You sent me a pretty concerning video, though. I'd like to know what's going on."

"Of course." Zarya pulled a sweater out of the pile on the bed and threw it over her head. "Let's go somewhere private and talk."

Sean's eyes wandered over the wallpaper with its fleurs-de-lis pattern. "Is this not private?"

Zarya shook her head. "Definitely not."

She led the way out of the Irving Hotel, past the resplendent Victorian cornices out front and the budding roses in the garden.

They kept going until the end of the street, where a Chinese restaurant shone an *OPEN* sign in the window. This would do. Zarya knew the owner, an old man who brought candy and coloring pencils to patrons with children. He spoke broken English but always wore a sweet smile.

"In here," she said, taking a seat by the window booth so that she could see if they were being followed. She must have seemed paranoid as her eyes probed the street.

The old man came over, handing them two laminated menus and a carafe of water.

"Thank you," Zarya said with a smile.

When the man had disappeared into the kitchen, she turned to Sean and told him everything. About the siren song that had started the night of their last encounter, about getting roped into the Defenders, about the tragic boat ride, and about her phone being bugged, possibly by a cop. Sean watched her intently. She hoped he had not written her off as crazy just yet.

As she stopped to catch her breath and take a gulp of water, Sean said, "And here I was, thinking you just missed me." A cheeky smile spread across his face.

Zarya wasn't sure what it meant to miss someone. She had enjoyed their one night of conversation, sure, and she relished the opportunity to see him again, but she could live just fine without him, thank you very much.

"I'm serious," she told him, gravely.

Before she had a chance to go on, a waiter came over to take their order. She ordered garlic noodles and zoned out while Sean inquired about the menu, her eyes fixed on a man waiting at the bus stop outside, trying to ascertain if he was following her.

Sean's voice snapped her back into the present moment. "You were saying?"

The waiter had long left.

"Right. I was saying that I recognized the thing from the water in a photograph at the Irving Hotel."

Sean seemed perplexed. "What do you mean?"

"There was a photo in the library, of a woman named Josephine Byrne. She was the lighthouse keeper's wife in 1850. And that was the woman I saw in the ocean."

"Are you sure?"

"Positive."

"But it was dark, and you were drinking that night—"

"Sean." Zarya leaned in and locked eyes with him. "Please believe me. I know what I saw."

It was all he needed to hear. "Okay." He tapped his fingernails across the paper tablecloth. "So, this woman who lived in the lighthouse in 1850 is now some sort of water-creature. Maybe we should go to the lighthouse, then—scope it out."

"It's been defuncted for decades."

"Okay. So, we break in, then." Sean smiled as if he had just suggested getting ice cream cones together.

Zarya let out a little laugh, caught off-guard by the coquettish timbre it produced. She was relieved when the waiter brought out two giant plates of steaming food.

For a while, they just ate. But when the movements of their chopsticks grew slower and Zarya found herself leaning back in the booth, she started back up.

"How do we break in?"

"Easy. Do you have a hairpin?"

She shook her head, suddenly self-conscious of her mussed hair. Sean must have been used to a more refined type of woman in LA.

"A paper clip, then?" he asked.

"Not on me. There might be one somewhere at the hotel…"

"No worries." Sean waved his hand in front of his face. "I saw an arts and crafts store across the street. We'll go there."

They toyed with the rest of their food as they waited for the check. Zarya had said everything she wanted to say for now, but the words played on repeat in her head. She wondered if there was something else she had missed.

After a while, Sean lowered his voice. "What did you do with the video recording?"

"I keep it on me at all times." Zarya motioned to the pocket of her pants. "The camera itself is in my room, in the safe."

"Normally, that would be good," Sean explained, "But it's not secure to keep it there if Mrs. Irving has access to all the rooms."

"I know. I thought about that, too."

"You should put it back where you found it."

Zarya's eyes widened. "Back in the cigar room?"

"Without the SD card," Sean finished.

She considered the suggestion. Then, she said, "You're right. It'll be less likely to raise alarms if she sees it where she left it."

"Let's put it back as soon as possible."

"When I get back in there, I want to open that secret drawer," said Zarya. "Can we pick that lock, too?"

Sean tilted his head from left to right as if unsure whether to nod or shake his head. "It'd be harder," he said. "At the lighthouse, there's less pressure. But in a room where someone could walk in at any given moment, I'm not sure."

Zarya constructed a mental map of Mrs. Irving's schedule, considering when the woman's next shift would be. "What about this?" She planted a palm against the table. "On my next shift with her, I'll come up with some reason to use her keychain. And right as I do that, you come to the concierge desk and keep her busy. I'll go into the cigar room, unlock the drawer, take photos of whatever's in there, and come right back."

Sean's luminous eyes glinted. "I like that. You should have been a journalist, too, you know."

With a shrug, she replied, "Maybe one day, I'll do something with my life."

She had expected him to chuckle, but Sean only frowned. "You shouldn't talk about yourself that way."

Zarya averted her gaze.

After they had dined and paid the bill, Sean pointed Zarya in the direction of the arts and crafts store. She must have passed by the place hundreds of times by now, but she had stopped noticing the little details. What was the joy of an idyllic nautical town without someone with whom to share it? There were only so many times she could walk down the main street, only so many places to eat, and only so many walks through the forest. At some point, the beauty of it all faded.

Inside, they bought a box of paper clips, then started towards the Rock. Sean ducked beneath a pink-and-blue awning on their way out.

Before long, the glittering ocean came into view through the canopy's fissures.

Here, in the forest, the energy shifted. There were no witnesses but for the giant trees on all sides, their trunks centuries-thick. Finally, the striped tower of the lighthouse emerged on the headland.

Perhaps it was silly to fear something like this. It was just an old building.

Sean's head swiveled from left to right. After he had ascertained that there was no one around, he snapped open the box of paper clips and unwound one of them, jamming one of its ends into the lock of the door. Zarya kept watch over the forest from where they had come. Her back was turned to the ocean, which she had vowed to never do, but desperate times called for desperate measures.

Sean grunted as the paper clip ricocheted into his finger, but it did not deter him. He kept twisting the wire inside the lock until finally, there was a clack, and the doorknob loosened in his grip.

As the lighthouse door cracked open an inch, Zarya swore she felt a shiver coiling its way across her spine. Decades of closed air must have poured out of that door. She exchanged a tense look with Sean, who kicked the door open a little further.

They stepped inside.

Inside was a kitchen and dining area, visibly old-fashioned from the make of the wood-burning stove and the décor. A cistern for collecting rainwater sat beneath the pantry. Zarya opened the cabinets to find a few items of heavy cast-iron cookware, as well as some wooden spoons and labels. A threadbare doily ornamented the dining table. One of its edges was folded onto itself as if someone had left the table in a rush.

"It looks like this place hasn't been used in a long time," Sean remarked. "Maybe not since the Victorian era."

"Yeah, it was a short-lived lighthouse." Zarya's eyes inspected the oil lamps affixed to the walls, their edges gathering dust.

"The town didn't at least turn it into a museum?"

Zarya shook her head. She ran her fingers across an ancient tea kettle. A layer of patina had taken over the old copper.

"Doesn't look like much in here," said Sean. "Just an old, creepy kitchen, as far as I can tell."

He started towards a connecting door. It creaked open, and Zarya followed Sean inside.

There, a wooden bedframe took up half of the wall. The bed was bare but for a dilapidated mattress. Bedsheets were folded and stacked on top of the mattress, cream-colored with some sort of faded pattern. Along the edge of the wall, Zarya noticed a wooden dresser, paint peeling off in wavy clumps. She opened the top drawer, but there was nothing inside it—nothing but a musty smell and a moth. Zarya patted the sides of the drawer for good measure. As she did, a dark piece of hair tickled the back of her hand. Zarya pulled it out of the drawer, but the piece kept going for longer and longer. By the time she pulled it out all the way, Zarya held between her fingers a piece of hip-length hair. Its wavy texture was rough to the touch.

"Sean." Zarya held the hair up to the light shafting through the window.

He looked at what was in her hand with disgust. "Oh, god. Whose is that?"

"I think it's hers." Zarya recalled those piercing, gray eyes from the picture. Her ears loudly pumped blood, as if the water inside her bloodstream was responding to something in the environment. She heard the whooshing of waves not far outside the window and felt the sudden prick of fear.

There was nothing else in the room, not even a hearth to keep its inhabitants warm during the harsh winters, so Zarya returned to the meager kitchen and tried the other connecting door. This time, there was no window light to illuminate the room, no furniture to gaze upon. There was only a narrow, spiraling staircase made of masonry. Trapped air hit Zarya's skin.

"This must be the tower," said Sean. Zarya struggled to make out his silhouette in the dark. "Shall we?"

"Yeah." She followed in his footsteps, slowly in case one of the steps collapsed, holding on to the walls on both sides.

Their footsteps echoed through the tower, each one adding to the previous echoes until together they made an eerie disharmony. And there was something else echoing through the walls—faintly, so very faintly—but Zarya could not be sure if it was the ghost of a scream or something in her head.

She knew they were near the top when light started to pour onto the steps. By the time they reached the lantern room, the brightness was blinding. The room was enclosed by glass panels. Zarya squinted her eyes, trying to make out the antique equipment. She could make out a giant, revolving lens connected to a clockwork system, but none of it made any sense. She stepped out onto the gallery, where gusts of air tossed her hair in all directions.

Zarya eyed the Pacific for signs of a creature coming up for air, but she saw nothing out of place. She gazed back at the roof of the tower behind her, a small cupola, before returning inside the lantern room.

"See anything interesting?" Sean was tilted over a desk-like structure by the window. He had found what looked like a hand-drawn manual, complete with diagrams and elegant cursive.

"Not really," Zarya responded. "You?"

Sean shook his head. "It looks like this place was scrubbed of most personal items whenever its last inhabitants left."

Zarya tried to hide her disappointment. "Okay, then. We should head out."

Back down the spiraling staircase they went, stopping only once they had reached the adjoining kitchen. Sean was halfway out the door, but something pulled Zarya back.

"Hold on a moment," she said.

She stood still, trying to make out the faint residues of a woman's voice. Sean did not make a peep, and the longer she held her breath, the clearer she could hear the words.

It was the siren song, a ghost of the past calling to her, singing its plaintive notes.

The noise was coming from the bedroom. Zarya walked into the bedchamber, the voice growing louder as she did. It drew her towards the mattress—no, underneath it.

Zarya upturned the mattress. There was nothing hidden inside the springs, but a cloud of dust expelled from the old thing. A reflexive cough pushed the dust out of her windpipe.

The notes continued to spiral melodically.

Zarya was close to giving up when she spotted a loose tile on the floor beneath the bed. She stepped on one of its corners with her boot, and in doing so, the other end popped open. Zarya kneeled beside the tile and pulled it off the ground with one hand.

"A trapdoor," she whispered, peering inside the dark crevice.

There was something there, a pale object among the darkness. She reached to grab it and felt the texture of crumpled paper at her fingertips.

The writing was cursive. The date was February 2, 1851.

Dear Thomas,

I have just received a letter from a Dr. John Ainsworth, expressing concern as to my sister's state of mind. He states that she is thin as a knife and alternates between periods of extreme lethargy and being on the go… That she swims indecently in the ocean and runs through town as if mad. Her appearance is quite sad, he says, and he is worried about her.

I do not presume to understand the inner workings of your marriage, but surely you must understand my concern at having received this news. You are well aware of my sister's history, and I should hate for history to repeat itself.

I beg of you to please look after her more carefully, to keep her occupied and well-tended. Dr. Ainsworth says he has prescribed pregnancy as the best course of action. I believe he is right that this would solve many of Josephine's ailments.

Sincerely,
Charlotte Williams

Zarya's fingers trembled as she scanned the last of the letter. She looked up at Sean, who had just walked through the doorway.

"What is it?" he asked.

"It looks like a letter from Josephine's sister to Thomas Byrne."

His eyes peered down. "What does it say?"

Zarya swallowed. "Josephine's doctor had written to her sister to say that Josephine was not well. It seems like there might have been some kind of mental illness involved."

Sean took the flimsy paper from her hands and read over it silently. His eyes raced across the page. When they had reached the bottom, he cast a jumpy look at Zarya. "February 2nd, 1851. When did you say Josephine died?"

Zarya looked at him darkly. "February 21st, 1851."

Josephine, 1851

Chapter 21

Josephine dragged the steel nib across the sheet of manila as she signed her name. The letter was complete now, stenciled with dark cursive. On some parts of the page, the ink still gleamed and pooled in clumps. Once it had mattified, she folded the sheet onto itself and tucked it inside an envelope.

Wax dripped down a beeswax candle, hot at first then hard by the time it reached the brass candlestick. Josephine dropped a chunk of wax into the spoon and held it over the candle flame. When the wax had liquefied, she drizzled it onto the edge of the envelope, then stamped a seal onto it. Wax spilled all around the seal. Josephine waited for it to harden before lifting the seal to reveal an adorned *B* shape. She wished it would say *J* for Josephine instead of *B* for Byrne. But it was no matter now.

Josephine prepared to head out. She wore her best attire today, better fit for a ball than a day out on the town. It was a gown made of blue taffeta, embroidered with dark beads, the bodice enclosed in the back with adjustable lace. The puff sleeves and the decolletage were rimmed with black lace, but they hardly kept her warm, so she threw a woolen cape over her shoulders.

She began her walk into town through the woods. The ground was sooty from rainfall throughout the night, but she did not lift her skirts. Soon, it would not matter anymore if her most precious dress were sullied.

The dress had been passed down to her from her mother. In fact, it was the only relic Josephine had of her parents. Years ago, her parents' clothes had burned in the housefire. So had Josephine's parents, for that matter.

But not this gown—no, this gown had been left outside to dry on the clothesline. Josephine wished her mother's lavender perfume still lingered on the fabric, but sadly, there were no traces of the scent. There had been at first, but this was the way of memories—the more she took them out of their drawers to behold, the more they wore away.

Charlotte, Josephine's elder sister, had tried her best. But without their parents' home and belongings, their inheritance had been worth very little, their previous life of glamour wiped clean. Charlotte, an unwed woman of eighteen, could hardly provide for a seven-year-old girl.

Josephine had searched for something to replace her parents' lost love ever since the day of the fire. She had searched for it in all the wrong places—men who looked at her like she was meat, men with wives back home, men who were thrown out of saloons for fighting… She had thought that, if she could find just one man to love her, it would make her whole again. That it would fill the gaping hole that her parents' abandonment had left.

But, in the end, all paths had led her back to the same place. As she trudged through the muddy forest, Josephine contemplated the fact that she was right back where she had started. With each man who made her feel like she was nothing, the belief sank deeper into her. None of the heartbreaks had hurt quite as much as Hurley, though, because her sense of emptiness had only grown with each failed love affair. His reciprocation could have been the confirmation she needed that she mattered, but instead, it had merely reinforced that she did not. How many times could a person be told they were worthless before it killed them?

She was out of the woods now, stopped by the side of the

cobblestone road. Passersby started to stare at her soiled dress. If they thought her mad, it did not matter anymore.

As she headed through town towards the Irving Estate, an image formed in Josephine's mind of Hurley sitting at his desk, looking dapper in a tartan suit, hair combed neatly to the side. And then an awful scene played, of Amelia greeting him with a tiny baby wrapped in linens. Of Hurley approaching the infant with a look of adoration.

Josephine had seen the way men looked at their children—they loved their offspring because they were a piece of themselves. And they revered their wives for giving them this reflection of themselves, much like their ancestors had fallen at the feet of statues depicting fertility goddesses. Josephine could imagine him now, reaching over to kiss the still-soft flesh of Amelia's belly, running a finger across her flushed cheeks. She imagined how he would yearn for Amelia even more once she was the mother of his child.

The image made Josephine's vision go green with envy. She was finding it difficult to hold back tears, and now even more townspeople were staring.

What about me? she thought. *Am I so forgettable, even to my own husband?*

There was one last trick she could try to make people care. She had lost all else, but at least this one thing could make them miss her.

But first, she had a decision to make—would she wreak havoc on Amelia's life before vanishing from this earth? Would she ask that her letter be delivered to Amelia, the love affair revealed to her, or would she ask for it to be delivered straight to Hurley? Josephine vacillated between the two options. She determined that, like with most of her choices, she would decide in the heat of the moment itself.

As Josephine reached the front steps of the Irving mansion, she wiped the tears from her face and thumped on the knocker. The same servant from last time opened the door.

"Hello, Mrs. Byrne."

"Hello—" Josephine hesitated as she realized she had never bothered to ask the woman her name. She dismissed the realization and began to pull out the sealed envelope from her cape pocket.

At the far end of the house, through the glass window of the kitchen door at the end of the corridor, she spotted Amelia. Amelia's hand rested tenderly on her belly. Her lips were parted in a smile for one of the servants in the kitchen. She was always the most charming, always the most delightful.

Josephine could not decide if she hated Amelia. She recalled the warmth with which the woman had welcomed her into her home and fetched her a physician. Amelia had ignored the stolen looks between Hurley and Josephine, perhaps because she had assumed other people were as honorable as she was.

Maybe it was better for Amelia not to know. It could not be good for the baby to bring that kind of stress onto her. Josephine's lashes fluttered as she peered down at the envelope.

It had been a long pause. But finally, she had made her decision.

Josephine told the servant, "I have an important letter for Hurley. Is he here at the moment?"

"*Mr. Irving* is not." The servant's lip quirked to the side.

It was exactly as Josephine had planned. With Hurley gone on business, it would be too late by the time he found the note. She handed the servant the envelope.

"Please give this to him when he returns. It's very important, so please make sure it gets into the right hands." This would be her last act of kindness—that she would leave Amelia out of it.

The servant gave one nod. "Anything else, madam?"

"No, that's all." Josephine started to pull away.

The kaleidoscopic colors on the stained glass eddied as the door closed on Josephine's face. Josephine descended the front steps, casting one last look at the mansion. She watched until even its highest spire vanished from view.

She could not have known what was to happen. She could not

have known that, later that evening, the servant would make sure to misplace her letter for Hurley, handing it instead to the lady of the house.

The route back to the lighthouse always felt faster than the journey into town. Before long, Josephine was back on the Rock, but she did not venture inside the building. Instead, she walked to the furthest edge of the bluff, where the ocean wind lobbed her hair in all directions. She wondered if Thomas could see her now from the watch room. If he could, she must have looked a fright—dark strands of hair blowing around her like a halo, the deep sapphire of her dress contrasting with pale skin, her eyes the same shade of grey as the tidal swell below.

But, of course, she knew that he was not looking at her. He never was.

Josephine took her time. She wondered, for the thousandth time, why her husband felt nothing for her. Perhaps he had heard of her reputation in Maine, perhaps he was uninterested in women, or perhaps he simply had no love in his heart—no love for anything except that godforsaken lighthouse meant to guide sailors to safety. It exasperated her, the not knowing why. But, sometimes, people died before ever discovering the why of things.

Next, she thought of Hurley. The curvature of his back, the tannic taste of his tongue after a glass of wine. That hungry look in his eyes, and the blue of his irises, so devoid of any warmth.

Hurley thought that he could hurt people. And that the consequences would never find him. But, if Josephine had learned anything in her lifetime, it was that hurting people had a way of ricocheting back. And the more people he hurt, the more it would catch up to him one day.

If nothing else would make Hurley love her, then this last act would. Josephine fantasized about the guilt-torn expression that would take hold of his face upon hearing news of her death. He would know it was his actions that had caused her death, and that knowledge would haunt him his whole life. He would finally realize that he had loved her. In death, her image would take on an idealized memory. He would be ravished by flashbacks of their lovemaking. Anytime he looked at his newborn son, he would blame the boy for the loss of his one true love. Only a lifetime of sorrow could make up for the suffering Hurley had caused Josephine.

It occurred to Josephine now, in her last few moments alive, that you can kill a person with your hands or with a cruel word, but you can also kill a person with silence. Letting them sink into an abyss all by themselves, until the very act of being alone feels like a prison. In that desolate abyss where there exists no kind word exchanged, no expression of affection, not even acknowledgment—there, a person can truly lose themselves.

Thomas did not need to lift a finger to kill her. Treating her like she no longer existed eventually made it so.

She edged closer to the ledge. Below, the ocean frothed against uneven-toothed pieces of bedrock. Further out, sea stacks protruded from the water like swords. It was a long enough way down that the impact would surely kill her.

As she prepared to take wind, a realization struck Josephine that she would soon be reunited with her parents. She had all but forgotten the shapes of their faces by now.

In the aftermath of their deaths, the emptiness had been unbearable. As a child, she had listened during the witching hour for the echo of their voices but heard nothing. She had peeked into dim, narrow glens hoping to see them there. She had fallen asleep with a breeze raising the hairs on her arms and imagined that it was her parents cradling her goodnight.

But each time, there had been only emptiness. The space inside her had collapsed into itself, eating her alive. It was a space that could be filled for a time—with distractions and thrills and fleeting affection—but as soon as she was alone, the emptiness was crippling again. Josephine could not stand to be alone with herself. The reminders of her countless losses were too painful to bear.

Meanwhile, the ocean called to her, whispering promises of an end to her misery. A return to the oceanic womb from which she had come. A return to her own mother.

It was time.

Josephine threw one last look at the lighthouse, with its beams of light spinning around. Then she jumped forward into hollow air.

Her stomach lurched beneath the pull of gravity. Wind slapped her face and twirled her skirts. The world was blue and grey, until her body met the ocean and everything went dark. The water was hard as basalt, and so very cold.

In her last split seconds alive, Josephine realized that she did not want to die—not truly. She wanted an end to her suffering, and she wanted love, not death.

She could not have known what was about to happen. She could not have known that the ocean would break its promise to her.

Part III

Zarya, 2023

Chapter 22

After their trip to the lighthouse, Zarya and Sean snaked their way through the thicket, back toward the hotel. Darkness befell the attic, only an edge of light shafting from the moon's beams.

"I'll take the couch, if that's alright with you." Sean was puffing up one of the ancient pillows, assessing how to best curl up on a couch three-quarters his height.

Zarya wondered if she should offer that he sleep in bed with her. After all, the idea of his warm body beside her sent a tingle of delight through her… But no, it could not happen. She had brought him back to her room to bed him once before, and something had stopped her even then. It was something about the way he looked at her. There was not only desire in his eyes but something dangerously close to affection.

"Sure, I hope it's not too uncomfortable," she said, gathering beneath her bedsheets.

She listened to the sound of Sean's breathing, at first accelerated from the walk upstairs, then even and languid. There was some solace in knowing that he was here, and soon she was able to fall asleep as well.

But it was not long before she awoke agape, nightmares still hovering over her. In the nightmares, she was running—away from a bevy of people with gaff hooks, headed toward the ocean. As she approached the body of water, an even more frightening sight materialized. The ocean was rising, a wall of water hundreds of feet high, approaching land at an unthinkable speed. And then Zarya was running away from the ocean, unsure where else to run. Trapped between one evil and another.

Her breath was so fractured that it awoke Sean, who lifted himself upright on the couch. His sleep must have been delicate, too, as he crouched in a fetal position on a too-small divan. Zarya's sight adjusted to the nighttime, and she saw the whites of Sean's eyes observing her across the room.

"Are you okay?" he asked.

She took a deep inhale. "Yeah, it's just a nightmare."

Sean paused. Then, he probed, "Does that happen to you a lot?"

"Lately, yeah." Zarya felt a sudden gush of air from the open window, and she rose to close it. The current had left her cold. "Do you think you can come into bed with me?"

She silently berated herself for articulating those words. She had managed the nightmares on her own just fine before Sean came along, and she certainly didn't need him to survive. But in the back of her head, a voice bit back, *And how well is that going for you?*

Sean didn't need to be asked twice. He slid into bed and, as Zarya approached to do the same, he held open the duvet for her to get under. It was a small gesture, but a thoughtful one. Zarya made a note of it.

He kept a respectful distance on his half of the bed, but already the heat emanating from his body melted the gooseflesh from Zarya's arms. Then, without warning, Zarya heard herself ask him,

"Will you hold me?"

"Of course, if that's what you want."

She gave an affirmative nod, and he turned toward her in bed. His arms spooled around her seamlessly—a perfect fit. She allowed her breath to slow down, in unison with his. With his arms around her, surely the nightmares could not get to her. She was safe behind a fortress. The pressure helped distract her from the song that wouldn't stop playing in her head.

The sun awakened long before it should have. But now that it was up, it roused Zarya, too.

There was no point in lounging around before her shift with Mrs. Irving. Zarya slipped out from under Sean's arms, surprised that he had not rolled away from her at any point throughout the night.

In front of the mirror, she pinned her hair into a bun at the top of her head. Casting a sidelong look at Sean in the bed, Zarya decided a hint of makeup was in order, too. She popped a smidge of pearlescent eye shadow on the inner corners of her eyes, drew a fluffy brush of blush across the apples of her cheeks, and accentuated her lashes with some mascara.

She looked at herself in the tiny bathroom mirror. The pop of color suited her quite nicely.

Sean was up now. He let out a sleepy groan and stretched across the bedframes. "Morning," he said.

"Morning." Zarya tried not to think about his embrace the night before. "So, let's go over the plan one more time."

She sat on her laundry chair, hands clasped over her thighs.

"I'll come to the front desk during rush hour," Sean rehearsed.

Zarya nodded.

"When is that again, by the way?"

"Around four o'clock. Check-in starts at three, so four is when most people head over."

"Okay." He started over. "So, I come over around four o'clock, and that's when you ask Mrs. Irving for her keychain because the lobby bathroom is out of toilet paper. Right when you ask her that, I come up to the desk and ask to book an entire fleet of rooms next month. I get very specific about the types of rooms I want and go on a tangent about how my brother is getting married and his guests must have the absolute best." At this, Sean flashed a mischievous smile.

"Good. And keep improvising until I'm back."

Sean asked, "What happens if she doesn't want to give you the keys?"

"Why wouldn't she?"

"I don't know, maybe she tells you to wait until after the two of you are done helping me."

"You should start by asking about the hotel's history," said Zarya. "She'll want to tell you all about it herself, and she'll be too preoccupied to deny me the keys."

"Okay." Sean smiled again, this time with excitement. "Ready?"

"Ready." Zarya started for the door. "I'll see you later. If you get hungry, I might have some leftovers in the mini-fridge."

"Okay. Thanks, Zar."

She headed downstairs, blushing the whole way down.

A dull day of work awaited her. Mrs. Irving was in a foul mood today, ignoring Zarya as she clocked in, even cursing under her breath. Zarya palpated her satchel to make sure that the video camera was still in there before sliding the satchel into a corner where it was out of Mrs. Irving's sight.

The hustle and bustle of the day took off, and Zarya watched the hotel guests swivel before the hearth, mimosas in hand. Summer was getting too close to make a fire anymore, but somehow, the guests all still felt a primordial pull to the fireplace, as if something in their bones knew this had once been the centerpiece of their ancestor's lives. They chattered gleefully, leaning against the mantle, exchanging introductions.

"Busy day," Zarya noted.

Mrs. Irving let out a curt, "Hmph."

The morning pulled toward the afternoon. Zarya cast a look across the wall behind her, and the porthole-encased clock ticked away, its arms hovering over 3:58 PM. Out of the corner of her eye, she saw Sean come out of the hallway shadows.

But then, something unexpected occurred. The front door swung open with a fierceness Zarya would have recognized anywhere, and her mother sprang through the lobby.

The petite Russian woman wore a satin blouse tucked into wide-leg palazzo pants. The soles of her sandals clacked against the hardwood, each step a warning shot. Anger drew her brows into high arches and her lips into a downward curve.

Unnerved, Zarya threw Sean a warning look across the room. His eyes found hers, then settled on the woman storming into the building. Slowly, Sean started backing into the hallway.

"Where have you been?" Zarya's mother nearly screeched. She was up to the concierge desk now, and she planted her elbows across the surface.

Zarya's gaze shot at Mrs. Irving, who was vigilantly watching the scene unfold. Something in the woman's stiff demeanor seemed to warn Zarya—*don't make a scene*.

"Here, working," Zarya answered.

"You vanished from the house without a trace. We were going to go for a walk!"

"Yes, sorry about that. I had an emergency come up, and I didn't have time for an entire discussion about it."

"What kind of emergency?" Her mother's eyes looked about to pop. "And you can't answer the phone when I call you twenty times?"

Zarya could not help herself. Faintly, she said, "Well, maybe you shouldn't be calling me twenty times."

Her mother's anger transmuted into black rage now. "I can't believe—"

Mrs. Irving must have reached her limit, because she flinched. "I understand you have some family business to discuss," she said, her voice pulled taut. "Perhaps you can do so at a later time, when Zarya is not at work."

Zarya watched the two women make eye contact with each

other. Her mother's eyes were still seething, but Mrs. Irving did not avert her gaze, holding her ground. Eventually, Zarya's mother broke the staring spell and pulled her elbows off the desk.

"Fine." She turned to Zarya. "When can we discuss this?"

Zarya cast a look at the monthly calendar on her computer screen. Today was May 24th.

No, it couldn't be.

The following Sunday was the Pentecost, which meant tomorrow was the first Thursday before the Pentecost.

Tomorrow was the day Rusalka Week started.

Zarya's head was spinning as she tried to estimate when the rocky events of the next week might end. Finally, she said, "I'll stop by next Friday."

Her mother peered at her still through pupils like molten lava. "That's in over a week, Zarya. You can't pick up the phone for your own mother in over a week?"

Zarya sighed, a sigh so deep it emptied her out. "No, Mama. I'm sorry, but I can't."

Her mother started to back away from the concierge desk. "Fine. Be at home next Friday and prepare to give the visit your full attention."

She left without a goodbye, the doorbell jingling for her on the way out. Zarya let out a big exhale. Beside her, Mrs. Irving cleared her throat.

The old woman kept her gaze forward as she said, "You know, Zarya, I think I know what you're going through."

Zarya had not been expecting a word of consolation from Mrs. Irving of all people. "Oh?"

"My parents were very strict with me also. They insisted that I take over the hotel and never sell it, even after their deaths."

"Why is that?"

Mrs. Irving pondered the question. She tilted up her chin, musing over the high ceiling. "Well, this place holds a lot of history, and I think they understood that history has a way of repeating itself.

The key to present conflict can be found in relics of the past."

"Are you talking about the siren?" Zarya sent a searing look through Mrs. Irving, but still, the woman did not turn to her.

"Yes, I am. My parents had good reason to hate sirens. They wanted to protect our bloodline, and the only way to do that was through ending the sirens. Once I find out what started the war, I can use it to stop the disappearances."

A surge of acid reflux burned through Zarya's chest. She was tired of the hate, so very tired of it all. "It doesn't matter what started it," she said. "There's nothing noble about hating someone just because your ancestors told you to."

Mrs. Irving looked at her now. "*Someone*? You speak as if those creatures are people. Make no mistake, Zarya—they are not. They're not from this world. They are half-dead because they come from the underworld."

"I don't believe in Hell," Zarya said. But even as she said it, she was not sure. Up until recently, she had not entirely believed in the creatures of the ocean, either.

"Then I envy you. Those of us who do believe in Hell live in constant fear of encountering it. I only pray that your disbelief doesn't bring you straight into the demon's trap."

Out of the corner of her eyes, Zarya saw Sean approaching the lobby once more. She nodded at him subtly to proceed.

Then, at a quicker pace, she asked Mrs. Irving, "Can I borrow the keys? I was in the bathroom earlier, and we're completely out of toilet paper."

Mrs. Irving's eyes slitted. "Are we? I thought there were a few more rolls beneath the sink."

"Nope, we're all out."

"Very well." The woman pulled a heavy set of keys out of her pocket, producing the sharp sound of metal scraping against metal.

Zarya grasped the keychain in her fingers, eyes already focusing on one silver key, hardly bigger than a quarter. Grabbing her satchel from the ground, she brushed past Mrs. Irving and out of the concierge area just as Sean approached with a wink. On her way down the corridor, she heard his baritone timbre already starting to schmooze the woman.

"Good afternoon. What a beautiful place this is! What year was it erected?" As Zarya pressed further, his voice drowned out behind her.

In the hall, she snuck through the door to the cigar room and turned the lock shut. It was even hotter in here today, and she could almost smell the ghost of cigar smoke curling through the air. Zarya crouched behind the big desk, once more opening the drawer where she had found the camera. She placed the device back at the same angle.

Moment of truth. Zarya fumbled with the keys, locating the tiny one out of the dozen others. She tried the key in the drawer lock with the ridge pointed left, and it did not fit. Then she tried it with the ridge pointed right, and the key slipped right in. She held her breath at the edge of her tongue. When the key turned in the lock, adrenaline raced through her.

The drawer pulled right open. Inside, she saw a scant number of objects. There was the same paperclipped stack of documents that Mrs. Irving had prompted her to leaf through, containing articles of all the ocean's victims over the years. Zarya took photos of each of the pages for good measure.

Then she spotted the manilla folder that Mrs. Irving had made sure to hide from her. Now, Zarya's hands swept deftly across its contents. There were many items to snapshot—photographs, legal documents, letters. But even as she snapped a quick photo of each, Zarya's eyes were drawn to one paper in particular.

It was handwritten, with expansive curlicues and even-spaced letters that indicated the author had taken a great amount of care in the letter. Once Zarya started reading, there was no stopping.

February 21st, 1851

Dearest Hurley,

I have decided that it would be best for all parties involved if I were no longer on this earth. After our last meeting, it is clear to me that my love for you is unrequited. With your upcoming child, you have more important matters of which to think. I had hoped for a baby of my own, but I suppose not everyone gets what they want.

There is one last request I would like to make. I ask that you please pass along the following messages to my loved ones:

To Charlotte—I apologize for the suffering this will cause you. My dear sister, you took me in when you were almost a child yourself, to spare me a life of orphanage. You granted me the best life you could. But some people are simply not salvageable. I happen to be one of those people. I love you forever.

Thomas—I know that our marriage was not the happiest of unions, and I apologize for the dishonor I brought to you. You will be far better off without me. I wish you happiness.

Mama and Papa—I miss and love you. I will be with you soon.

With eternal love,

Josephine Byrne (née Dubois)

So, Josephine had taken her own life. Zarya did not even have time to process her shock before she was jolted back to the present moment by the sound of Sean's voice coming from the lobby. She snapped a photograph of the letter and quickly tucked it back where she'd found it. After checking the drawer for any missed items and determining that there was nothing else there, Zarya locked it back up. She left the cigar room with her heart pounding in her chest and the siren song growing nearer in her ears. It was so close now, she could finally make out the words.

Hush-a-by baby, babe not mine,
My woeful wail, do you pity never?
Hush-a-by baby, babe not mine,
A year ago I was snatched forever.

Zarya scuttered down the hallway. She thought she had recognized that melody, but now she knew it for sure—it was a lullaby playing on repeat in her head. She closed her eyes firmly together, willing the song to leave her, but it would not.

It was a beautiful soprano voice that sang it, each note punctuated by an olden accent. When she could not get it out of her head, Zarya returned to the lobby, hoping the distractions might help. Sean was still craned over the concierge desk, his mouth fixed into a charming laugh at whatever Mrs. Irving was saying to him. When he saw Zarya return, his laugh trailed away. Perhaps he saw the fear that gripped her.

"Well, Mrs. Irving, thank you very much for the information. I'll tell you what—I'll have my brother call you directly next week and book the rooms. How's that?"

Mrs. Irving nodded emphatically. "Very good. I'll be expecting his call."

Sean nodded at her, then at Zarya. "Hello," he said to Zarya, as if just meeting her for the first time.

"Hello," she responded, her voice breathless. She handed the keys back to Mrs. Irving.

When Sean was gone, she tried to throw herself into work, but her hands shook over the console keys.

Noting her difference in mood, Mrs. Irving asked, "Is everything alright?" Her tone suggested caution.

"Mmhmm." *Breathe, Zarya, breathe.*

But everything was far from alright. How could it be, when she had just discovered that the *rusalka* in the ocean was a woman who had ended her own life over an affair with Mrs. Irving's predecessor? She had been scorned by an upcoming baby, and now she whispered lullabies in Zarya's ear, as if hoping to lure her out at sea—to finally have the child she'd always wanted.

Josephine, 1851

Chapter 23

At first, there was nothingness. Darkness. And cold. So much cold.

Then, from that nothingness, something unfolded. Josephine's eyes adjusted to the darkness, made out little glitters of sand floating through the water. Her flesh adjusted to the cold until the thorn-sharp iciness felt tepid. Her pinky finger twitched, the first sign of life.

But she was not alive. It could not be.

She was floating at the bottom of the ocean, amongst serrated rocks and strange fish with diaphanous fins. Her hair was strewn all around, soft as silk underwater. Her skirts, too, were pushed up by the pressure of the ocean, forming a bubble around her legs. Josephine's toes felt around the base of the ocean, making sure that it was truly legs she inhabited and not a fish tail. When she determined that it was, she reflexively exhaled. But she felt nothing in her chest, no sense of release. She put a hand to her heart and felt nothing there.

She was not alive. And yet, she was not dead. What was this in-between?

The ocean was not as quiet as she imagined it. There was a heavy, rhythmic pulse running through it, deafening her ears. It sounded almost like a heartbeat. She imagined this was what it must have felt like to be in her mother's womb.

Josephine's dress was beginning to feel like a cage, and she tore it from her limbs. Once the sapphire-blue cloth was off her body, Josephine cradled it in her hands. She could not leave it at the bottom of the Pacific, this last vestige of her mother. She folded it as best she could undersea, then pushed up from the ocean floor with all her might. Her legs were so cold now she could hardly feel them, a sickly yellow color, but they beat against the water until she made it to the surface.

The water had pulled her away from the Rock. Here, she could see only the lighthouse's beam rotating further down the peninsula. The shore was within reach but would have been treacherously far had Josephine still harbored a heartbeat in her chest.

Luckily for her, that was no problem anymore.

She swam with the tidal waves, their undulations far taller than she had expected. They tossed her up toward the sky before bringing her back down. Near the shore, the waves broke, casting foam into Josephine's mouth and eyes. She felt no sting, only tasted the concentrated brine upon her lips.

Before death, she had loved the taste of salt. Her mother had told her about the purifying properties of the element, how it kept meat from going rotten. Apparently, it had done that with her own flesh. Josephine was a vessel buoying through the ocean, one with no souls carried aboard.

By the time her feet reached sand beneath the water, night had fallen. It came suddenly tonight, no sparks of pink or flames of orange burning. A curtain of twilight covered the sky, then an even thicker curtain of dusk.

The soles of her feet sank into the beach. There was a copse of trees up ahead, and she went to it. Her skin felt no pain as she passed over rough pebbles and snapped twigs. Josephine continued, past a blueberry bramble, until she found a place fit for a grave.

It was underneath a giant redcedar that she found the right patch of soil. Josephine dug through the dirt with her hands, digging a hole large enough for a dress. Once excavated, she tucked the dress in. She gave it one last pat, feeling the texture of beads and lace and taffeta beneath colorless fingers. Then, she buried the dress in the loam.

Josephine was beginning to wonder if she could return to town in her current form. But before the idea had even fully materialized, she felt a choking in her throat, as if there was not enough oxygen.

There *was* oxygen, but it was not oxygen her body craved. Instinctively, she ran towards the ocean, something deep inside telling her it would provide what she needed.

Once she had flung herself into the water and inhaled a big gulp of it, the choking sensation diminished. It was like taking a deep breath after three minutes underwater—and somehow, it was the very opposite. Things were upside-down here, in this world of neither death nor life. She belonged to the ocean, and it would not permit her to go very far.

The subaquatic world was so very dark at nighttime. Josephine swam through it, marveling at the creatures that glowed through the darkness. For a while, she rested at the bottom of the ocean, waiting for something to find her.

Finally, it did. A shadow whisked by her.

Something told her to follow the shadow. And she did just that, watching the ocean slowly light up, until she was sure that the creature before her was a seal.

The seal looked over its shoulder now and then, as if to check whether Josephine was still trailing behind. Josephine kept her pace as best she could.

She discovered the reason for the ocean lighting up when the seal finally stopped up ahead, beneath a ceiling of electric blue. Josephine approached it, twisting her fingers into the phosphorescent tassels in all their splendor. They were bioluminescent algae, lighting up the ocean like a starry sky.

The seal looked at Josephine with what could only be described as a smile. Josephine ran her hands across the creature's slippery body now, and she recognized it. The seal had seen her as a human, and now it saw her as something else.

Josephine cried as she embraced the seal. Its giant body pressed up against her, she felt affection for the first time in too long.

Days and nights dragged on like this, eventually turning into years. Josephine hovered near the seals and the light show whenever possible. She watched storms ravage the ocean ceiling, waves crashing monstrously overhead.

Eventually, she realized that it was her moods stirring the weather. The sense of darkness had not left her even in death.

And the emptiness was far worse.

It was a gray-skied day when she discovered it. Josephine had been crying for weeks, tormented over her loneliness in the vast Pacific. The seals and the other creatures were not enough to satisfy her desire for a lover, for a child, for even just a friend. There was a pit of desperation inside of her, and now it grew so powerful that the ocean was beginning to spin.

It spun and spun until a massive maelstrom whisked her in circles. An underwater tornado, a whirlpool. It plundered everything in its trajectory.

From the eye of the storm, Josephine could see the sky up above. She broke free of the whirlpool and popped her head out of the water. Up here, the storm looked like water guttering down a drain. It did not do justice to the force of the vortex. A ship could head towards the eye of the maelstrom and not know the power about to thrust its bow down to the bottom of the ocean. That emptiness that ate away at Josephine could manifest in the ocean, promising to drag all passersby into the pit.

And then, a most curious idea struck her.

Zarya, 2023

Chapter 24

Sean's eyes drifted over the letter's penmanship from the four-by-six, glossy photograph in his hands. Zarya watched him absorb the letters' contents, eyes growing wider by the second.

She took big gulps of her burger and even bigger gulps of her beer. The beer bottle was getting light, just a sliver of amber liquid fizzing at the bottom. She would need all the courage she could muster as the clock ticked midnight in a few hours, announcing the start of Rusalka Week.

"She killed herself," Sean said, more to himself than to anyone else. "She was having an affair with Hurley Irving, and she killed herself."

"There's more." Zarya grabbed the deck of photographs from his hands and shuffled through it. She had captured another letter with the instant camera, though it contained different handwriting. "This is a diary entry from Amelia Irving."

March 14th, 1851

Today was better than the last, though not by much. I have asked Hurley to move back into our bedchamber as the baby's delivery date grows near, though the sight of him still makes me flinch. When I see him, all I can imagine is his body wrapped around Josephine—whose name I dare not speak, for I do not trust myself to not speak ill of the dead in this situation.

She vanished without a trace, leaving my life upturned. Even though I know she was an ill woman, may God forgive me, I am glad she's gone. She was a poison to our family, turning everything she touched putrid.

What makes matters worse, is that I cannot tell a soul about her suicide. They do not even know where she's gone. If I tell them, it will all connect to Hurley, and our family will bear great shame. Lord knows he deserves it, but our unborn child does not.

Dare I say it? I do not deserve it, either.

The baby is kicking ferociously as I write this. Dr. Ainsworth says he is due to be a healthy child, despite the stress of recent weeks. At least I have this one solace—this one little creature who is with me throughout it all, sending flutters of love across my belly.

I grow weary. I think I will head to bed. No doubt, Hurley will join me once he is done discussing business, and I will know it from the smell of cigar smoke and scotch. If I am not asleep yet, I will pretend to be, so that I can feel the touch of his hands around my belly without asking him to stop. I still yearn for him, despite his errs. He is a good man underneath it all.

Now, I really must sleep.

I will write more tomorrow.

Zarya and Sean exchanged a glance.

"She forgave him," said Sean.

Zarya shrugged. "Not something out of the ordinary at the time." She added, "Not something out of the ordinary today, either."

"It should be," responded Sean.

Zarya drained the last of her beer, and now she sat back in the laminate booth. She watched Sean impatiently flip through the photographs, his eyes scanning every detail. It occurred to Zarya that she knew very little about this man who sat before her. Sure, he was a journalist-in-the-making, and he lived in LA. But who *was* he, really? Who was the man cradling her to sleep?

"You think so?" she asked, observing his mannerisms. "You

think people should leave when the other person cheats?"

Sensing a conversation starter, Sean stacked the photographs and slid them into the inner pocket of his jacket. "I do, yeah. It's what my mom always said to me growing up and, when she caught my dad with another woman, she left him for good."

Zarya fought off the hint of a smile. It was a good answer.

"What about you?" he asked.

"Oh, I always encourage people to break up," she answered. Her tone may have been flippant, but she meant it.

Sean chuckled. "Really?"

"Oh, yeah. You're not 100% happy? Leave. Moving in different directions? Leave. No longer compatible? Leave."

His eyes squinted slightly. "I can't tell if you're joking."

Zarya shrugged mysteriously.

"Are you one of those people whose parents should have divorced but didn't?"

She again shrugged mysteriously.

"You don't think there's something valuable about working through issues together? Making a commitment to another person instead of just replacing the relationship with a new one?"

"Sure, in the same way repairing a shoe is admirable instead of buying a new one. But I pity the person who has to do it. I think there's nothing worse than feeling trapped by another person."

"A shoe is very different from a relationship," Sean pointed out.

Across the room, the busboy approached to take their empty plates. Zarya gave him a quick thank you. She felt Sean still staring at her, his gaze steady.

When the busboy was gone, she decided to change the subject. "What made you come here?"

Sean seemed perplexed by the question. "You asked me to."

"Yeah, but you could've said no. Instead, you got right on a redeye and drove however many hours without so much as a place to stay the night."

"As you said in your email, it's a big story to break. I recognize what the people of this town are doing." He paused. "Also, I like you. I wanted a reason to see you again."

Zarya felt the creep of panic up her spine. Eager to fill the silence, she asked, "What do you mean you recognize what the people of this town are doing?"

Sean let out another chuckle, but this one was bereft of any feeling. "You know, I'm mixed," he explained. "My mom's black, and my dad's white. And when you're mixed, you have the unique opportunity to see things others can't. You don't belong in either group completely, so neither group wants you. And it becomes very clear just how determined people are to split themselves into Us and Them."

"Or Defenders and sirens," Zarya said, her voice barely louder than an echo.

Sean gave one slow nod. "Exactly."

Zarya's head was swimming in the lullaby. She tapped her foot against the leg of the table, making a rhythmic *clack-clack-clack* sound.

"I gotta be honest, Sean—I don't know how we're going to get out of this." She peered down at the napkin in her lap. "Or how I'm going to survive this week."

Sean reached for her hand across the table. "I'm right here with you. I won't let anything bad happen to you."

It should have been a lovely reassurance, but Zarya wanted to crawl out of her skin as he said it.

After the bill was paid, they returned to the hotel. Zarya was cautious of any prying eyes, suspecting even the peacock feather eyes on the walls. As the light leaked from the sky, she shuddered. She had been frightened of the nighttime before, with its nightmares and siren song, but now it was an altogether different kind of fear. Zarya kept her eyes locked on the clock as if doing so would prevent midnight from striking. When it finally struck, Rusalka Week would start, and soon Josephine would be here, fingers ready to clench around her throat.

"Why does she want me?" Zarya whispered. She was surprised

to have said the words aloud.

They were lying side-by-side in bed, barely an inch of space between their bodies. Zarya considered tying her ankles to the bedframe again, but it seemed an embarrassing thing to do in front of an audience. Hopefully, Sean's presence would be enough to keep her safe.

"Josephine?" asked Sean. "I don't know." He contemplated. "Some people decide they want another person, and nothing can stand in their way. They say it's love, but it's not. Love isn't possession. And other people don't exist just to make us whole."

He wound his fingers through Zarya's hair, making her eyes roll into the back of her head. Somehow, Sean knew exactly where she wanted to be touched, without her needing to say it. He noticed how she melted in his hands when he scratched certain parts of her scalp. Before long, Zarya was fast asleep.

She was jolted to consciousness by the song blaring through her ears.

Hush-a-by baby, baby not mine…

She could hear it so closely, it was as if someone were singing it right in her ear.

No. It was as if someone were singing it from *inside* her head.

Heart aflutter, Zarya looked around the room. Every shadow looked like it could have been humanoid, the laundry pile on the chair dreadfully similar to a broad-shouldered man. Sean slept deeply beside her, his arm drawn across Zarya's chest. As her eyes adjusted to the darkness, she searched for the hands on the clock across the room.

Two in the morning.

Zarya scampered to the edge of the bed, tussling the sheets by her ankles. Her breath grew heavy, so heavy it filled the whole room. She thought she caught sight of a moving shadow by the window, but when she looked towards it again, there was nothing there, nothing but the curtains blowing in the wind like plumes. She tiptoed out of bed to close the window, eyes lingering over the dark garden. If there was something out there, she could not tell.

Zarya prepared to scurry back into bed. But as she turned around, there was motion again in the corners of her eyes. This time, it came from the door. And this time, it was not just the wind.

The doorknob was rattling, someone trying to get in despite the lock. Zarya held her breath, trying not to make a sound. She strained to squint at the sliver underneath the door, but it was too dark to make out whether someone was standing on the other side. Tears welled in her eyes.

Then, from the other side of the door, came a child's voice.

"Mama?"

Zarya froze.

Again. "Mama, are you there?"

It was so silly, Zarya thought. She had been so terrified, but this was just a child lost in the hotel. He must have gone exploring the common rooms while his parents were asleep, and now he couldn't figure out which room was his.

She forced an exhale. Zarya approached the door and unlocked it.

But before she could open the door herself, it creaked open from the other side. There was a moment's pause. The air was thick with silence.

Then, a head peeked through the door, so suddenly it made Zarya take a jump back.

It was the head of a small boy, certainly no older than three. He had a swarm of blonde hair and wore a sweet, little smile. But he smelled rancid, so very foul. How could such a sweet-looking child smell so awful?

Zarya covered her nose with the back of her sleeve. "Are you lost?" she asked, her voice muffled by the fabric.

"I'm looking for Mama."

Zarya pushed the door far enough to see the whole boy standing in the corridor. He wore a sailor-themed pajama, dark stripes across a ruffled, white blouse. Tiny fingers poked out of the hems.

"Do you remember what room you're staying in?" asked Zarya, crouching down to the boy's eye level. Up close, she could see the cerulean blue of his irises.

The boy giggled. "I want Mama."

"Okay, let's help you find your mama."

Zarya lifted herself from her knees and offered her hand to the boy. He took her hand, and his tiny fingers were cold to the touch.

"What's your mama's name?" she asked.

They were headed down the corridor, to the stairs. Zarya decided she would turn on the concierge computer and find the boy's mother in the system to locate the room number. But as they reached the top of the staircase, the little boy took off, a flash of pale hair and pajamas across the spirals. His giggles reverberated against the walls.

When she reached the lobby, the boy was gone. Zarya peeped her head through all the rooms, unsure how to call after him. But there was nothing in any of the common rooms, no soul as far as she could see. There were just the silhouettes of age-old furniture pieces standing stark against the hotel walls.

She guessed that the boy must have found his mother or the room from which he had come. Zarya returned to the attic, where Sean lay still in bed. She curled up beside him and tried to drown out the lullaby in her head. It seemed to grow louder by the minute.

Sailor aboard the Vandalia, 1853

Chapter 25

They boarded the barquentine at half past noon. It was an unusually bright day in San Francisco, sunshine reflecting off the water like diamond dust. A fair wind blew from aft. The ship was rigged, the anchor hove up, the topsails set out. They were underway at five knots, headed north. The ship was practically flying over the seas.

The steward gave one last look at the port, at the red-roofed houses on the hills beyond. It was a glorious city, home to storehouses and steeples, courthouses and hospitals, wharves with thousand-ton clipper ships… But for him, the empty ocean awaited. He would have been lying if he pretended not to love the rocking of the ocean, the squalls that felt like they would never end but always did.

Wind lashed the sails and whipped his face. The steward inhaled briny air, clamping his hands down along the banister. Eight bells rang out, the crew's call to watch on deck. But he was not one of them—they had made that much abundantly clear. The steward was not here to be a sailor. The mates did not so much as look at him—neither of the watches, neither larboard nor starboard.

He went inside to Captain Beard's quarters to complete his duties. Once he was done preparing the cabin, he returned to the deck.

That first night, the skies were open wide, littered with stars. From out here, he could hear the crew laying in the forecastle—smoking, singing, playing cards, telling stories, laughing… He knew the words to the sea shanties by heart at this point, and he would have very much liked to join in, but it was no matter. In two weeks' time, the voyage would be over. He would return to his beloved with her hair like threads of gold. In her arms, all would be well.

From behind, there came footsteps on the deck. The steward turned over his shoulder to see the chief mate standing there, unsmiling.

"Captain asked for you."

Whatever Captain said was law out on the water, but this was especially true for the steward. He bid farewell to the stars that punctured the sky and went inside.

Captain Beard clutched a pipe between his teeth. Upon seeing the steward, he gave a nod. "Did you prepare the pantry for breakfast tomorrow?"

"Yes, captain."

"Good, good." The captain removed his pipe and exhaled a puff of smoke. "It's a beautiful night."

"That it is." The steward thought of something else he might say. "Do you expect rough seas further north?"

Captain Beard shrugged in a way that suggested it was a foolish question. Embarrassment stung at the steward's cheeks. "We are at the mercy of Neptune, young lad. Not even a captain can say for certain."

For tonight, the seas were smooth. The apex of each swell glistened in the moonlight. The steward slept soundly while the night watches made their rounds.

The following morning began with the washing down, scrubbing, and swabbing of the decks. The cook had prepared hard tack and hot porridge, which the steward had alongside coffee. The sea was starting to rock the ship a bit more heavily, though nothing he could not manage. When his cup slid down the table, he hastened to catch it.

By the end of the first week, the sea was running higher. Slowly, almost imperceptibly, the swells had gone from small and frequent, to tall, infrequent masses of water. Still, the deck was filled with sailors' songs, their laughter raucous.

At a week and a half, clouds rolled overhead. At first, just a few puffs of them, but they piled on top of each other until the sky was gone from sight. The sea was black, and a chill spun through the air. The ship dropped between swells, and the steward's stomach lurched in anticipation as the Vandalia crested each one. When it dipped particularly hard between swells, white foam sprayed the starboard.

Captain Beard had instructed the mates to secure for heavy seas. It was a wester, he said, so he steered the ship east, so close to shore that they could see the edge of the distant mountains. He gave the cape a wide enough berth, but the steward wondered if there was cause for concern. They had never been this close to shore before, so it must have been a big storm brewing. The steward heard someone cry out, "Land, ho!"

He waited for the skies to start coming down, but they took their time, as if gathering their strength. At long last, the first drop splattered against the deck. Within minutes, the whole ship was slick with rainwater. The steward could no longer see the outline of the coast in the distance, so dense was the air with water.

The second mate came forward and told one of his watchmen to haul down the jib.

"Aye, aye, sir," replied the other mate.

But as the westerly gale started, the ship began bobbing more violently upon the water. Captain Beard walked across the deck, his footsteps slow as he assessed the ocean. He called out for the mates to clew up the main top-gallant-sail.

Then, he looked at the steward and said, "Go to the cabin."

The steward obeyed. The cook was already there, seated uneasily. They both watched the waves grow monstrous through the porthole.

"A big storm is coming," said the cook, in a Norwegian accent so thick the steward almost asked him to repeat himself.

Overhead, the wind whistled. Even the chair underneath the steward slid side to side. He steadied himself against the walls to keep from falling. As the barquentine crested a swell, a leather trunk slid across the floor, cracking open at contact with the opposite wall.

"Aye," responded the steward. "Seems it's reached us already."

Through the porthole, the waves grew monstrous. A pit of dread burrowed in his stomach, but the steward shook his head. Soon, he would be home to his precious lady. It was a sure thing.

He had closed his eyes, but now a bellow startled him from above. "All hands on deck!" It was Captain Beard's voice.

The steward rose from the chair, unsure what to do with himself.

"I don't think he means us," the cook told him, but the steward was already out. He needed to be with the others, to hear the comforting sounds of their shouts.

Back on deck, it was chaos. A goliath swell sent the bow of the ship pointing at the sky. Moments later, the ship lurched down the swell, tangling the steward's stomach into knots. There were a few shouts of amusement from the crew, but the steward did not laugh. He could tell this was only the first of many close calls.

The sailors had double-reefed the topsails and furled the other sails, but still, the ship labored against the ocean. They were at the mercy of the storm, riding each wave in hopes that the seas would be merciful.

As the swells grew to fifty feet tall, the steward gripped the handrail for dear life. He kept his eyes glued to the ocean—or what he could see of it.

A song had begun to float across the water. At first, he thought it was one of his shipmates attempting to lighten the mood—which surprised him, for even the shouts of excitement had been replaced by cries of despair—but this was not a man's voice he heard.

It was a woman's voice, bright and feathery, coming from the ocean.

The steward leaned over the edge to see from where it came. Its echoes tricked his ears, swirling from all sides, making it impossible to know from where the voice originated.

But as the Vandalia mounted another wave, he found what he was looking for in the water. A woman's skin, pallid as moonbeams, floating along the swell effortlessly. She disappeared into the wave as the ship came roaring down the swell. This time, the ship crashed into the ocean so hard that water sprayed all over the forecastle deck.

"Did you hear that?" asked the steward, to no one in particular.

"Hear what?" one of the watchmen yelled over the sound of the ocean.

"The song!"

"What song?"

Before the other man could respond, the chief mate started crying out instructions, something to do with hauling the reef tackles and reefing the topsail. It was all gibberish to the steward, even after so many voyages. He could only concentrate on the woman's song.

There she was again—a dark-haired maiden lurking in the water. Her eyes were focused on him, silvery and slitted.

He had heard the tales of sirens, of course. No sailor ever boarded a ship without hearing the sea shanties written for ladies of the high seas. But he had always told himself that it was just a legend, something his mates told themselves to ward off the loneliness of missing a woman's touch. Something to explain the unpredictable gales that endangered their lives. Now, as he saw the woman in the water, the steward could not believe the tales had been true.

The siren's mouth was open and full of song. Like a constrictor snake, her call wound around his head, tightened its grip, and would not let go.

"We cannot continue in this direction," he said, loud enough for all to hear.

The mate looked at him as though he were mad. "Have you

lost your mind? Go back to the cabin! You know nothing about sailing."

"But we are headed straight into the heart of the storm." Somehow, it felt like that was where the siren wanted them.

"Go back to the cabin!" roared the mate. The gale had taken away whatever little patience he had.

This time, the steward did not obey. His hands gripped the taffrail, eyes locked on the ocean. "Don't you see her?"

He motioned to the water, but the siren had already vanished. The mate followed the steward's gaze to the empty water.

"See what?"

"We are sailing right into her trap." The steward braced himself as the ship hurtled into the base of another wave.

"Whose trap? Where've your wits gone?"

The steward did not answer, for his eyes were drawn to something out up ahead of the bow. It was a hole in the ocean, with a diameter nearly as large as the barquentine itself. Water spun counterclockwise into the hole.

He thought his heart would stop beating in his chest. This was like no whirlpool he had ever seen before—a maelstrom so giant it belonged only in religious texts. The Vandalia was headed right towards its eye, and it was sure to be sucked right in.

Finally, the mate followed his gaze, and his eyes befell the underwater cyclone.

"Steer right!" he cried, mustering all the volume he could find. "Steer right! Steer right!"

The helmsman, hearing the panic in his voice, had begun shifting direction on the helm, but it was too late. The ship grew dangerously close to the whirlpool. Already, a current underneath the ship had started drawing it straight into the eye of the eddy.

In that split moment when the ship was neither on the surface of the water nor underwater—when it was pointed down into the vortex—the steward thought that perhaps there was still a way out. Certainly, he could not die today.

But before he even had a chance to blink, water gushed into the Vandalia from all sides, ripping apart the boat.

Water swallowed the steward. It swallowed even his shipmates' screams of anguish.

Instead of fighting the current, he tried to swim along with it. He had heard once before that, if a man could get to the base of a whirlpool, he could try to break free from it.

But stakes of wood thrashed into him, wiping the air out of his lungs. He stopped fighting the current and waited for death.

She came for him with those unnerving eyes. She was so close now that he could see her bare flesh underwater. Her form was womanly, but undeniably sickly. Her breasts were bare, but the nipples were gray. She smiled at him, but it was through rotten teeth.

Lord, have mercy on me, he prayed.

But it did not spare him from joining the graveyard of the Pacific.

In her arms, all would be well.

Zarya, 2023

Chapter 26

Zarya repeated her mother's instructions in silent Russian.

On the Thursday before Pentecost, sing songs and pick flowers. Use the flowers to make wreaths. Find a clearing in the forest, choose a girl to be the rusalka, and put flowers in her dress and hair.

This was ridiculous. Zarya did not even have a group of girlfriends in whom she could confide, let alone friends she could convince to frolic in the forest with her. Growing up, her mother had made certain of it—why did Zarya need to see friends today if she had seen them last week? Why did she need to sleep over at their house? Why did she need to go camping with the other girl scouts? No, she would stay home. Spend some quality time with family.

Pick a birch tree. Name it after the rusalka. *Cut a branch from it and bring it home. Bring it offerings—fried eggs, beer, butter, garlands. Whisper incantations.*

This, Zarya could try. But was it a crazy thing to do?

At the end of the week, go to the tree. Dress it like a woman, tie colorful ribbons around it, and drown it.

Yes, it was definitely a crazy thing to do.

Zarya's chest heaved. In the morning sun, the Victorian attic did not seem quite as frightful. The paisley pattern on the rug beneath her no longer resembled a thousand evil eyes. The pile of clothing on the chair revealed itself to certainly be no monster.

She could hear Sean in the shower, the white noise of running water washing away her fears. But despite this morning's reprieve, she knew the nighttime would return soon enough. There could be no minute of daylight wasted.

Sean was out of the shower now, a towel wrapped around his hipbones. Zarya forced herself to look away, pretending to be wrapped up in her journal, across which she scribbled nonsense.

"What are you up to?" Sean asked her. Steam poured out of the bathroom and enveloped him, eventually making its way to Zarya.

"You shouldn't take such hot showers," she said, her tone biting. "I told you, the attic is the hottest part of the hotel, and I don't have an AC unit."

"My bad. Is that why you're so annoyed today?"

Zarya groaned. "Sorry, I don't mean to be annoyed. I just can't remember the last time I slept through the night, and I'm still trying to figure out what the hell I'm supposed to do." *And watching you stand there without a shirt isn't making things any easier.*

"About Rusalk—Rusalka Week?" Sean fumbled with the word.

"You can just call it Green Week."

As if reading her mind, Sean slipped into a shirt. "Green Week," he repeated after her. "Is that what you're talking about?"

She nodded. "The only thing my mom mentioned was a Slavic Pagan ritual."

"Okay," said Sean. "Well, I think we should do that—even if just for good measure."

Zarya threw a disbelieving glance in his direction.

He continued, "I also think we should learn everything we can about Josephine and Hurley, and work on that article."

Right. The article. The pretense that Zarya had given to lure Sean out here. She had framed it as a beneficial opportunity for him, but really, she had been too scared to deal with it all on her own. A moment of desperation had brought Sean to her doorstep.

"Okay."

After Sean had dressed all the way, they headed down to the breakfast buffet. Zarya piled scrambled eggs and roasted potatoes on her plate, hoping to silence the rumbling in her stomach. But once they were sat in a booth, her appetite vanished, as if toying with her. She picked at the potatoes with the tip of her fork, each bite making her nauseous.

Across from her, Sean peered at her over the rim of his mug. "You alright?"

"Fine," she said. "You almost done?"

There was still coffee at the bottom of his mug, but Sean nodded affirmatively. They headed back toward the Rock, to the nearest forest where they might find a birch tree for the ritual.

This time, Zarya was acutely aware of her mother's warning. *Well, definitely avoid bodies of water. Especially during Rusalka Week in early June, when they come out from the water to swing from the willows at night.*

It was daylight now, but the ocean was foreboding. She roved through the forest, making sure to remain cloistered among the trees and never turn her back to the ocean. Sean followed her lead, occasionally peering up at the lime-green leaves blooming aloft.

"What are we looking for?" he asked.

"A birch tree."

"Why a birch?"

"I don't know."

Zarya looked for the narrow trunk and pale bark of a birch, for its dark pattern reminiscent of the eye of Ra, but there was none in sight as far as she could see. This was not Russia, where birch forests spanned hundreds of miles. It was coastal Washington, where firs, alders, and pines reigned.

She stepped through the mulch toward a copse of evergreens, where she took a pause and peered at the horizon.

Thick fog was coming in from the ocean. It swallowed everything in its trajectory. In a matter of minutes, a sheet of white was pulled between the earth and the sun overhead, and the temperature dropped. Zarya felt Sean's sleeve brush up against her arm, and she wished she could reach for his hand. Instead, she practiced self-restraint.

"Something's not right," she said. Fog had shrouded the ocean's surface, making it impossible to keep her eyes on it. She had the same distinct feeling that she'd had on the boat, right before the Defenders had taken the seal's life. It was the feeling of being tricked by the ocean.

"You want to go back?" asked Sean.

She was about to respond, but something caught her eye from the depths of the fog. Zarya made way to the edge of the headland, the lighthouse coming up not far on her left. From here, she had a view of Dead Man's Cove. She peered down at it expectantly.

"There's something there," she whispered.

Through the fog had materialized a vessel. It was a vast sailboat, but the sails were pulled down, donning only bare masts like a dark skeleton. It seemed to be struggling on the water, bobbing up and down on the wind waves. Whatever captain was on board, he was not doing a very good job.

"I think they're in distress," Zarya realized. Just as Sean had finally caught up to her, she ran down the edge of the headland toward the cove.

"Zarya, I thought we were staying away from the water!" Sean called after her, but his voice drifted into the mist.

She was immersed in fog now. Her feet planted into greige sand, and she approached the water, careful not to come into contact with the water.

Zarya squinted through the fog. It had grown so thick, she could no longer see the ship. The air was eerily quiet—even the lapping of waves seemed to have gone silent. She held her breath, waiting for some sign of the vessel.

Suddenly, something broke the silence. There was a giant gasp from the water, and out of the cove burst the shape of a man. Zarya could see him only up to the shoulders at first. His face wore the creases of many summers in the sun. His cheeks were bloated and purplish-blue. He took a gulp of air as if it was the first he had taken in years, then swam further ashore until the water came up knee-high. There was something not right in the way he swam. He looked like someone pretending to be human, someone whose legs hardly worked.

"Are you alright?" Zarya exclaimed. She knew she had not imagined the boat in distress.

The man dragged himself out of the water, his legs rickety. Water had pressed a frilled shirt against the skin of his torso. He wore duck trousers on his bottom half.

"Help," he cried out, his voice thin with desperation. There was something unusual in his accent, thought Zarya. Even this one word had betrayed it.

Zarya did not come any closer. "Was there a shipwreck?"

The man only repeated the same note, as if he did not hear her. "Help."

Up on the bluff, Sean's voice came tumbling down. "Zarya, get away from there!"

Zarya looked up at him. Sean's eyes were shot with fear.

"He needs help!" she yelled back.

"Help," the seafarer repeated. He was up close now, the water only up to his ankles. Zarya smelled a fetid stench, the same as she had smelled last night on the little boy. It was like sardines gone bad, like something that had been decaying for centuries in the water.

Suddenly, Zarya's voice was reedy. "Who are you?"

Before the seaman had a chance to answer, a dark shape emerged behind him in the fog. It was the vessel, coming straight towards the cove. Zarya got a better look at it now, with its bow pointed forward like a wooden stake.

There, below the bow, two words were carved into the ship, the dark shadows of letters.

The Vandalia.

Zarya remembered the name from the book on shipwrecks. This barquentine had vanished 170 years ago.

Before she had a chance to bolt, the sailor grabbed Zarya by the wrist. His touch was clammy and cold as the ocean, his grip tight. He was inches from her face now, so close she thought she might retch from the smell of his breath. He peered at her through midnight-black eyes. Without any words exchanged, his eyes spoke of the horrors they had witnessed.

"What happened to you?" she asked, her voice somewhere between terror and pity.

"It came out of nowhere," he said, his words feverishly fast. As he spoke, his fingers clenched tighter around Zarya's wrist, overgrown nails digging into her skin. Then, his eyes shifted slightly, as if seeing Zarya for the first time. He cocked his head to the side and, in a faint voice, said, "You're her, aren't you?"

Zarya wrenched herself out of his grasp. "What are you talking about?"

He reached for her wrist again. "You're the one she wants next."

Zarya stared at him in shock. She did not know whether to strike him or to scream. He was hurting her, but it was not cruelty she saw in those eyes. No, they were the eyes of a man gone mad with grief.

"What are you talking about?" she asked, and this time tears started to well in her eyes.

The crazed look in his eyes subsided all at once, and his grip on her wrist turned into a caress. Sweetly, he whispered, "It's alright. In her arms, all will be well." But it did not look like he was speaking to Zarya. Rather, he looked through her, to the land beyond, as if he had spotted a long-lost lover and was speaking to himself.

The more he petted her with that death-cold hand, the more it frightened her. Terror pulled a scream from Zarya's lips.

As soon as the scream left her lips, she saw a flash of motion in her periphery. In just a few moments, Sean ran down the outcropping to the cove. Before she knew it, he was kicking down the dead seaman.

It did not deter the seafarer, who rose from the ground as if the kick had been a mere mosquito prick. But it bade Zarya enough time to go running toward the woods, and Sean caught up with her soon after. As he outpaced her, he grabbed her by the hand.

Her feet could hardly keep up. She nearly tripped, but the fear fueled her giant leaps forward. She and Sean did not stop until the edge of the forest, where cars whizzed past on the road.

Zarya felt fire in her lungs. She stopped to catch her breath and looked over her shoulder at the forest, but there was nothing there. They must have lost him.

"What the fuck was that?" she asked. The words brought bile to her lips.

"You were right," said Sean. "I wasn't sure if I believed you before, but you were right."

They crossed the street toward town. The fog was only now spreading through the pastel buildings, as if following them home. It glowed in the headlights of cars winding down the road. Zarya's heart thumped rapidly in her ears.

At the gates enclosing the Irving Hotel, she finally allowed her pace to slow down. Zarya's fingers shook against the handle.

They walked up the sidewalk to the front door. Zarya had forgotten all about the need to slink through the side door with Sean by her side, but it did not matter anymore. Hiding from Mrs. Irving was not as important as hiding from whatever was out in that ocean.

When they entered the lobby, it was a new face behind the concierge desk—a woman with elfin features, brightly colored hair, and a crop top that barely reached her navel. Mrs. Irving must have been desperate for someone to cover her shift, because she would have never hired this girl otherwise.

Zarya was about to walk past her when the girl behind the concierge desk addressed her. "Mrs. Irving was asking for you," she said.

Zarya cast a suspicious gaze in her direction. "Do I know you?"

"I'm filling in for Mrs. Irving today. She had something

important come up, and she specifically asked to see you."

The last thing Zarya needed today was for Mrs. Irving to have discovered the missing SD card from the camera. But if she had, there was only so long Zarya could postpone the confrontation.

"In the cigar room, I imagine?" she asked, already sinking into the doorknob.

The girl nodded.

Behind her, Sean shrugged his shoulders. "What should I do?"

"Fuck it. Come with me," replied Zarya. "Cat's out of the bag now."

They entered the cigar room, at first spotting Mrs. Irving behind her desk. Her brows were pulled close as if by an invisible drawstring.

But she was not alone in the room. On every loveseat, armchair, and ottoman sat members of the Defenders. Before Zarya opened the door, there had been the faint humming of voices coming from the room, but now the voices all quieted.

"I'm glad you've decided to join us," said Mrs. Irving after the moment's pause. Her eyes lingered on Sean. "Ah, it's you. You know, I'm still waiting for your brother's call," she said to him, her voice dry. The ruse was up.

"Sean is staying with me," said Zarya, already armoring herself for battle.

Mrs. Irving rolled her eyes to all sides of the room. "I can see that, Zarya. I figured he was with you when I saw the two of you having breakfast this morning."

Zarya blushed. They had gotten sloppy.

She prepared to save face, the excuse fresh on her tongue. "I just—"

"Save it," Mrs. Irving cut her off. "We have more important things to tend to."

Across the room, Bruno threw an oblong look at Zarya and her presumed beau. There was the usual glint of curiosity in his eye, but something else was interlaced with it today—hurt, perhaps? He averted his gaze as soon as Zarya made eye contact.

"Mallory was just telling us about the night she had," said Mrs. Irving, passing the figurative baton to the woman sitting before the mantle.

Mallory looked like she had not slept through the night. She did not wear her usual face of makeup, donning instead a mottle of freckles across her cheeks and nose, as well as a bottom lip that looked bloodied from biting.

"I saw Jessica last night," she said, and right away her voice crumbled in on itself.

Defenders gasped and muttered amongst themselves, but Mrs. Irving ceased the commotion with a sharp wave of her hand. "Let's listen to what Mallory has to say."

Sean shot Zarya a confused look. She replied in a whisper. "Jessica is the most recent victim at Dead Man's Cove."

"It was one in the morning," Mallory went on. "I got up to go to the bathroom, and just as I was washing my hands—" She choked on her words.

"Go on, Mallory." Mrs. Irving went over to her and put a comforting hand around Mallory's shoulder. "Be strong for us."

Mallory had closed her eyes to hide the tears, but now she opened them abruptly. There was madness in them.

"I saw a shadow in the doorway. It was dark, and I was startled, but the shadow came out of the darkness and into the bathroom light." Her voice went soft. "It was Jessica."

Not even Mrs. Irving could quiet the next uproar that arose from the group. Zarya said nothing, merely trading a knowing look with Sean.

The commotion only grew louder, and now Mrs. Irving pounded her palm into the desk. Three times, like a judge. "Hush!" Their voices fell to a mere collective whisper. "Mallory, what happened next?"

Mallory gave a helpless shrug. "I did what any mother would do! I reached to hug my daughter. In my mind, she had been found.

She looked like death, but she was there, in flesh and blood. I figured we must have been wrong about the sirens. I took her in my arms, and my Jessica was so cold, as if she'd just now gotten out of the water."

Zarya waited breathlessly.

"She didn't hug me back. She wasn't the same Jessica. She just leaned in real close and, in a voice I didn't recognize, said, 'She won't stop. She won't stop until she finds her baby.'"

"*She*?" It was Joe the fisherman who interjected. "Who the hell is 'she'?"

Mallory shrugged. "I was wondering the same thing."

Mrs. Irving pursed her lips together before asking, "Well, how did it end?"

"I kept asking Jessica what she meant, but she wouldn't answer me. I saw a tiny crab coming out of the corner of her mouth, and that was when I absolutely lost it. Seeing that sent chills down my back."

Mallory's face sank into her hands.

"Then, I ran to the kitchen to grab something I could clean her up with—a paper towel, a bar of soap—but by the time I was back in the bathroom, she was gone. Vanished without a trace. I looked for her throughout the house, I even called Dan…" Her gaze trailed towards Dan the police officer, who had been listening intently with his hands folded in his lap. "She wasn't there," she concluded.

Mrs. Irving paced in circles around the room before leaning against the edge of her desk. Lost in thought, she looked up at Zarya.

Finally, she said, "Zarya, it's time for you to tell us what you know about this."

Zarya shifted her weight uncomfortably. She looked to Sean for help, but he had fallen speechless.

She sighed, deeply. Then, she said, "They go by different names. In my mother tongue, we call them *rusalki*—people who have died violent deaths in the water. My mom said they're women, but I saw a man today, too."

"You saw a man do *what*, exactly?" The hoods around Mrs. Irving's eyes draped lower than usual.

"I saw a sailor from the Vandalia wash up ashore," said Zarya.

Empty stares met her gaze.

"The Vandalia shipwreck that happened in 1853," Zarya explained.

Murmurs filled the high-ceilinged room.

"But the sailor wasn't dead—he was something else." Zarya went on before they could cut her off. "Once a year, during the week of the Pentecost, they can come ashore." She scanned the room, waiting to see if they had connected the dots. When it was not apparent that they had, she added, "That week started today."

Mrs. Irving's cheeks went pale.

Across the room, Bruno said, "You can't be serious."

"I am." Zarya gave him a look as hard as stone. "And they can get into the hotel, too."

"What?" Mrs. Irving snapped. "How do you know?"

At this, even Sean arched a brow. She had not had an opportunity to tell him about the boy. Not since realizing what the boy was.

"Last night, a little boy knocked on my door," she said. "At first, I thought he was just a guest, but he had the same smell of decay as the man who washed up at Dead Man's Cove."

Sean was slack-jawed. The others were not quite as subdued in their reactions, chaos unfolding across the room like a symphony of instruments. Mallory's voice was the violin, the fisherman played the bass, the others drummed away, and Mrs. Irving's voice trumpeted above them all.

"Gather yourselves," she said. "I'm just as surprised as you to hear what Zarya has been keeping to herself, but we must move past it now."

"Keeping to myself?" Zarya sent a scorching look in the woman's direction. "Am I the only one that has been keeping secrets, Mrs. Irving?"

Mrs. Irving did not shy away from her glare. She beheld it for a moment before responding, "What have I been hiding, Zarya? Tell me! I know nothing that you don't."

"You know about Josephine," said Zarya, her voice low now.

She had expected the others to look confused, but not Mrs. Irving. The woman's brows furrowed together for a long time before recognition finally smoothed them out.

"Josephine—Byrne?" Mrs. Irving's breathing grew splintered.

Zarya nodded.

"The lighthouse keeper's wife who tried to bring shame to my family?" Anger gathered strength behind her voice. "What on God's green earth does she have to do with this?"

Zarya could not believe the woman hadn't pieced together the puzzle. The evidence had been right under her nose this whole time.

In a soft voice, Zarya replied, "Josephine is the woman I saw in the water, Mrs. Irving. I believe the woman your ancestor drove to suicide is the reason this is all happening. She's the only one luring people out to sea."

"No, that can't be." Mrs. Irving grew distant, her mind rifling through distant family memories passed through the generations. "Because, if you're right, then that means she also—no, it can't be..." Her voice collapsed in on itself before she had a chance to finish.

Josephine, 1854

Chapter 27

She first saw him in the spring.

From the water, she watched him—the little boy with a button nose and hair like spun gold. He looked like the perfect mixture of his parents, with his father's slightly wavy hair and his mother's peach-round cheeks. Josephine had no heartbeat left, but if she'd had one, it would have pulsed madly in her chest.

The boy and his nursemaid came to the beach once a week. Josephine swam as close to shore as she could without being spotted by the nursemaid. She did not need to be very close to make the boy hear her song, but the nursemaid was very strict. She would not let the boy get too far in the water, just a bit of splashing at the edge of the sand.

Every time she heard the splashing of little feet in the cove, Josephine swam to shore. Week after week, she awaited her opportunity.

Once, the boy saw her. His nursemaid was turned away, unpacking a picnic basket for them, and his eyes fell on the lady in the water. A smile looped across the boy's lips, followed by a laugh so wholehearted it could have melted ice.

"Come to me, precious boy," Josephine whispered.

But before the boy could stumble deeper into the cove, his nursemaid turned back around and whisked him onto land.

"I warned you about that!" she yelled at him, raising her palm to him as if about to hit him.

Rage seethed inside Josephine. She hissed while ducking underwater. She would be back another day and save the boy then. Give him all the love in the world. When it came to happily ever after, the ends justified the means.

Summer drew nearer. Josephine waited by the edge of the cove, listening for the sound of infectious laughter.

But it was not laughter that she heard first. Instead, it was a familiar voice—husky, polished, impeccably charismatic. A voice that had sent her into the throes of ecstasy.

She peeked around the corner. There, walking along the beach, she saw Hurley, followed by Amelia and their little golden-haired prince.

It had been so long since she had even uttered Hurley's name. He seemed to have lost a bit of weight, and a few silver hairs had left their mark. But he was handsome as ever. It occurred to Josephine that her desire had never fully burned out. How could it have? They'd never had a proper goodbye.

Amelia, too, looked dashing in a loose, chemise-style gown the color of lemon cake. It brushed against her supple ankles as she occupied herself with the boy. And there, beside her, was a ruffle-edged baby carriage containing twins.

They had three children, then. It would not be the end of the world if one was taken from them. Before she had known about the twins, Josephine had felt guilty knowing that Amelia's only child—a seeming miracle, given how many years she had been barren—would be taken from her. But now, seeing that Amelia had three children, Josephine knew it was the right choice to make. What need did some women have for multiple children when there were those like Josephine who could have none?

She convinced herself that this was her reason for taking the boy. Not the fact that she saw Hurley kiss Amelia with great tenderness. Not the fact that they seemed to have forgotten her. Not the fact that she still reminisced about the way Hurley had kissed her—forcefully, with no care for the violet marks he left across her body—which seemed to be nothing like the way he kissed Amelia.

Perhaps there are just some women worth loving, and others who are not, Josephine thought to herself. She had spent years of solitude trying to figure out why she was one of the latter, never quite finding the answer. Somehow, every man she'd ever known had smelled it on her—she was not a woman who deserved love.

Long after the Irvings had left the beach, Josephine sang. She sang as beautifully as she could, hoping to draw the boy out at sea. It was an Irish song she had heard her mother sing many times before, back in the times when she had still felt like someone who deserved love.

Hush-a-by baby, babe not mine,
My woeful wail, do you pity never?
Hush-a-by baby, babe not mine,
A year ago I was snatched forever.

When night fell on the Thursday before Pentecost, Josephine rose from the water. She did not know how she knew it, but she could feel in her bones that this was the one week a year when she could again walk on land. Something told her to wade to shore. Just this week, she was allowed to emerge from her prison.

Her flesh was crumpled as a raisin from years underwater. She did not recall how to walk properly, but she tried her best. Hobbling on one foot, then another, Josephine went to the place where she'd buried her mother's dress. The soil had stripped some of the color from the blue material, but the fabric was relatively intact. She put it on, clumps of earth still caked onto the skirt. Then, she headed into town to scrounge the child from his home.

Torchlights illuminated the cobblestones. As she walked by, a trail of saltwater dragged behind her. She paid it no mind. There was no one around to see her, for even the saloon patrons had long ago yielded to sleep.

Soggy fingers found the wrought-iron gates around the Irving estate. The gate screeched ever so slightly, but Josephine snuck inside before anyone inside the house could peer through the stained glass. She climbed up the English ivy that snaked up the side of the house, feeling none of the prickles from its rough vines. Once she was at the top of the vines, just below the gables, she peered in through the window, at the nursery inside.

The boy lay in his bed, eyes shut to the world. Josephine started her lullaby again, and she scraped a long, yellow fingernail across the window.

The boy's eyes opened. He sat up in bed, watching the woman who sang through the glass. If he was afraid, he did not show it.

But of course, there was no reason to be afraid. Josephine was only here to save him. In her arms, all would be well.

Zarya, 2023

Chapter 28

After the Defenders meeting, when all the others had started pouring out of the room, Mrs. Irving pulled Zarya aside.

"I need to speak with you. Privately."

Zarya looked at the hand gripping her forearm with its diaphanous skin. It reminded her of the sailor's grasp, and she shuddered.

Pulling her arm away, she said, "Okay."

Beside her, Sean threw Zarya a searching look. She gave him one subtle nod.

"I'll be up in the room," he said, leaving them to it.

Once the door had shut and everyone was out, some of the oxygen seemed to return to the cigar room. Zarya sat across the arabesque rug from Mrs. Irving, permitting herself a moment of rest. It was all too much at once. She let out a sharp exhale.

"You mentioned a ritual," said Mrs. Irving. "I think we should do it."

Zarya shifted in her seat. "That's what Sean said, too."

"For God's sake, forget about the boy." Mrs. Irving looked disturbed. "You're so sure you can trust him? How long have you known him, exactly?"

Zarya held her tongue—an answer would have only confirmed Mrs. Irving's point. Instead, she answered the question with another question. "You and I have been working together for years, and how well do we know each other, exactly?"

"That's not all my fault," Mrs. Irving maintained. "You sneak away as soon as you can. Your contempt for the job is so marked, it's a miracle you haven't quit by now."

Zarya shook her head to herself. "It doesn't matter, really. I don't need to be friends with my coworkers, let alone my boss." In fact, she had been telling herself that she didn't need to be friends with anyone for a long time. She'd had no choice in the matter growing up, and at some point, it had gotten easier to just pretend it had been her own decision.

Mrs. Irving started walking over to the bookshelves. Her fingers lingered over a marble globe, spinning it gently on its axis. "That much is clear." Then, her hands found the spine of what looked like a photo album, parchment and ancient photographs encased inside a hardcover. "Let me show you something."

Zarya sat upright as the woman approached her with the book. Mrs. Irving's desiccated fingers swept over the pages, stopping on a photograph where family members posed before a garden. She handed Zarya the book, and Zarya took in the image.

She already recognized Hurley Irving standing tall beside a curly-haired dog. He leaned his weight into a cane, for time had aged him. Zarya's gaze drifted to the bottom of the page, where the date 1868 was inscribed. Beside Hurley sat two girls, identical in both their facial features and dresses. Behind them, a prepubescent boy stood proudly. And on the other side of the children sat Amelia Irving, with eyes radiating warmth despite the austerity of the photograph. Next to her was a carriage with two more twins sleeping soundly.

"What do you think of this image?" asked Mrs. Irving.

Zarya shrugged. "Big family."

Mrs. Irving clacked her tongue against the back of her teeth. "I know you've read about the original Irving family. Think, Zarya."

Zarya reflected on what she had read of Mrs. Irving's

descendants. Amelia Irving had initially been believed to be infertile, but she went on to have six children. Judging by the fine crow's feet around her eyes, she had borne children well into her forties. One after another, as if compulsively. As if she were afraid they might be taken from her.

Then, it struck Zarya. There were only five children in the photograph. She ran some calculations in her head.

"Where is their sixth child?"

"Exactly," said Mrs. Irving, in a didactic voice as if egging on a student. "Where did their firstborn child go?"

Zarya's neck burned hot. She scratched at the itch, certain it must have looked flaming pink by now.

When it was clear Zarya did not know what to say, Mrs. Irving answered her own question. "I know only what has been told to me. Amelia and Hurley Irving's first boy disappeared from his nursery at age three. Police never discovered the truth of what happened. No body was ever discovered."

It could not be. Suddenly the room felt drafty, and Zarya crossed her arms below her sternum.

Mrs. Irving went on: "What has also been passed down through my family is a deep hatred for the sirens, and a deep hatred for Josephine Byrne after she vanished from the lighthouse." Her eyes met Zarya's. "I never imagined the two were connected until today, when you told me the siren you saw was Josephine herself."

"You think Josephine took the boy?"

Mrs. Irving nodded, slowly and severely. "I never thought the boy's disappearance might be related to the sirens, since he vanished from his own home. But he disappeared in early June. I'm willing to bet, if we look at a calendar right now, it was the week of the Pentecost."

Zarya's thoughts were spinning. "Do you have a photo of the missing boy?"

Mrs. Irving leafed through the photo album some more. When she had found what she was looking for, she handed the album to

Zarya once again.

Zarya's breath froze in her chest. She recognized the little boy with his rosy cheeks, those pale eyes rimmed by thick lashes.

She had held hands with him last night, and he had felt cold as death.

She jumped in her seat, startling not only herself but Mrs. Irving, too. The hotel heiress clutched at the neckline of her blouse as if to steady herself.

"This is the boy who came knocking at my door last night." Zarya's voice was paper-thin.

Mrs. Irving pulled even tighter at her neckline. At last, she said, "If he can get in the hotel, so can she." This next word, she hissed. "Josephine."

She was right. And this time, Zarya was the target.

"Tonight, we'll lock all the doors and windows," Mrs. Irving decided, her eyes darting from left to right as if trying to catch onto her thoughts fast enough.

"What about the hotel guests?" asked Zarya.

"We'll keep a Defender on watch in the lobby all night. We can stay up in shifts. If a guest leaves in the middle of the night, there will be someone there to lock back up." She looked to Zarya, breaking the spell of her own thoughts. "If you see or hear anything at all, ring me. Keep your phone on you, and keep the sound on. Understood?"

Zarya did not much like the idea of the woman being able to track her, but there were more important matters to consider now. If she wanted to make it through the week alive, she needed to do what the woman asked.

She gave a nod.

"Okay. I'll alert the rest of the group," Mrs. Irving said. "But for now, we need to gather the supplies you mentioned for the ritual."

The garden that spanned the Irving estate was vast, though Zarya had only ever seen a shaving of it. The limbs of gnarled oaks contorted overhead, their edges fading in the oncoming mist. Beneath her soles, the ground was soft with moss, and mushrooms sprang from the soil. There were lobster mushrooms in their vibrant orange, curly-edged chicken of the woods, and even fly agarics with their red, dotted umbrellas that could make a human fly—into either hallucinations or death.

They walked past a wooden gazebo, constructed with the same intricate cornice carvings as the hotel itself. The wooden panels had been painted a dark, muted green, not dissimilar to the color of the fir towering over it.

Zarya followed Mrs. Irving deeper into the garden. Along the trail, knee-high fireweeds nodded in the breeze like delicate little amethysts. Daisies and devil's nettle bobbed in white and pale yellow.

"There's bound to be a birch tree around here, I know it," muttered Mrs. Irving to herself. The deeper they ventured, the thicker the fog.

Zarya remembered her mother's words once more. *Sing songs and pick flowers.*

There was one melody she could not get out of her head, its echo still fresh in her mind, and Zarya hummed it quietly under her breath. She reached over into the stalks of purple and twisted flowers from their stems until her hands were filled with a bouquet of purple and white.

Choose a girl to be the rusalka*, and put flowers in her dress and hair.*

She spun a stray fireweed behind her ear.

Mrs. Irving had stopped up ahead. Zarya peered up from her bouquet to see a birch just a little taller than her height, with its typical ashy bark and ridged leaves. Mrs. Irving had been holding a bowl in her hands, and now she placed it at the foot of the trunk. Inside the bowl was a most unusual combination of eggs, beer, and butter.

Pick a birch tree. Name it after the rusalka*. Cut a branch from it and bring it home. Bring it offerings—fried eggs, beer, butter, garlands. Whisper* *incantations.*

Under her breath, Zarya whispered a prayer three times.

"This will do," said Mrs. Irving.

Zarya touched the peeling bark. "Its name is Josephine, then."

Mrs. Irving shot her an ugly look, as if the very name was forbidden.

In the distance, a gust of wind blew through the garden, rattling the leaves from their boughs. Zarya watched the wind draw nearer through the trees. When it was the birch's turn to sway, the squall pricked the hairs on the backs of her arms, its touch unusually cold for this time of year.

"Well, go on, then," Mrs. Irving told her. "Let's get back inside before the storm comes."

Zarya picked up the ceramic bowl from the ground. Its contents swished around in clumps. The mixture was cream-colored and smelled like no recipe that should ever be crafted. She bit her bottom lip to keep from gagging and started pouring out the potion at the base of the tree.

The soil, despite already being saturated with moisture, lapped up the offering thirstily. Once all that remained of the mixture were strands of fried egg on the ground, Zarya took her bouquet of flowers and began girdling branches with flower stems. She took her time, even as the first droplet of rain plopped onto her forehead, until the bouquet was gone and she took a step back. The birch was adorned like a pretty lady with flowers in her hair.

There was one more step to take. Zarya pinched one of the finer branches of the birch, clipping a bough for herself. She doubted this ritual would help much at all, but stranger things had happened. She had to give it a try.

"Alright, then." Mrs. Irving tilted her head in the direction of the house. "Let's go back in."

They walked side by side for a while, Zarya still holding the empty bowl and the birch bough. Rain started coming down in clumps, streaking the sky.

For a while, it seemed like Mrs. Irving was determined not to speak. But then, just when the hotel's castellated edges and dormers came into view, her voice emerged from the silence.

"I know what you must think of me, Zarya."

Zarya pondered whether to deny the oncoming accusation. "What do I think of you, Mrs. Irving?"

"That I'm heartless in my grudge against Josephine. That I have no empathy."

Zarya looked at the woman sidelong, noticing her wraithlike pallor and the bleary edges of her eyes. If anything, Zarya pitied her.

"I don't think you have no empathy," she said. "I just think you distribute your empathy unevenly."

Mrs. Irving took in her estimation. In a tone that suggested genuine curiosity, she asked, "How do you mean?"

"You care so much about protecting your family, that you forget to care about anyone else."

The woman considered this. "You could be right. You have to realize—my family practically founded this town. The people of this town are my family." She squandered a teardrop gathering in her eye. "With my husband gone, and no children or grandchildren, this town is all I have."

"Family isn't everything," Zarya said.

Mrs. Irving looked at her—*really* looked at her—and there was a glint in her eye. "I know, Zarya."

"You know?"

"People talk. We all see it—you've had a rough go of it with your parents."

There was tension clenching across Zarya's jawline. "That's nice that you all saw it and did nothing about it."

"It wasn't our place to say anything."

Zarya just shook her head.

"No family is perfect, but you really can't trust anyone outside of family, either," Mrs. Irving added.

Zarya had heard it all before. *Blood is thicker than water*, her mother had repeated endlessly. *You cannot air out our dirty laundry to other people. No one has your best interests at heart like I do. No one will tell you the truth like I will.*

Some people were lucky to be born into loving families. Others were not. Some people found themselves a family that did not share the same bloodline. And some even stole family from others—like Josephine must have done, her heart so achy for someone to call her own.

Had it worked? Zarya wondered. Had Josephine found herself a family after all?

Judging by the little boy who had come knocking for his mother even in death, no. And judging by the graveyard of innocent victims out in the ocean, no. Josephine seemed determined to never learn her lesson—that one cannot take love by force, that love must be freely given to be real.

The storm had arrived now. Zarya peered through the arched windows of the Irving Hotel, where electric chandeliers cast a warm glow upon the guests. Her eyes were drawn to the dormer in the gable. It jutted out like an eye, ever-watching, and at the window, she saw Sean peering toward the garden. Her chest drew tighter as they spotted each other. A smile wound across his face. She wasn't sure what made the tightness in her chest worse—her excitement or the wave of fear that followed.

She and Mrs. Irving stepped into the building, beneath the vaulted ceiling of the lobby. A brocade drapery billowed from the open window, and Mrs. Irving rushed to lock the window.

As Zarya headed up the stairs, the old woman threw her one last glance. "Remember what we talked about," she said. "Don't go outside no matter what."

Josephine, 1854

Chapter 29

Just like marriage had not been what Josephine had expected, neither was motherhood. She had imagined something idyllic—a quiet, loving child who wanted nothing more than to be held in her arms. Who would cry for her when he was frightened and be comforted when she cooed at him. Who would always be with her, keeping at bay the feelings of emptiness. Who would make her whole.

What she had failed to consider was that the child had needs and desires of his own. He cried when he did not get his way. He pouted and screamed. Oftentimes, he pushed away her loving arms. He wanted to explore the deep, dark ocean without her.

The rejection wounded Josephine all over again. She had been spurned on land, back when she'd still had air in her lungs, then she had been spurned underwater by the sailors she'd lured to their deaths, and now she was being spurned by a small child, too. Not even the pure, good heart of a child could find something worth loving in her.

She continued to try. The good part about being a mother was that nothing would ever break the bond between them. Try as the boy may to run from her, he would never get far. He was frozen in time at three years old. His dependence made up for the moments when he rebuffed her love.

Sometimes, she lost her patience. She plunged toward him through the water with her decaying teeth bared, and those little eyes widened so much that she understood she had frightened him terribly. Then, she demanded to comfort him, to take away the bad feelings she had created in him. To take away the feeling that *she* was bad.

Sometimes, it felt like she needed his comfort more than he needed hers. The boy was reluctant, but he had little choice in the matter. She was all he had in an ocean of eternity.

She would try again to find someone who could make her whole. If it was not this boy, she would find someone else. What other option did she have? She, too, needed someone to fill an ocean of eternity.

Zarya, 2023

Chapter 30

The door to the attic opened as soon as Zarya's footsteps reached the top of the staircase. Sean stood in the doorway.

"Everything alright?"

Zarya brushed past him into the room. "Yeah. She doesn't know I stole the camera."

"So, what did she want, then?"

Zarya cast a peek through the crack in the curtain. The garden was doused in rain, and the storm cast a gaudy light across the greenery, as if someone had turned on a fluorescent light in the sky. Zarya fastened the birch bough to the curtain rod, hoping it would keep the spirits at bay. Then, she closed the curtains tighter.

Finally, stepping away from the window, she answered him. "She suspects Josephine took the Irvings' first child during Rusalka Week."

Sean didn't look too surprised. Frowning, he said, "I was doing some research while you were gone, and I started to suspect the same thing."

"I don't understand how Mrs. Irving didn't connect the dots about Josephine being a siren until now."

"Probably because the suicide letter never specified how Josephine was going to kill herself."

For the first time since stepping in, Zarya noticed the dozens of tabs open on Sean's laptop, the photographs sprawled out across the desk. He must have snapped them downstairs in the library. Photos of old newspaper clippings and historical textbooks also lay spread out, like a charcuterie board of history and tragedy.

"What did you find?"

Sean clicked one of the tabs on his laptop to the forefront. "Read this."

Zarya approached.

The Dark Legacy of Hurley Irving

Each year, the Irving Hotel in coastal Washington oversees thousands of guests. What most of these guests fail to realize is that the immaculately waxed floorboards beneath their feet were made with blood money.

Hurley Irving was a Scotsman who settled in Washington during the days when not many had made their way out West. He began to dabble in many lucrative businesses: mining, dyking, railroads, and eventually politics. Within five years, he built a fortune and used that fortune to construct the mansion on his estate.

In the beginning, Irving was known as a respectable boss. On multiple occasions, he headed into the mines himself to pull out miners from accidents. But as his empire grew, his greed grew along with it, and eventually it outweighed his beneficence. The Irving family threw lavish parties at their estate and cut corners with the mining safety precautions while workers continued to die.

In 1851, seventy souls were suffocated in a mine or crushed amidst the smoke, some of them only boys. Workers went on strike, which Hurley deflected by putting his brother Clyde in charge of the business instead. Clyde's refusal to acknowledge the unsafe mining conditions, combined with Hurley's refusal to raise wages, resulted in further strikes. European miners were evicted from their homes at Hurley's instructions and replaced with Chinese miners, who accepted far lower wages. When the accidents continued, the Chinese miners were then scapegoated.

As Hurley turned away from the mining business altogether, he set his sights to the railway business and politics. He continued to demonstrate his greed when, in 1859, he constructed a railway that cut through indigenous land. Much of the local natives' loss of land in the subsequent years can be attributed to the construction of Hurley's railway.

If you ever find yourself in the dark-paneled, Victorian-style Irving Hotel, make sure to remember the avarice that helped construct it.

"So, this is the man Josephine Byrne fell in love with," said Zarya. "Charming."

Her eyes drifted to a newspaper article underneath Sean's knuckles. This one was older, far older than the modern-day exposé she had just read. On the cover, a black-and-white illustration of a young boy was encased inside columns of writing. Zarya tugged the article out of the stack.

It was certainly the boy she had seen wandering the hotel last night—soft stencil strokes depicted pale hair and eyes, atop them the words *IRVING BOY MISSING* in Gothic font. The date was June 6th, 1854.

"This is the boy I saw last night."

Sean followed the trajectory of her gaze down to the drawing of the boy. There was a moment's pause, then a sharp inhale of air.

"So, the kid who knocked on your door was—definitely the missing Irving boy?"

She nodded. "You know what that means, don't you?"

Sean's brows were furrowed with incomprehension.

She went on, "If the boy can get into the hotel, so can Josephine."

Zarya cast one last look at the image of the boy. She wondered what had possessed Josephine to take him from his parents. Had Josephine been longing for a child of her own? Did she want to punish Hurley for living happily ever after despite her suicide? Worse yet, had she wanted to punish Amelia for having the life Josephine wanted?

Zarya shook her head. How could she possibly know the answers to these questions? She did not understand people like

Josephine. Zarya could not relate to the desire to engulf another person, to restore a sense of wholeness by burrowing under their skin. If anything, she had the opposite problem—a compulsion to flee from anyone who might get too close.

And yet, Josephine reminded her of someone. Someone from this age.

"That's interesting," Zarya mumbled, to no one in particular.

"What is?" asked Sean.

"I wonder if Josephine keeps drowning people because she thinks it will get her love."

Outside the window, rain started to splatter against the glass. The air was streaked with raindrops. Sean peered out at the storm, then pulled the curtains shut. He paced across the room, a hand nested deep into his pant pocket.

At last, he asked, "You think she keeps picking victims because none of them end up loving her?"

Zarya nodded. "It makes sense, no? She jumps from person to person, thinking this time will be different. This time, she'll be loved. But every time she takes love by force, it only adds to the loneliness she tries to fill."

"Seems plausible."

"And maybe she continues because no one ever discovered what happened to her. Amelia never told anyone about the suicide letter."

"That's very insightful." Sean beheld her gaze.

Now, with the curtains drawn, darkness pressed between the beamed gables. Zarya could see the whites of Sean's eyes aglow, and she willed herself to break his gaze.

"I think we should take turns sleeping tonight," she said, clearing her throat. "Mrs. Irving said there will be someone to keep watch in the lobby, but I don't want to risk it."

"Sure." Sean motioned to the heaped duvet on her bed. "You go first. I think I'll stay up a bit longer."

Zarya changed into a pair of pajama pants and a camisole

before slipping under the sheets. Across the room, Sean typed fervently on his keyboard, only the light from the computer screen dancing against the walls.

Maybe the clicking of keys lulled her like a metronome, or maybe Sean's presence gave her the impression of safety, but by some miracle, Zarya managed to fall asleep.

When she awoke, Sean was gone from the desk, curled up beside her underneath the duvet. He must have been unwilling to wake Zarya up when it was her turn to keep watch. Under her breath, Zarya cursed him for his chivalry.

Rain continued to splatter against the roof. It was so dark, she could hardly make out the furnished contours in the room.

The lullaby's echo was sharp now, and it came from outside in the garden.

From the high rooftops, down to the sea…
No one's as dear as baby to me.

Zarya tore the duvet from her limbs and walked toward the window. She held her breath, cracking the curtains open an inch.

Rainwater sprayed against the window, and the trees outside swayed as if someone had grabbed them by the trunk and shaken them.

But there was something else out there—a flash of motion, a human shape.

Zarya hitched her breath even higher into her chest. She thumbed with the curtain to open it a little further.

There, in the garden pathway, a person hurtled away from the hotel. Zarya had to squint her eyes to make out the shape, but once she did, she saw a woman's backside. The woman was clad in a long, dark dress, and rain-soaked hair clung to her back. Zarya saw the figure for only a fleeting moment before it disappeared among the trees. So quickly had it vanished, that she wondered if she had seen it at all.

But the siren's song echoed in her skull, and she knew it must have been Josephine. No doubt, Josephine had come to take what she considered to be rightfully hers. Were it not for all the reinforcement tonight and the birch bough hanging from the curtain rod, it might have been Zarya's last night alive.

Without thinking, Zarya slipped into a pair of sneakers and dashed down the attic stairs, leaving Sean asleep in her bed. She wanted to get one good look at the woman terrorizing her, even if just a glimpse. If she hurried, perhaps she could make it to the parlor in time to see Josephine out the window.

She nearly tumbled down the stairs, knees buckling with adrenaline. Zarya made it to the bottom of the grand staircase only to see Bruno sitting behind the concierge desk, wide-eyed and morose.

"Oh," she said. "You're here."

Bruno looked her up and down, from her disheveled hair to the sneaker laces she hadn't had a chance to tie. "Are you okay?"

"I'm fine," she said.

With Bruno there, staring at her, the opportunity to steal a glimpse of the *rusalka* was surely gone.

She cleared her throat. "Is this your shift?"

"Yes." He averted his gaze.

For the first time, she realized there was anger lurking beneath those dark eyes of his.

"Did you—see anything unusual?" she went on, reluctantly.

Bruno's gaze returned to her, but it was unfeeling. "Nope."

"Okay, then." Zarya turned back towards the staircase, preparing to return to the attic. "I'll see you lat—"

"That's it, then?" Bruno's voice was sharp as a blade.

Zarya turned her head in his direction. There seemed to be more coming.

"You're done being my friend?" he continued.

There it was.

It had been naïve of her to think she could avoid this conversation forever. Swallowing a sigh, Zarya turned away from the stairs.

"We just have different values, Bruno," she said.

He scoffed, a big scoff of indignation that couldn't quite hide the hurt underneath it. "And what values are those?"

Zarya shrugged. Did he really want to know?

"What, you don't know?" Bruno ran a hand along the black ponytail at the base of his head. "You can't even give me a straight answer?"

Zarya had learned a long time ago to not take the bait in situations like these. She had listened to her mother scream at her during car rides to school. She had learned that any response would be used as fuel. If Zarya justified herself, her mother would just come up with a witty counterargument. If Zarya apologized, her mother would feel righteous in beating a dead horse. But if Zarya said nothing? Well, that was her only power. Sometimes, withholding a reaction was the only way to preserve her sanity. Why would a person beg to be heard over and over again, when it was clear that the outcome would always be the same?

Zarya just stood there. She did what she always did in times like this, which was to withhold what she would have liked to say. After all, it had kept her alive all these years.

"What is it?" Bruno's voice almost reached the threshold of a shout. "Tell me! What is it that I did?"

The words spilled out before she could draw them back in.

"You know, I realized something," said Zarya. She met his shout with a soft cadence. "All these years, I've been telling people you're like family to me. That you're like a brother." She couldn't help but smile—a sad, small smile. "But it wasn't because we're close or comfortable with each other. It was because, on some level, I think you remind me of someone from my family."

Bruno scratched his scalp. "Huh?"

"The way you boss me around. The way you take jabs at me.

The way you don't hear the word *no*." Zarya lifted a finger for each item she listed. "At some point, I think I reached the point of no return."

There was a crack of thunder outside, and it made the stained-glass windows tremble. The storm from the Pacific surrounded them now.

"I've been nothing but good to you," Bruno retorted. "I bring you Gatorade when you're too hungover to get out of bed. I give you expensive makeup. I'm even the one who got you this job—"

For the first time, Zarya truly saw him. He had been keeping her dependent on him with favors and breadcrumbs, hoping for the day he could throw it all back in her face.

But Zarya had an advantage. She was all too accustomed to the manipulation. All her life, she had heard, *One day, you'll see. When I'm gone, you'll regret not treating me better.* And, *Every time I buy you something, you act out. You're so ungrateful.*

For the longest time, she had believed her mother's words. She had bought into the story that she was a selfish, ungrateful girl.

But lately, Zarya was starting to believe a different story. The story of a little girl who had been indoctrinated by her mother's unspoken rule—the rule that, when you let someone do something nice for you, it means that person now gets to control your life. Every time she had gone about her day or said no to a hug, that little girl had been breaking the conditions of an invisible contract. A contract someone else had signed for her.

"Don't worry," Zarya said to Bruno. "I'll get you your lipstick back."

She started back up toward the attic. It would be the last favor she had ever accepted from him.

Josephine, 2023

Chapter 31

How many times could a person be spurned before giving up on a chance at ever tasting reciprocal love? As it turned out, the limit did not exist for Josephine. She had tried putting an end to her misery, but it had been futile, only leaving her disfigured in this half-dead form.

She had, on many occasions, wondered why the ocean had turned her into this. Perhaps the medic had been right all those years ago, that it was a sin to take one's own life. Perhaps sin required punishment.

But there was another possibility that made more sense to her—that a soul could not rest until it felt love, and until wrongs were righted. It was unnatural for a person to go through life never having experienced the tender touch of someone who could see them for who they were, truly *see* them. Until she felt that love, Josephine would never be able to rest.

So, as she hulked over the bed of flowers in the backyard of the Irving estate, she refused to give up her quest. She saw the lights that shone from the windows—so much brighter than the oil lamps and candlelight she remembered the house harboring—and she approached like a moth, circling the mansion for an open entry. It was wet out here, but she was used to the water. She hardly noticed how cold the rain felt against her dress.

She could see a man standing in what had been the parlor, short of stature with olive skin and black hair. Josephine did not understand what had happened to the estate, why so many people came and went from the doors of its mansion. None of it made sense. It did not seem to be a party, and the guests did not seem related to the Irvings.

Except one. The old woman waiting at the side door, peering into the night with eyes as blue as her forefathers. Josephine wondered which of Hurley and Amelia's children she was descended from. She wondered whether to love or hate the woman. Should she hate her for being related to Amelia, or love her for being related to Hurley?

To a person like Josephine, there was seldom anything in between love and hate. Oftentimes, her hate was fueled by love. And oftentimes, her love felt more like hate to the receiver.

When it became clear that there was no route into the house, Josephine retreated into the thicket. She kept her eyes fixed on the window of the attic, where the curtains were drawn. Then, she began singing her sweet lullaby, even as the rain patter drowned out the lyrics.

From the high rooftops, down to the sea…
No one's as dear as baby to me.

There was a shuffle at the curtain. Despite the dark, Josephine could see the outline of a girl in the window.

It was not the night to take her to the ocean. There was no way in, and the doors were guarded. But Josephine would find the girl before the week was done. And when she did, the girl would be her baby forever.

Zarya, 2023

Chapter 32

Though morning had come, sunlight did not come with it. The storm pounded on, flooding the streets and the creeks. Gray water gushed down riverbanks, and Zarya wondered how much longer the rain could go on before tiring itself.

She and Sean took turns on the laptop writing up the life and death of Josephine Byrne. In his excavations, Sean had managed to uncover Josephine's birth records. According to her birth certificate, Josephine was born to a French father and Irish mother in Maine, during the year 1830. Interestingly, her parents' death certificates had been written on the same day, a day when Josephine was seven years old. The listed cause of death was a fire.

Zarya scrolled through a list of Maine's historical fires on screen, blinking away the dryness of her eyes until she got to the year 1837. Records indicated that several souls had perished in a fire sparked by Independence Day fireworks. The daily paper on July 5, 1837 wrote of a young girl and her eighteen-year-old sister who were rescued from the house, but not before hearing the tormented screams of their parents burning to death.

Zarya shuddered. Josephine had been orphaned, then.

There was another family member in the genealogy, a certain Charlotte Dubois who had married into the name Charlotte Williams. The other girl from the fire. Zarya could only presume that Josephine had been adopted by her older sister until the time when she was married off to the first man who would take her, a lighthouse keeper named Thomas Byrne.

Zarya shut the laptop with a thump. She pressed her fingers into the muscles at her temples, which were so tense they resisted her touch.

"Tired?" asked Sean. He sat on the floor with his back against the wall, one leg bent and the other sprawled out.

Zarya nodded. "I need a break."

"Maybe we can grab some lunch."

She agreed, and soon they found themselves in a sandwich shop, sitting at a table by the window from where she could see clouds quickly scudding across the sky. Zarya dug into her turkey provolone sandwich, but her thoughts were too preoccupied to notice the taste. In her mind raced flashes of what Josephine's life must have been. A high-collared dress itching at her neck. The stench of flesh burning. The sight of that lighthouse on the outcropping of the Rock. Such were the memories of a woman long dead.

Across the table, Sean ate his sandwich slowly, eyes occasionally settling on Zarya. "You seem miles away," he said.

Zarya remembered that she was supposed to blink. She put down her sandwich and wiped the grease from her fingers, crumpling the napkin into a ball when she was done with it.

"I just keep thinking about her."

Before she could grasp what was happening, Sean wove his fingers through hers.

Zarya's heart hastened in her chest. She sat motionless, waiting to see what Sean would do next. When he offered a smile and retracted his hand to take another bite of his meal, she finally let out the exhale she had been hoarding.

"How long do you think you'll stay here?" she asked, suddenly.

Sean shrugged. "I only had a one-way ticket. I'm not going until after Green Week is over." He added, "Once I know you're safe, I mean."

"And what if that never happens?"

"I'll make sure it happens."

They were quiet again, listening to the shop's little sounds—the doorbell ringing as a customer walked in, the cook slapping slices of ham onto buttered pieces of bread, the cashier printing out a receipt on his register. Zarya had heard these sounds so many times, they were like background noise to her. There was nothing new left for her in this town. Many times, she'd dreamed of running away, but would she be able to withstand the siren's song calling her back? Would it drive her mad?

"Maybe I'll leave this place one day," she said, fingers curled beneath her chin as she gazed out the window.

"Is that something you want to do?"

"Of course. But I don't know if I can handle the guilt."

"The guilt?" His brow perked.

"Yeah, you know…" Zarya fished for a vague platitude, but when one eluded her, she just shook her head. "It's nothing."

Sean was done with his sandwich now. He clasped his fingers together contemplatively. He said, "When the article is done, I'd like to credit both of us for writing it."

"That's kind of you."

He shrugged. "Kind would be to credit you if you didn't write it. I'm just giving credit where credit is due."

She supposed that was true.

After they had both finished, they crossed the street back to the Irving Hotel. Zarya jumped over puddles like a child playing hopscotch. She could not avoid them all, and her foot splashed into a puddle up to the ankle, the cotton canvas of her sneakers drenched. She whispered a curse under her breath before lurching inside the hotel lobby.

Before she had a chance to rattle the rainwater from her jacket, Zarya noticed the eerie quiet of the lobby. There was no one behind the concierge desk—something unusual given the check-in time quickly approaching.

Sean had started down the hall, and she followed him. But no sooner had she passed by the cigar room, that the heavy, wooden door opened a crack, and a pair of eyes peered at her.

When the eyes spotted her, the door swung open full throttle. Mrs. Irving stood in the doorway, and any of yesterday's warmth was gone from her face. She seemed to be gnashing her teeth together behind those pursed lips.

"You." Her voice was tinny.

Zarya took a step backward. In front of her, Sean had stopped in his tracks and turned to look in her direction.

"You okay, Mrs. Irving?" Zarya asked.

"Did you go through my belongings?"

By now, Sean had joined Zarya's side.

"Oh good, you're here, too," Mrs. Irving said, this time directed at Sean. "I'm sure you're the one who put her up to it in the first place."

Zarya did not look at Sean, confident her gaze would have betrayed their secret. Instead, she took comfort in the back of her hand brushing up against his side, the warmth of his skin permeating through his shirt.

"I can't give you an answer if you don't tell me what you're talking about," she told Mrs. Irving, surprised by the steadiness of her own voice.

Mrs. Irving's face creased into a knot. "I doubt that very much." She moved aside so Zarya could see the opened drawer of her desk. The camera was there, just as Zarya had left it. "The recording from the night of the boat. Where is it?"

"Wherever you left it," Zarya replied, but this time her voice shook.

"Be honest with me, Zarya. I have a key to your room, to your safe—to anywhere you might have hidden it."

"To my phone?" Zarya wondered. She couldn't help herself. Her voice was slippery with contempt.

"Don't be ridiculous." Mrs. Irving raised a finger at her. "Whatever you've done with it, that recording could get you in as much trouble as the rest of us."

But before Zarya could formulate a response, Sean stepped in front of her. With that sumptuous voice of his, he said, "Yes, Mrs. Irving, we have the recording. And, if you don't leave Zarya alone, a good friend of mine will make sure that recording is released on every major news outlet. You'll have the environmental advocates knocking on your door in no time. You could spend up to a year in prison, from what I hear."

Mrs. Irving let out a laugh, cold and stony. Ignoring Sean, she directed her response at Zarya instead. "You're afraid of all the wrong people, Zarya. You trust outsiders more than people you've known your whole life. It's no wonder you're in danger."

Zarya had heard enough. She could still feel the edges of the SD card in her jeans pocket. She pulled Sean aside by the hem of his sleeve, back out toward the lobby. If Mrs. Irving intended to go through her room, Zarya did not want to be there when it happened. She pulled Sean past the front door and back out into the rain.

The splashes of water were so loud, they drowned out the squeaking of tires against asphalt.

"Where are we going?" Sean shouted over the sound.

It was a good question. Zarya was trying to figure out the answer herself. Already, the water had slicked her forehead.

The truth was that there was nowhere they could go. Her room at the hotel wasn't safe. Her parents' house wasn't safe. She had no friends at whose place they could spend the night. Suddenly, the years of solitude and pushing people away seemed to have piled on top of her. They pressed from all sides, leaving her nowhere to go, just floating aimlessly through space.

Growing up, there had been nowhere to run, either. Mama had made sure to limit Zarya's outings with friends, to punish her for going out with disappointed looks and guilt trips. *No one will ever love you like I do*, she would say. She had said it so many times that, eventually, it became true. Eventually, there was no one to whom Zarya could run.

Zarya was getting tired of trying to run. She couldn't run from Mrs. Irving and her parents and Josephine and her feelings for Sean at the same time. Maybe that was the irony of it—that sometimes, in order to run away from something, you have to pick something to run *towards*.

"Fuck it," she said. "Let's camp out at the lighthouse."

Sean's eyes looked like they were about to bulge out of their sockets. "The lighthouse? You're sure that's a good idea?"

She didn't answer him, just took his hand in hers and led him towards the Rock. Beyond the shops closing for the day and the diners starting to fill up. Past the edge of town, to the place where no one lived.

They were so close to the water now, her head abuzz with the sound of lullabies, piling on top of each other, echoing through her head like a chorus of voices. The ocean was the *rusalka*'s lair most days of the year, but nowhere was safe this time of year. Whether on the mainland or by the sea, they'd have to risk it.

Zarya heaved through the grove of trees, rain still running down her head in runnels. The ocean came into view in the gaps of the foliage, looking misshapen today as the waves battered the shore. Even the sand at Dead Man's Cove had vanished beneath a high tide. With each wave that smashed into the headland, the water seemed to rise higher and higher. Foam hissed against the Rock.

The lighthouse was embowered by forest, but finally, it emerged amongst the trees. Zarya ran up to the door and motioned for Sean to pick the lock again. Whether to get out of the rain or to please her, he abided by her wish, twisting the same paperclip into the lock.

The door came open with a push, and they both tumbled inside. Outside, it had been dark and dim, but indoors was a different kind of dark and dim. Drafts of old air brushed up against Zarya's wet skin, sending a shiver through her. She squeezed the water from her hair before peering down at her sopping clothes. It would take hours for them to dry in this humidity.

Zarya took off her jacket first, followed by her jeans. The latter clung stubbornly to her thighs, but finally, they fell in a soaked heap at her feet. Suddenly, Zarya was very aware of Sean's presence behind her. She saw him step through the entryway to the bedroom, undoubtedly to give her some privacy.

But it was not privacy that she wanted anymore.

Zarya went after him, and when she had passed over the sill of the door, they locked eyes. He had never seen this side of her before—this bolder side. Truthfully, neither had she.

"I can't run away from everyone at once," she told him. And, more importantly, he was the one person she didn't want to run away from.

Keeping her eyes still on his, Zarya took off her shirt. There was no more confusion in his look after that. Sean drank her in.

Her shirt fell to the floor, and she approached him by the window. Sean's arms welcomed her openly and, despite the wetness of his skin, he felt like a furnace. Zarya pushed herself against him and let her lips find his.

He tasted like shea butter somehow, sweet and smooth. As the kiss intensified, his arms wound around her shoulders, hands planted at the nape of her neck. Strands of wet hair ensnared his fingers.

Zarya pulled Sean to the bedside. She sank into the mattress as he hovered over her. The mattress expelled clouds of dust, but she did not care. There was only one thing she wanted in that moment, and that was to remember how it felt to be touched by another human being.

Sean did an excellent job at reminding her. His fingers trailed down her neck, to her breasts, where he kissed her. His arms were sinewy to the touch—as were other parts of him, which pressed up against her in ways that left her yearning for more. She pulled her undergarments down her legs and flicked them off with her toes.

As he entered her, a small gasp fled her lips. Sean thrust as he kissed the side of her neck. She dragged her fingertips across his spine as her pleasure intensified.

His thrusts quickened. His panting grew shallow.

Her skin was alive and tingling, every inch of it. Zarya had forgotten what it felt like to join her body with another person. She'd had one-night stands and casual encounters, of course, but they had felt more like a handshake—an exchange of pleasantries, a fleeting moment of pleasure.

This was different. She could feel it in the way he touched her—not like he was trying to rouse himself, but like he was trying to rouse *her*. Her pleasure was his pleasure. Her satisfaction somehow heightened his.

When she felt a surge of warmth between her legs and her thighs shook forcefully, Sean, too, lost control of himself. One last grunt and his body melted into hers.

The rainwater had evaporated from their skin. Zarya lay there, caressing the back of his head, feeling his heartbeat dawdle against her breastbone.

When at last he lifted his head from her shoulder, Sean smiled at her. "I've been wanting to do that for a long time."

He lay down beside her on the mattress, his fingers once more finding their way to hers. For a while, they sat like that, staring at the peeling ceiling paint and listening to the sound of each other's breathing.

In fact, they lay there until gloaming darkened the storm clouds outside the window—and that was when dread inched its way back into Zarya's chest. When night fell, the *rusalki* would come roaming from the water—and this time, there was nothing to keep them out.

Josephine, 2023

Chapter 33

Josephine saw the girl heading into the lighthouse. To the very place that had been her prison back in 1850. She must have known, thought Josephine. The girl must have known now what the place had done to her.

She was different from the others. This one understood.

Josephine waited until nightfall to rise out of the water. She brought the boy with her, holding his clammy little hand all the way out to the cove where she'd first seen him. He stumbled on a piece of driftwood but was undeterred, excited to explore the earth he had once traversed freely.

They climbed into the weeping willows along the shore and swung from their branches like pendulums. Josephine laughed in delight. She sang. She looked towards the lighthouse and prepared for the girl to come to her.

They always did.

Zarya, 2023

Chapter 34

"This time, I'm serious." She looked at him resolutely. "We can't both sleep at the same time."

Darkness had overtaken the lighthouse. There was no electric switch, just a candle holder on the bedside table. Traces of melted wax had hardened at the base.

There must have been light somewhere in this building, thought Zarya. It was a lighthouse, after all. But all she had was a small set of matches she had snatched from the host stand at the Irving Restaurant.

The storm had been pounding at the walls for so long that rain was starting to penetrate the edge of the window, little beads trickling in with growing intensity. The wooden bedpost, too, was decaying from years of damp, salty air. Water was starting to win this war.

"Agreed," Sean answered, though Zarya had already forgotten what he was agreeing to. Her eyes were transfixed on the ocean whorling outside the window.

He cocooned himself atop the bed, not daring to get underneath the century-worn sheets. When his breath went from jagged to placid, Zarya watched Sean sleep, watched the rising and falling of his chest. Her worst nightmare was starting to come true—she was starting to grow attached to him, just like she had predicted she would.

After a while, she rose from the mattress to sentry all the windows. In the kitchen that abutted the bedroom, she peered out through the glass at the labyrinthine forest. Trees swayed madly in the gale, their branches like the sleeves of ballroom dresses mid-dance.

She went up to the tower next. The spiraling staircase was so dark that she could not even see her own hands feeling up the walls. Zarya held her breath, hoping there would be no creature waiting for her up ahead. But there was no way to know, and maybe there would be a candle up in the lantern room—so on she climbed.

It was deadly silent but for her footfall on each step. The wet soles of her sneakers squeaked against the uneven surface of the steps. Zarya went on like this for some time, ascending into the darkness. There had to be salvation at the top. There had to be.

When at last she reached the lantern room, the lambent, blue light from the storm was a most welcome sight. It was nothing compared to the darkness beneath.

Zarya patted down whatever surfaces she could get her hands on—the table, the lens itself, the lens, the clockwork attached to it. Dust clung to her fingertips. When she found nothing, she sat in the dilapidated chair overlooking the view. The seat was threadbare, the wood splintering along the sides, unlike the elegantly upholstered chairs back at the Irving Hotel. Zarya brushed a splinter out of her palm.

Outside, the ocean raged on.

She was starting to see how a place like this could drive a person mad. And, combined with Josephine's traumatic loss of her parents and a husband who was determined to withhold all affection—it was an almost certain recipe for disaster. Josephine had never stood a chance at happiness.

Zarya wondered if maybe some people were just born to live out a tragedy. Like in the old Shakespearean plays, their lives were a cautionary tale. Their life stories held no other purpose but to warn others.

And then, Zarya wondered, if perhaps she was one of those cautionary tales, too. Her life was dull. She had been born to a cold father and a soul-devouring mother. She had little ambition. Every day was more of the same. In a way, setting her sights on Josephine had been the best thing to happen to her—or at the very least, the most interesting. Was it wrong that a part of Zarya wanted to join the *rusalki* in the ocean?

Yes, Zarya decided. It was wrong. And crazy.

She readjusted her foot and, in doing so, knocked into something beneath the desk. Zarya peered beneath to see what hard, metallic surface she had bumped into.

It was some sort of canister, and she dragged it towards her across the floor to get a better look. Its contents were heavy. Zarya squinted in the dark.

WHALE OIL.

This must have been what was used to light the lens, then. Zarya swiveled the canister to its side, assessing it. She knew nothing about how to turn on a lighthouse lantern, but she knew the general gist of using oil was to light a wick. The lens must have had a wick, though she was sure it was no longer in function after centuries of disuse. Zarya looked around for a candle, but there was none in sight.

Just as she was about to sit back up, Zarya heard the rustle of something underneath the canister, a sound like paper brushing against paper. She leaned down to fumble at the sheaf.

In the dark, she could feel it better than she could see it—a stack of papers folded together, with edges creased and indentations from the place where nib had pressed against paper. She pulled it up before her eyes, eyeing the letters as best she could.

More diary entries, dated as far back as 1851. Unsigned, though Zarya did not recognize the penmanship as consistent with any of the handwriting she had read up until now. It did not have the measured curlicues of Josephine's writing, nor the similar rhythm of her sister Charlotte, nor the slightly chubbier letters produced by Amelia Irving. No, this writing was sharper and more angular, with staccato sentences. It belonged to a man—and, by the looks of it, a man desperate to put his story in writing before it was too late.

October 12, 1851

I saw her again today. Out by the cove.

She saw me, as well. She did not smile at me. In fact, I do not think she cared to see my face at all.

I must tell someone.

But who? They think her dead. I think, in some sense of the word, she is. But, in another sense, she is anything but.

They will send me away. Maybe it's best that they do. They will think I've lost my mind. Maybe I have.

They think that I've killed her. Maybe I have.

Aye, maybe I have.

Zarya flipped to the next paper, fingers dragging over the letters.

October 15, 1851

She hates the light beams. When they shine, I sometimes see the glint of her eyes in the water. They contain a look of hate.

She has reason to hate me, of course. As I have reason to hate her.

Was it my fault that I never wanted to wed? It is simply the way I am. I have no interest in people. Never have. That's why I picked the life of a lighthouse keeper, is it not?

But to not wed was never an option.

I think I do hate her.

Companionship is one thing. I would not have minded a companion. But she wanted love. She wanted desire. She wanted our souls to join like the river meets the sea. I could not give her this. Why could she not just leave me be? Why can she not leave me be even now, in death?

I grow weary of this place. I cannot keep seeing her every time I look out at the ocean. I am inattentive toward the ships. I am not myself.

I must leave. Go back to Maine, or anywhere else. Far from the ocean, if I can.

There was one page left. Zarya continued, ever more hungrily with each word.

November 26, 1851

Whatever man keeps this lighthouse after me, you will think me mad after finding these letters. You may not understand what I mean by the following words. But, if you do, it means you, too, have seen her. And, if you have seen her, you are in great peril.

I have spent many long, sleepless nights trying to figure out how she can be put out of her misery. In order to unearth what weapon can be used against her, I must figure out what she is.

She is not alive and yet she moves. She was killed by water. She ravages the earth come summertime.

It seems to me that she can only be killed by something that contains the same properties as her yet is diametrically different from her. Mechanically speaking, that makes the most sense. For example, sound waves of opposite frequencies can cancel each other out. Colors that sit opposite each other on the color wheel cancel each other out.

But then, that begs the question: what weapon contains the same properties as her, and is also diametrically different from her? What is not alive but still moves, is killed by water, and ravages the earth come summertime?

No matter how hard I try, I cannot find the answer to the riddle.

I cannot be the one to end her. And I will not let her be the one who ends me. I am leaving this Godforsaken lighthouse.

Zarya read and reread the words, hoping this next time would bring along the clarity she needed to solve Thomas' riddle. *What is not alive but still moves, is killed by water, and ravages the earth come summertime?* She simply could not figure it out. Plants could move and be killed by water, and they sprang across the earth during summertime, but plants were also alive. Rocks could not move. The sun could move. What on earth was the antidote to the *rusalka*?

Zarya sank back into the chair's spindles, ready to give up.

As a rogue wave crashed into the Rock, foam splayed across the glass panels of the lantern room. Zarya covered her head, half thinking the wave would shatter the windows. When the sizzling sound of the water retreated, she peered over the edge and saw that the ocean had climbed to monstrous dimensions below the headland. It almost reached the base of the lighthouse.

And then it came.

A melody so angelic, each note perfectly clear, coming from outside. Josephine was drawing nearer.

Hush-a-by baby…

There was a brittle laugh, followed by more of the lullaby. Zarya gathered the strength to look in the direction of the song, near Dead Man's Cove. She saw a mere flash of movement. But it was enough to know Josephine was there.

She bolted down the stairs, tripping over her shoelaces and sliding down the steps three at a time before gathering herself to descend more measuredly. Now she flitted through the darkness, unsure where she was even headed. All she knew was that, if she stayed in the lantern room and Josephine started up the tower, there was only one way out—and that was the ocean, hundreds of feet below.

As she reached the bottom of the stairs, Zarya bent over her knees to catch her breath. The song grew clearer.

Hush-a-by baby, babe not mine,
My woeful wail, do you pity never?

The voice lingered on tall notes, then slid seamlessly into a lower octave. It sounded like butter melting before candlelight. Josephine's voice was womanly, with a high timbre not like that of a girl but like a beautiful creature not from this world. It called to Zarya, cajoling her outside. Despite her self-restraint, Zarya could not resist the siren song forever. Her legs acted without her permission, stepping towards the door. They ached more strongly than they had ever ached before.

The door swung open of its own accord, and Zarya stepped outside.

The rain came down thick, silvery and translucent as spider-silk. Zarya begged her legs to stop stepping forward, but she had lost all control of them. Right foot stepped before left foot, and then left foot followed.

Hush-a-by baby, babe not mine,
A year ago I was snatched forever

She was walking parallel to the edge of the bluff, toward the place where the forest met Dead Man's Cove. Already, she could see dark figures ahead, movement between the trees. But it was not until she was at the edge of the glade that she truly understood what she was seeing.

A weeping willow quivered like tinsel. And from its branches swung a woman that must have been long dead, her skin pale and sepulchral, with a dress that hung beneath her in bustle folds. Her gown looked like it had been entombed along with her, torn open in some parts and caked in soil. It was nearly falling apart.

When Josephine peered down from the willow, her eyes met Zarya's, and Zarya felt once more as she had that night during the lightning storm. The whites of the *rusalka*'s eyes were yellowed like parchment paper, though her irises had taken on a hoary sheen that glimmered despite the missing moon. The skin along her collarbone was encrusted with barnacles, like a rough scab that had hardened.

And that was not the worst of it.

From Josephine's hands dangled Hurley Irving's son, swaying in the same motion as the willow branches themselves. The two looked as though they were playing—though Zarya did not know what game, nor the rules needed to win it.

As Josephine swung from the willow and thrust the boy back and forth, her song went on.

From the high rooftops, down to the sea…
No one's as dear as baby to me…
Wee little hands, eyes shiny and bright…
Now sound asleep until morning light.

As soon as the song came to a close, Zarya was snapped out of the trance. Like coming out of a sleepwalk, a surge of shock mounted inside her. She looked from left to right, suddenly realizing her whereabouts. Slowly, she started to back away, hoping her retreat would go unnoticed.

But, if Josephine knew anything at all, it was to spot a person about to abandon her. In an instant, her head snapped in Zarya's direction, eyes pale with fury. She dropped from the willow, the boy falling out of the treetop along with her. As soon as her feet planted into the soil, the *rusalka* started careening towards Zarya, her movements irregular as if she had forgotten how to walk on land. The boy scuttered away into the distance.

Zarya had always wondered if, in times of danger, she was the type of person to scream. She liked to think of herself as a person immune to such melodrama. But now, with the creature hurtling towards her, the scream left Zarya's lips of its own accord, piercing the forest for miles and miles. And then, Zarya did what she did best—*run*.

The world was a blur. The roots of trees snagged her shoes, and rocks underfoot left her footsore. But Zarya persisted, avoiding the thicket and tussocks and trunks as best she could. She was certain she had never run so quickly in her life.

She had forgotten in which direction to run. She could have been headed towards the lighthouse, or the street, or the ocean, but it was hard to tell in the dark. There was no time to think, to plan out her next strategy. There was only time to flee.

Just as she was beginning to think she could hear the whizzing of car engines in the near distance, a fallen branch caught Zarya's shoe, and she tumbled forward onto all fours. Josephine skittered not far behind, her silhouette emerging from behind the trees.

This is the end, thought Zarya. *This is goodbye.*

In that span of just a few seconds, thoughts raced through her mind, one after the other. She thought about all the things she had wanted to do as a child—to paint watercolors in a sunny park, to board a plane and glide across clouds to unknown destinations, to sip coffee from a place she could maybe call home.

And yes, to find a boy she could love and who loved her back. To have a family of her own, a place where she belonged. To stop watching families from the outside in, to finally feel the lively bustle of Sunday brunch in the dining room. To hear laughter and chatter instead of what she had always heard growing up—shouting and, worse yet, all-encompassing silence.

All of these had been wishes she'd made as a child. Back when they had mattered.

Somewhere along the way, she had forgotten about those dreams. But now that she was at risk of losing them all, she wanted them more than anything. She had changed her mind about surrendering to the ocean. She wanted to live.

Her eyes grew cloudy with tears. She shut her eyelids.

And then, there was a gunshot, so loud that even its echoes jolted her. Zarya's ears were ringing.

Her eyes flung open. A bit further down among the trees, she saw Mrs. Irving, standing in a wide-legged stance, hands wrapped around the grip of a pistol that pointed straight at Josephine.

Josephine had stopped in her tracks. She peered at Mrs. Irving with a smirk on those bluish lips of hers. Wherever Mrs. Irving had sent the first gunshot, it did not hit the *rusalka*.

But Mrs. Irving was not one to quit. She clenched down on the trigger a second time, and this time Zarya saw the bullet go straight through Josephine's shoulder. A flower of black blood bloomed beneath her clavicle.

Zarya waited to see what would happen, horrified. Had Mrs. Irving killed the creature once and for all?

Josephine staggered backward just slightly, but she regained her balance soon after. She looked down at the blood dripping down her dress, and a devilish smile overtook her mouth. Her gaze lifted from the wound to Mrs. Irving. She seemed to have forgotten all about Zarya.

What happened next was like a carpet being pulled out from under Zarya's feet. Josephine launched at Mrs. Irving, toppling her over in the grass. Gurgles of pain arose from the dark shapes wrestling on the forest floor.

Mrs. Irving did not stand a chance. Her cries of pain subsided with each strike.

Soon, once she was done with the old woman, Josephine would turn her sights to Zarya. It had been silly of Zarya to think she could kill someone who was already dead.

Zarya picked herself off the forest floor and began running again, racing to the lighthouse as fast as her legs would take her.

Zarya, 2023

Chapter 35

The lighthouse door slammed behind her, so loud it sent Sean rushing from the bedroom. His eyes were still glassy with tiredness.

"What happened?" he asked, just starting to piece together that Zarya had come from outside.

Zarya's back slid down the door until she was pressed up against the threshold. She hid her face in her hands and let out a sob.

In an instant, Sean was beside her. "Tell me, Zarya. Why were you out there? Did you see her?"

Zarya nodded, her eyes closed as if she couldn't quite face the world yet. In between chokes, she managed, "She got Mrs. Irving." Finally, she found the strength to open her eyes.

Sean reached for the lock on the door, flicking it shut with more force than necessary. Then he stumbled towards the window, trying to spot any signs of *rusalki* coming toward the lighthouse. His vacant gaze indicated that there were none, but Zarya knew that would soon change.

"She'll be coming here next," said Zarya. Her voice was matter-of-fact, as if she had long ago accepted the issue at hand.

Sean's head whipped in her direction. "What? Well, what are we supposed to do?"

Already, the siren song started its echo back up, growing louder with each moment that passed. Zarya lifted herself from the ground and peered out the window. In the distant trees, Josephine approached. Small of stature and bony-limbed as she was, the sight of her still froze Zarya's heart. Josephine marched assuredly, in no rush as she prepared to finally get the one person who would love her.

Every victim was the one person who would love her—until they were not.

As she watched the creature approaching, Zarya knew there was nowhere left to run. Soon, the walls of the lighthouse would be breached. For the first time in her life, she would need to stop fleeing and actually *fight.* Her life depended on it.

Zarya's jaw tightened. "We need light in here."

She thought back to the whale oil upstairs in the tower, their only hope of illuminating this night as dark as death.

And then, it dawned on her.

What is not alive but still moves, is killed by water, and ravages the earth come summertime?

It was the antidote to all of this, the one thing that could kill Josephine.

Fire.

Of course. Fire could be killed by water, but fire could also kill water. Fire ravaged the forests in these parts during the summertime, sending clouds of smoke across the earth. Fire produced light, in the most primordial sense. And light killed darkness.

A smile overtook her. "Fire," she said, this time out loud.

Sean's forehead was dimpled with confusion. He waited for her to explain, but Zarya did not.

All she managed was a rough, "Stay here," as she hastened up the winding staircase, two steps at a time, then three, her legs powered by a surge of energy. She reached the top of the tower in no time, where she unspooled the cap from the oil canister and started pouring its contents onto the floor in heaps.

Would this even work? The tower was built of stone, but the

interior seemed to be made of wood. She saw panels of it in the places where the paint peeled.

It was worth a try. So, she waited.

For a moment, silence was suspended in the air. Zarya heard only the pounding of the storm and the shrieking of wind outside, but nothing coming from within the lighthouse. She held her breath in anticipation.

She expected that there would be footsteps from the staircase, each getting louder. But there was no sound from the steps. Zarya held her breath for so long, waiting to hear the slightest shift in the atmosphere, until she felt blue in the face. She was facing the door to the staircase, her back to the ocean.

She should have remembered. *Never turn your back on the ocean.*

But the next sound she heard did not come from the staircase—it came from the gallery. Zarya's heart nearly leaped out of her chest. She turned to face the ocean.

When she looked toward the water, she saw Josephine on the gallery, crawling up the handrail with all her might. She must have somehow climbed up the masonry with her bare fingernails, using her preternatural strength. The wind was blowing her hair every which way, and her dress billowed like a loose mast. When the *rusalka* spotted Zarya, she smiled.

It all felt eerily familiar.

The door separating the gallery from the lantern room was shut, but it suddenly occurred to Zarya that she had not locked it after her the last time she was up in the gallery with Sean. She lunged toward the knob, fumbling with the ancient lock, but Josephine was making way. Already, she had swung herself over the handrail, her left foot in contact with the gallery.

Zarya could not see the lock too well in the darkness. She fumbled with it one last time before Josephine threw herself at the door, body-slamming it open an inch. The door screeched.

Through that little opening in the door, Josephine forced her hand in and grabbed Zarya by the wrist. Her grasp was deathly cold.

Zarya retreated, pulling away her hand.

As soon as she did, the creature won. The door swung open, and Josephine now stood in the doorway, arms dangling idly at her sides. She grinned that skeletal grin of hers, exposing her corroded teeth. There was something almost innocent in her smile, as if Josephine were reuniting with a lost friend. She must have had no idea how frightening she looked.

But then again, how could she? She was so consumed by her hunger for love that she had forgotten to consider anyone else.

"Please," said Zarya, deciding she would first try to reason with the creature, "I know what it is you want." She looked from side to side. There were two ways out—through the staircase, and through the gallery. But if she chose the latter, she would surely fall to her demise in the stormy, rocky waters below.

Josephine cocked her head to the side, but she did not take another step forward yet. Tufts of hair dangled down her chest like seaweed. At last, her mouth opened, and she answered in that gilded voice of hers. "And what is it I want?"

"Love," replied Zarya. "A child of your own. Retribution."

Josephine's face melted with joy. "Exactly," she lilted. "You truly see me for who I am. With you, I will finally be happy."

She prepared to step forward now, and Zarya had to rush out the rest of her speech.

"No, it wouldn't work," she blurted out. "Only love that is given freely can save you. Not love taken by force."

The joy evaporated from Josephine's eyes now. Her brows flattened. "You will learn to love me, in time."

"I'll give you something even better," Zarya offered. "I'll write an article about you. I'll tell everyone your story—about Hurley, about Thomas, everything. They'll know the truth about what happened to the lighthouse keeper's wife."

Josephine produced a small chuckle. "It's kind of you to offer. But I would really rather have you."

The *rusalka* took another step forward with those bony, wan feet. Her soles made a spattering sound against the wooden floor.

In an instant, Zarya pulled the set of matches from her back pocket and slid one from the box. With each footstep, Josephine closed the gap between them. Zarya floundered with the first match, dropping it to the ground. Then she grasped a second match between her fingers, scratched the side of the matchbox, and heard the deep inhale of fire coming to life.

Orange light danced across Josephine's face. Zarya felt heat at the tips of her fingers. She looked down and saw a teardrop of fire burning at the match. For a moment, Josephine looked at her in surprise, as if none of her victims had tried this before.

Before the *rusalka* could stop her, Zarya tossed the match onto the ground, where the inky puddle of oil turned the teardrop into an ocean of fire. The wooden floorboards, furniture, and wall panels were already catching.

She felt warmth at her ankles, at first just a delicate caress, followed by hotter burning. From where she stood, there was only one way out between the flames—a sliver of stonework leading to the door. Between her and Josephine, the flames fanned all around.

It was then that the *rusalka* reached over the flames and once more grasped Zarya's hand. But this time, it was not with force. Zarya peered into the creature's eyes and realized that she was clinging in fear. All the rage had gone out of her eyes. She just needed a hand to hold in her last moments.

The fire was starting to dance across Josephine's dress and skin, but Zarya let her hold on a moment longer. She stared into those silver eyes filled with so much sadness and grief. It was only once she felt a burning sensation on her forearm that Zarya finally realized the fire had taken a life of its own. If she wanted to make it out alive, she needed to go, *now*.

Zarya broke free of Josephine's hand and leaped across the room, nearly falling to her knees as she reached the threshold.

The *rusalka* simply stood there, frozen as if the stench of smoke had reminded her of someone she loved. She did not fight the fire—

not even as the sleeves of her dress caught and her skin was enveloped in amber light. Instead, she just looked at Zarya with a melancholic stare.

Zarya would have told Josephine that her suffering was about to end. That she promised to avenge her death. But there was no time. Instead, she scampered down the staircase, feeling the heat of flames follow her, letting the fire light her way. She choked on smoke but carried on, not allowing herself to fall until the moment when she reached the last step.

There, she thunked onto the floor in an uncontrolled landing. She lost consciousness before she could feel the fire at her fingertips.

Josephine, 2023

Chapter 36

After the Irving descendant had stopped resisting her scratches, Josephine rose from the ground and started towards the lighthouse. She snarled, remembering those countless days at the Rock enveloped in fog, the lonely nights she had spent alone in bed while Thomas was up in the lantern room. This would certainly need to be the last time she ever stepped foot in the lighthouse.

An idea struck Josephine. The lantern room.

The young woman would surely secure the downstairs door and the windows, but she might forget to secure the door in the lantern room. It was Josephine's best bet to penetrate the walls of the tower. She would climb up the side of the structure just like she had done the night she'd taken the boy.

The boy. Where was he now, anyway? Running back to the Irving estate, most likely, like he did every summer. Josephine had managed to keep him away while his parents were still alive, but each year it grew harder. No matter how much she tried to raise him as her own, the boy never quite accepted her as his mother.

Josephine had loved him to the best of her ability. She had played with him and held him in her arms and whispered lullabies to him. Sometimes, she wanted to shake him senseless, to yell at him and demand an answer for why he was always running away from her. He was so ungrateful.

It had taken her a few years to realize that the boy would never truly love her. He was just like the sailors, with his mind on another woman. And so, she had kept trying. Josephine had continued luring people to the ocean, convinced that this time would be different. She had learned to identify those with a sad look in their eyes, those who would more easily be drawn out to sea.

With this young woman, she had spotted a sense of longing. Josephine needed a child, and this young woman needed a mother. She could sense it. She did not even know the girl's name, but she recognized the grief inside her.

Josephine crawled around the side of the lighthouse, to the outcropping of bedrock separating the tower from the ocean. The storm raged on, sending waves up so high that Josephine could feel their spray on her skin.

She started up the side of the lighthouse, her fingernails digging into the places where the paint had peeled, her feet finding little nooks between the stones. The stonework was slick, but she had no fear. After all, if she fell, she was already dead.

She reached the top of the tower in no time. There, her hands curled around the gallery handrail. She pulled herself up to see inside the lantern room.

Despite the moonless night, she saw the girl inside, through the glass. Josephine hurled herself up the handrails and planted her feet on the gallery. She approached the door to the lantern room.

The girl had also rushed to the door, though, by the looks of it, she was trying to lock it. By now, Josephine was used to forcing her way into people's hearts. She threw her entire body weight against the door until it gave way an inch. Then, she slinked her hand through that inch and grabbed the girl by the wrist.

The girl pulled away her wrist and fell away from the door. Josephine had not expected a warm homecoming, but she would win the girl's affection in due time.

She swung open the door and stood in the doorway, smiling. She looked upon the girl, who now seemed much older than

Josephine had initially estimated.

"Please," the girl said. "I know what it is you want."

Josephine was intrigued. "And what is it I want?"

"Love. A child of your own. Retribution."

For the first time, Josephine had picked the right person to bring with her to the ocean. This girl knew her innermost desires!

"Exactly," she said. "You truly see me for who I am. With you, I will finally be happy."

She stepped forward to embrace the girl.

But the girl continued, "No, it wouldn't work. Only love that is given freely can save you. Not love taken by force."

Josephine's elation just moments prior dissolved all too quickly. Why was this little girl being so insolent? Why would she not give her love freely?

She batted away the urge to cry. "You will learn to love me, in time."

"I'll give you something even better. I'll write an article about you. I'll tell everyone your story—about Hurley, about Thomas, everything. They'll know the truth about what happened to the lighthouse keeper's wife."

Josephine chuckled. This girl knew more about her life than anyone had. And it was one thing to be known, but quite another to be loved. Josephine preferred love.

She said, "It's kind of you to offer. But I would really rather have you."

She took another step forward into the room. As she approached, the girl pulled some strange-looking matches from her strange-looking trousers. She fumbled with a match, dropping it on the floor before once more fumbling for another match.

Then, fire flickered from between her fingers. Josephine had not seen fire in many, many moons. It did not exist underwater. In fact, she had forgotten its existence.

When the girl tossed the match onto the floor, something liquid caught fire. Right away, the scent transported Josephine back to the year 1837—the sound of her home crackling in the flames, Mama screaming for her life, Papa already too dead to scream out. The emptiness gripped her all at once, and Josephine could not bear to be alone with it once more.

She reached for the girl's hand across the fire. The girl had looked frightened before, but now there seemed to be something else etched on her face. Pity? Kindness? Sympathy?

Tears welled in Josephine's eyes. This was the closest she had ever gotten to love in centuries, since the moment she had bid her sister goodbye in Maine. What was this girl's look of goodwill, if not love?

Now that she had felt even a dollop of love, Josephine let the flames engulf her. The girl extricated her fingers from Josephine's grip and bolted toward the staircase. Josephine let her go.

Once the girl was gone, Josephine watched her own reflection in the windows, her limbs alight with fire.

She did not feel pain. Instead, she let out a laugh. This tower of gloom was finally about to burn down, just as she'd always desired.

And then, beyond the glass, on the gallery, two figures materialized from thin air. Josephine had long ago forgotten their faces, but now she recognized them with ease. They were waiting for her, on the other side of the glass.

"Mama," she whispered, as the flames took the last of her spirit from this world.

Zarya, 2023

Chapter 37

Zarya awoke beneath a sterile overhead light that somehow seared into her eyes more blindingly than the fire had. An electric monitor beeped in the corner, mapping out her heartbeat onscreen.

Becoming aware of a stinging sensation on her left forearm, Zarya craned her neck to look down. Her arm was wrapped in some sort of bandage, a slippery salve glazing the skin beneath it. Aside from her wound, she could feel the bleach-white bedsheets underneath her, coarse from overwashing. She could wiggle her toes under the blanket, could adjust her eyes in the glaring light. She was alive, alright.

On her right, Sean sat in a chair, head lolling against the wall with his eyelids closed. Above him, a clock showed the time 12:45. Zarya did not know if it was morning or night, or today's date. Just as she was about to ask, the sound of her ruffling beneath the sheets awoke Sean from his dozing.

When he saw Zarya's eyes open, Sean vaulted from his seat. In a moment, he was bedside, his hands clasped around hers.

"Finally, you're up," he said, placing his palm on her good arm—the one not wrapped in bandages. "You've been out for so long."

"How long?" Zarya asked, half afraid of his answer.

"Ten hours."

"Am I—okay?" Zarya lifted her bad arm. "What's under here?"

"Second-degree burns. You're fine otherwise. The doctors said you inhaled a lot of smoke, but you're going to be just fine."

Zarya swallowed. "What do the doctors think happened?"

"Well, the police guy was here earlier. The one from the Defenders."

"Dan."

"Yeah. He said he'd take care of it." Sean raised an eyebrow, seeming unimpressed. "The story is that there was a strange woman out by the cove last night. You and I had broken into the lighthouse for a romantic evening, and she set the place on fire. After attacking Mrs. Irving, of course. The police guy said our cover will be corroborated by Mrs. Irving's story."

Zarya propped herself up on her elbows. "Mrs. Irving is alive?"

"By a hair, but yes. She's just down the hall."

"How is she?"

Sean shrugged. "I don't know. Want to see for yourself?"

Zarya looked side to side across the room. Aside from the powdery, white-painted walls and the medical equipment, she spotted her mother's handbag on the ground, below the chair where Sean had been napping.

"Are my parents here?"

Sean gave a nod. "They went down to the cafeteria not long ago, but they're here."

That was all she needed to hear. Zarya ripped the monitors from her wrist and tore the covers off. She planted her feet on the cold vinyl flooring, then got up from the bed. "I'm going to see Mrs. Irving before they come back."

Sean proffered a hand, but Zarya denied him, shaking her head.

"Let me talk to her alone."

He didn't argue with her. After all, the woman hated him.

Zarya ambled down the hospital corridor, trying to look

inconspicuous as nurses and doctors walked past with stethoscopes draped around their necks and patient charts in hand. She peeked through each door to see if it was Mrs. Irving's room, but it wasn't until the very end of the hall that she found the hotel heiress.

Zarya could tell it was Mrs. Irving from her head of white hair and translucent fingers. When she knocked on the door, Mrs. Irving shot a look at the window, and her face was swollen with purple bruises and fresh gashes. She lay swaddled in blankets.

Zarya stepped in, her heart already heavy from the battered sight of the woman. The door made a clicking sound as it shut behind her.

"I'm as surprised to see you alive as you must be to see me," the old lady croaked.

Her room was a replica of Zarya's room down the hall. Zarya sank in the chair pushed up against the wall.

"I admit, I didn't think I'd see you again," she said.

"That *thing* tried its best to kill me, but it was distracted." Mrs. Irving peered at Zarya through the one eye that wasn't shut in a bulge. "You're the one it wanted. So, how did you get away from it? I hear you burned down the lighthouse?"

Zarya nodded. "With her in it."

"Bit cruel, isn't it? You're the one always yapping about empathy."

Zarya ignored the woman's sardonic tone. "Empathy doesn't mean letting someone take over your life," she said. "Sometimes, empathy means saying enough."

"Well, that you did." A smile spread across Mrs. Irving's face, which looked like it must have hurt, because she winced right away. The stitches were fresh on her skin.

"And besides," Zarya went on, "It was an act of mercy. Her existence was misery."

Josephine had never found rest when her soul passed through the element of water. Perhaps, now that her soul had been initiated into the next stage by the element of fire, she could at last be with her parents.

"You finally understand." Mrs. Irving raised an admonishing finger at Zarya. "You finally understand why I was so hellbent on killing her, don't you?"

Zarya considered the question.

She recalled the other day in the garden, when she had seen for the first time how much Mrs. Irving was willing to go to war for the people of this town. Behind her tough exterior, there was something softer there. She would have battled anyone who threatened her family.

The silence between them had grown almost intolerable. At last, Zarya broke it. "I'm glad to see you're alive, Mrs. Irving," she said. "And thank you, by the way."

"For what?"

Zarya smiled. The old woman was always so preoccupied with plotting her next move, that she found it easy to forget even recent events.

"For saving my life?" Zarya reminded her.

Mrs. Irving rolled her eyes. "And you made such a fuss about me tracking your whereabouts. If I hadn't, you'd be at the bottom of the ocean now."

"I'm sure you're right." Zarya gave a lackluster smile as she stood up. "By the way, I'm giving my two weeks' notice."

Mrs. Irving threw her a baleful look. "Now that we finally get along? Why on earth?"

Zarya shrugged, already sinking into the doorknob. "It's time for something new. I'll move out my stuff from the attic." She did not linger to hear Mrs. Irving's rebukes.

When she was halfway out, Mrs. Irving inquired, "And what about the video recording, Zarya?"

Zarya cleared her throat before saying, "I've decided not to release the footage from the boat."

The woman blinked through bloodshot eyes. "What changed your mind?"

"No one outside of this town will believe the full story. But they don't need to. I'll tell them the half of the story they need to hear, let their imaginations run wild at the rest, and I'm sure they'll come to the conclusions on their own."

Zarya returned to the hallway, gave one last wave through the glass, and turned on her heels.

The corridor was a blur of faces. At the end of the hall, two familiar faces had just entered through the double doors. The woman had a fine, pointed nose, pale hair, and freckled cheeks, while the man towered over her, blue eyes bespectacled above a straight nose.

They saw Zarya right away and bolted across the corridor, stopping only once she was in their arms.

"Zarychka, what happened?" her mother asked, pulling back to get a good look at Zarya. "Why were you out there?"

Zarya said nothing. She simply smiled. After the news she was about to give them, they would need this tender moment to remember.

Zarya, 2023

Chapter 38

The garden was very different from the last time Zarya had seen it. Instead of storm clouds and rain, there was nothing overhead but the cyan-blue sky. Even the leaves in the trees seemed to have matured overnight, the once-lurid green replaced by dark, thick foliage that cast shade beneath its canopy.

Sean walked beside her, a basket dangling from his hand. Inside the basket, Zarya had packed the supplies they needed for the rest of the ritual—brightly colored ribbons, a dress, and an axe.

When they got to the birch tree with ribbons in its hair, Zarya knelt beside the trunk and started rummaging through the basket. She wrested a dress out of the basket, thick chiffon weighing down her arms. It was in a similar style to what Josephine had been wearing, dark blue with puff sleeves.

Zarya pinned the dress around the tree's trunk using twine, and then she took a step back to assess the creation.

The tree was a far less frightening sight than the *rusalka*, but even seeing the same style of dress made Zarya shiver.

"Ready?" asked Sean. He lifted the ax in his hands and squatted in front of the tree.

Zarya nodded.

Sean whacked the bottom of the trunk with the blade of his ax. Such a young tree, the birch craned backward from the very first impact. At the second impact, it made a snapping sound, and at the third, it fell onto the forest floor.

They carried it to the parking lot together, though it was admittedly quite light. Sean wrapped it atop the roof of Zarya's car with bungee cord, and then they hopped inside. Passersby would surely think they were out of their minds for carrying a tree dressed in women's clothing atop the vehicle, but soon it would not matter what the townspeople thought of Zarya.

It was a short drive to the Rock. Once there, Sean cut the cord, and then they were hauling the tree down to Dead Man's Cove together. The forest was not quite as menacing as before. The storm had made the greenery vibrant with life.

There, up ahead, the Victorian lighthouse was almost unrecognizable. Many of the stones had fallen apart in a charred heap. The tower no longer loomed over the horizon. Now, the black stones and the outcroppings blended into each other, giving the Rock a naked look.

There was, however, a cordon of police tape around the circumference. After all, the police had found the bones of a woman amongst the ruins—though Zarya was fairly sure they would never identify her. As far as the law was concerned, Josephine's remains belonged to an unidentified woman who had self-immolated, presumably someone not from these parts.

Zarya's gaze loitered over the wreckage, still unsure whether Josephine's figure would rise from the ashes. When no figure emerged, she gathered the courage to avert her gaze.

This time, there were no undead sailors roaming the sand, no ghost ships careening on the horizon. There was only the gentle lapping of water beneath Zarya's toes as they stepped into the cove, the prickling of sunshine soaking into her skin.

They waded into the water thigh-deep, then gave the birch a strong push out to sea. Zarya walked back to shore, Sean not far behind, and the two sat on a piece of driftwood until the ocean took the birch out past the cove, to wherever the ocean took things.

Zarya dragged her fingers across the water-polished surface of the driftwood beneath her hips. "I wonder where this one came from. How far it must have traveled to get here. What it must have seen." Maybe this wood was from a forest that had lived thousands of years ago. Maybe it had come from Russia, where it had seen *rusalki* of its own.

"You have a unique way of looking at things," said Sean. Across the driftwood, his fingers crept up on hers. "I want to ask you something."

She detected a hint of nervousness in his tone. His voice didn't have its usual velvetiness.

"Okay," Zarya responded, warily.

"I'd like to take you out to dinner."

The words hung between them, punctured only occasionally by the sound of songbirds in the forest behind them. Zarya considered what this meant. A date here? A date in LA? A long-distance relationship, eventually? And he didn't even know yet…

"I'm moving to the city," she blurted out.

Sean's eyes widened a smidge. "Which city?"

"I'm not sure yet. I just know I'm leaving this place."

"Okay." Sean bit his bottom lip, deep in thought. "Well, can I still take you on a date?"

"Yes," she answered, before she had a chance to talk herself out of it.

The answer seemed to have assuaged his fears, because Sean's body relaxed, and he put his head on Zarya's shoulder. She listened to the rise and fall of his breath, which was becoming increasingly synchronized with the rising and falling of crests on the water.

After a while, Sean lifted his head. "West Coast Media won't publish the article," he blurted, as if he had been waiting for the right time to utter the words.

"Why not?"

"It hints at mysticism, it's vague about the sources, and it blends history with an opinion piece." The muscles along his jaw were tight.

"In their words."

"Well, we still have to publish it," Zarya maintained. She had made Josephine a promise, and she intended to keep that promise even if Josephine was gone for good.

"I know. Which is why we'll post it on a blog."

Sean reached into his pocket, from where he pulled out his phone. After scrolling through a couple of pages, he handed the phone to Zarya.

She peered at the letters on the screen.

The Life and Death of Josephine Byrne
By Zarya Petrov & Sean Hays

Off the coast of Washington is a place known as the Graveyard of the Pacific, where hundreds of shipwrecks have vanished, and dozens of locals have gone missing by the water. Town lore warns of undead spirits in the ocean. Townspeople call them sirens, vengeful and bloodthirsty creatures that lure victims out at sea.

In my mother tongue (Russian), we call them rusalki, *and we appease them in early June with an annual ritual, so that they will take mercy on the living. During the seventh week after Easter, it is said the* rusalki *can roam freely on land, swinging from willow trees and drowning anyone who comes near the water with their hair.*

But what lies beneath the surface of this legend is a true story—one of tragedy, loneliness, and sin. It connects the lighthouse to the Irving Hotel, both of which were erected by Scottish businessman Hurley Irving during the late 1840s.

Hurley emigrated from Scotland and made a fortune settling in the Pacific Northwest during a time when not many populated the area. He built himself a business in mining, railroad engineering, ship manufacturing, real estate, quarrying, saw milling, and eventually politics. By 1949, he had accumulated dozens of acres of property, upon which he built a mansion. Today, this estate is known as the Irving Hotel, where hundreds of patrons sojourn each year.

In 1850, Hurley decided to build a lighthouse at the peninsula

Rock, thinking it would secure the safety of his freight ships in the stormy Pacific. He hired a lighthouse keeper known as Thomas Byrne. Thomas, who had been serving as head keeper in Maine, was transferred to the Rock to be its first keeper. He brought along his newlywed wife, a woman named Josephine born to French-Irish parents.

But Josephine did not have a happy history. Orphaned by a housefire at age seven, Josephine had been adopted by her older sister, Charlotte. Barely old enough to adopt her, Charlotte made do with what she could. Their parents' inheritance was destroyed in the fire, so together the two lived in poverty. Charlotte married when Josephine was an adolescent. As for Josephine, it was rumored that she was promiscuous, and no one but the lighthouse keeper would agree to marry her.

Life in Washington was not easy for Josephine. Unaccustomed to the dreary weather and the isolation of living in a lighthouse, she fell into what was at the time called melancholia. Bouts of sadness plagued her. Married life was no solace, either, since Thomas had little interest in the partnership. He had married because it was expected of him to continue his family's legacy, but correspondence between him and the local medic, Dr. Ainsworth, indicated he put little effort into starting a family with Josephine. Dr. Ainsworth believed quite firmly that Josephine's ailments would be resolved once her womb was no longer barren.

When the most powerful man in the Pacific Northwest, Hurley, took a liking toward Josephine, a love affair quickly unfolded. Josephine slid deeper into darkness, in love with him but unable to have him. Reports mention her storming through town unattended, looking frenzied and unwell. She was sometimes seen swimming naked in the cove beside the lighthouse. Other times, she could not get herself out of bed.

Upon discovering that Hurley's wife, Amelia, was with child, Josephine decided that there was nothing left for her on earth. In 1851, she wrote Hurley a suicide note and jumped from the Rock into the ocean. When Amelia came across the note, a dark family secret was born.

Amelia told no one about the suicide note, so that Hurley's reputation would not be sullied in the community. Her descendants also kept the secret. But evidence linking Hurley to Josephine's death was discovered this year when an anonymous source found Josephine's suicide letter in the Irving Hotel.

The tragedy does not end there. Following Josephine's suicide, ships began sinking along the coast. Sailors' bodies washed ashore near the lighthouse, in the place now known as Dead Man's Cove. Not long after, beachgoers also began disappearing in the water, with no earthly explanation. Thomas stashed away erratic diary entries for the next lighthouse keeper. Eventually, he returned to Maine, convinced his dead wife was watching him from the water. But the following lighthouse keeper did not stay long either, citing that he could hear a woman's voice singing at nighttime. After several tries, Hurley was forced to abandon his dreams of a lighthouse to guide his ships.

In 1854, tragedy finally struck the Irving family personally. On a night in early June, the youngest Irving boy vanished from his bedroom without a trace. The open window suggested someone had taken him, but it was a long way down from the tall-ceilinged second story of the house. No one considered that this disappearance might be related to the death of Josephine three years prior. No one knew how much she had desired a child of her own, nor that she had declared her love for Hurley.

Are the happenings of this small town unrelated? Are the locals' disappearances explained by natural causes, such as violent ocean currents in these parts? Was the Irving boy simply kidnapped? Is local legend merely a way for people to make meaning of a series of tragedies that otherwise seem too incomprehensible? Or are the events all connected, knotted together by lovelessness and sorrow?

Today, history still leaves its mark on the present. Just days ago, the abandoned lighthouse burned down after a woman attacked Joan Irving, heiress of the Irving Hotel, before self-immolating in the lantern room. Last month, Jessica Robinson was the most recent victim of the Graveyard of the Pacific, having disappeared from Dead Man's Cove without a trace. This town will never heal until it brings into the light the generational secrets swept under the rug.

Josephine Byrne wanted to be loved more than anything. She searched for wholeness in another person. She searched for wholeness in a baby. But love isn't selfish. Until we discover that, none of us will ever be free.

Zarya smiled. "It's too bad we can't tell them it's over now."

Sean chuckled. "That's alright. You'll have paranormal podcasters coming around these parts for years to follow."

They waited awhile on the beach. Seagulls flew overhead, picking at traces of mussels along the beach. The afternoon sun warmed her skin, as did Sean's hand across her knuckles.

Tomorrow, Sean was boarding a plane back to LA. Zarya did not know what the future held for them, but for once, she had decided to let things unfold as they would.

For now, she had an even harder task at hand.

The house smelled of minced meat, thyme, and carrots as Zarya stepped in. She could hear the sizzling of food on the stove, of hot oil crackling against cast iron, of her mother's feet shuffling in the kitchen. Zarya's mother must not have heard her come in over the loud whirring of the vent.

Zarya hung her jacket on the coat hanger by the door. She stepped into the kitchen, stopping to kiss her mother hello.

"My sweetheart!" her mother exclaimed, wearing the look of joy one might have found on a three-year-old. "You're dressed so scantily! Aren't you cold? You'll catch a draft."

"It's, like, eighty degrees in here."

"I feel like it's been so long since we had dinner together."

Zarya said nothing. It had been less than two weeks, but she and her mother had different definitions of a long time. Instead, she sat by the dining table, toying with the table runner. It had been brought straight from St. Petersburg, handcrafted from white linen, and stitched with blue thread.

Across the room, her mother turned down the vent. "We've been so worried about you, Zarya. There's nothing worse for a mother than to hear her own child is in the hospital. Promise me you'll never do that to me again, okay?"

"How can I promise that, Mama? I can't predict what might happen."

Her mother came by the dining table to remove the table runner and replace it with a tablecloth depicting lemons. It was Zarya's favorite tablecloth—and surely no coincidence. Her mother was trying. She had no idea what Zarya needed, but she was giving her best guess.

"Now that it's just the two of us, before your father comes..." Zarya's mother cast a furtive look over her shoulder. "You can tell me, Zarya. What really happened that night?"

Zarya sighed. She had her story memorized forward and backward, but there was no point reciting it to her mother. The woman always knew when she wasn't telling the whole truth. And besides, a part of her longed to finally be out with it. Despite everything her mother had done wrong, she was the one who had warned her of *rusalki* in the first place.

She said it plainly, as if she were reading off ingredients from a food label. "The *rusalka* attacked Mrs. Irving. I hid in the lighthouse, and I set her on fire."

Her mother's turquoise eyes had widened. Her lashes batted against the tips of her eyebrows. No louder than a whisper, she asked, "It was really a *rusalka*?"

Zarya gave a terse nod. "It's over now."

"Are you sure? I mean, maybe you should move in with us for a while, just to be safe—"

"I'm sure," Zarya interrupted, her tone a little more brusque than she had intended.

Her mother blinked a few times, then went to retrieve the pans from the stove. "I'm glad you're safe, Zarya, but I really do worry about you."

"Is Papa coming, too?" Zarya looked around, as if her father might be hiding in the crevices of the kitchen. She would need them both here for what she was about to say.

"Yes, he's coming." Increasing her volume by several decibels, Zarya's mother cried out, "Oleg! Time to eat!"

Zarya heard footsteps coming from the office, her father

burbling under his breath. When he saw her, he stopped to give her a kiss on the forehead. Perhaps the hospital scare had thawed his heart a little.

Zarya's mother had just finished adding the last few details to the table, and now she pored over the buffet bowls. "Let's eat," she said.

They ate quietly at first, though Zarya could not say whether it was out of hunger or unease. She relished this last moment of silence before the news she was about to break. As their chewing grew slower, Zarya took a deep breath and clasped her hands together under the table. Her heart was racing. Surely, that wasn't a good sign.

"I need to tell you both something."

Their eyes met hers. Panic instantly found its way onto her mother's face. "What is it, Zarya? Is everything alright? Don't keep us in suspense, please."

"Let her tell us," her husband chided her.

By now, Zarya's heart rate had increased even further. Her voice trembled as she announced, "I'm moving."

Blank stares faced her.

"Out of the hotel?" her mother probed. "Where to? Are you moving back in here?"

"Yes, out of the hotel… And out of town."

More blank stares.

"Wha—to where?"

Zarya shrugged. "I'm still figuring that out. I have my eye on the cost of rent in a couple of different cities, and when I find a good deal, I'll pick that one."

Her mother looked like she had just been stabbed with a dull knife. Her brows pointed downward girlishly. "You can't be serious. You're going to be so impulsive?"

"It's not impulsive. It's something I've been considering for a while—"

Zarya's mother had picked up steam. "Is this how we raised

you, to just pick a place on the map and upend your life? And you're just *telling* us, without even running it by us first?"

Zarya squeezed her fingers tighter under the table. "I'm telling you and not asking you because it's my decision." These last words, she barely had the courage for. "Not yours."

Her father, as always, was mute.

Across the table, her mother had overcome the metaphorical stabbing and was now determined to stab back. "This doesn't just concern you! Haven't you thought about how this will affect all of us? You'll be thirty soon, and I assume you want a husband and kids. Haven't you thought about what this will mean for us? Who will look after your children?"

Ah yes, her unborn children. As ridiculous as it felt, Zarya had indeed considered them. When she'd seen Josephine swinging from the willow with the little boy in hand, singing her lullaby, Zarya had realized something: Josephine must have thought she was a good mother. She must have thought she was just looking after her baby.

But all along, she had been looking after her own interests. Her own needs had come first, her desperate need to fill the void inside her. She had been so incapable of distinguishing between self and other, that she had assumed what was good for *her* was also good for the baby.

It was not.

Zarya's mother did not wait for a response before continuing. "You're going to do what you always do, which is run away."

"I'm not running away," said Zarya, and for the first time it was true. "I'm doing what's right for me."

Time seemed to stand still for the rest of the dinner. Zarya tried to swallow as quietly as possible while forks scraped against dishes and a bird chattered outside the window.

Afterward, when Zarya's mother was loading the dishes into the dishwasher with shaking hands, Zarya reached for the stack of plates, but her mother pulled it away gruffly.

Normally, Zarya would have run to the bathroom to hide. She

would have avoided her mother's gaze. Her voice would have been mousy and small, hoping not to trigger Mean Mommy.

But this time was different. She smiled and looked her parents in the eye as if nothing had happened. She pretended not to hear the jabs her mother murmured under her breath.

"Will you be staying the night?" her mother asked through clenched jaws.

Smiling, Zarya shook her head. "I have to go get my things in order."

Zarya gave her mother a hug goodbye, which her mother tolerated listlessly, after which she headed for the door.

As she stood on the threshold of her childhood home, peering back at her parents, Zarya finally understood. There was no one who could fill the emptiness inside her mother. She was done living her life as a placeholder in someone else's soul.

Then Zarya got into her car, started the engine, turned the corner, and was gone. No lullaby echoed through her head, luring her back to the ocean. No lullaby lured her back home, either. The waters were still. The spell had been broken.

Zarya's mother had called them *rusalki*. Josephine's mother had called them *selkies*. Her father had called them *melusines*. They went by various names all over the world, these spirits of the water, with each mother passing down the legend in her own mother tongue. What they were called was not important. They all spoke of the same thing, the same pull of the ocean.

Once, Bruno had asked Zarya why the siren had picked her. At the time, she hadn't known. But now, she understood.

It hadn't merely been by chance. Josephine had smelled the vulnerability on Zarya. She had sensed that Zarya needed a mother just as much as she needed a child.

But it had all just been a ghost. Nothing could ever give Zarya the mother she had deserved, just like nothing could ever give Josephine the mother she had lost.

A tear budded in the corner of Zarya's eye. She was about to wipe it away, but she let it linger a moment longer. It crawled down her cheek, making its way to her mouth, where Zarya licked away the taste of saltwater. She cried not for the mother she was leaving behind, but for the mother that could have been.

Grief could be a funny thing. Sometimes, the biggest loss of all was for a person who had never even existed.

Afterword

Behind the History

A year and a half before writing this novel, I moved to Seattle. Right away, I fell in love with the raw nature of the Pacific Northwest—the giant evergreens, the jagged mountains, the mist, the crystal-blue alpine lakes…

Much of this novel's setting is a fictionalized amalgam of various places I visited along the Pacific Northwest coast. The lobby of the Irving Hotel was inspired by the Shelburne Hotel in Seaview, Washington, while parts of its interior and exterior were inspired by the Craigdarroch Castle in Victoria, British Columbia, as well as the countless other Victorian homes on Vancouver Island.

The coastal town where the novel takes place is based on the main strip of Seaside, Oregon, which lives in constant threat of tsunami if The Very Big One strikes. The lighthouse was inspired by the one beside Dead Man's Cove in Cape Disappointment. The town in the novel is never named because it is meant to synthesize the history of various places along the Northwestern coast.

Along my travels in the Pacific Northwest, I heard the echoes of tragic stories. Although the novel you have just read is entirely fictional, the following historical details inspired its first seeds.

The ocean floor along the coast of Washington is indeed known as the Graveyard of the Pacific, due to the countless shipwrecks in the area. The Vandalia was one of them. The captain was indeed named Captain Beard.

Early settlers developed expansive business empires in the area, sometimes at the expense of those less fortunate. For example, Robert Dunsmuir was a Scottish-Canadian businessman who built a fortune in the city of Victoria. Though he was initially regarded as an underdog who cared about his miners, an article from 2020 written by Ann Edelstein titled "The Dark Money That Built Victoria's Craigdarroch Castle" suggested Dunsmuir's enterprises involved the scapegoating of Chinese workers, forceful evictions, and railways whose construction shrank indigenous territory. I do not pretend to know the truth about Dunsmuir's character, but Edelstein's article inspired some of the details of Hurley's business endeavors.

Dusnmuir's daughter, Anne Euphemia "Effie," had troubles of her own. Letters from her friend Kathleen O'Reilly describe symptoms that might echo our modern-day understanding of mania: "Effie has simply been on the go since we came here… She is not looking well… She is as thin as a knife. The people here seem to think she is rather mad to hunt all day and dance all night, any spare time being filled up by bicycling, at homes, or skating!!... Her appearance is quite sad and Jessie is worried about her."

Josephine's character was in part inspired by the haunting portrait of Effie, but also by a tragedy further south, at the lighthouse near Dead Man's Cove in Washington. There, the lighthouse keeper's wife was suspected to have jumped from the edge of the cliff not long after being diagnosed with melancholia in 1923.

Tragedy also struck further inland, near Lake Pleasant, to a woman named Rose Rucker in the 1890s. According to *Women to Be Reckoned With*, a book about remarkable Washington women throughout history, Rose found herself embroiled in a love triangle on more than one occasion. Her fate ultimately ended in a double-murder suicide committed by a jealous suitor.

These little seedlings of inspiration eventually amassed into a full work of fiction. Aside from the historical occurrences I just listed, the characters and all other details in this novel are fictionalized, and any resemblance to actual persons, living or dead, is purely coincidental.

Behind the Psychology

I intended to write Josephine as a character who suffers not from Bipolar Disorder, nor from "melancholia," the predecessor of what is now called depression. Rather, this novel is meant to explore the inner workings of a different affliction called Borderline Personality Disorder (BPD). Its core components include a bottomless feeling of emptiness and a terrifying fear of abandonment.

Of course, BPD comes with many different facets and presentations. The depictions shown in Josephine and Zarya's mother are only two such examples, and they are not meant to be taken as representative of everyone's struggle with this disorder.

BPD most often develops due to early trauma. Sometimes, its sufferers have experienced an early loss or a series of attachment ruptures. Other times, they grow up in chronically invalidating homes which, combined with a temperamental predisposition for emotion dysregulation, creates this heartbreaking personality structure.

People who struggle with BPD go through extreme anguish every day, but it is not an incurable disease. The biggest antidote is a stable, secure attachment with at least one individual. In realizing that they will not be abandoned, the sufferer gradually releases their frantic attempts at clinging to others. This secure attachment must also be accompanied by validation and boundaries, a balance that is slippery to strike for both professionals and laypeople. A person with BPD must be made to feel like their emotions are heard, and they must at the same time understand that they cannot engulf other people. Boundaries and safety must coexist.

I have great compassion for individuals with BPD, and I also have great compassion for those who were raised by parents with untreated BPD. Many individuals with BPD do not cause harm to their loved ones, and the disorder is treatable. The issue, however, arises when a person is unaware of their affliction and/or does not have the resources to seek help.

A parent with unaddressed BPD may sometimes take part in enmeshment, codependency, emotional incest, control, parentification, and emotional blackmail, among other things. The child quickly learns that they exist to make their parent full, a task that is sure to fail every time, because no one can make a person full except themselves. The child is treated like a "best friend" upon whom the parent dumps their grown-up issues.

In such parent-child dyads, the roles are upside-down: the parent takes on a childlike level of helplessness and neediness, while the child must take on the responsibilities of a parent at a very delicate age. The child may go on to become an adult who chronically feels they must take care of other people, thus attracting partners and friends who are unwilling to care for themselves. Alternatively—like Zarya's character—they may avoid attachment at all costs, afraid of being engulfed by other people.

The child may feel guilty when they try to individuate, seek out privacy, honor their personal agency, or pursue their own needs. They might struggle to regulate the parent's emotions, not understanding that it is not their responsibility to do so. They may develop BPD themselves if the combination of trauma, invalidation, and temperamental predisposition to emotion dysregulation activates the disorder.

It is a paradox that relationships can heal us, but they can also be what breaks us.

Acknowledgments

First and foremost, thank you to my husband Nikolai, the first person to read my manuscripts—who always catches bizarre word choices that reveal English isn't my mother tongue—and the only person I trust enough to read my first drafts.

Thank you also to Oishika and Ginny for their beta-reading feedback. I'd also like to extend my gratitude to Nicola from The Literary Consultancy, whose editorial feedback helped me get this novel ready for publication.

And of course, thank you to you—the reader—for taking the time to pick up my novel. As an indie author, every purchase means the world to me. I still cannot believe I get to pursue my lifelong dream of writing, and it's all because of your support. If you enjoyed the book, passing along the word to someone else who might enjoy it would be greatly appreciated.

Book Club Discussion Questions

1. In what ways do Josephine and Zarya approach loneliness and attachment?

2. What do you think each of the following symbolizes in the novel?

   The ocean
   The lighthouse
   The siren call

3. What do you think drew Josephine to Hurley? What are your own thoughts on Hurley?

4. Issues of class are threaded through the novel. How would you describe each character's relationship with wealth?

5. How does the past haunt the present throughout the novel?

6. The novel presents a glimpse into how mental illness was treated historically, especially for women. In what ways does Josephine experience medical gaslighting and misogyny? Do any of her experiences still ring true today?

7. What do you think Josephine and Zarya's mother have in common?

8. Why do you think Thomas was uninterested in Josephine?

9. Why do you think Josephine ultimately decides not to hand her suicide letter to Amelia?

10. How are mother-child dynamics explored among the characters?

11. What does Zarya learn over the course of this novel, and how does that inform her decisions at the end?

12. The novel touches on several water-spirit legends from various cultures. Why do you think so many places around the world speak of these legends? What do water-spirits reflect about our fears and values?

13. What are your thoughts on Mrs. Irving's character? What does she reveal about tribalism and empathy?

14. What does Zarya learn about herself as a result of her friendship breakup with Bruno?

15. In what ways does the harsh, isolating setting of coastal Washington affect the characters?

16. What does it mean that a spirit of the water can only be killed by fire?

17. Describe what you think this novel is about without detailing any of the plot.

More from the Author

To find out about future novels and journaling workbooks, make sure you're subscribed to my email newsletter at:

www.dranayudin.com

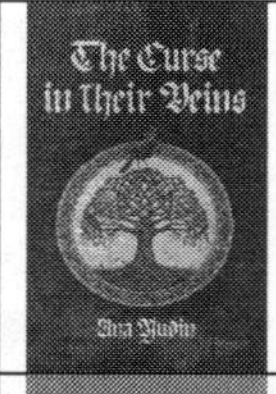	**The Curse in Their Veins (2023)** A novel about witchcraft, narcissism, and severing the cycle of intergenerational trauma.
	**A Season of Life: Daily Journaling Practice for Emotional Wellness (2023)** A 90-day journaling workbook that promotes joy, kindness, gratitude, and productivity.
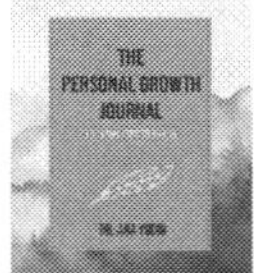	**The Personal Growth Journal: 75 Templates to Thrive (2023)** A journaling workbook for emotion regulation, processing difficult interactions, and self-improvement, with prompts based on 75 different situations that could arise.
	**Get It Done: A Quarterly Productivity Planner (2024)** A year-long planner split into quarters, with evidence-based techniques to help you achieve your goals.
	**Living in Alignment with Nature's Cycles (2024)** A spirituality journaling workbook to stay aligned with the seasons and the phases of the moon.

Psychology YouTube channel: Psychology with Dr. Ana
Cozy YouTube channel: Book & Hearth
TikTok: @PsychologyWithDrAna

Made in the USA
Columbia, SC
20 June 2025

6266b86b-dd26-4a2f-b0a2-f6b8c251cf0aR01